David Hodges joined the Berkshire County Constabulary in 1964 and became a member of the Thames Valley Police on amalgamation in 1968. During his long and varied police career he gained wide operational and management experience before retiring as a superintendent after thirty years service in 1994.

A keen family man, with two grown-up daughters, he lives in Oxfordshire with his wife, Elizabeth.

Flashpoint is his first published novel.

FLASHPOINT

David Hodges

To Dave & Sue
With very Best
Wishes.

David Hodges.

FLASHPOINT
ISBN 1 901 442 047

First published in 1999 by Pharaoh Press

Typeset in 10/12pt Linotype Times by
Kestrel Data, Exeter, Devon
Printed by Short Run Press Ltd, Exeter, Devon

To my wife, Elizabeth, and our two daughters, Caroline and Suzanne, for all their patience, understanding and support over so many years,

to my mother, father and 'big' brother, John, who introduced me to writing in the first place and gave me the encouragement to persevere,

and finally to my good friend Roger Parkes, who 'showed me the way' and also provided much of the red wine.

Author's Note

Flashpoint is about a totally fictitious policing crisis of the future. Much of the background to the story broadly reflects the service as it is today – including references to the Police & Criminal Evidence Act, the Crown Prosecution Service and specialist services like the National Identification Bureau, the Police National Computer and the recently formed National Crime Squad – but I have introduced a number of innovations which are entirely the products of my own imagination.

As yet, we have no national police system in this country, but a service that, in England and Wales, comprises over forty individual police forces. Outside London these forces are headed by chief constables, instead of regional commissioners, and there is no connection between my fictitious regional commissioner and the rank of commissioner currently held by the chief officers of both the Metropolitan and City of London forces.

We have no quasi-military style regional public order groups either. Police support units (commonly referred to by the media as 'riot squads') are often deployed in times of serious public disorder, but these units are normally made up of personnel drawn from existing police establishments. Whilst some forces may already maintain highly-trained specialist public order teams within their own areas, these are not part of a separate police organisation, as is the case in many other parts of the world.

The service certainly does not have the sort of militant National Police Union I have described, but a highly respected Police Federation, which represents all officers from constable to chief inspector level. Police officers themselves are specifically prohibited from taking any form of industrial action.

My Regional Complaints Department is also an imaginary body. At present forces have their own complaints departments which investigate allegations against police officers and the procedure is overseen and often supervised by an independent Police Complaints Authority. However, although at the time of writing there are moves towards employing civilians to assist with such enquiries, responsibility for the actual investigation process still rests with senior police officers and not with some cadre of high profile civilian investigators, working directly to an independent investigatory authority, as suggested in my story. Coupled with this, the rather draconian new Police Act I have quoted, which, amongst other things, requires the automatic suspension of a police officer for alleged criminal conduct, even before an investigation has been started, remains for the moment the stuff of bad dreams.

Yet who can tell what will happen in a decade or so from now? With centralisation the apparent philosophy of a rapidly evolving federal Europe, with the trade union movement clamouring for the right of union representation for all workers, including the right to strike, and with an under-staffed and constantly criticised police service becoming increasingly demoralised and resentful, perhaps the situation I have described in *Flashpoint* may be just around the corner.

David Hodges

1

The night was hot and sticky, the police car a metal casserole that had hardly cooled after yet another blistering day. Sergeant Jim Calder flicked his half-finished cigarette through the window into the canal, then eased his stocky muscular frame into a more comfortable position. He grimaced as his shirt peeled off the back of the seat and clung to him, cold with sweat. The forecasters had predicted a warm summer, but so far temperatures had exceeded even their wildest expectations. Three months of withering heat had baked the ground into concrete and reduced the rivers to a trickle. There was not the remotest hint of rain. Something to do with fronts and pressure systems, the man on television had said. Calder neither knew nor cared what that technical garbage meant. It made things no easier to bear. He still had to drive around all night in this mobile oven, barbecuing in his own perspiration.

He switched on the interior light for a moment and, after adjusting the rear view mirror, delicately pulled back the lid of one eye to check for any further remains of the storm fly he had removed with his handkerchief a few moments earlier. 'Damned thing,' he muttered to himself as the eye continued to itch and prick, suggesting there was still something in there. He could find nothing to account for the irritation and in the end he was forced to admit defeat. He reached up to switch the light off, then paused momentarily to consider the face that stared back at him from the mirror. It was a battered lived-in face with a hard square jaw-line, a generous mouth and a slightly crooked nose. There seemed to be more lines than he had noticed before and the grey eyes looked tired and heavy. 'You're getting old, Jim,' he muttered, inspecting the receding line of his closely cropped fair hair. 'Time you packed it all in, my son.'

He quickly snapped the light off and turned his attention to the tow-path, studying it intently through the fly-spattered windscreen. It was deserted. That should have pleased him, but it didn't. Where the hell was Nash? The luminous dial of his wrist-watch stared coldly at him and his mouth tightened. The young patrolman was late and in an organisation that regarded punctuality as the eleventh commandment this was practically a hanging offence.

The personal radio in the leather harness attached to his belt rasped once, then went dead. On impulse he depressed the transmit button of the remote microphone clipped to a tab on his shirt.

'Bravo-Alpha-Sierra One-Zero to Control.'

The set held its breath for a moment. The answering voice was flat, unemotional. Phil Davies in the control room rarely displayed an interest in anything save his collection of police uniform badges. With twenty-six years service under his belt, however, he was an ideal operator. There wasn't much that the chubby poker-faced Welshman did not know about police work in general and the town of Hardingham in particular.

'Location of Bravo-Alpha Three-Zero,' Calder demanded.

'Put you on talk-through, skipper,' Davies returned. 'Go ahead with Three-Zero now.'

The next moment Calder could hear his own voice amplified in the cramped confines of the car. 'PC Nash, where are you?'

A burst of atmospherics and a tiny voice came back. 'Approaching you . . . tow-path . . . north . . . Hillier's Bridge.'

Calder smiled grimly. The cheeky little sod had almost certainly been across to the festival site. No wonder he was late. Couldn't really blame him though. It was pretty ball-aching working twelve-hour shifts because of a rave festival you weren't officially even allowed to see.

Still, the Deputy Commissioner had been quite emphatic about it. A nucleus of personnel from the local area would maintain police coverage of Hardingham town on the west side of the canal, whilst officers drawn on a *pro-rata* basis from all operational areas of the force would police the festival site itself, working to a separate radio communications control on a dedicated channel. Orders were orders, even if they had been written by some jumped up inspector for the Deputy Commissioner's signature. But you had to make allowances for human nature. There was a lot of talent on the heath just now and the weather being what it was, bare boobs and belly-buttons would be in profusion. His tone, however, did not reflect such liberal thinking when he snapped back into the radio.

'Get a move on, Nash, you're late!' A second burst of atmospherics served as a reply. 'Talk-through concluded, Control,' Calder finished.

'Stand by,' the flat voice answered and the radio went dead.

Calder jerked the door open and stumbled out onto the tow-path, his seat-belt buckle clinking on the sill. Almost immediately, as if this had been a signal, the throb of beat music started up on the far side of the canal, supported by an extravaganza of brilliant, flashing lights. 'Noisy bastards,' he breathed.

Why should the ratepayers of Hardingham have to put up with that racket all night? True, the local council had insisted on a close-down at midnight each night, but he knew from past experience this would not happen. Other years, the pop groups had played on well into the early hours and nothing had been done about it. To be fair, what could anyone do? There were more fans on the thirty-acre site than coppers on duty in the entire force. Any attempt to enforce such an unpopular regulation would be sure to provoke a riot which the police had no means of controlling.

So why did the authorities allow the festival on the heath in the first place? For much the same reason as they didn't interfere with it once it got started – the sheer weight of the opposition. The kids would come anyway, whether it was banned or not, and there were not enough bobbies to go round to stop them. Law enforcement was no longer a question of right and wrong, but arithmetic and the calculation of odds.

On this occasion the odds had been adjudged as too great to risk a confrontation. A 'Hardingham Incident' was the last thing the unitary authority wanted, especially as even a healthy sneeze was likely to dislodge it from the knife's edge on which it perched. Softly, softly, a policy of appeasement. That was the official line, but to the ordinary man or woman in the street, especially the ratepayers of Hardingham, it seemed their elected council representatives had abdicated their responsibility. There had already been several anti-festival demonstrations and in the continuing heat tempers were running high. This year there was going to be trouble; Calder could feel it in his water.

He tossed his cap through the car window on to the back seat and wiped his face and forehead with a handkerchief. If only it would rain, that would put paid to their bloody festival. He could not help feeling bitter. It was bad enough to have lost your only weekend in the month by starting twelve-hour night duties on the Saturday instead of the Monday. But then to be told by means of a carefully-worded memorandum from the top that, because the government had demanded cut-backs on police spending, there would be no payment for the overtime worked, that was just too much. A shoddy trick had been pulled which he, in common with the rest of the lads and lassies, strongly resented and bobbies suffering from resentment certainly did not make the best diplomats in a difficult situation. The two-year-old National Police Union, or NPU, had already warned of possible strike action if the Commissioner did not change his mind, so heaven alone knew where it would all lead.

He leaned on the railing bordering the canal and stared across at the lights of the festival site reflected with the moonlight in the black water. They had to be screwy, he reasoned, some of them travelling two to three hundred miles simply to sit in a field and have their eyes turned inside out by flashing lights and their eardrums perforated by screaming amplifiers. But screwy or not they had been pouring into Hardingham over the past few days in their hundreds; long-haired youths carrying guitars they could not play, accompanied by skinny girls in skimpy tops and jeans, many of them barefoot and bra-less with dyed hair and haunted white faces. An army of zombies, drugged up to the eyeballs and intent on a weekend of bedlam and debauchery. None of this was new, of course, the whole scene had happened many years before in the sixties. But to this generation, the hippy revival was the very latest trend and they had gone for it with all the abandon of youth.

Calder's thoughts were interrupted by the crunch of feet in the tow-path grit and out of the corner of his eye he caught the glint of a tin badge. 'Evening, skipper,' a voice drawled at his elbow. 'Sorry I'm late.'

Calder straightened up with a grunt and studied the young constable sourly. Trevor Porter-Nash, PC 2294. Twenty-six years old, barely 5' 8" in height, with silky blond hair, pale aquiline features and a frame more suited to a ballet dancer than a copper, he was one of the graduate-entry recruits. Son of a merchant banker and an ex-public schoolboy, he had come to the force direct from university with a head crammed full of academic theory and a working knowledge of life that could be safely accommodated on the back of a postage stamp. One of the Commissioner's pets this one, Calder thought, with the golden career of a whizz-kid ahead of him.

Calder didn't hide his dislike for Nash. The twist of the thin lips, the expression of thinly veiled contempt in the pale blue eyes and the smug condescending manner all smacked of insolence. Nothing you could nail down, but it was there just the same. Nash belonged to a privileged minority that had seized every morsel of education the state had been able to set before it, but in consequence had developed an overrated opinion of itself and a built-in contempt for the very establishment that had made such education possible. As far as Nash was concerned, Calder was a bit of a joke; a member of the old guard who would one day have to call him 'Sir.' That's as maybe, Calder thought, his grey eyes hardening, but for the present the clod was on top and this flaxen-haired wonderboy would have to do as he was told!

'Pocket book, skipper?'

'Eh?' Calder stared like a man in a trance at the wallet thrust under his nose.

'I thought you might want to examine it?' Nash continued smoothly. 'It's all up to date from that job last night.'

Calder's mouth shut tight. Yes, it would be, you little snide, he thought, remembering the young teenager Nash had arrested for a very minor breach of the peace. 'Not necessary,' he said aloud. 'You know damned well we don't check those things as a matter of routine anymore.'

Nash gave a little cough. 'Yes, I realise that, but I thought you might want to check mine anyway.'

Calder frowned, but chose to ignore the implication in the remark. Instead, he ducked through the car window and reached for his flashlight and side-handled baton on the back seat. 'I reckon it would be a lot more productive to check a few derelicts than to read about your arrest of the century,' he said, clipping the baton to the harness on his belt.

Nash gave another little cough. 'Do you think that's wise?'

Calder stiffened. 'Do I think what's wise?'

'Well, those places are dangerous; they're falling down.'

'So?'

Nash sighed. 'Oh nothing. After all, you are the sergeant.'

His tone suggested that there was some doubt about that fact and Calder's grip tightened on his flashlight. 'Listen, laddie,' he said softly, 'you have just three years service. Don't presume to question the judgment of someone with over twenty-two behind him.'

'No, Sergeant,' Nash drawled with exactly the right amount of exasperation in his voice. 'Of course not.'

Calder felt like hitting him, but resisted the temptation. It wasn't worth the aggravation. Besides, he thought, mellowing a little, perhaps some of the antagonism he got from Nash was self-generated. Maybe he asked for it. Deep down he knew he begrudged the man the opportunities that he himself had never had. To be honest, an education did not prevent a man from becoming a good copper, but it did not necessarily make him one either and that was the whole crux of the matter as far as he was concerned.

'Bravo-Alpha Two-Three receiving?' The bark of the radio jolted him back to the present and he listened intently. 'Yes, Two-Three. Attend Sixteen Lawson Street. Mr. Ali. Someone's lobbed a brick through his front window.'

Calder smiled without humour. Despite the rave festival, life in Hardingham went on just the same. They had already had the usual series of late night punch-ups, a couple of cars stolen and the customary invasion of the hospital casualty department by injured drunks. You couldn't blame the festival for that sort of thing; it would happen anyway. Someone would probably try though.

He tested the flashlight and turned towards the dilapidated properties that lined the tow-path from Hillier's Bridge to the gas works. Nash was right; they were dangerous, bloody dangerous. For some reason known solely to the local council, Wharf Cottages had escaped demolition, probably because in a couple of years they would fall down of their own accord anyway. Their only tenants now were winos and legions of rats, neither of whom seemed to object to the others' company.

Most of the down-and-outs were regulars and though a persistent nuisance with their wine and cider bottles in the town square during the day they were otherwise completely harmless. Every so often, however, there was a stranger among them whose arrival coincided with a series of robberies or burglaries in the area or whose name was on a wanted persons' list somewhere. An enterprising copper could get lucky at Wharf Cottages and make a name for himself . . . if he didn't break his neck in the process.

Calder pushed the first door he came to. It lurched back on one groaning hinge, the stench of the place holding him back for a moment. Then he thought of Nash behind him and that made up his mind. He switched on the lamp and swung it slowly round a small square room. The floor was littered with debris and the place smelled of excrement and stale cider. To his right and directly in front of him were open doorways. To his left a rickety looking staircase climbed stealthily up into the darkness.

'You check down here,' he snapped at Nash. 'I'll take a look upstairs. But watch your step.'

He didn't wait for an answer, but edged his way round an overturned settee towards the stairs. Out of the corner of his eye he saw Nash's torch studying the right-hand door. He grinned fiercely in the darkness. An economics degree should prove invaluable in this sort of situation, he thought vindictively.

'Bravo-Alpha Two-Four,' the radio barked. He snapped it off quickly. No sense in advertising the presence too much. He listened for Nash's radio, but there was silence. One up for wonder-boy. Unlike himself, Nash was either using one of the special earpiece attachments now issued to all patrols to cut out external transmission noise or he had had the sense to turn his set off to start with. That annoyed Calder and he almost put his foot through a hole in the staircase in his bad temper. Careful Jim, he thought, you're getting careless in your old age.

There were three of them in the first room, flat out on mattresses amongst a litter of cider bottles. He nudged one with his foot and stepped back quickly as a furry shape flashed past his leg and vanished into the shadows. The wino did not so much as stir. There was congealed vomit on his face and over his shirt front, but he was snoring loudly. 'Drunken bastard,' Calder murmured with a soft chuckle.

A quick inspection revealed that the other two were in a similar condition. Nothing short of an exploding brewery would wake up this gruesome trio. He knew them all as regulars and thought it better to let them sleep it off here than to foul up the cells back at the nick. Common sense really.

It was at this point that Calder became aware of the peculiar scent, a scent so strong that it was apparent even above the smell of the winos. He knew at once what it was and his heart-beat quickened perceptibly. He swung his lamp in an arc until it caught the glint of a brass handle. One of the winos stirred and began to talk loudly in his drunken sleep. Calder ignored him and cautiously approached the door.

The sickly scent was stronger now. He carefully tried the handle. The door was wedged in some way, but he knew just the cure for that. Drawing back a few paces, he put his boot against it and the whole flimsy structure, including part of the frame, caved in with an almighty crash.

The scent suddenly became a nauseating stench that rushed out of the room, forcing itself up his nostrils and down his throat, making his insides heave. His smarting eyes took in the overturned butane gas lamp, the rucksacks strewn everywhere and the figures struggling at the single window. Then he lurched forward. One of them made it – just a shadow momentarily silhouetted against the face of the moon before it dropped out of sight – but he collared the next in line, grabbing him by the hair and hauling him off the window-sill on top of the pair still trying to climb up.

He waited whilst the tangle of arms and legs sorted itself out. Heavy boots were now thudding up the staircase behind him and he smiled thinly in the darkness. So Nash had finally decided to put in an appearance, had he? That was nice of him.

He played the beam of his flashlight over the floor around the butane lamp. 'Quite a party, eh, fellers?'

he remarked dryly and stooped to pick up a still smoking cigarette. He was conscious of Nash at his elbow, but did not turn round.

'Hey, man, what's the hassle for, huh? We ain't done nothin'.'

Calder swung the lamp to pinpoint the speaker, a skinny black man with an incredible 'Afro' hair style. He pinched out the cigarette and slipped it into his pocket, commenting: 'No wonder you couldn't get through the window with hair like that.'

White teeth blazed. 'Hey, the pig cracked a funny!'

Calder bent down and scooped up a tobacco tin from the floor, but he had the good sense not to take his eyes off the trio. It was just as well, for the person standing behind the Afro haircut moved with sudden speed. Calder was quicker and the other stopped short. Rimless spectacles, framed by shoulder-length blond hair, glittered in the bearded face. 'Yours, Moses?' Calder held up the tin.

Glasses didn't answer, but regarded him fixedly as he flipped open the lid. For some unaccountable reason that unwavering stare made Calder feel strangely uneasy. He raised the flashlight a fraction. Glasses hurriedly averted his gaze and stepped back. Calder breathed again. Glasses was a big lad.

'You going to bust us or what?'

Surprise, surprise. The third member of the trio was female. Calder studied the emaciated features and haunted eyes, then shook his head slowly. Cannabis had not done that. Heroin maybe or a little cocaine, but not the evil-smelling weed the tobacco tin undoubtedly contained. 'Something like that, love,' he murmured.

'On what charge?' Glasses had found his voice at last and it was quiet and educated.

'How about on suspicion of possessing a controlled substance?' Calder replied pleasantly.

'Pig!' said the female.

'Shit!' said the black man.

But Glasses said nothing at all.

Calder switched his radio back on and depressed the transmit button of his remote microphone. 'Bravo-Alpha-Sierra One-Zero to Control. Transit, please, to Wharf Cottages. Three overnight guests for you.'

Glasses smoothed his golden locks back from his face. 'He that is without sin among you, let him first cast a stone,' he intoned.

'Amen,' replied Calder and Nash in unison. For once they were both in perfect agreement.

Calder made the police canteen at just after eleven and fought his way to a corner table that was sticky with spilled coffee and sugar. Steve Torrington, the local detective inspector, nodded briefly as he sat down beside him, his dark eyes hooded and watchful as usual. Bit of passionate Latin blood in this one, Calder had always reckoned, and certainly a man whose adventures with the opposite sex were about as legendary as his record as a thief-taker. Lucky sod, Calder thought ruefully, but there again, he was still single, so why shouldn't he make the most of it?

'Got yourself a bust then, Jim?' Torrington queried, scratching his nose.

Calder grunted and snatched a biro from the top pocket of the other's expensive looking jacket to stir his tea with. 'Bit of weed, that's all,' he replied. 'Left young Nash with it.'

The little weasel-faced detective chuckled throatily and leaned back in his chair. 'Couple of real shitty junkies I suppose, eh? Our future commissioner will love that.'

'Three actually,' Calder corrected. 'One's a bird.'

'Even better. Does Nash know the difference?'

Calder grinned. 'Janice Lawson will explain it all to him, I'm sure. She's custody officer.'

Torrington whistled, his eyes widening appreciably. 'What big Janice?' He cupped his hands in front of his chest in an obscene gesture. 'The wopsie with the arthritis?'

'The same.'

'Poor old Nash. He could end up going blind!'

Calder drained his tea cup and changed the subject. 'How did the meeting go?'

'Meeting?'

'Yeah, the so-called union conference.'

Torrington's face twisted into a contemptuous grimace. 'No idea. Never went. Too busy nicking villains to play children's games.'

The detective leaned forward, his dark eyes suddenly very serious. 'You know, Jim, I can never get used to the way things have gone in the last few years. I mean, who would have thought the Police Federation would one day give way to a fully-fledged trade union?'

Calder nodded. 'Who would have thought the country would end up with a national police force run by regional commissioners instead of chief constables either, but it has. It's called progress, governor.'

Torrington snorted. 'Progress, my arse! Now we're

a pukka union, it will be downhill all the way, you mark my words. The young hotheads we're getting in the job today will soon see to that.'

Calder sighed. 'Can't say as I like the idea myself, I must admit, particularly as we now have the right to strike like everyone else.'

Torrington gloomily played with the fine black line of his moustache. 'The last government must have been loco to let such a thing happen.'

'They were just politically naive, that's all' said a third voice. 'To a bunch of woolly-headed liberals, civil rights take precedence over common sense and it's too late for the present shower to change things now.' The speaker, a tall fair-haired man in his late forties with a neat military moustache, slid into the seat beside Torrington, unbuttoning his beige linen jacket at the same time. Detective Chief Inspector Richard Baseheart, the Special Branch man from headquarters, looked very tired and there were dark smudges under his blue eyes which suggested his head hadn't touched a pillow for far too long.

'What's new then, sir?' Calder queried. 'What does our secret squirrel have for us tonight?'

Baseheart pulled out a handsome Meerschaum pipe with the bowl carved into the shape of an Arab's head and filled it with the energy of a seventy-year old. 'Conference, you mean?' he replied. 'No idea, Jim. I've been elsewhere today. But from what I hear things don't look too good.'

Torrington stared at him. 'You don't mean they'll go ahead with this daft idea of a strike?'

Baseheart shrugged and lit up. 'Who knows? Damned force is full of firebrands now. And with our very own Willy Justice leading the regional executive and the Commissioner refusing to budge an inch, anything could happen.'

'Then we'll just have to hope that the government steps in before things get out of hand,' Calder said grimly.

Baseheart shook his head. 'They can't afford to,' he replied. 'Not after all the jibes they made when they were in opposition about the previous government being run by the trade unions. And don't forget too that all the other public services are in the same boat as us over budget cuts. If the police were seen to get their own way because of the threat of strike action, everyone else would soon be knocking on the Chancellor's door to try the same tactic.'

There was a look of frustration on Torrington's face. 'But even with the present stop on paid overtime,' he exclaimed, 'we've got a damned sight more money than we've ever had.'

Baseheart laughed cynically. 'It isn't really about money anymore, Steve. It's about politics and brinkmanship . . .' He broke off, his eyes suddenly wary, as if he had started to say too much. 'Anyway, how goes the festival? Many bodies in yet?'

Calder grunted. 'Around thirty today the site documentation centre tells me, but you should know what it's like. You've been down there, haven't you?'

Baseheart laughed again, almost with relief at the change of subject. 'What, dressed like this? Hardly unobtrusive gear for infiltration, is it?'

Torrington's eyes narrowed. 'Where then? You look as though you haven't slept for twenty-four hours.'

'You should know better than to ask me that, Steve.'

Baseheart broke off for a second time as a raucous

cheer erupted from across the room. A large ungainly looking man with a red beard and tight curly red hair, dressed in a creased grey suit that was a size too small for him, had swept into the room carrying a bulging briefcase.

'Well, well, well,' Torrington remarked dryly. 'Constable Willy Justice, our very own union chairman.'

'With bad news from the conference, judging by the grin on his face,' Calder added.

Good or bad, Willy Justice had the floor immediately and as all heads turned in his direction he raised one podgy freckled hand like John the Baptist addressing his flock. 'Talking's over, comrades,' he announced in a deep booming voice, his small piggy eyes gleaming, 'Commissioner won't see sense, so we've re-stated our deadline and he's got until 2200 hours, normal shift start time, on Friday. Then it's all out!'

Another rousing cheer from a group of young uniformed officers in front of him and Willy Justice was accepted into their midst in an orgy of back-slapping.

Calder turned away, sickened by it all. 'Bloody sprogs,' he growled. 'What do they know about anything? Their numbers aren't even dry yet.'

'Maybe, Jim,' Baseheart agreed, 'but they're the future; we're the last of the old guard.'

'Then God help the service . . . and the country,' Torrington commented. He took a final gulp of his coffee and climbed to his feet. Then with a short, 'See you later,' he headed for the door.

Baseheart watched him go with a humourless smile, then studied Calder for a moment as if trying to make up his mind about something. Finally, he nodded towards the door. 'Fancy a walk in the fresh air, Jim?' he said. 'Something I want to say.'

Calder glanced at his watch. 'Maybe ten minutes,' he replied. 'I'll get my civvy coat.'

Calder found the SB man standing by the notice board at the front of the police station, studying the empty lamplit street that curved away between rows of shops and offices towards the town centre and the bejewelled line of the by-pass in the distance. 'Let's walk,' Baseheart murmured and moved off in the opposite direction towards the municipal park.

Only when they were among the trees, following the gritty path that skirted the lake, did Baseheart speak again and his first question came as a complete surprise to his colleague. 'How long have we known each other, Jim?'

Calder grinned in the darkness, thinking of times gone by. 'Too bloody long, Richard,' he said, dropping the formality of rank now that they were on their own.

'No really, I'm serious.'

Calder shrugged. 'Since we joined this outfit, as you are well aware.'

'So you reckon we can trust each other then?'

Calder stopped dead. 'Richard, what is all this?'

'Please, just answer the question.'

'I should flippin' well hope so.'

'Good, because I need to confide in someone and I can't think of a better man.'

'Need?'

'That's what I said, just in case.'

'In case of what?'

Baseheart didn't answer, but found a wooden seat and sat down. Calder hesitated, staring at the moon reflected in the lake, his hands thrust deep into the pockets of his anorak. 'Richard,' he said abruptly, 'are you in the shit or something?'

'Sit down, Jim,' the other said quietly. 'I don't want the whole park to hear what I have to say.'

Calder sat and waited expectantly, but for a few moments Baseheart said nothing else. Then there was the flare of a lighter as he re-lit his pipe. 'Funny how this job's changed over the past few years, isn't it?' he commented.

'I don't follow you.'

'Well, everything used to be so simple, didn't it? You did as you were told, kept your nose clean and earned yourself a few brownie points. Now,' he sighed, 'it's all wheels within wheels, politics, double meanings . . . '

Calder snorted. 'You've certainly got it bad tonight, Richard. What brought all this on? Willy Justice?'

Baseheart laughed, a soft mellow sound. 'Now there's a name to conjure with. No, old man, it's not Willy Justice, though he is part of the overall equation.'

'Then what?'

Baseheart stood up and Calder followed him curiously as he strolled to the lakeside and stood there, staring at the water lapping the concrete edge. 'What do you really think to this strike business, Jim?' he said suddenly.

Calder shrugged. 'Sign of the times, I suppose.'

'So you're ambivalent about it?'

'Of course not. I think it's all a bloody disgrace. But there's nothing I can do about it, so I just try to soldier on and not get too involved.'

Baseheart appeared to consider his answer for a

moment, then nodded. 'But who do you think is behind it?'

Calder looked puzzled. 'Well, we know that already don't we? Willy Justice and his bloody cohorts in the union.'

'That's what I thought you'd say and you're half right. But the union is only part of the problem.'

'Meaning?'

Baseheart's pipe had expired again and, knocking it out on a nearby wastepaper bin, he began to refill it from a leather pouch, spilling some of the tobacco on to the path in the process. Calder glanced impatiently at the luminous dial of his wristwatch. 'Meaning that there are certain other non-union people who also have a vested interest in seeing this strike happen,' the SB man said, 'powerful people, some external to the force, who see the strike as a way of achieving their own political ends. Willy Justice and his militant crew are merely pawns in a much bigger game.'

'And who are these people?'

But Baseheart was no longer listening and had turned to study the section of path which continued on past the seat further into the park. The sound of singing was very close and following his gaze Calder saw two figures stumble into view round a bend. It was obvious, even from a distance, that the pair were very drunk and as they drew closer he recognised them as a couple of local winos. 'It was a mistake coming here,' Baseheart snapped. 'It's much too public.'

'Mistake?' There was more than a trace of exasperation in Calder's voice. 'Richard, can you stop all this secret squirrel stuff and just tell me what's going on?'

Baseheart shook his head firmly. 'Sorry, Jim. Catch you again,' he promised. 'But for the moment, forget I ever spoke to you.' Then without another word he strode off briskly along the path, heading back the way they had come towards the park entrance, and soon disappeared from view among the trees.

For a moment Calder remained where he was, uncertain whether to go after him or not. In the end he decided against it. If Baseheart wanted to tell him something he would do so when he was good and ready and if he had made up his mind that now was not the right time, then that was it.

He frowned and fumbled in his anorak pocket for his cigarettes. This was a damned funny business though. What the hell was Richard into that made him want to confide in someone? And who were these other people he had spoken about?

He lit up and inhaled deeply. It all sounded more like the ingredients of some far-fetched paperback novel than anything else. Either Richard was having him over, which was certainly out of character for the quiet ex-army intelligence officer, or his old friend was up to his neck in something really heavy. Whatever the truth was, however, it would have to wait until the SB man chose to confide in him and the frustrating thing was, he had no way of knowing just how long that would be.

He scowled at the two drunks who had unwittingly cut the lakeside conversation short. They had now deposited themselves on the seat a few feet away to share a large bottle of what looked very much like cider. Suddenly the cigarette he was smoking tasted more acrid than usual and, snatching it irritably from his mouth, he tossed it away into the darkness. Time he was back at the station before they sent out a search-party to look for him.

The foot patrols on early meal break were already returning to their beats when he climbed the steps to the big double doors of the police station, but his thoughts were elsewhere and he hardly noticed anyone at first. Then as he brushed past two uniformed constables in the doorway he was abruptly brought back to earth with a bang. 'Hey, Sarge,' the taller of the two called after him with a grin, 'Torchy's looking for you.'

He felt his stomach tighten apprehensively, all thoughts of Baseheart now swept from his mind. Torchy, more properly known as Douglas Charles Maybe, was the shift inspector, a tense unsmiling individual, who had been given his strange nickname because of his alleged reluctance to go out on his own after dark, which had resulted in some anonymous wag loading the entire top of his desk with scores of torch batteries. He was not a man to engender liking or respect and about the only thing he could be relied upon to do was put a blot on even the most auspicious day by always popping up in the wrong place at the wrong time.

Now was a classic example and the gangling inspector confronted Calder in the corridor even before he had had the opportunity to hang up his civilian coat. 'A word in my office please, James,' he said.

Calder nodded. 'I'll just drop my anorak in the locker-room, governor.' he began.

'Now!' Maybe snapped. 'And don't call me governor. We're not in the Met!'

'Pity you're not!' Calder muttered under his breath as he turned to follow him.

2

'Take a seat, James,' Maybe snapped, marching briskly into the drab little office at the end of the corridor he shared on a shift rotation basis with the other three inspectors. 'And shut the door, please.'

Calder frowned as he closed the door after him and collecting a metal framed chair from a corner of the room, he placed it in front of the desk behind which the other had now settled himself like a judge about to pass sentence on the prisoner in the dock.

For a few moments Maybe said nothing, but, slipping on a pair of gold-framed spectacles, he studied a bulky file lying on the desk in front of him, his lips compressed tightly as he flicked through the documents. Then abruptly he removed his glasses and twirled them in one hand, looking past Calder and apparently studying the broken venetian blind hanging at a crazy forty-five degree angle across the single window.

'I have a bone to pick with you, James,' he said at length, meeting his gaze with difficulty.

Calder raised his eyebrows a fraction. 'Have you, sir?'

Maybe fidgeted in the chair and cleared his throat. 'Yes, it's about young Porter-Nash.'

Calder's eyes narrowed suspiciously. 'What about him?'

'I understand you instructed him to carry out a search of Wharf Cottages with you tonight.'

Calder nodded curtly. 'Been bleating to you about it, has he, sir?'

Maybe's thin lips twitched and he slipped his glasses back on. 'Never mind about that,' he said testily, drumming his index finger on the desk top. 'You had no business taking him in there. You know those properties have been declared out of bounds to patrols.'

'Perhaps someone should tell the villains the same thing!' Calder interjected dryly.

Maybe glared at him, blinking repeatedly. 'Don't you get facetious with me,' he snapped. 'You were out of order and you know it. Those places are falling down. Nash could have been injured or worse.'

Calder scowled. Apparently the fact that he could also have been injured was not even taken into consideration. 'Nash is supposed to be a copper, sir. It's part of his job to take risks, just like the rest of us.'

Maybe drew in his breath with a sharp exasperated hiss. 'Nash is not here to take risks, and you know that only too well. He's a first-class graduate and he wasn't recruited to spend his time wandering round unoccupied houses nicking social misfits. The Commissioner has already earmarked him for future senior rank under the accelerated promotion scheme and it's part of your job to make sure he gets the proper kind of support and practical experience.'

'Nothing is of more practical value than basic beat

work,' Calder countered. 'What you're really saying is he mustn't be allowed to get his hands dirty.'

'I'm saying he is to be given every sensible opportunity to gain the experience he needs, in line with the development plan agreed by headquarters. Is that clear?'

'With respect, sir, I've been trying to do just that since I joined the shift and with very little success. In fact, it's about time someone told headquarters and the Commissioner that Nash is an arrogant useless prick, who will never make a copper as long as he's got a hole in his arse!'

'Now that's quite enough!' Maybe snapped. 'It's patently obvious to me that you have taken a personal dislike to this man, possibly because he has a first-class honours degree and will go a lot further in the service than you have been able to. But the matter stops right there. Understand? You will give him your support and I shall be watching very carefully to make sure you do. Furthermore, in future you will not force him, or anyone else for that matter, to disobey local instructions and follow you on some hair-brained pointless activity, like the search of Wharf Cottages.'

'Are you aware that we arrested three druggies as a result of that pointless activity?' Calder said quietly.

'Druggies?' Maybe retorted with a short derisive laugh. 'Three kids in possession of a bit of weed? Can't our great ex-detective do better than that?'

The barbed reference to Calder's previous departmental job was totally unnecessary and he controlled his rising anger with an effort. 'Those were not kids, sir, and they were up to a lot more than smoking pot.'

Maybe raised his eyebrows. 'Oh? And how do you

know that? Find a couple of Armalite rifles on them, did you? Or maybe four or five pounds of Semtex?'

Calder ignored the jibe. 'I just know, that's all,' he said. 'Call it a feeling in my water, if you like. There was definitely something very wrong there and one of the trio, a big lad with blond hair, certainly didn't fit the bill as a run-of-the-mill pot smoker. Once we've interviewed them I'm sure you will see there was every justification for the arrests.'

Maybe took momentary refuge behind his file which he held upright, shuffling the documents unnecessarily. 'You won't be able to interview them,' he muttered, clearing his throat uneasily. 'I've already released them with a caution.'

For a moment there was a stunned silence as Calder mentally digested the statement. 'You've done what?' he breathed.

'My prerogative,' Maybe said defensively, now studying the keys of the computer terminal on the corner of his desk. 'Cannabis is only a minor drug, not much worse than smoking tobacco really, and under the new legislation an inspector or above can issue a caution for using. There was no evidence of supplying and keeping those three in would only have meant tying up critical cell space. They weren't worth the hassle.'

'Weren't worth the . . .' Calder began, then breaking off he lurched forward in his chair and gripped the edge of the desk top. 'We hadn't even interviewed them. How the hell could you make a decision like that without knowing the first thing about the case?'

Maybe visibly flinched. 'I knew all there was to know after I had spoken to Nash.'

'Nash?' Calder rose half out of the chair. 'That

supercilious little prat was only following my instructions. I was the arresting officer. You should have spoken to me!'

Maybe jumped to his feet, his face a delicate shade of pink and his mouth working silently as he fought to get the words out. 'Don't you dare talk to me like that,' he choked. 'I don't have to explain myself to a jumped-up patrol sergeant.' He swallowed hard as he tapped the file in front of him, then went on in a rush, his voice trembling with suppressed anger. 'Oh we know all about the great Jim Calder, don't we? It's all in your personal file here. Never done a day's proper police work in your life, have you? Too busy playing the great detective and swanning around on one specialist squad after another; first CID, then Regional Crime Squad, Drug Squad, Criminal Intelligence and finally the magic mushroom itself, the grandly named National Crime Squad.'

'Proper police work?' Calder shouted, kicking over his chair and stabbing an accusing forefinger at his superior. 'I've forgotten more about real police work than you've ever learned.'

'Oh is that so?' Maybe sneered, the gloves off and his personal animosity towards Calder now nakedly exposed. 'Well, from what it says in here you've forgotten all you have ever learned. Face facts, Sergeant, you can't hack it anymore; that's why you were slung off the NCS and put back in uniform. You're a washed-up, out-of-date has-been nobody wants and it's about time you came to terms with what everyone else already knows.'

'You pompous arse-hole!' Calder snarled, now forgetting himself completely. 'At least I don't hide myself away in the nick as soon as it gets dark. You even need a torch to cross the bloody police station yard!'

'What on earth's going on here?' In the heated exchange between the two men neither had heard the door open and both turned quickly to face the young woman standing there with one hand on the door knob.

In her early forties with a tall slender figure and jet black hair worn in an attractive page-boy style, she had all the appearance of a barrister or company executive in her smart grey suit and black, patent-leather high-heeled shoes, but she was nothing of the sort. Chief Inspector Rosalind Maxwell (or Rosy to her few close friends) was a shrewd and very experienced police officer, who had earned considerable respect in her two years as second-in-command of Hardingham Police Area. And now, as she studied the two men squaring up to each other across the desk, her pale finely chiselled features registered an expression of absolute incredulity.

'I said,' she repeated icily, 'what is going on here? I've never heard anything like it. Do you realise the pair of you can be heard all over the station?'

'Sorry, ma'am,' Calder muttered, straightening and staring down at the floor in embarrassment.

'So you damned well should be,' she snapped. 'I only dropped in here tonight on my way home and what do I find? Two of my supervisors indulging in a slanging match like a pair of nine-year-old kids. I wonder what else has been going wrong while I've been away on my college course?'

'My apologies, ma'am,' Maybe said, recovering abruptly and forcing his best smile. 'I'm afraid

Sergeant Calder disobeyed a local instruction prohibiting . . .'

'I don't wish to know, Inspector Maybe,' she cut in sharply. 'The management of the shift is your responsibility and I expect you to get on with it.'

Maybe's smile faded and he began to fidget with the papers on his desk, throwing her quick nervous glances. 'Yes, ma'am, but I wanted to assure you that this will not happen again. I shall be putting a discipline report through to the superintendent concerning Sergeant Calder's insubordination and . . .'

'Enough, Inspector!' she snapped. 'I said I don't wish to hear it. But I warn the pair of you, I shall be back on duty for your next night tour and if there is any repetition of this nonsense, I will deal with it in the severest possible manner. Is that understood?'

Then like the fairytale Ice Queen, she turned her back on them and marched off up the corridor, her high heels tapping smartly on the woodblocks as she went.

'I'll have you for this,' Maybe promised as Calder made to follow her.

'Not if I have you first!' he grated in reply and slammed the door behind him.

A slight but welcoming breeze fanned Calder's face through the open window of the police car as he drove out of the police station yard and headed for the town centre. He was less angry with himself for losing his temper with Inspector Maybe than incurring the displeasure of Chief Inspector Maxwell and he felt he had let himself down badly in her eyes. The fact was that he had a lot of time for Rosy, even though she was a woman and in his sexist view women and rank didn't generally mix. A close friend for many years, she had worked with him on the Crime Squad when they had both been detective sergeants and she had certainly shown herself to be a match for anyone else on the team. He had to admit it really was hard for a woman to make it in the service (and he grinned to himself), particularly when working with old-fashioned sexist bastards like Jim Calder. But Rosy hadn't complained or asked for any favours; she had simply got on with the job, notching up one of the best arrest records on the squad and earning five commendations in four years. She had deserved all her promotions and, surprisingly, he had been only too pleased to find on his return to uniform that she was to be his new boss. Perhaps he wasn't the sexist bastard he imagined himself to be.

Negotiating a large roundabout, he went straight over into Lower High Street, then slowed as he approached a group of youths squatting on the pavement outside the public library amidst a litter of take-away boxes and what looked like beer or lager cans. He recognised several local tearaways among them and made a mental note of who they were. He could have stopped and given them a roasting for the mess, but experience had taught him that sometimes it was best to leave well alone. The youngsters weren't doing any real harm, apart from making a bit of noise and creating a mess the street cleaners could clear up later. At least while they were there they weren't vandalising the shop fronts and street furniture. Speaking to them in their present state was only likely to cause more trouble than it solved. Nevertheless, it was worth letting the station know they were about in the town and, while his eyes studied them in his rear-view mirror as he drove slowly by, he pressed the transmit button of the remote microphone of his personal radio.

'Bravo-Alpha-Sierra One-Zero to Control.'

'Go ahead, Sarge,' returned a female voice. Phil Davies was obviously on meal break and the civilian operator, Jackie Holt, was in the chair.

'Just a mention, Jackie,' he said. 'Jimmy Talbot, Ice Robinson and the McCready brothers are with a few cronies outside the library. They're bevvied up and we could have trouble with them later, but they're best left alone at present. Pass to all patrols for a watching brief only please.'

The youths were on their feet now, raising their beer cans in a raucous abusive toast, and he smiled grimly to himself, listening carefully as Jackie passed out his message. At least Jimmy and his mates knew he was out and about and that he had seen them. Showing the flag was often all that was necessary, prevention rather than cure, and if it didn't work on this occasion, well, they could always come in later. After all, he had the whole night at his disposal.

He spotted the shadow pushing a bicycle as he drew level with the Queen's Shopping Mall and swung across the road into the disabled parking area outside. Constable Maurice Stone (Bravo-Alpha Three-One) had already seen him and was waiting just inside the entrance to the pedestrianised precinct, his bicycle tucked in neatly beside him.

Six foot two and a former resident of Barbados, Stone was one of the force's newest and most promising acquisitions as far as Calder was concerned. Sharp as a razor, with a sense of humour that coped easily with all the racist comments he got from the yob fraternity, the twenty-two-year-old already had an impressive arrest record for crime and he made no secret of his respect for Calder, who he saw as a real copper's copper.

'Evenin', Sarge,' he said as Calder parked the car and joined him. 'Just doing a bit of door shaking.'

Calder nodded. 'Good for you. But don't shake too hard, will you? We don't want you triggering off half the alarms on the estate.'

Stone grinned broadly, well aware of his reputation in that quarter. He knew he was sometimes a bit too enthusiastic and there were occasions when he had completely removed a door handle or two.

'How's the wife then?' Calder went on seriously.

Stone's grin vanished. 'Still waiting,' he said with a frown. 'Hospital told me tonight that they're going to try and bring her on. If that don't work, it could mean a caesarean.'

'Don't you think you should have some time off?'

Stone shook his head. 'Nothing I can do and the hospital's only just down the road if anything happens. I'd rather work. It takes my mind off things. Anyway, the nick's a bit short on manpower at the moment.'

'Don't you worry about that; that's my problem. Your wife comes first. Sod the job!'

'Thanks, Sarge, but if it's all the same to you I'll just carry on. See what happens.'

'Okay, but should anything happen, you're to drop everything and go to the hospital. Understand?'

'Yeah, 'course.' Stone seemed about to say something else, but then hesitated and Calder raised a questioning eyebrow.

'And?' he encouraged.

The other shuffled his feet uncomfortably. 'This strike thing, Sarge.'

'What about it?'

'Do you think it will happen?'

'I damned well hope not, but with the NPU spoiling for a fight and Willy Justice stirring things up, who knows? Why do you ask?'

'Well, it just don't seem right, that's all. I mean, how can we just walk off the job and leave the town to get on with it? The yobs and those weirdos at the festival will tear the place apart.'

Calder shrugged and turned back towards his car. 'But that's up to you, isn't it?' he replied half over his shoulder. 'No one can force you to strike. Everyone must follow their own conscience. It will be hard for anyone who ignores the call, though. Bloody hard.'

'What will you do?'

Calder opened the car door and stared back at him over the roof. 'Now there's a question. Carry on as usual, I suppose. But then I always was a contrary bastard. Ask Inspector Maybe.'

He swung into the driving seat and, after fastening his seat-belt, was just about to start the engine when Stone came over to the open passenger window, his grin suddenly back with a vengeance and devilment in his eyes.

'Hey, Sarge?'

Calder raised his eyes to the roof in mock exasperation. 'Now what?'

'The baby? You know? If it's a boy we thought we might call him Jim.'

Calder kept a straight face as he started the engine and slammed the gearstick forward with the finesse of a tractor driver. 'Poor little sod!' he retorted through the open window and, executing a rapid U-turn, rejoined the main road.

The youths were still sprawled on the pavement outside the library as Calder drove past, though he noticed the group had shrunk and the ginger-haired McCready brothers and Jimmy Talbot were missing. His face hardened. 'So where have you three gone?' he murmured to himself. 'Screwing somewhere, I bet.' The usual cat-calls followed the passage of his car, but he made sure he was well out of sight before swinging off the road into the mouth of a narrow alleyway to radio his information through to the station. Even as he was passing his message, however, Phil Davies, who was now evidently back in the control room, cut him off.

'Anyone vicinity of the Carlton Club? Serious disturbance.'

'Bravo-Alpha-Sierra One-Zero attending,' Calder snapped, reversing out of the alleyway and racing back down the High Street.

'Thank you,' Phil replied, confirming the responses that only he could hear. 'I have Bravo-Alpha-Sierra One-Zero, Bravo-Alpha Two-Two and Bravo-Alpha Two-Four.'

Calder nodded appreciatively. Good old Phil. He wasn't putting the radio on talk-through, which would at least stop the confusion of garbled voices over the air, allowing the station to keep control of radio communication. It was certainly worthwhile having an experienced bobby in the chair. Then as he turned off the High Street and headed towards the canal where the club was located he frowned. Where was Porter-Nash (Three-Zero)? The incident was on his bloody beat, for heaven's sake.

He saw the bundle of figures in the brilliant moonlight outside the club when he turned the corner. Two-Two, Daphne Young, was already there and jumping out of her area car. 'Steady, girl,' he breathed. 'Don't wade in on your own.' But he was too late and she disappeared into the melee even before he lurched to a stop. From behind him the flashing blue lights of other police cars were reflected in the windows of the club and he heard a dog barking frantically. Brilliant, they'd got hold of one of the dog vans.

The fight began to break up as he got to it, several of the combatants tearing themselves away and making for the bridge leading to the tow-path, but two of the others were still at it and a third was merrily putting the boot into the prostrate figure of Daphne Young on the ground. Calder went straight for him, but quick as he was, someone else was quicker. Two-Four, in the stocky shape of Keith 'Taffy' Jones, almost knocked his sergeant over as he tore past him across the rough ground and cannoned into the man, hurling him back against the wall of the club close to where dinner-suited stewards and a group of young women watched the proceedings excitedly. With a snarl of rage the man bounced back off the wall, stooping in mid-charge to snatch up what turned out to be a length of lead piping from the ground. But the tough little Welshman already had the measure of him and, producing his baton with amazing sleight of hand, he drove the end of it low down into his body. He then changed his grip to bring the formidable weapon down hard across the side of his head, laying him out on the grass.

'Not a nice man, Sergeant,' Taffy understated in his

soft Welsh accent, and bending over him he efficiently snapped a pair of handcuffs on his prisoner's limp wrists.

Calder nodded grimly and went quickly over to Daphne Young who was now sitting up on the grass watching her colleagues leading two other prisoners to the waiting police Transit Van. 'Steady,' he said, gently. 'Don't try and get up. We'll call an ambulance.'

She shook her head vehemently. 'Sorry, Sarge, but I don't want a bloody ambulance. I'm not a sodding pensioner!'

He grinned, used to the plucky ex-Wren's colourful language, and carefully helped her to her feet. In the moonlight he could see that there was blood on her face, her tights were in tatters and her blouse had been ripped from shoulder to waist. She clung to his arm, trying to keep back the tears as he guided her to the open door of his car and sat her down on the edge of the seat with her feet on the grass.

'Bloody-well exposing myself now,' she said, pulling the torn fragments of her blouse together.

'I'm not looking,' Calder lied, turning to watch the dog van and Transit pull away. 'But you need to go to the hospital. I insist. Just for a check-up.'

'Okay. But not in a flaming ambulance, Sarge.'

'I'll take her,' Taffy volunteered, strolling over with a broad grin on his face. 'Can't have her walking about like that, can we?'

Calder nodded. 'Thanks, but then straight back to the nick to see your prisoner in, okay?'

'What about her car? You'll have a job driving two.'

Calder grunted; something he'd forgotten. Then he stiffened, his face hardening as the uniformed figure

44

of Porter-Nash appeared, walking quickly from the direction of the bridge. 'I see just the man to do that,' he said softly.

'Cowardly bastard,' Taffy breathed, then bent down to help Young to her feet. 'Right my girl, time to get you out of the public eye, eh?'

The little Welshman and his casualty were actually pulling away in the area car by the time Nash reached the scene and Calder eyed him fixedly. 'So where have you been?' he said, suppressing his anger with great difficulty.

Nash looked surprised. 'Been, Sarge?' he echoed. 'Why, what's happened?'

'You know damned well what.'

The constable removed his personal radio from the harness attached to his belt and shook it a couple of times. 'Sorry, I didn't hear anything. My radio's been playing up. I was . . . er . . . just making my way in to change it.'

'Give it here.'

Nash shrugged and, unclipping his remote microphone, handed the lot to Calder, who immediately depressed the transmit button. 'Bravo-Alpha-Sierra One-Zero to Control.'

No response and Calder was distracted for a second when the sound of rock music started up from the festival site across the canal, apparently after a lull. He repeated his transmission, now having to raise his voice because of the music. Still nothing. Then his own radio rasped and Phil Davies' voice came over as clear as a bell. 'Bravo-Alpha Two-One, attend smash-and-grab, Wade's Electrical, South Parade.'

He tried again with Nash's radio and thought he caught the suggestion of a smirk on the young officer's face when there was no response. 'Sorry, Sarge,' Nash drawled. 'I appear to have missed all the fun. Whatever it was.'

Calder wound the wire of the microphone attachment round the dead radio set and tossed the equipment on to the back seat of his car. 'Ask Daphne Young whether it was fun receiving a good kicking, Nash,' he said. 'Especially as it happened on your beat and you were the only one who didn't respond!'

'Now just a minute, Sergeant,' Nash exclaimed with just about the right amount of annoyance in his voice, 'I hope you're not implying . . .'

'Implying?' Calder snarled, squaring up to him. 'I imply nothing. I know you ignored that call. I haven't yet sussed how you swung it with your radio – maybe you took a dud with you deliberately – but I'll find out, I assure you. Even a clever little prick like you will drop himself in the shit one day. In the meantime you can get your bloody pocket book out and start making a few enquiries at the club while I call for CID support. Names and addresses, Nash, that's all we want. Witnesses to an affray. Do you think you can manage that?'

Nash was too astute to speak out of turn now and he nodded, swallowing hard.

'And when you've done that and CID are satisfied they've got all they want,' Calder finished, 'you can take Daphne's car and cover her area. You'll be delighted to know her radio is still in the car and it works!'

'Are . . . are you not staying here then?' Nash queried hesitantly and threw quick glance at the club entrance, still crowded with onlookers.

Calder smiled fiercely. 'No, Nash, I'm not staying.

46

I'm going to the hospital to see how Daphne is. But you're a star pupil. Inspector Maybe told me that. You should have no trouble interviewing a few witnesses, should you?'

Daphne Young was sitting on the edge of the examination table, clad in a white cotton dressing gown, when Calder was shown into the curtained booth at the busy casualty unit. Her face was cut and bruised and it looked as though she was developing a real classic of a black eye. There were also long scratches and the first signs of ugly bruising on her legs, and the crooked way she was sitting, with one arm pressed tightly into her side, suggested that the rest of her was not much better.

'Surviving?' Calder queried, turning away from her for a moment to book off the air with Control.

She gave a slightly lopsided smile which accentuated the swelling on one side of her face. 'Well I wouldn't win any beauty contests just now, Sarge, that's for sure,' she commented as he switched off the set.

He smiled back at her, though inwardly his blood boiled at the state she was in. A reasonably pretty young woman with short blonde hair and candid blue eyes, her main attraction lay in her bubbly mischievous personality which endeared her to everyone and usually enabled her to defuse the most difficult situations. She was an excellent ambassador for the force, comfortable with people from all walks of life and one of the mainstays of the shift. He knew he would be sorry to lose her, but he didn't need to be a doctor to see that she was likely to be out of action for some time now.

'What you did out there was very courageous,' he said sincerely.

Another grin. 'Because I'm a woman, you mean? Poor little thing and all that?'

Even in her present condition she couldn't resist trying to wind him up. She and Stone were a right pair. 'Don't you come that feminist crap with me,' he retorted. 'You know damned well what I mean.'

She nodded, then winced with pain and adjusted her position. 'Yes, I know, skipper, thanks. But Taffy certainly gave him what for, didn't he?'

Calder frowned, thinking about the little Welshman's contribution. 'A bit too much of a what for, I'm thinking. I just hope we don't get a complaint.'

She stared at him in astonishment. 'A complaint? From that bastard? After what he did to me?'

Calder sighed and dropped his cap on to an adjacent chair. 'Yes, but you know what the job is like nowadays. Got to be squeaky clean and all that. Giving people a belt with a baton, even if they deserve it, is not part of the image and it's certainly not in the Commissioner's glossy new charter!' He smiled again and patted her arm. 'Anyway, don't you worry about young Taffy. He's quite capable of looking after himself. You just concentrate on getting well.'

'We'll be keeping her in overnight for observation anyway,' another voice said briskly and Calder turned as one of the nurses appeared in the doorway.

'It's because of this bloody headache,' Young explained, with a grimace. Then she smiled again, her irrepressible humour bouncing back in spite of herself. 'And the real rub is I haven't even been on a bender.'

The nurse also smiled briefly. 'She has a nasty bump on the back of her head,' she went on, watching her patient carefully, 'and there's the possibility that she's suffered some mild concussion, so we're just playing it safe. In addition, we think she may have cracked a couple of ribs, but we won't know for sure until she's had an X-ray.' Then abruptly she became more business-like: 'Now, Sergeant, isn't it about time you were out on the street arresting someone or something?'

Calder nodded and quickly retrieved his cap. Nurses had always frightened him, especially the matronly variety like this one. 'I'll have someone ring up to see how you are in the morning,' he said to Young as he jerked the curtain aside and stepped into the corridor beyond.

'Not too early,' her voice called back. 'I might decide to have a lay in!'

'Bravo-Alpha-Sierra One-Zero,' the radio barked the moment Calder booked back on the air. 'From Inspector Maybe, attend Number Three, Fairacres Drive, a Mr. Sharp. Complaint of noisy party. Please note, he rang ten minutes ago, but we were unable to raise you.'

'Then why didn't you send someone else?' Calder snapped back. 'I had already booked off the air with you.'

Silence for a moment. Then the radio barked again. 'Bravo-Alpha-Sierra One-Zero. Further from Inspector Maybe. He wants you to deal personally. Mr. Sharp is a member of the Police Authority. Please expedite attendance.'

Calder swore. Police Authority? Why the preferential treatment just because of that? Anyone else would end up with a beat constable when he or she had time to attend. Noisy parties were a nuisance, but certainly low on the list of operational priorities.

He swung out of the hospital entrance on to Seymour Road, heading for the outskirts of the town, and as he did so there was another radio call, this time carrying more urgency.

'Any mobile vicinity of Cooper's Store . . . ABA!'

Calder answered immediately. ABAs (or automatic burglar alarms) often went off accidentally and they could be a damned nuisance, but sometimes there were actually intruders on premises and for this reason the calls always justified a rapid response. 'Bravo-Alpha-Sierra One-Zero, Seymour Road. Two minutes away.'

Control acknowledged two other mobiles, then replied. 'Bravo-Alpha-Sierra One-Zero. From Inspector Maybe. Disregard Cooper's. Attend Fairacres, as instructed.'

'What?' Calder shouted to himself in the confines of the car. Ignore a burglar alarm to deal with a noisy party? Like hell, he would. Mr. bloody Sharp could wait even if he were on speaking terms with the Queen herself.

With this in mind, he swung into an alleyway three hundred yards down the road and switched off his lights, thereafter driving solely by the light of the moon. Cooper's alarm was actually connected to a central monitoring station run by a private security company thirty miles away and it was the security company who were responsible for advising the police the moment it was triggered. The system had been cleverly designed to ensure that when it was activated by an intruder, the alarm bells would initially remain silent, but only for a few minutes. After that they would sound with a vengeance. In this way, whoever was breaking in wouldn't have a clue that their forced entry had been detected until it was too late. The place was always getting burgled and the idea was to give the police a reasonable opportunity of getting to the premises before any would-be breaker could make off into the night. The very last thing Calder needed therefore was to advertise his presence with the lights of his car.

He didn't have to travel far, however, and shortly after turning into the alleyway, just a few yards from a barely visible cross-cut, he stopped and switched off the engine. The premises, he knew only too well, lay at the end of the intersection to his left, but due to their close proximity he reasoned that it was more sensible to finish his approach on foot.

The radio rasped again as he was getting out of the car and he snapped it off before plugging in the wire of the hated plastic earpiece attachment he carried in his pocket. He usually avoided using the kit, because he found the earpiece uncomfortable and irritating, but there were occasions when it was essential to silence the noise of the radio and this was one of them.

Switching the radio back on again, he quickly turned the volume down with a grimace as a transmission from Control blasted his eardrum: 'X-ray-Delta One-Four (the dog van), can you back-up units at ABA, Cooper's Store.' Then, feeling for his big rubber torch on the back seat of the car, he gently closed the door and headed off into the shadows, his rubber-soled boots making no sound.

'Bravo-Alpha Two-Zero, attend ABA, D'Arcy's Wine Merchants, Cromwell Street. Believed smash-and-grab . . . Bravo-Alpha Two-Six attend East

Street multi-storey car park. Report of winos breaking into cars.'

The radio continued to bark out its instructions as he walked, but he only listened with half an ear, concentrating instead on the ominous looking building partially illuminated by the face of the moon at the far end of the alleyway. His heart was pounding up into his throat, making a funny squishing noise, and he grinned fiercely. Nothing changed, not even after twenty-two years. Still the same old feelings you always got from a shout like this: the sudden intoxicating surge of adrenaline; the increase in heart rate; the dryness in the throat; the strange mixture of apprehension and excitement; and the acute sharpening of the senses. This was what police work was all about and, at fifty years of age, he knew he wouldn't have it any other way.

Then abruptly he froze all the way down his spine as a hand reached out from the darkness and grabbed him roughly by the shoulder, stopping him in his tracks and taking ten years off his life.

'Evenin' all!' a voice mocked softly.

3

Shaken though he was, it didn't take Calder long to recover from his fright and shock quickly turned to anger. But as he turned with a curse and clenched fists towards the sound of the voice, the grip on his shoulder was quickly removed and a torch, shielded in a ghostly red hand, directed its faint light upwards into Detective Inspector Steve Torrington's grinning face.

'You bastard, sir,' Calder breathed as the torch was extinguished. 'I could have had a heart attack.'

'Inspector Maybe will have a lot more than that when he finds out you've ditched his Police Authority man for this,' the DI chuckled.

Calder stepped quickly into the open gateway where Torrington was standing with another plain-clothes man. 'Who's with you?' he queried.

A second torch flashed briefly and he recognised the heavy bearded face of Detective Sergeant Dennis Sale, Hardingham's patent door-removing machine; a man whose exploits on building searches had cost the force almost as much in civil actions as they paid out on his creative overtime claims. The real problem with Dennis was that it seldom occurred to him to check whether the door of a premises named in a warrant was unlocked before he put his shoulder against it and a man of Dennis' bulk didn't just remove the door, but usually the frame as well.

'What a likely pair,' Calder commented dryly. 'So why haven't you gone in yet? Don't tell me you've caught old Torchy's complaint?'

'If you think I'm going to clamber over a chain-link fence in a three hundred pound suit you're out of your tiny mind,' Torrington replied. 'Anyway, we thought we'd wait for the cavalry to scream up to the front with their blue lights flashing as per usual. Then we'll nab whoever's in there as they come flying out the back. Bit like beating for pheasants really.'

Calder grinned. 'You underestimate my shift,' he retorted. 'You've been watching too much television.'

But his faith in humanity was suddenly and dramatically dashed in mid-sentence for, at that precise moment, the sound of a high-revving engine approaching along the High Street on the other side of the building, was followed by the scraping shudder of rubber as brakes were violently applied. Then, as at least two doors banged almost in unison and heavy feet pounded the pavement, the upper structure of Cooper's was brilliantly illuminated by the pulsing of a powerful blue light from the street below, neatly framing the small clocktower like some form of St. Elmo's fire.

'As I said,' Torrington remarked with a chuckle, 'all we have to do is wait for the cavalry!'

Just two to three minutes later three intruders hit the chain-link fence at the back of the premises, scrambling over with an agility born of panic, and with nowhere else to go they ran straight into the arms of the three waiting policemen.

The struggle that followed was violent, but very

brief, for almost at the same moment the pounding of heavy feet along the lane from the direction of the cross-cut announced the arrival of Maurice Stone and Special Constable Dick Weaver. The would-be breakers were soon overpowered and handcuffed and as Torrington radioed for transport Calder hoisted his own prisoner to his feet and had a quick look at him with the aid of his torch. A contorted pock-marked face, framed by a mass of tangled red hair, snarled back at him and he chuckled.

'Well, well, well,' he exclaimed while the youth continued to struggle in his grasp despite the hand-cuffs, 'if it isn't Danny McCready. Now there's a surprise. I wondered where you'd got to earlier on. Get bored with your mates, did you Danny?'

Torrington directed his torch at the man he had arrested, now held securely by the two uniformed constables. 'And here we have good old twin bruv', Ivan,' he said. 'Who've you got, Dennis?'

'Probably Jimmy Talbot,' Calder interjected.

'The very same,' Sale growled, studying the skin-head he was holding with one large hairy meat-hook. 'You must be psychic.'

Calder grinned. 'Not psychic, Dennis. Just beat-wise, that's all. It comes from spending more time out on the street than in the bar. You should try doing it yourself sometime.'

Sale's unprintable reply was drowned by the revving of the police Transit's engine as it carefully reversed along the narrow cross-cut towards them, doors opened wide in readiness to receive its passengers. Jimmy Talbot made one last futile effort to break away, but the McCready brothers had had enough and all three were soon loaded on board and into the custody of the two uniformed bobbies in the back, with Dennis Sale bringing up the rear.

As the Transit lumbered off on its way back to the station Torrington turned to Calder and made him an offer he could not refuse. 'I'll stay on here for a bit to make sure there's no one else still inside the building,' he said. 'I've left my car round the corner anyway. You can then get off on your other job.'

Calder nodded his thanks, then turned briefly to Maurice Stone. 'Who's at the front?' he said softly, staring at the roof of Cooper's Store, which was still illuminated by the pulsing blue light.

'Terry Watson on Two-One and Grandad,' Stone replied, referring to Dick Potter, one of the area beat constables whose shaggy beard and eccentric habits had earned him this unfortunate nickname. 'They're with the keyholder now.'

'Bloody idiots,' Calder breathed to himself. 'Okay, stay here until DI Torrington releases you. I've got another commitment.'

'Enjoy the party, Sarge,' Stone said with a short laugh.

'Don't push it, Maurice,' Calder retorted over his shoulder as he headed back towards the cross-cut, 'or I might even take you with me.'

There was a black cat sitting on the bonnet of the car when Calder got to it and he hissed at it sharply, sending it streaking off into the shadows.

'That will bring you bad luck.'

He turned at Torrington's voice and waited until the DI reached him. 'I thought you were staying on here until the premises had been fully searched, governor?' he queried.

'So I am,' Torrington replied, 'but seeing as I'm a

CID man like Dennis and more used to the bar than the beat, I thought I might take my car round to the front in case I got lost.'

Calder winced. 'Touché! I suppose I was a bit hard on Dennis, but after your comment about the cavalry, I just couldn't resist it.'

'Oh, he'll get over it. You can always buy him a drink later,' Torrington returned with a chuckle, 'but I rather suspect that your sensitivity stems from a secret yen to get back on CID, eh?'

Calder shrugged. 'Nothing secret about it, but it'll never happen now; I'm too long in the tooth.'

Torrington ran a comb through his hair. 'Oh I don't know. Sometimes experience can be the most important factor.'

'Why, are you offering me a job?'

Torrington's gaze met his. 'No,' he said slowly, 'but I thought Richard Baseheart might have had that in mind when you two went for your little stroll in the park.'

'Baseheart?' Calder exclaimed with another laugh. 'Whatever gave you that idea? And how did you know we went for a walk?'

Torrington laughed. 'My spies are everywhere, but seriously, is an SB job in the wind?'

Calder pulled open the door of his car and climbed in. 'Hardly. And as an ex-SB man yourself, you should know better than anyone that Richard Baseheart wouldn't be in a position to make me an offer anyway.'

Torrington nodded. 'Well, I can't think what else you and Richard would have found time to talk about, except maybe why he's nosing around here.'

Calder firmly closed the car door and, disconnecting the irritating radio earpiece, he gave a short sigh.

'Governor, you are so transparent. That's what all this interrogation is about, isn't it? Personal pride. It's hurting your CID ego not to know what's going on.'

Torrington bent down and leaned on the open window frame with both hands, staring at his colleague with an almost predatory intensity. 'Maybe you're right, but it's my bloody patch after all, so I should have been told.'

'Did you tell the local DI what you were about when you were on SB with Richard Baseheart?'

Torrington laughed again. 'That was different. Come on, Jim. Give us the SP. There's a bottle of scotch in it for you.'

'What, a miniature?'

But Torrington was not about to give up so easily. 'Not still chasing ghosts, is he?'

'Ghosts? What are you talking about?'

'Well, Richard always had a thing about anarchists. Spent most of his time chasing some misfit named . . . what was it? Ah yes, Solomon. Nasty bit of work, he was. I don't think Richard ever managed to put him away.'

Calder shook his head. 'Why should someone like that be here?'

Torrington shrugged. 'Fertile ground at the moment for the dedicated activist, I would have thought, rave festival and all that.'

'I wouldn't know about such things, me being just an ordinary woodentop.'

Torrington ignored the sarcastic reference to the nickname given to uniformed officers by the CID and straightened up. 'Well, he must have told you something. After all, you've been friends for years.'

Calder shook his head and started the engine.

'Sorry to disappoint you, but friendship doesn't extend that far. I know as much as you do.'

'Bravo-Alpha-Sierra One-Zero, are you receiving?' The bark of the radio put paid to any further conversation.

'Shit!' Calder muttered, then quickly acknowledged Control.

'From Inspector Maybe. He has had yet another call from Mr. Sharp and is asking why you haven't arrived there yet.'

Calder thought quickly and depressed the transmit button. 'You did say Fairfax Road, didn't you?' he queried innocently, while Torrington walked away shaking his head and chortling.

A pregnant pause, then Phil Davies responded dryly. 'No, Sarge, I did not say Fairfax Road. I said Fairacres Drive.'

'No wonder I couldn't find it. Attending now.'

'Understood, and Inspector Maybe would like to see you when you have dealt with that commitment.'

'I bet he would,' Calder said savagely to himself and, turning the car into the other end of the cross-cut, he drew level with Torrington as he was opening the door of his own vehicle. 'You can have my collar if you like, governor,' he said. 'I'm going to be tied up for awhile with this other commitment.'

Torrington nodded soberly. 'Yes, I suppose it could prove embarrassing trying to explain to Inspector Maybe how you managed to get yourself a prisoner when you were supposed to be on the other side of town at the time,' he said, then added: 'Are you sure Richard Baseheart didn't tell you anything?'

Calder grinned. 'I've already said he didn't. And blackmail is a criminal offence, you should know that.'

59

Torrington climbed into his car and pulled on his seat-belt. Then shaking his head slowly he gave an exaggerated sigh. 'Okay, Jim, for you I will do just this one thing, but you owe me, remember that. Draft me a statement of arrest when you get back and I'll square it with Janice Lawson in Custody. Dennis can do the rest. Have a nice time at the party.'

Fairacres Drive was in a plush part of the town Calder seldom visited, except following the odd burglary or robbery, which was usually found to have been committed by some professional criminal team, putting the investigation out of his shift's league anyway. It was a small tree-lined close of eight Georgian style houses, each with a large manicured garden and a swimming pool. He could hear the music as he turned into the close and saw the lights blazing from every window of the house at the end. The big front garden, lined with oaks and chestnuts, was jam-packed with vehicles and not one of them was less than twenty-five thousand pounds in price. On the opposite side of the road, another large house also had its upstairs and porch lights lit and as he drew up outside a small balding man, wearing a dressing-gown and slippers, strode down the driveway to meet him.

'So you've arrived at last?' he commented acidly as Calder climbed from his vehicle. 'I telephoned your station an hour ago.'

'Sorry, sir,' Calder replied, 'but we're having a busy night at present.'

'I'm not interested in your problems, Sergeant,' the other snapped, gesticulating angrily towards the house opposite. 'I want that racket stopped immediately.'

'Understood, sir,' Calder replied. 'I take it you have

60

already spoken to the people about it without success?'

'Spoken to them? Certainly not. That's your job to sort out. I wouldn't demean myself by going over there.'

'But surely if you had spoken to them, sir, the problem might have been resolved by now? Most people will listen to reason if approached in the right way.'

Sharp's eyes glittered behind the lenses of his spectacles. 'Don't you try to lecture me,' he grated. 'Just get over there and put a stop to it.'

'Right, sir,' Calder replied, controlling his own anger with an effort, 'I'll go and have a word with them.'

'A word? A word? I am not asking you to have a word, Sergeant. I want the music stopped completely and the whole damned rabble turfed out of there. Do you understand?'

'I'm sorry, sir, I can't do that. All I can ask them to do is to turn the noise down. If they refuse, I can report the facts to the local authority and have a notice served on them.'

The little man placed his hands on his hips and thrust his face towards Calder. 'Do you know who I am, Sergeant?' he breathed.

'Yes, sir, I know who you are. But that doesn't make any difference. I can only do what the law allows me to do. Now if you will bear with me, I will pop across and speak to your neighbours about the noise.'

It took Calder a few moments to find his way between the maze of cars to the open front door. He rapped the door-knocker and rang the bell repeatedly before a young man appeared from what was obviously a downstairs toilet, doing up his trousers. Treating Calder to a sheepish grin, he staggered off down the hall shouting: 'Dawn, police are here!'

The young woman who appeared shortly afterwards was about twenty-five years old with a willowy figure wrapped in a short black dress, long blonde hair and large liquid blue eyes. 'Good evening, Sergeant,' she said politely. 'Don't tell me you've come to join the party?'

Calder smiled briefly. 'No, ma'am, but there has been a complaint about the noise from one of your neighbours.'

She stepped on tip-toe and peered over his shoulder at Sharp who was still standing by his front gate. 'Oh him,' she said. 'I thought it might be. Do you know, he's the only neighbour who objected to the party when I told everyone about it. Bit off for him to call the police. This is the first one we've ever held.'

'But it is rather noisy,' Calder pointed out.

'Only for another half hour, honestly, then everyone will be going home. Would you like to come in for a moment?'

Calder shook his head firmly. 'No, thank you, ma'am, but I must ask you to turn the music down and close the windows. That way, you can still enjoy your party and Mr. Sharp can get some sleep.'

'And if I refuse, bearing in mind that it is rather a warm night to be closing windows on people?'

Calder sighed. 'I hope you won't put me in that position. It would be a bit embarrassing for you and I don't think your parents would be very pleased when they returned home from abroad.'

Her jaw dropped. 'And how on earth did you know this was my parents' house and that they were abroad?

Did Mr. Sharp tell you? He's such a nosy unpleasant little man, I don't suppose he misses anything.'

'Mr. Sharp told me nothing, ma'am. I simply drew my own conclusions.'

'Then you should be on CID.'

Calder smiled faintly. 'My thoughts entirely, ma'am. Now are you going to do as I've asked?'

She sighed. 'Oh very well, Sergeant. If it makes Mr. Grumpy happy.'

'Well?' Sharp snapped when Calder got back to him. 'What did she have to say?'

'They will turn the music down, sir, and close the windows. I could see the place was double-glazed so that should reduce the noise considerably. And I'm assured the party closes down in half an hour anyway.' He turned to stare back at the offending house where the volume of the music had suddenly dropped. 'There you are, sir, they've done as I asked, so you should be able to get some sleep now.'

'Pity they didn't do that before,' Sharp retorted. 'Then my wife and I wouldn't have been kept awake half the night. And what happens when the whole damned crowd leave, with their doors banging and their engines revving, eh? Is it going to take you another hour to get here?'

'I hope not, sir, but it will depend on our commitments at the time. It's all a question of priorities. We are very short-staffed at present and we have to grade our response to incidents according to their importance.'

'Meaning that my complaint is unimportant?'

Calder took a deep breath. 'No sir, I wasn't implying that at all. But obviously, if we have a report of a serious crime or road accident that will take precedence over a noisy party. Anyway, hopefully you will have no more problems tonight.'

'Well I'm not satisfied with the service I've received from my local police station, Sergeant,' Sharp snapped, 'and I certainly don't like your manner. I shall be speaking to your superintendent about it later today.'

'Your prerogative, sir,' Calder replied quietly, turning back to his car. 'Now, if you don't mind, I have other matters to attend to.'

Calder didn't cool down until he had left the close well behind him and was back in the commercial area of the town. Then he parked up in a lay-by for a few moments to light a cigarette, listening to the pop music still blaring out from the festival site a quarter of a mile away. Finally, with a weary sigh he took hold of the remote microphone and depressed the transmit button. 'Bravo-Alpha- Sierra One-Zero to Control.'

'Go ahead, Sarge.'

'Incident at Fairacres resolved. Music turned down at police request.'

'Understood. Don't forget to see Inspector Maybe on your return to the station though, will you? Stand by.'

Calder finished his cigarette and tossed the stub out of the window. That's what he liked about this job. There was always something to look forward to!

Maybe was easy enough to find. He was where he could always be found, in his office doing paperwork, and he hardly looked up when Calder knocked on the half-open door.

'Come in, Sergeant,' he snapped.

No 'James' this time, Calder thought, we're suspiciously formal this morning. He was even more uneasy when Maybe finally sat back in his chair with a frosty smile on his face. 'Well, you've really dropped yourself in it this time, haven't you?' he said, tossing a telephone message form across the table. 'Read that.'

Calder did not give him the satisfaction of picking it up, so Maybe shrugged his shoulders and retrieved it. 'Mr. Sharp has telephoned me to say he will be coming in to make a formal complaint against you later today. He alleges you arrived late and were' (he consulted the telephone message) 'both insolent and negligent.' Maybe's smile became even more pronounced and he leaned forward across the desk. 'You certainly know how to do things, don't you, Sergeant? Of all people to upset, fancy picking a member of the Police Authority. This, coupled with a report I am submitting to the superintendent about your earlier scandalous behaviour and your disobedience to my orders in failing to attend Fairacres immediately, will take some explaining, even for an ex-detective!'

Calder said nothing and Maybe's smile faded. 'Lost your tongue, James?' he queried testily.

'No, sir,' Calder replied. 'But I want to know whether I am actually being reported for discipline and if so, why you haven't cautioned me properly, as required by regulations.'

Maybe's mouth hung open for a moment, then closed sharply into a rat-trap. 'You know the rules as well as I do, Sergeant,' he snapped. 'Yes, you are being reported for discipline, for offences of insubordination, disobedience to orders and neglect of duty. And yes, you are under caution, but I don't intend reeling the caution off to you since by now you should know it by heart! As for Mr. Sharp, his complaint will obviously be dealt with separately and in accordance with the normal complaints procedure once it has been officially recorded.'

Calder nodded. 'Is that it, sir?'

'No, not quite. There is another matter concerning one of your officers which is even more serious. You seem to have had a good night tonight.'

Calder's eyes narrowed. 'Which officer?'

'Keith Jones. Sergeant Lawson in the custody office tells me that a prisoner brought in from the Carlton Club tonight, a Mr. Donald Harris, has complained of being assaulted by a police officer. He has visible injuries consistent with being struck on the head, allegedly by a police baton. I understand Jones was the arresting officer. Mr. Harris is too drunk to be interviewed properly at the moment, but the duty police surgeon has been called to look at him. Do you know anything about this incident? I gather you were at the scene when it took place.'

Calder took a deep breath. He'd had a feeling this would happen. 'Yes, I was there and the man was violent. He attacked and injured Daphne Young. She is currently in hospital, possibly with cracked ribs and concussion. PC Jones arrested him after a struggle.'

'But did he hit him with his baton?'

'Blows were exchanged, yes. Taffy had no alternative. The man was violent.'

Maybe shook his head irritably. 'There is no excuse for this sort of conduct. I will not have my officers assaulting people in revenge for assaults on their colleagues. Obviously there will have to be an investigation and I will be informing headquarters at once to get the process underway.'

'And what about Daphne Young, sir? Have you visited her in hospital yet?'

Maybe gave a puzzled frown as if he couldn't see the link between the two issues. 'No, but I understand you have and that should be sufficient.'

'Nevertheless, I am sure she would appreciate a visit from her shift inspector to indicate his concern for her welfare.'

'I don't have time at the moment and it's not as though she's at death's door, is it?'

Calder regarded him with undisguised contempt. 'Perhaps if senior officers like yourself took as much interest in the welfare of their own personnel as the drunken louts who violently assault them,' he grated, 'they might earn a bit more respect.'

'And you'd do better to watch your tongue,' Maybe snapped. 'You're in enough trouble at the moment as it is, without adding to it. Now get out before I lose patience with you completely.'

Janice Lawson was sitting at her desk in the custody suite when Calder walked in and the sound of shouting and swearing, accompanied by a distinctive clanging sound from the direction of the cell passage behind her, indicated that one of their guests was not entirely satisfied with his accommodation. The smell of stale vomit and urine wafted through the security gate and Calder made a grimace as he sat on the corner of her desk.

'Janice, young Taffy Jones?' he began.

The plump little brunette looked embarrassed. A twenty-eight year old ex-nurse with just two years in the rank of sergeant, she was nevertheless new to the difficult job of custody officer which she had filled only a month before and she was still finding her feet.

'Jim, I'm so sorry,' she replied, 'but I had to report that man's complaint to Inspector Maybe. It was more than my job was worth not to. Besides which, he did have obvious injuries which had to be noted on the custody record.'

Calder shook his head. 'I'm not blaming you Janice,' he said. 'I would have done the same thing in your situation. Were his injuries bad?'

She pushed the custody record across the desk towards him and glanced round her nervously as he scanned the sheet. 'Don't let Mr. Maybe catch you in here looking at that,' she warned. 'I would really be in it then.'

Calder smiled bitterly. 'I'm in it already,' he replied.

'Yes, I heard on the bush telegraph that you had had a bit of a disagreement with him over those three druggie prisoners. I did try to tell him that they needed interviewing, but he just wouldn't listen. All we managed to do was search and document them, then it was a case of chucking them out.'

Calder looked up from the custody record he was studying, suddenly interested in what she was saying. 'I take it we did the usual NIB and address checks?'

She hesitated before answering. 'Well, their address checked out. They gave some flat in Riverside which they've apparently just rented for six months. It was visited and verified by Grandad as it's on his area beat, but we couldn't get anything from the National Identification Bureau. The Police National Computer's down and isn't expected to be back in operation until later today.'

He grunted. 'So much for our wonderful PNC. I wouldn't mind having a look at their custody records some time though. I still feel there was something wrong about that big blond guy.'

She shivered. 'Yes, I know what you mean. He gave me the creeps. You're certainly welcome to see their sheets when the LIO's finished with them.'

'What, Sergeant Grady?'

'Yes, as you know custody records are always routed via the local intelligence officer before they're filed so he knows what's going on.'

Calder nodded. 'Thanks. I'll do that.' He returned to the custody record in his hand and stabbed a finger at one of the written entries. 'Bruising and a deep cut to the right side of the head?'

She nodded. 'Taffy didn't muck about, did he?'

'Anything else?'

Her face reddened noticeably and she gave a little smile. 'Claims to be a bit tender in the lower bits.'

'Our man's not too drunk then, not if he can feel that?'

She shook her head. 'Well, the doctor's been and won't carry out a full examination because of his present state. The awkward sod's certainly had a few, but I think he's putting on the drink bit a lot more than he needs to so he can use drunkenness as mitigation for the assault on Daphne when he goes to court.'

'Bastard!' Calder grated. 'Meanwhile we've got a bloody good policeman hanging by his fingernails just for doing his job. I often wonder what the public would say if they really knew what was going on today.'

'How is Daphne?' Lawson queried.

Calder sighed heavily. 'She'll do, but she's suffering a bit at the moment. Not that Maybe gives a shit. Do you know, he hasn't even been to the hospital yet? Too busy trying to make sure he does all the right things in relation to your prisoner's complaint. We're certainly getting some arse-holes in the force now.'

Lawson smiled. 'Why should you worry? With your army service you'll soon be able to grab your pension and run. Think of the rest of us still here.'

Calder nodded and headed for the door. 'If Maybe has his way I won't stay in long enough to collect my pension. Keep taking the tablets.'

There was a large pile of reports in Calder's tray when he got to the sergeant's office and he scowled. He had never liked paperwork and he usually left it as long as he could, but there was a penalty for that and he was looking at it now. Unclipping his radio harness and laying it on the desk beside him, he deposited himself in the broken swivel chair and made a start, listening with half an ear to the radio as he did so.

Concentration was difficult, however. He was more interested in what was going on outside than in the mundane reports and files on his desk, coupled with which, his mind kept going off at tangents, dwelling on the disciplinary action now hanging over him and the injustice of the complaint against Taffy Jones. He was also constantly disturbed by the coming and going of police cars in the yard at the back and footsteps in the corridor passing his closed door. Even when there was a momentary lull, the heavy clank of the old-fashioned clock on the wall in front of him, as the hands advanced slowly through the final hours of his duty tour, got on his nerves. Finally, he could stand it no longer and, pushing the pile of reports away from him, he pulled out his right-hand drawer and reached for the box of cigars he kept there for special occasions.

It was then that he noticed the small brown envelope lying on his desk, one corner trapped beneath the plastic out-tray. It must have been placed there during the course of the night; there had been nothing on his desk when he had first arrived for duty. Obviously it had been buried under the mountain of paperwork he had taken from his tray a short time before. He never liked sealed envelopes, especially handwritten ones like this which bore just his name on the front and had a large 'Strictly Confidential' endorsement in the top right-hand corner. He frowned heavily as he slit it open with his paper-knife. There was just a single sheet of lined paper inside, obviously torn from a spiral-bound notebook and carrying a simple if intriguing message:

Meet me Peter's Pantry 1900 tonight (21st).
Destroy note after reading.
Baseheart

Calder sat back in his chair and stared at the piece of paper incredulously. What the devil was Baseheart playing at? Had he gone completely round the bend or what? Secret notes like this didn't happen in police stations, only in fictional spy thrillers. As for Peter's Pantry, that was an old bakery down by the railway line they had both used as a tea-spot when they had first been on the beat together as rookie constables. To his knowledge the place had closed at least ten years ago and was now just a derelict shell, occupying a triangle of land that no one could do anything with.

He tapped his teeth with the handle of the paper-knife. First Baseheart's strange conversation in the park and now this. What was going on? He would probably have pondered further on the issue had he not heard Bravo-Alpha Two-Two (PC Nash in Daphne Young's area car) booking off on the radio and, glancing at his watch, he saw that it was dead on quarter to six. Trust Nash always to be the first one in at the end of his duty tour at six. Anyway, it was now time for him to see that the rest of the shift were booked off safely and then hand over responsibility to the early-turn sergeant who was due to appear any second.

Almost as the thought occurred to him, the door swung open. He just had time to slip Baseheart's note back in the drawer under a pile of recruiting pamphlets before Sergeant Tom Lester appeared, his lunchbox under his arm.

'Morning, Jim. Quiet night?'

Calder smiled faintly. 'Busy enough.'

As Lester hung up his coat and dropped his lunch-box into the drawer of the desk opposite, Calder related the occurrences of the tour in as much detail as necessary, omitting only the disciplinary action being taken against him personally.

'Could you visit young Daphne, see she's okay?' he asked.

Lester nodded, dropping into the opposite chair. 'Pity about Taffy. He's a good lad. He wouldn't thump anyone who hadn't asked for it.'

'He'll have a job telling the investigating officer that when one is appointed.'

'I suppose all the necessary has been done? You know, doctor's examination and photographs of the prisoner's injuries etc.? I don't want to have the thing left in the air for me to sort out later.'

Calder stood up. 'Up until a couple of hours ago our man was allegedly too drunk to do anything with, so I have no idea what's been done. It's all down to Inspector Maybe but, knowing him as I do, he will have made damned sure everything is covered to protect his own arse.'

Lester's grey eyes studied him fixedly for a moment, one finger thoughtfully stroking his moustache. 'You okay? You look like shit.'

Calder laughed, but there was no humour in it. 'Getting old, Tom, that's all.' He grabbed his anorak off the back of the chair. 'I'll just see that my troops are all in and then the town's yours.'

'Have you thought anymore about Friday night?'

Calder turned slowly, his face puzzled. 'Friday night?'

'The strike, man. Have you forgotten? Unless the Commissioner capitulates over this damned overtime business, it's everyone out.'

'I really haven't had time to think about it.'

'Well, will you or won't you?'

Calder stared at him. 'I think you already know the answer to that, Tom.'

'Then you're a bloody fool.'

'Yeah, but there again I always have been, so why change now?'

By the time Calder got to the briefing room most of his shift had already signed-off and gone, so he made a point of following their example. It was only when he was almost home that he remembered he had stuffed Baseheart's note in the drawer of his desk. 'Damn and blast it,' he said aloud in his car. 'Richard told me to destroy it.' Instinctively, his foot went for the brake, but by then he was already turning into the tree-lined avenue leading to the estate where he had his small bungalow and he took his foot off and accelerated towards home.

'I don't suppose it will do any harm to leave it there anyway,' he said wearily.

4

Calder woke just after one o'clock in the afternoon to a loud ringing sound. For several seconds he fumbled with the alarm clock before the fog cleared from his brain and he realised it was the telephone beside his bed. 'Yeah?' he barked, still half asleep.

'Sergeant Calder?' queried a haughty female voice.

'This is he.'

'Miss Turnbull, Superintendent Rhymes' secretary.'

Calder sat up quickly, visualising the thin bird-like woman in her smart two-piece grey suit sitting behind her word processor, eyes as hard as flint behind the large tortoiseshell glasses.

'Sorry Miss Turnbull, I was asleep.'

There was no expression of sympathy or under-standing from the cold politically-correct guardian of the inner sanctum, who was feared by new recruits more than the superintendent, merely a brief pause before she continued. 'Superintendent Rhymes asked me to ring you. He would like to see you in his office this afternoon. Shall we say three o'clock?'

Calder shook his head to clear his still befuddled brain. 'Three o'clock? Could you make it later, say four, only I have to . . . er . . . have lunch and . . .'

There was an impatient cough at the other end of

the line. 'This appointment is not negotiable, Sergeant,' she replied, the reproof evident in her tone. 'I have the task of slotting appointments into Mr. Rhymes' diary and he's a very busy man. I'm afraid it will have to be three o'clock. Oh yes, and in uniform please.' The telephone went dead.

'Cow!' Calder said savagely as he set the receiver back on its rest, knowing that it was she and not the governor himself who had actually arranged the time.

So it had happened. The preliminary interview with the head of the police area for the formal issue of the regulation discipline forms, after which the investigating officer would almost certainly arrive to carve him up. 'Nice one,' he breathed.

Swinging his legs over the edge of the bed, he sat there for a few moments and lit a cigarette from the packet on the bedside cabinet, making a mental note to kick the filthy habit one day. The sound of children playing outside drew him to the window and he peered out.

His brown front lawn, bordered by drooping shrubs, met his gaze and he made a grimace, glancing vindictively at the cloudless blue sky, but looking away almost immediately as the glare of the sun seared his eyes. They desperately needed rain, but there was not the slightest hint of it and the temperature had to be around thirty degrees Celsius, even though they were only just into the afternoon.

Next door the two little girls were playing with a gushing hose on their green neatly trimmed lawn and on the other side of the street one of his neighbours was washing down his car. Calder turned away from the window in resignation. Some people never took any notice of anything. Despite the water shortages and the well-publicised need for individual restraint they just carried on as usual, as if such self-imposed privations only applied to other people and not to themselves. That's why he had a brown lawn and theirs' were like manicured bowling-greens. Still, it wasn't up to him to be everyone's moral watchdog and one good thing about the situation was that at least the recent hosepipe ban introduced by the regional water authority did not fall to the police to enforce, so he could ignore the most flagrant transgressions with a clear conscience. With that comforting thought in his mind, he stepped into his en-suite shower and turned the water full on!

Half an hour later his Number One uniform, kept solely for important interviews and royal visits to the force – old army habits died hard – was laid out neatly on his bed and, still clad in his dressing-gown, he rustled up some lunch for himself in his small galley kitchen.

Bacon, eggs and baked beans hardly made a proper nutritious meal, but they were quick and easy and besides, he didn't much care anymore. Had his wife, Margaret, been there she would have insisted on providing something more substantial, but then she wasn't and never would be again. God, or whoever was responsible for such things, had taken her from him three years before.

Breast cancer was always a risk for women of her age, the hospital had told him by way of consolation, but it hadn't helped at all. She was still dead and he was still on his own, missing her like hell. The pair of them had been everything to each other, rookie bobbies who had fallen in love and, somewhat unusually for the service, stayed the course for seventeen wonderful years. Ironically, in the year she died they had been planning to buy a plot of land for a bungalow in the Scottish Highlands, ready for the day he decided to retire. They had wanted nothing more than a place that had good fishing where they could take long walks together. Then she discovered the sinister lump in her breast and nine months later she was gone.

He only wished there had been children. Her spirit would have lived on in them, but somehow they had never got around to starting a family. Strangely enough, one of his worst fears since her death had been that in time he might actually end up forgetting what she looked like. They had never been ones for photographs and those he had of her now were poor in quality. But no, deep down he knew he could never forget Maggie. In fact, she had been his whole life and he could still see her vividly in his mind's eye: the black shoulder-length hair, greying slightly with middle-age; the dimpled chin; and those level grey eyes that had once sparkled so much with life, but in the end had lost their lustre, seeming to say to him, 'Jim, I've had enough. I can't fight anymore.'

Shaking his head to clear the mist from his eyes, he cursed himself for a fool. If the lads and lassies on shift could see him like this they would never believe it. Tough old Jim Calder, who didn't give a damn about anything, reduced to tears like some bloody kid on his first day at school. That would do his macho image a power of good, wouldn't it?

Trouble was, the pain was still there and he couldn't understand why after so long. Wasn't it supposed to heal or something? To be fair, the hospital had originally offered him some support through Social

Services, counselling they had called it, but he had soon rejected that. Social Services? The organisation he had been at logger-heads with for much of his service? It would have been the ultimate humiliation to have had to ask that crowd of woolly-headed do-gooders for help. So he had stubbornly soldiered on alone, keeping himself to himself and sharing his grief with no one; tired, lonely and with nothing to look forward to but a job that right now he wasn't sure he wanted anymore.

Turning off the gas hob, he sat down to eat his 'Egon Ronay masterpiece,' but after a few mouthfuls and a sip of tea he pushed the lot to one side in exchange for another cigarette. The faded photograph of Maggie on the breakfast bar wall stared at him critically.

'You're killing yourself, Jim,' he seemed to hear her say in that peculiar Geordie accent of hers. 'Give it up, man, give it up!'

He studied the unlit cigarette for a moment and nodded to himself. Yeah, well he had given it up once, packed it in just like that after getting through thirty-plus a day since his early teens, but then it had been easy, because he'd done it for Maggie and she'd been there to help him. He'd only gone back to it after her death, succumbing to his old weakness as a way of coping with the trauma of his loss. The ironic thing was, he didn't actually enjoy the damned things anymore. The nicotine often tasted foul and made him feel sick, and smoking was no longer as socially acceptable as it had once been, which meant he felt guilty every time he lit up. So why did he still do it? Maybe because he didn't have a good enough reason to stop. Or was that just a feeble excuse because he lacked the willpower in the first place?

Scowling at the line his thoughts were taking, he abruptly slipped the cigarette back into the packet and returned it to his pocket. Then gulping down some more tea, he turned on the radio to give him something else to think about and immediately regretted it.

'So, Mr. Justice,' snapped a voice he recognised as that of the local radio presenter, Danny Pierce, 'what you're really saying is that the pay packets of your members are more important to you than the public you and your colleagues have sworn to protect?'

'Absolutely not,' Willy Justice's deep booming voice replied. 'We didn't ask for this confrontation and we certainly don't want to take industrial action.'

'Then why do so?'

'Well I think I've already explained that to you. My members have a right to be paid for the overtime they have to work and don't forget, this can involve very long hours in very stressful situations.'

'Don't the public have rights too though, Mr. Justice?'

'Of course they do, but . . .'

'Which you and your members will be ignoring if they go ahead with this strike?'

'It isn't a question of ignoring anything.'

'But you won't be responding to any calls or providing patrols to police the streets if the strike goes ahead, will you?'

'No, but . . .'

'In other words, it will be open season for the criminal? There'll be no one around to stop them?'

'That's just not true.'

'Oh? Then are you saying that there will be some officers on duty; the strike won't be one hundred percent as you claimed earlier?'

'No, I'm not saying that at all. We expect the union's action to be fully supported in this region.'

'So you are expecting officers to be brought in from other regions perhaps?'

'No, I'm not saying that either.' Willy Justice sounded as if he was starting to get rattled and when he continued there was a harsh edge to his voice. 'It would be totally against the new trades union laws for a strike to be broken in this way and if the official side tried it they would have a national strike on their hands, I promise you that!'

'The government could always bring in troops to do your job for you.'

'They wouldn't dare. They would have to declare martial law first and the public wouldn't stand for it.'

'So we're talking about vigilante rule on the streets of Hardingham from Friday night onwards then? Everyone for themselves, is that it?'

'No, of course not. That sort of talk is just media scare-mongering.'

'Media scaremongering or not, Mr. Justice, if your union decides to go ahead with its threat to shut down the local police force it could happen, couldn't it? How would you and your union executive feel then?'

'As I said earlier, Mr. Pierce, the union has been forced into this situation and cannot be held responsible for what happens as a result.'

'Mr. Harding, the Commissioner, doesn't see it that way though, does he? In my interview with him earlier this morning he made the point that this strike is totally irresponsible.'

'Well he would say that, wouldn't he? With the greatest respect to Mr. Harding, this strike is a direct result of his policy to refuse to pay my members for the overtime they are being required to work.'

'But he says there's no more money left in the budget and in the light of the government's latest cuts he has to make savings somewhere.'

'But not at my members' expense; he should understand that.'

'Do you think the public will understand, Mr. Justice? Do you think they will sympathise with your union's action when they are assaulted and there is no reply to their emergency calls? Or when their homes are broken into and there's not a sign of a police officer anywhere?'

Calder shook his head slowly. Willy Justice was on to a hiding to nothing and at the same time he was dragging the image of the force down with him.

'I'm sure people will see that we have a just case,' the union man blustered pompously, but Calder didn't wait to hear anymore and turned the radio off in disgust.

So the Commissioner had been on the radio, had he? That had to be a rare event for John Harding. A policeman in the more traditional mould, he was well known for his anti-media views and normally avoided contact with what he called 'the gutter press' unless he was actually cornered or wanted to use them for his own propaganda purposes. It had always amazed Calder that someone like Harding had managed to survive in the present political climate when Home Secretaries seemed to be looking for younger more dynamic clones as chief officers, especially female graduates or members of the so-called ethnic minorities. Maybe the Police Authority couldn't find a good enough excuse for terminating the old man's contract and were waiting for him to drop himself in it? Calder smiled grimly as he returned to the bedroom to change into his uniform. Well if they were, this impending strike could be the very rock on which his ship foundered and then the sharks would be in for the kill!

He tried not to think about the deteriorating situation as he climbed into his car and set off for the station, reasoning that he had more important personal worries to occupy his mind than to dwell on things he could do nothing about. But the radio changed all that the moment he flicked on the button and caught the tail-end of the familiar news-time jingle. This was followed by the brisk announcement that there would be an extended news bulletin, 'with Judy Grace,' and the rich voice of the popular newscaster then plunged straight in without further preamble:

'For the first time for over a hundred years a British police force is set to take industrial action. At 10pm on Friday night, the Central Region branch of the National Police Union will be calling its members out on strike over the non-payment of overtime allowances. The Commissioner of the force, Mr. John Harding, has put the blame for the situation squarely on the government. In an interview with our own Danny Pierce this morning, he made the following comments:

'This is the second time in twelve months,' Harding's voice suddenly growled from the twin speakers, 'that this government has seen fit to impose additional spending cuts on the police service. As commissioner, I am responsible for the efficient policing of the Central Region, but I need proper funding to do it and yet I am constantly being required to make savings on a shrinking budget. Those savings have to come from somewhere and, whilst I understand the feelings of my officers over this issue, some unpleasant decisions have had to be taken.'

'So you don't blame them for striking?' Danny Pierce's voice queried.

'I said I understand their feelings, but strike action is not the answer and in my view, to take such a course would be totally irresponsible.'

'But if this strike happens, who do you think will be to blame for the situation?'

'I am not in the business of apportioning blame and my senior officers and myself are doing all we can to avert the possibility of industrial action. But I strongly recommend to the government that it should reconsider its demand for the present financial cutbacks and do so as a matter of urgency in the interests of public safety. As I have already said, it is not possible to provide efficient policing without proper funding. What my region needs, in common with the rest of the police service, is more money, not less.'

'In other words, if you pay peanuts you get monkeys?'

An embarrassed cough.

'Your words, not mine, Mr. Pierce.'

There was a faint laugh in the studio and Judy Grace was back.

'Well, that was John Harding, Commissioner of the Central Region Police Force, during an interview with Danny Pierce earlier this morning and we shall be hearing the response of Mr. Willy Justice for the National Police Union shortly. But before that, what has the government got to say about Mr. Harding's comments? To find out, we approached the Home Office, and Home Office minister, Derek Playford, is on the telephone now. Mr. Playford, you have heard what Mr. Harding has said. What is your reaction?'

'Well, I have to make it clear that I have not heard all the interview, but I would like to take up the Commissioner's point about funding. This government has always considered law and order a high priority and in real terms funding for the police has increased considerably since we came to office.'

'Yes, but you're cutting back on it now.'

'That's not strictly true. We are anxious to ensure the police service, like every other public service, delivers real value for money and that economies are made where appropriate.'

'How can you justify approving a budget at the start of the financial year, then clawing the money back afterwards?'

'That is an exaggeration. All budgets, in whatever industry, should be flexible and subject to adjustment as an ongoing process. That is good business. We are merely seeking to make chief officers more accountable by regularly reviewing their expenditure requirements.'

'What if there is a police strike as a result of these cut-backs? Won't your government feel responsible for any crime-wave that might result?'

'Policing is a matter for the relevant chief officer.'

'It could prove a bit embarrassing for the Prime Minister though, couldn't it? After all, Hardingham is his own constituency!'

'I must repeat, policing is a matter for the relevant chief officer and I am quite sure Mr. Harding has the situation well under control.'

'Thank you, Mr. Playford. We hope so too. Now a short time ago, Willy Justice, the Chairman of the National Police Union, was in the studio and he had this to say . . .'

Calder snapped the radio off and swung into the police station yard, his eyes searching desperately for a parking space. The place was packed with a whole variety of vehicles, some of them parked at crazy angles as if the drivers had simply abandoned them. He found a space between the oil storage tank and one of the police Ford Transits that looked as though it had been driven through a ploughed field. No bloody pride anymore he thought to himself as he locked up. At one time it was a 'discipline job' to leave a police vehicle in that state. Now no one seemed to care.

'Hey, Jim!' a voice suddenly bellowed, shaking him out of his reverie. Turning, he saw the podgy, bald-headed figure of Sergeant Bob Grady, the local intelligence officer, or LIO, leaning out of his ground-floor office window. He had a sheath of papers in one hand and waved them at Calder as he headed for the back door of the station. 'Got something for you, me boy,' he encouraged.

'Have to wait, Bob,' Calder snapped back, glancing at his watch.

'It'll do when you've seen the old man,' came the reply.

Calder half half-turned. 'How did *you* know I was going to see him?'

Grady laughed. 'Whole nick knows, me boy. See you afterwards, eh?'

'Bloody bush telegraph,' Calder muttered as he inserted his warrant card into the security lock of the back door. 'It's a wonder I'm not on local radio as well.'

The area commander's office was at one end of a long corridor on the first floor and the only access to it was via the office of his formidable secretary. Calder knocked once on the half open door of the secretary's office and almost immediately strode in. He knew that Miss Turnbull disliked anyone entering her kingdom before receiving an invitation to do so and he enjoyed provoking her. Most secretary's in the service were pleasant, helpful people, but she had an elevated sense of her own importance and he felt she needed taking down a peg or two from time to time. On this occasion, however, he was disappointed, for the ogress was not at her desk. She was obviously off somewhere photo-copying or lasering some unsuspecting probationary constable with her eyes.

For a moment he stood in the centre of the room, wondering whether to sit on one of the chairs arranged along the right-hand wall or to knock on the superintendent's tightly closed door to announce his arrival. He glanced at his watch and frowned. Only five to three, so he was early. Better to wait a few moments.

He listened. Someone was in Rhymes' office; he could hear the murmur of conversation and the clink of cups. Maybe Miss Turnbull was receiving some dictation? He grinned. Well, she wouldn't be receiving anything else, that was for sure. Poor old George Rhymes would run a mile! Checking the corridor first he strolled round to the other side of Miss Turnbull's desk and studied her diary, trailing one finger across the neat list of appointments and mentally noting each one in turn. 0900 morning conference; 1015 Meeting

Chief Inspector Maxwell (Post-college briefing); 1100 Douglas Sharp (PA). So the little sod had come in to complain after all; 1200 Inspector Maybe. Well now, he had obviously got up bright and early and no prizes for guessing why; 1300 lunch; 1400 Deputy Commissioner Stephen Turner. So that's who was still in there, Harding's favoured batman. Now what on earth was he doing in the nick? He was officially the force's head of operations and deputy to the boss himself; the only other policeman at chief officer level, since the remainder of the top echelon were civilian . . . what did they call them? Oh yes, principal officers, that was it.

Unable to contain his curiosity Calder returned to the safe side of the desk and after checking the corridor again and seeing no sign of anyone he crept to the door of the superintendent's office and pressed one ear against it. The panelling was only thin and he was able to follow the conversation inside even above the clink of cups and the creak of chairs.

'Let's get this straight, sir,' Rhymes said. 'What you're really saying is that if I don't do what you want I won't have my service contract renewed. That's about the strength of it, isn't it?'

'Not at all, George,' a second voice patronised. 'I was merely pointing out how difficult it will be for a man of your age to convince a review board he has the necessary qualities to justify an extension of service. After all, competition for the superintending ranks is very strong indeed. I just thought you might like the chance to . . . er . . . prove yourself.'

'And if I do prove myself what are my chances then?' Rhymes queried dryly. 'You know very well I can't afford to retire for another three years.'

'By which time you will be fifty-six, going on fifty-seven?'

'Exactly and under the old system it wouldn't have mattered, because I could have stayed on until I was sixty, as of right.'

A heavy exasperated sigh cut him off. 'Yes, George,' his visitor snapped, 'but we're not under the old system anymore, are we? Now it's five-yearly renewable contracts and yours is up in six months, simple as that!' Then abruptly Turner's tone became more conciliatory. 'Look, George, all I'm saying is that you need a friend on the review board to give you an edge; someone sympathetic to your needs.'

'And to get that friend, I've got to sacrifice my principles?'

Another loud sigh. 'George, George, you're looking at things all the wrong way.'

'Maybe, but I don't like this proposal, I don't like it at all.'

'You don't have to like it, George. Just do your bit, that's all.'

'And what about the press?'

'What's it got to do with them?'

'Well, the union's proposed industrial action has attracted a lot of media interest and if what we've discussed were ever to get out . . .'

'That's exactly why I impressed on you earlier the need for extreme tact and diplomacy. The Commissioner is very keen to make this work. He sees it as a golden opportunity to redress the balance and after all, it is ultimately for the good of the service. Just look on it as your chance to demonstrate your value to the organisation. I'm sure you can rely on your contribution being taken into consideration when your contract is reviewed, eh? I can't be fairer than that, can I?'

'I don't think fairness comes into it, sir. It sounds more like blackmail to me.'

'Rubbish, George; it's nothing of the sort. Now, will you speak to our man and reassure him or what?'

'Do I have a choice, sir?' Rhymes said bitterly.

There was a cold humourless laugh. 'Splendid. After all, we don't want any wavering, do we? Well now, I must be off.' The scrape of a chair. 'Keep me posted, won't you? And in the meantime, George, let's make sure justice does prevail, eh?'

Another cold laugh, but it was noticeable that Rhymes did not join in.

Calder frowned heavily, wondering what on earth was going on. Plainly it had something to do with the strike, a hidden agenda that only a chosen few were privy to, but what? Perhaps the Commissioner had an ace up his sleeve that was designed to queer the union's pitch at the penultimate hour, but if so, George Rhymes was certainly not too happy about it and the Deputy Commissioner had had to resort to a form of career pressure to make him go along with the plan. That in itself made Calder feel strangely uneasy.

He wasn't given long to think about the issue, however, for the next moment there was the sound of a hand on the door handle. He just had time to dart across the room and deposit himself in one of the chairs before the door opened and the thick-set figure of George Rhymes stood to one side to allow his visitor past.

The latter was a short wiry-looking man, with gold-framed glasses, thin gingery hair and a small moustache that ironically, made his fair youthful face look even younger. But for the moustache, Calder thought uncharitably, he might at first sight have been mistaken for a senior member of the Boy's Brigade in his smart uniform, but there was nothing youthful about his expression. The small blue eyes were cold and hard and the brief smile he directed towards Calder, when he nodded perfunctorily in greeting, held the sort of warmth to be found in the gaze of a cobra.

Now just thirty-eight years of age, Deputy Commissioner Stephen Wilson Turner MA, BA Hons, had joined the police service only fourteen years before as a graduate entrant and had climbed the ladder very rapidly indeed, according to internal gossip, dislodging a number of his more trusting colleagues on the way. An import on promotion from the Met, he had in ten short months earned an unenviable reputation for himself as a ruthless and devious tactician, interested solely in the furtherance of his own career and exhibiting about as much charisma as an android.

Briefly meeting that cold gaze as Turner donned his flat cap and strode briskly from the office, Calder slowly shook his head. A nice beauty, he thought, and not the sort of man he would want to rely on when the chips were down, as Rhymes obviously intended doing. It would be like making a pact with the devil and he wondered whether the police force deserved Turner or Turner deserved the police force. Either way, there didn't seem much hope for those doing the job on the ground anymore, or was he just feeling depressed and sorry for himself?

'Are you going deaf, James?'

Calder started, immediately shaken out of his reverie. Rhymes' voice had an irritable edge to it and he suddenly realised that the other must have already spoken to him at least once. 'Sorry, sir,' he exclaimed. 'My mind was wandering.'

Rhymes grunted from behind the desk in his office. 'Well, perhaps you would kindly get it to wander in here,' he snapped. 'I haven't got all day.'

Calder nodded and taking a deep breath stepped through the doorway, his gaze automatically scanning the teak desk top for the familiar discipline form he knew must be there.

'Shut the door and sit down,' Rhymes directed, studying Calder narrowly for a moment before returning his gaze to the file in front of him.

A chunky balding man, with a perpetual worried frown and haunted blue eyes, George Rhymes always seemed to have the weight of the world on his shoulders. That was hardly surprising given his personal circumstances which had become common knowledge, not just around the nick, but, sadly, throughout the whole police region. His wife had walked out on him several years before, leaving him with the job of bringing up twin teenage sons and coping with a rebellious twenty-year-old daughter who, as a fiery anti-establishment miss, had ended up in all sorts of minor scrapes with the police until she had settled down. Now at fifty-three, with a negative equity mortgage forcing him to remain in a house that cost him an arm and a leg to run and all three of his offspring requiring support at universities in different parts of the country, he had a financial millstone round his neck that would have frightened lesser men to death. No wonder, Calder mused, that he was so eager to stay on in the job. Retiring on pension, even with the salary he earned, would have been ruinous for him.

It was all such a bloody shame, because George Rhymes was a decent hard-working bloke, liked and respected by everyone under his command for his humanity and his approachable style of management. A copper's copper, he always showed genuine concern for the welfare of his staff despite his own problems and he was usually one of the first to visit officers who had been injured on duty or were on long-term sick-leave. This trait became apparent now as he dumped the file he was studying into one of the plastic desk-trays and sat back in his seat, studying Calder fixedly.

'Daphne Young,' he said.

Thrown for a moment, Calder just stared at him.

Rhymes sighed heavily and leaned forward. 'Daphne Young?' he whispered. 'One of your officers? Injured last night? Remember? Damn it, man, you're not going senile as well as deaf, are you?'

Calder recovered with a jolt. 'My apologies, sir, but I was expecting . . .'

'We'll come to you in a moment, James. Now, about Daphne. I went to see her this morning. She's being released from the hospital later this afternoon and though she is likely to be off sick for a time it seems she's suffered no serious damage, apart from cuts and bruising.'

Calder breathed a sigh of relief. 'Well, that's good news, sir. When I saw her myself the hospital still had to do tests.'

Rhymes grunted. 'Did Inspector Maybe visit her?'

Calder's mouth tightened. 'I don't know, sir,' he

lied, wondering at the same time why he couldn't bring himself to be disloyal even to an arse-hole.

Rhymes' eyes gleamed. 'You know damned well he didn't, James. Anyway, I've dealt with that matter already. Now tell me about young Taffy Jones. What really happened there?'

Briefly Calder related the story, this time being completely candid about the incident, and Rhymes scowled.

'Well, for your information, he was dragged out of bed at ten o'clock this morning on the instructions of the the Regional Complaints Department and suspended from duty on an allegation of Assault Occasioning Actual Bodily Harm.'

'The bastards!' Calder breathed, unable to stop himself.

Rhymes raised his eyebrows. 'Only doing their job, James,' he replied grimly. 'And you know as well as I do that under this year's new discipline regulations suspension for a bobby accused of a criminal assault is now automatic. I gather young Taffy was lucky he wasn't actually arrested and put in the cells.'

'You're joking.'

'Not at all, James. However, the complainant was found to have only superficial injuries when he was examined by the police surgeon and due to his own violent behaviour being a contributory factor, the CPS felt such a course of action was unwarranted, although a full prosecution file will still be required for consideration.'

Calder's eyes blazed. 'A file . . . against Taffy? The CPS want to take a look at Daphne. See what was done to her by the animal he nicked.'

Rhymes shook his head wearily and sat back in the

chair again. 'It wouldn't make any difference, James, and you know it. I don't like it anymore than you do, but times have changed and we have to go along with them. We're the villains now, not the criminals, so what do you expect to happen?' His eyes gleamed again and he reached forward to pick up another report. 'Talking of which, I trust you had a restless sleep and your ears were burning all through it?'

Calder's stomach churned.

'At eleven o'clock this morning I entertained a certain Mr. Douglas Sharp for coffee. Name ring a bell?' Calder nodded. 'Good! Well, Mr. Sharp was not at all happy with you or the time it took you to get to his house.'

'No sir.'

'No sir! Well fortunately for you, Mr. Sharp had cooled down by the time he saw me and after two cups of my excellent Colombian ground coffee and three, not two, bourbon biscuits he agreed to leave the matter in my hands and went away rejoicing.'

Calder breathed a sigh of relief. 'Thank you, sir.'

Rhymes raised his eyebrows again.

'Oh don't thank me yet, Sergeant, for there's this as well.' He held up a report that looked to be several pages long. 'Inspector Maybe was obviously most put out when he prepared this little novelette and I can well understand his feelings.'

Calder's mouth tightened again, but he made no comment and Rhymes slammed the report down on the desk top. 'You had a busy night, Sergeant,' he rapped. 'Is there anyone out there you didn't manage to upset during your tour of duty? Well?'

'I've nothing to say, sir.'

'You never defend yourself, do you, James? Proper old soldier, aren't you?'

'I've nothing to defend, sir. I do my job to the best of my ability and I expect others to do the same.'

Rhymes smiled thinly. 'I know you do, James, and so does someone else.' He pushed another report across the desk towards Calder. 'Read that. It certainly saved your bacon.'

Puzzled, Calder picked up the report and scanned the contents. It had been submitted by Detective Inspector Steve Torrington on the incident at Cooper's Store and several phrases jumped out at him.

'But for the prompt attendance of Sergeant Calder on the scene, the three offenders might well have got away . . . local target criminals with a long history of offences of burglary, taking and driving away and assault . . . as a result of these arrests, it is anticipated a large number of local burglaries will be cleared up.'

'I . . . I don't understand,' Calder began, returning the report to the desk.

Rhymes grunted. 'It seems Mr. Torrington has a much better opinion of you than Mr. Maybe,' he replied, 'and it's certainly a relief to know you've done something right for a change. For your information, following CID raids on the addresses of those three Herberts so much stolen property was recovered it took three trips by two of our Transits to recover it all!'

'But sir, I have to say I didn't . . .'

Rhymes cut him off with a wave of his hand. 'Now don't go and spoil it all,' he snapped and held up one of the reports in each hand. 'As far as I'm concerned they both cancel each other out. No fizzer and no commendation. So take it you've been bollocked and congratulated all in one go. Okay? And listen, I don't want to see you in here again on this sort of thing. I realise you're under a lot of pressure at the moment with some of your shift, plus the other patrol sergeant, on loan to the rave festival, but everyone else is in the same boat and you'll just have to manage as best you can. I know I have got more important things to worry about, with my area on half-strength and the possibility of a police strike in the offing, than sorting out internal bickering among supervisors. Got it? Now clear off, I've got work to do!'

Calder rose from the chair and turned for the door like a man in a dream. Good old Steve Torrington. He owed him for this.

'Oh by the way, James.'

Hand on the door knob, Calder turned quickly. 'Sir?'

Rhymes forced a smile. 'Do try and get on with Mr. Maybe in future, will you?'

Only when Hell freezes over, Calder mused and as he passed through the outer office where Miss Turnbull was now back behind her desk, he directed an extravagant wink in her direction and had the satisfaction of seeing her stiffen with indignation.

Bob Grady was seated at his beloved computer terminal when Calder dropped by his office and he swivelled his chair round to face him, a big grin on his face. 'How was it, Jim? Bum still sore from the strapping?'

'Piss off,' Calder said pleasantly, 'and just tell me what you've got for me.'

Grady reached across the desk beside the computer and disentangled a sheaf of papers from a bundle of computer print-outs and photographs in one of his many plastic trays. 'This,' he said triumphantly, wheezing at the exertion.

Calder took the papers from him curiously.

'Got this little novel off the box when I put through a check this morning,' Grady explained between loud gulps of coffee from a Mickey Mouse mug. 'I got a note from Janice Lawson to say the PNC was down last night and she couldn't get any information on the three junkies you had in.'

Calder hardly heard him and he felt his heart already begin to race as he studied the papers in his hands.

'That should bring tears to the eyes of that prat Maybe,' Grady went on. 'The girl and the black guy were just a couple of small-time pushers-cum-users, but your blond hippy is evidently a real bad dude!'

More as a means of shutting Grady up so he could concentrate, Calder started reading aloud from one sheet. 'John Joseph Preston . . . born in Manchester . . . aged twenty-nine . . . numerous addresses, yeah, yeah, yeah . . . NIB number. Well, that's a foregone conclusion. Aliases, shit, he's got enough of them . . .'

'Only one since last year when he got religion apparently,' Grady interjected and, half standing, pulled the corner of the page towards him and pointed. 'See? Now calls himself Solomon.'

'Well, I'll be damned,' Calder breathed, remembering what Steve Torrington had told him, 'I've certainly heard that name before.' He read on, feeling a crawling sensation at the back of his neck as he did so: 'Six foot two inches tall, thin build, full beard, shoulder-length blond hair, recent tattoo of "Jehovah" on left arm. Usually wears rimless spectacles with plain glass. Warning signals? Extremely violent. Believed psychotic. Convictions? Bloody hell, how many has he got?'

'Sixteen,' Grady replied in the middle of trying to demolish a chocolate bar. 'GBH, robbery, arson, supplying heroin and cocaine, car theft, buggery, sodomy. You name it, he's done it. Versatile boy, this one.'

Calder tapped his arm and pointed to a reference number at the top of the first sheet. 'What's that?'

Grady twisted his neck and screwed up his eyes to see. 'Special Branch interest,' he replied, returning to his chocolate bar. 'That's their reference, but I can't get hold of the file without special clearance.'

'But he's not wanted?'

'Nope. Your mate in SB, Chief Inspector Richard Baseheart, did a number on him two years ago. Raided a house in Birmingham after some info' that he had an arms and drugs cache there and was planning a big job. But our man was on his toes before the boys in blue arrived and all they found was an empty house and some reefers. Richard Baseheart apparently reckoned Solomon was tipped off from the inside.'

'What by one of the raid team? Surely not?'

'Something like that, but they never got anywhere with it and it died a death . . . except as far as Richard Baseheart was concerned, that is. Solomon had become a bit of a *cause celebre* for him and he chased the guy all over the country for three more months before the big cheese in his department told him to cool it and find himself some other anarchist.'

'Anarchist? Is that what he's doing now?'

Grady couldn't answer until the artificial abscess

created by his chocolate bar dissolved, then he nodded. 'Yeah, as I said, he's got religion; quotes from the Bible and all that. Apparently thinks he's the new Messiah sent to punish us sinners. He'll find plenty of those at the rave site anyway. If you want to know a bit more, I'm sure DI Torrington will oblige. He was on the raid too, when he was a DS on SB, and he should certainly be able to fill in any blanks.'

Calder rolled the sheets of paper up into a tube and regarded him with disbelief. 'Do you always eat like that?'

Grady stopped licking the chocolate off his fingers and belched. 'Like what?'

Calder shook his head slowly and swung back to the door. 'Thanks for all your hard work, Bob,' he called over his shoulder. 'Much appreciated.'

'Oh, Jim?' Grady called after him.

Calder turned slowly and Grady grinned again. 'Calamine,' he said.

'Calamine what?'

'It's a lotion you get from the chemists. My old grandmother swore by it. It's very good for stings and heat rashes if your bum is still sore.'

'Go fry your nuts!' Calder retorted and left Grady shaking with laughter over his keyboard.

Torrington wasn't in his office and Tracy, the young administration clerk, said he was 'out on enquiries', which probably meant he was down the golf club with Dennis Sale, considering the merits of the various brands of ale on offer.

'Tell him I called, will you?' Calder said.

Tracy gave him her best smile. 'Of course, Sergeant. Any other message?'

Calder nodded and as Tracy put down her nail-file

and picked up a pen he dictated quickly. 'Leave him a note to say: "Thanks for the accolade and speak to me soonest. Maybe you were right re Solomon." Okay?'

Tracy finished writing, studied the note and frowned. 'That's a funny message,' she said.

'Isn't it?' Calder replied and left the office with a grin on his face.

5

There was a strange atmosphere at the station when Calder reported for duty at six o'clock that night. As he drove into the yard he noticed four or five uniformed bobbies standing in a group by the oil tank, apparently arguing about something. The group broke up and the officers strolled away in different directions the moment they saw his car. One of them was Maurice Stone and he recognised at least two officers off the day shift.

Then, poking his head round the door of the briefing room, he saw another collection of mixed day and night shift officers standing together in one corner, talking in low voices. Again, all conversation stopped when they saw him and as the members of the day shift hurriedly departed, no doubt for the bar at the top of the building, his own crew suddenly found the pressing need to study the updated beat information provided on the new computer terminals placed at intervals around the room or to check their paperwork dockets in the adjacent office.

He found Tom Lester in the sergeants' office already donning his anorak. 'Much?' he queried as he dumped his lunchbox and civilian anorak on an adjacent chair.

Lester raised his eyebrows and nodded towards the computer terminal in the corner of their own office. 'Well there's plenty of scandal on the magic box if you've got a couple of hours to spare. Festival's certainly been hotting up all day. They've had a number of punch-ups there and a nasty stabbing. Girl responsible apparently. She put a blade into some young lad's stomach.'

'Serious?'

'Could be. He's in intensive care and they're still looking for the girl.'

'Any description?'

Lester shrugged. 'It's all on the box. Skinny blonde apparently. The suggestion is she was a junkie and approached the kid for some money to feed her habit in exchange for sexual favours. When he refused she did the business on him.'

'Nice lady. Anything else?'

Lester sat down for a moment with a heavy sigh. He was well used to Calder's liking for the old-style verbal hand-over and his distrust of the computerised self-briefing system that had now been introduced and he knew from past experience that it was better, and quicker, to humour him than to try arguing the toss about it.

'Yeah, as I said, quite a bit of trouble at the festival and it seems to have spilled over into the town. We must have dealt with at least twenty incidents involving festival drop-outs and locals – most of the latter from our unemployed yob fraternity – and there have been a dozen walk-in thefts at town centre shops.' He thought a second. 'Also three cars stolen – one found on the festival site burned out – and an attempted arson at a farm near Saxby Village.

Apparently the farmer refused to give some weirdos free milk and eggs and they took exception to it. Fortunately he spotted the smoke in one of his barns in time and put a small blaze out.'

'You've had a busy day.'

Lester nodded, but made no move to leave.

'Something else?'

The other frowned. 'Yeah, bit of worrying intelligence actually. Drug Squad have a couple of people on the rave site and they suspect that most of the incidents we've been having are the result of a deliberate attempt by someone to whip things up. There's a lot of cannabis, ecstasy and LSD in circulation and we've got unconfirmed reports that some of the hallucinogenic stuff is now being given away free for this precise purpose.'

Calder whistled. 'Free? Someone obviously does mean business.'

'Exactly. A lot of the kids we've had in have been totally out of their minds and the hospital casualty unit is already running at nearly full stretch. I suspect things will get worse after dark tonight.'

'Thanks a lot.'

'That still isn't the end of it.'

'Go on.'

'Well, a substantial number of the local residents who opposed the festival in the first place, mainly those from the Warren Estate, have set up an action group.'

Calder half-closed his eyes, visualising the Northern section of the canal beyond Wharf Cottages and the large middle-class housing estate bordering it. 'Hardly surprising really,' he remarked. 'Theirs is the closest residential area to the site. That continuous racket from across the canal must be driving them crackers.'

'Agreed, but their representatives have since been into the nick with a warning that unless the festival is closed down they'll close it down themselves by force. There has already been one skirmish between a small group of them and some festival-goers in front of the main entrance to the site. Fortunately, security called the police festival control in time and the residents were sent packing, but the thing could have turned pretty nasty.'

'Is that it now?'

Lester grinned and stood up. 'More or less. All twelve of our cells are full, two of them doubled up, but it's expected that at least half of our guests will be bailed in the next two hours and three of my crew are staying on to run another six over to Gratling nick in the prison van, so you should have room for some more customers later.'

On his way to the door he half-turned. 'Oh yes, and you might find yourself a bit short on radio batteries.'

Calder looked puzzled. 'Why? Someone been eating them? We had plenty last night.'

'Yeah, I know you did, but it turns out that one of the chargers has been up the shoot for a couple of days at least and no one sussed it. Apparently half the batteries we've been using haven't been charged properly and the older ones have been prone to failure. I gather you had problems last night.'

'Only young Porter-Nash.'

Lester shook his head. 'No, Grandad had to change his twice, so I'm told, and John Powell had a similar problem.'

'No one told me about it.'

'They probably didn't think it was worth

mentioning. We're always having trouble with the damned things anyway. But I would go careful tonight. My shift had to use some of the batteries reserved for your lot.'

Calder scowled. So he had been wrong about PC Nash after all. If his battery had packed up on him, he owed the little sod an apology. Blast it! Nash was really going to love seeing him choke over that. 'Brilliant,' he grated, 'It never rains, but it hisses!'

Tom grinned, obviously enjoying his chronicle of bad news. 'On that note, I expect the boss told you about young Taffy Jones' suspension when you saw him earlier, eh?'

Calder's scowl deepened. 'Is there anyone who doesn't know I saw Rhymes?'

Lester scratched his nose. 'Well, I don't think it's got to Gratling nick yet.'

'But it will when your crew get over there with the prisoners no doubt. See you, Tom.'

'And the strike?'

'We discussed that a few hours ago. Situation hasn't changed, all right?'

Lester shrugged and left the office. 'Your funeral,' he called over his shoulder and went off along the corridor whistling loudly.

Calder was hardly aware of his departure, for he had suddenly noticed the big pile of reports stacked on the corner of his desk beside his already over-flowing tray. Those hadn't been there at the end of his last duty tour, so obviously someone had been very busy since. It didn't take him long to find out who that someone was, for there was a large typed memorandum addressed to him in the middle of his desk:

Please clear your tray as a matter of priority. Some of this paperwork is already well overdue. Please also note I have now routed Sergeant Dalton's paperwork to you, since she can hardly deal with it while she is away at the festival.

Douglas Maybe
Inspector.

Calder swore several times. So now he was not only expected to do his own work, which with everything else that had been happening he just hadn't had the time to tackle properly, but to take on the work of the other shift sergeant as well. Torchy certainly had the knife into him this time and no mistake.

Snatching up the area deployment sheet from his tray, he stamped from the office towards the briefing room, his face set and angry. His mood wasn't improved either by the sight of his shift gathered round one corner of the briefing table, talking in low voices.

'Okay, so what gives?' he snapped as the group broke up and made for the nearest chairs. 'I've had enough of all this intrigue and childish whispering behind hands. This is a police station, not a bloody primary school!'

Silence, save for the shuffling of feet and one or two embarrassed coughs as gazes were lowered to study the table top. His face hardened even more and he glowered at each member of his crew in turn.

'We have no secrets on this shift,' he continued softly, 'so out with it. Now!'

Jenny Major, a mature redhead who had been with the force for over fifteen years and was one of the linchpins of the shift, nodded. 'Sorry, Sarge, nothing against you, but everyone's worried about what's going to happen Friday night when the strike is supposed to take place.'

Calder's anger left him and his eyes narrowed as his gaze roved round the dozen or so tense anxious faces that were now raised expectantly towards him. He had a serious morale problem on his hands, he could see that immediately, and if he was honest with himself, he had seen it coming for several days, but had tried to ignore it. Trouble was, he couldn't think of anything he could do to solve it. A bit of leadership support from the shift inspector would have helped, but he'd given up crying for the moon long ago.

'I realise you're all in a state of flux over this business,' he began carefully, 'and I sympathise, I really do. But the decision as to whether or not you join the strike has to be yours. I can't make it for you.'

'That's a cop-out, Sarge,' Major replied sharply.

Calder sighed and nodded in agreement. 'Yeah, I suppose it is. All right, if it's my opinion you're looking for I'll give it to you.' He thrust out his jaw aggressively. 'I don't believe in police strikes and never will. We have all taken an oath to serve and protect the public and that's what we should be doing. I know that might sound naff in this wonderful modern era with all its so-called human rights and freedom of speech, but if it does that's tough. I shall be on duty as usual every night I am rostered to work and if that means I shall be policing the bloody town on my own on Friday, then so be it.'

'If we work, we'll be called scabs,' Maurice Stone pointed out uneasily.

Calder nodded again. 'And if we go on strike, we'll be called a lot worse. Any of you looked at the magic briefing box yet or have you all been too busy talking about industrial action?'

There was a unanimous nodding of heads round the table which he took to mean that they had already fully briefed themselves.

'Then you'll know the problems the day shift have already had. Things are hotting up and we can anticipate an escalation of those problems tonight. Fights, drug abuse, assaults, smash-and-grabs; you name it, we can look forward to it. By Friday night it will probably be even worse, especially as the whole world will then know from the press that the police are on strike. Can you visualise what will happen to this town and every other town in the central region once the scum we have to deal with realise we aren't around anymore?' He shook his head grimly. 'I'd rather be called a scab than have that on my conscience.'

Silence once more greeted what had unintentionally developed into an emotive speech and Calder sat back in his chair for a moment, annoyed with himself for baring his soul to such an extent.

'Thank you, Sarge,' Major said quietly. 'That was all we wanted to hear.'

Her eyes gleamed with admiration and even Porter-Nash looked impressed. Inspector Maybe, on the other hand, had an entirely different view of the proceedings when he chose that particular moment to stalk through the open doorway, his thin face wearing an even more disagreeable expression than usual.

'Isn't it about time this shift was out on patrol, Sergeant?' he snapped. 'You're already ten minutes late.'

Calder, who had been sitting with his back to the door, stood up and turned to face him. 'They're just about to go out, sir,' he replied quietly. 'There was a problem that needed to be dealt with while they were all together.' He turned back to the waiting officers. 'Okay, let's get moving. You should already know from the magic box what areas you are covering, except that Jenny Major, Bravo-Alpha Two-Three, will also be looking after Two-Four's area, due to the absence of Taffy Jones, and Maurice Stone will be covering Two-Two's area, plus his own foot beat, whilst Daphne Young is on sick leave. '

Amid the scraping of chairs and the general movement towards the door he added: 'Oh yes, and make sure you choose the right radio batteries. We've had a problem with one of the chargers.'

'Chaos!' Maybe grated, casting a critical eye over each of the officers in turn as they filed past him uneasily. 'Absolute chaos, Sergeant. Heaven knows how long this briefing would have taken you under the old system. And tell me, why have you put Stone on Two-Two's area instead of Nash? Bit of favouritism there, I suspect.'

Calder studied him coldly. 'Nash took over Daphne Young's car last night, after she went to hospital,' he replied. 'Maurice Stone hasn't been given the opportunity of covering an area car beat before, even though he got his driving ticket two months ago.'

'Never mind that. Stone has plenty of time, but Nash hasn't if he's going to go anywhere. Change them round please.'

'You're joking? Don't you see what that will look like to Maurice Stone now that I've told him he's covering Two-Two's area?'

Maybe raised his eyebrows. 'I never joke, James and I'm not particularly concerned about the personal perceptions of junior officers under my command. Change them round before they go out and that's an order, unless you want another visit to see Superintendent Rhymes, that is.'

'You're determined to make me look a prick, aren't you?'

Maybe turned for the door. 'I don't need to do that, James,' he replied with a faint smirk. 'You do it so well all on your own without any help from me.'

Calder found both officers still in the locker-room, kitting up. Maurice Stone took the news badly and even Nash looked uncomfortable.

'So I'm not to be trusted, Sarge, is that it?' Stone exclaimed.

Calder sighed. 'That's not it at all, Maurice.'

'Then why make the change at all? Bloody Torchy's behind this, isn't he?'

Calder didn't confirm or deny the fact and Stone swore angrily. 'It's the old skin thing, isn't it? Keeping the nigger in his place!'

'Don't you come that colour nonsense with me!' Calder snapped, his eyes blazing angrily. 'There's no racism on this shift and you damned well know it. I'm surprised that you of all people would try that one on. Now get out on patrol before you say something really stupid!'

Stone glared at him, his fists clenched angrily by his sides as he fought to control himself. Then, suddenly throwing the car keys at Nash, who was standing uneasily on the sidelines, he grabbed his helmet from his locker and headed for the door.

Nash fidgeted with the keys as if they had just come

out of an oven and looked down at his feet unhappily. For the first time he looked unsure of himself and there was not even the suggestion of an arrogant smirk on his face, only an expression of embarrassment.

Calder frowned. He was almost starting to feel sorry for him. 'Pity you had to witness that,' he said gruffly in an effort to break the ice. 'I didn't expect Maurice to react in the way he did.'

Nash looked up at him. 'You can hardly blame him, can you, Sarge?' he said bitterly. 'And I suppose this is another black mark the shift will have against me.' He smiled thinly. 'If you'll pardon the pun.'

Calder's eyes narrowed. 'Black mark? What do you mean?'

Nash sighed and reached for his flat cap from the top shelf of his open locker. 'Well, you don't think all this mollycoddling by Mr. Maybe is helping me in the popularity stakes, do you?'

Calder hardened his heart. 'And whose fault's that, Nash? If you will keep running to him telling tales.'

'That's a lie!' Nash's face was white with anger and for a moment, Calder was taken aback. 'I've never run to Inspector Maybe about anything.'

'Not even to complain about me?'

'I haven't made any complaints about you. I know we don't get on particularly well, but I wouldn't stoop that low.'

'Then how did he know about the search of Wharf Cottages?'

Nash gave an exasperated sigh. 'Inspector Maybe came down to the custody office when Sergeant Lawson and I were documenting the prisoners. What made him come down, I don't know, as he rarely pokes his nose in there – perhaps he heard your radio message about the prisoners – but he was in a right old mood and he asked me why I had disobeyed local instructions by carrying out a search of Wharf Cottages. Naturally I told him I had been required to do it by you.'

'Thanks.'

Nash smiled briefly. 'He then said that the prisoners were to be released with a caution and that's what happened. I made no complaint to him and never have. It's just that, if I might say, your name seems to be like a red rag to a bull with him.'

Calder grunted. 'Tell me about it.'

'And, Sarge? I know I come across to you as an arrogant bastard, perhaps I am, but I haven't asked Inspector Maybe or anyone else to give me privileged treatment and it's doing me no favours on shift, I can tell you. Furthermore, although I may not be the best copper in the world I'm not a coward. My battery genuinely failed on me last night and I didn't hear the call to the Carlton Club, otherwise I would have been there.'

Calder nodded and scratched his nose. 'I was coming to that. I know about the battery now, as you must have gathered from my comments at briefing.' He cleared his throat. 'I . . . er . . . owe you an apology for accusing you in the first place. I shouldn't have spoken to you the way I did anyway.'

Calder looked for the anticipated smirk of satisfaction on Nash's face, but it didn't appear. Instead his expression was one of obvious surprise.

'It must have been very difficult for you to say that, Sarge,' he said quietly, 'but I certainly appreciate it.'

Calder cleared his throat noisily, anxious to extricate himself from the situation as quickly as possible. 'Well, don't let it go to your head,' he said gruffly. 'Now it's about time you were out on your area.' He paused in the act of turning for the door. 'And Nash. Let's see what you can really do from now on, eh?'

'I'll try my best, Sarge.'

'That's all I ask of anyone.'

Calder's brain was working overtime as he drove from the station for his rendezvous with Richard Baseheart. It seemed he had been wrong about Porter-Nash all along and he was annoyed with himself for having unwittingly allowed Inspector Maybe to use the young officer as a means of getting back at him. Torchy had always hated him for something that had happened between the two of them way back, something he himself just wanted to forget. He knew he should never even have been posted to Hardingham in the first place, let alone actually put on the man's shift, but he had never realised until now just how paranoid Maybe's animosity towards him must have become. Apart from undermining his own authority on the shift, it had already led to the release of three prisoners who should have been detained, caused unnecessary hostility between himself and Nash and now served to alienate a first-class officer like Maurice Stone, who for the first time in his career had started to think that he was the victim of racial discrimination. Calder shook his head grimly as he turned the car into the narrow lane at the back of the railway sidings which led to Peter's Pantry. This bloody nonsense would have to stop or the shift would be torn apart, but how the hell could he manage it on his own, that was the point?

Richard Baseheart was standing just inside the main entrance gateway of Peter's Pantry when Calder drove into the rubbish-strewn yard and parked up. The SB man's Meerschaum pipe was in his mouth and his gaze was directed towards the faded sign still clinging to the front of the building. 'Thanks for coming, Jim,' he acknowledged as he strolled over to him. 'Doesn't seem like twenty years since we were last here, does it?'

After all the recent aggravation he had suffered Calder was in no mood for reminiscences. Furthermore, he felt ridiculous enough taking part in a secret meeting like this without wanting to prolong it. 'I can't be long, Richard,' he said in a much sharper tone than he had intended. 'There's too much happening.'

Baseheart nodded and threw him a sympathetic sideways glance. 'Yes, I can imagine. But this won't take more than a few minutes.' He glanced at his watch. 'And I have an appointment myself in just over an hour anyway.'

Calder's radio blared, making him jump. 'Bravo-Alpha Two-One, attend ABA, Johnson's Upholsterers. Bravo-Alpha Two-Three attend . . .'

He snapped the radio off. 'Five minutes, Richard,' he said firmly.

Baseheart nodded and waved a hand towards the far corner of the yard where a brand new silver-grey Mercedes was parked. 'I've got a present for you in the car.'

'A present?'

The other grinned. 'Well, sort of anyway.'

Calder waited while he opened the boot and bent inside, his eyes roving appreciatively over the sleek lines of the powerful car. 'Nice new motor, Richard,' he commented.

Baseheart produced a large padded envelope and slammed the boot lid shut with a boyish grin. 'Actually bought her three weeks ago,' he replied. 'But the garage crunched her as they were getting her out of the showroom and they needed to order and fit a new wing. I finally collected her this afternoon, but she was well worth waiting for. Goes like a dream.'

He locked the car and handed Calder the envelope. 'Would you mind keeping this somewhere safe for me?' he said, 'And produce it at a moment's notice if I ask for it? Sort of personal favour.'

'What's in it?'

The SB man studied him through the smoke curling up from his pipe, but instead of answering the question he nodded towards the building. 'Let's just go inside for a moment where we can talk, eh?' he said and without waiting for a reply led the way to a low doorway at one end.

The door itself was missing and the large room that lay beyond was gloomy and uninviting, with shafts of sunlight probing the shadows through broken sky-lights. The ovens that years ago had sweetened the air with such delicious baking aromas had long since been removed, but surprisingly the big walk-in refrigerator, flanked by two yawning store-rooms, seemed to have been left intact, it's door, complete with the manufacturer's original logo, tightly shut and secured by a large rusted padlock, no doubt put there as a safety measure to keep out inquisitive children. The remaining fixtures and fittings had all suffered the usual fate that befalls long-term unoccupied buildings and the vandals had indulged themselves to the full. Every single window appeared to have been smashed, sinks and piping torn out and the long tables, where Peter and his staff had produced the best sticky buns and doughnuts in the business, wrenched from the iron brackets that had screwed them to the floor and ripped apart. Even the ceiling had been pulled down in places and exposed electric cabling now hung there in untidy liquorice-like festoons.

'Remember the tea and cakes we used to get in here?' Baseheart reflected, studying the devastation with an expression of sadness. 'Old Martha Broderick's bread pudding certainly went down a treat on early-turn, didn't it?'

'Richard!' Calder interjected impatiently, his feet crunching on broken glass as he followed him inside. 'Let's just forget Martha Broderick's bloody bread pudding, shall we? What's this business all about? You seemed to suggest yesterday that you were investigating something to do with the strike.'

The other nodded. 'Well I am now, but that wasn't part of my original brief. I actually stumbled on to this bit of mischief by accident during another enquiry.'

'So what's in the envelope you've given me?'

The SB man hesitated. 'Tapes, documents, photograph negatives, that sort of thing,' he replied. 'Most of it surveillance material.'

Calder gave a low whistle. 'Then shouldn't you be keeping the stuff under lock and key in a police crime property store?'

Baseheart gave a short humourless laugh. 'That's the last place I would want to keep it.'

'Why?'

'Because it would very likely go walkies and disappear for good.'

'From a police property store? Do you realise what you're saying?'

'Only too well, Jim.'

'But who the hell would want to do a thing like that?'

'Obviously the people who actually feature in the material.'

'But that means you must be investigating some sort of conspiracy within the service.'

Baseheart sighed and, leaning back against one tiled wall, knocked out his pipe on the nearby window sill and returned it to his pocket. 'You get no prizes for stating the obvious, Jim,' he said dryly.

Calder ignored the sarcasm. 'Then surely this whole thing should be handed over to the Regional Complaints Department? You shouldn't even be dealing with it.'

'It's not as simple as that. As I indicated when we had our chat yesterday, there is a very sensitive political dimension to the business, including powerful external influences, which put it way outside the province of a normal internal investigation.'

'So call in my old department, the NCS. That's what they're there for.'

Baseheart shook his head firmly. 'That wouldn't be appropriate either. There are other complicating factors, associated with the identity and role of the participants in this conspiracy, which need very careful handling. Furthermore, although the conduct of those involved may be morally reprehensible, I'm not even sure that it amounts to any provable criminal offence.'

Calder frowned in puzzlement. 'But if they haven't committed any criminal offence, why are you bothering with an investigation at all?'

'I said provable criminal offence, Jim,' the SB man corrected and began restlessly pacing the room, his hands thrust deep into his pockets. 'As I also intimated to you yesterday, the purpose of this conspiracy is to initiate a police strike, but on the face of it, there is nothing illegal in that. Under the new trade union laws the police have the right to strike like anyone else and people cannot be prosecuted simply for supporting that principle. But it is one thing to back a union's fight for overtime pay and quite another to try and engineer strike action as a means of achieving a personal political objective.'

Calder shook his head quickly, his frustration painfully evident. 'Now you've completely lost me,' he snapped and pulling out a packet of cigarettes he lit up and took the smoke right down.

'All right,' Baseheart went on patiently, 'to put the issue in simpler terms, these people want a police strike for its own sake – they're not interested in a settlement and will do all they can to frustrate one – and they are using Willy Justice and his executive committee as the tool to enable them to get what they want.'

'Well, they couldn't have found a better tool than Willy Justice, and that's a fact,' Calder commented dryly. 'But exactly what is it these people hope to gain from a police strike, apart from possible mayhem?'

Baseheart hesitated for a moment, his lips pursed in thought. 'They're all motivated by different considerations,' he replied, seeming to choose his words with great care and skilfully evading the question in the process. 'Life is all about agendas, Jim. We each have our own and we don't necessarily disclose them to other people. That's what's happening here and to make matters even more complicated, not all of those involved in this conspiracy are aware of the involvement of some of the others, simply because the latter are pulling the strings through intermediaries.'

Calder shook his head irritably and it was apparent from his expression that he was even more confused than before. 'Okay, okay,' he snapped, 'but forgetting the old Len Deighton/John Le Carré stuff for a moment, who are these people?'

'I can't tell you that. Not yet, anyway.'

'Why not? You've gone this far. What difference can it make?'

'It's best you don't know at present.'

Calder's scowl was back. 'Maybe I already know who one of them is anyway.'

'I sincerely doubt it.'

'An anarchist called Solomon, for instance?'

To Calder's satisfaction Baseheart visibly started. 'Now there's a blast from the past,' he breathed. 'Where on earth did you get that name from?'

'I have my sources too, you know.'

Baseheart made a wry face. 'Yes, but only out of a bottle these days and if I had to hazard a guess on this particular source it would have to be Steve Torrington, since he was with me on SB when Solomon was being targeted by the department. Been sniffing around as usual, has he? Trying to find out what I'm doing on his patch?'

Calder smiled faintly in spite of himself. 'You know how CID hate to be kept in the dark about anything, Richard,' he replied. 'It offends their elitist ego. Steve probably sees this affair as a challenge.'

'And he thinks I'm still chasing Solomon, does he?'

Calder shrugged. 'Personally, I reckon he was on a

fishing expedition when he dropped the name. He'd convinced himself that you had confided in me and thought he'd test my reaction. Let's face it, with this bloody rave festival in progress and talk of a police strike in the offing, it's logical that SB would send someone down here to keep an eye out for likely trouble-makers like Solomon. And who better to look for the arch-villain himself than the man who's pursued him with the zeal of the crocodile who tracked Captain Hook?'

'I'm not sure I like your literary analogy, Jim,' Baseheart replied. 'But since our local super-sleuth has always made a habit of putting two and two together and making five I suggest we encourage him to continue.'

'So Solomon is definitely not part of this conspiracy then?'

'Not even remotely, Jim,' he replied. 'The people I am up against here are in a totally different league. As for Solomon himself, I lost track of him a long time ago and I have absolutely no idea what happened to him.'

'Well wonder no more, for we had him in last night.'

'You did what?'

'Young Nash and I busted him with two others for suspected drugs offences just before I saw you in the canteen, though at the time I didn't realise who we'd got hold of.'

'And where is he now?'

'Back on the street somewhere. Torchy, good old Inspector Maybe, chucked the three of them out before they could be interviewed. I only discovered your man's identity when the LIO showed me his Descriptive File this afternoon and I remembered what Steve Torrington had told me.'

Baseheart showed his agitation. 'You must find him, Jim,' he exclaimed. 'Pull him in for something. Anything. He's real aggravation, believe me, and if he's on your manor you can expect major disturbances soon. This is obviously something those involved in the present conspiracy did not foresee at the planning stage and some of them could well end up with a lot more than they bargained for.'

Calder nodded. 'Exactly my point, which makes it all the more necessary for me to know who is involved in the business to start with, particularly if the police strike actually takes place.'

Baseheart shook his head. 'Nice try, Jim, but my answer remains the same. I can't tell you.'

Calder threw his still lighted cigarette into a dark corner with a muffled curse. 'Richard, this is not on and you know it. You're asking me to look after an envelope containing incriminating evidence against other colleagues, which you have decided for the moment to actually suppress, and yet you won't tell me who's involved or exactly what they've done. I could lose my pension over this or worse, end up on the wrong side of a cell door!'

Baseheart studied him intently. 'It won't come to that, I promise you. As far as you're concerned, you are simply holding on to a sealed envelope for me. You're not to know what's inside it.'

Calder sighed heavily. 'Look, Richard, I've always been as straight as a dye. There's never been the slightest doubt about my honesty. This whole thing stinks to high heaven and you've no right to put me in this position.'

'I have no choice, Jim. Apart from one other person

who is actually working with me on this enquiry, you're the only one I can trust . . .'

'But what about your own governor? Don't tell me he's mixed up in all this as well?'

'What? The Detective Superintendent, you mean?' Baseheart gave a short humourless laugh. 'Not as far as I know anyway, but John Briggs is not in a position to be consulted at the moment. The last postcard he sent the office was from somewhere in the Australian Outback where he's on a month's holiday. He's not due back for another two weeks and by then it will all be too late.'

'I don't believe this. He went on holiday with this conspiracy enquiry going on?'

Baseheart shook his head. 'The present business surfaced after he had gone. As far as he is concerned I am still following up the long-term enquiry for the Home Office I was allocated just before he left.'

'What a mess! So who is the other person working with you on the investigation or is that a trade secret as well?'

'No, it's necessary you should know, just in case I need someone else to contact you. Her name is Jane Sullivan. She's a detective sergeant with SB and she's doing some leg work for me right now.' He hesitated again. 'Look, Jim, I can't force you to help me. If you want out, then fine, but I would ask you to consider what's at stake. If this strike happens the balloon will go up in a very big way and an awful lot of people are going to get hurt. At least give me the chance of stopping it now.'

'And how do you propose doing that?'

'I have someone to see at eight-thirty tonight. Don't ask me who. He has the necessary pull to halt the process and I'm hoping that I can make him see sense. If I can't, then I promise I will take that envelope to the appropriate authority when I get back. All I'm asking you to do is to hold on to it for a couple of days. What's it to be?'

Calder weighed the envelope in his hands for a few moments, his scowl deepening. In the gloomy depths of the building the loud plopping of water escaping from a leaking tap or pipe was suddenly drowned by the blare of a siren from the railway sidings close by, followed by the thunder of a slow-moving diesel engine. 'I must be a bloody fool to get involved in this,' he said. 'Just don't drop me in the shit, Richard, that's all I ask.'

'I'll do my best, Jim,' Baseheart replied. 'Now isn't it about time you turned your radio back on? They might be wondering where you are.'

6

Calder left the premises before Baseheart, turning his radio back on as he eased the car through the gateway and out into the lane leading to the main road.

'Nothing for you, Sarge,' Phil Davies confirmed when he called up Control to check for messages and he breathed a sigh of relief. He must have been off the air for ten to fifteen minutes and he felt very guilty when he thought of the criticism he had levelled at Porter-Nash the night before over his own radio silence.

A flock of small birds skimmed the car's bonnet and disappeared over the hedge to his left, no doubt winging their way to nests in the scrub and withered hawthorn bushes that covered the strip of rough ground between Peter's Pantry and the railway sidings.

'Bravo-Alpha Two-Zero, attend RTA junction of Dean Street and Ronalds Way. Believed injury. Ambulance en-route,' the radio barked. 'Bravo-Alpha Two-Six, start making Dale Bridge, report of yobs throwing stones at trains . . . Bravo-Alpha Three-One, attend Odeon Cinema, fight in progress; Bravo-Alpha Two-One and Two-Five back him up please . . .'

Calder reached the main road and turned left,

intending to call by his bungalow on his way back to the town centre. He had to drop off Baseheart's envelope before it burned a hole in the back seat. But he had only travelled about half a mile when a further message from Phil Davies in the control room forced an immediate change of plan.

'Any mobile vicinity Fox Way. Two-Two needs urgent assistance.'

Calder had spun the wheel almost as a reflex action, swinging the car round to head back the way he had come. 'Sierra One-Zero two minutes,' he responded as he flashed past the mouth of the lane leading to Peter's Pantry.

Fox Way bordered wasteland on the opposite side of the derelict bakery to the railway sidings and it led to the council refuse tip. What Nash was doing there he couldn't imagine, but he had evidently found something to amuse him!

As he turned into Fox Way at speed the car slammed into a large pothole, no doubt left by the refuse lorries, and the steering wheel was almost wrenched from his hands. Clouds of dust enveloped the car, forcing him to slow down and stones rattled viciously on the underside and against the lower wings. The ragged chain-link fence which bordered the track on both sides was at times barely discernible and twice he mounted the low grass bank on his left, tearing nettles and brambles away with him as he went.

But then through the dust clouds he glimpsed a flashing blue light and swung hard to his right on to the concrete apron in front of the gates to the tip where several figures, one in police uniform, were rolling about on the floor in what appeared to be a violent struggle. He didn't bother to set the handbrake, but, stalling the car in gear, snatched his side-handled baton from the front passenger seat and wrenched the door open.

A ginger-haired man, wearing just a pair of jeans, came at him even before he got round to the front of his car. The man was holding a long piece of wood in one hand and he obviously meant business. Calder's expertly wielded baton struck him a resounding 'whack' across the shoulder and he dropped on to one knee with an agonised cry as Calder then cannoned into him, sending him sprawling. The screeching of brakes announced the arrival of other mobiles, including Steve Torrington in a CID car, and the frenzied barking of a dog had a sobering effect on the proceedings. Even before Don Gearing, the police dog-handler, could get his alsatian out of the back of his van figures were disappearing in all directions. One, a black man with a familiar Afro-Asian hairstyle, drew the short straw, however, and the dog brought him down before he had managed to cover twenty yards. The rest managed a fleetness of foot that was little short of the spectacular, scrambling through gaps in the chain-link fence and bowling each other over in their panic to get to the other side of the tip. One of them was Calder's would-be assailant and he noted with grim satisfaction that the man was holding his arm with his other hand as he ran.

'You okay, Nash?' Calder snapped as the young officer climbed to his feet, pulling his still struggling prisoner up with him.

'Fine, Sarge,' the other exclaimed, trying to smile through his pain. 'But this one's a bit of a handful.'

His face was covered in dirt, his short-sleeved shirt

was torn and blood streamed down his wrist from a wound on his forearm, but he refused to let go of the young woman who snarled spat and kicked out at him as he tried to hold her at arm's length.

'Give her to me,' Jenny Major snapped grimly, pushing past Calder. In a moment she had forced the woman to her knees in an arm-lock, then on to her face in the dirt. Placing her knee in the girl's back to hold her there, she snapped one cuff on her wrist and with seeming little effort jerked her other wrist across her back to complete the process.

'Well, well, well,' Calder murmured, recognition dawning as Major hauled the now much more subdued prisoner to her feet. 'I think Nash and I have made your acquaintance before.'

'Cock-sucker,' the girl snarled.

The eyes which stared back at him through the strands of dyed blonde hair were crazed and venomous and he studied the pale emaciated face and skeletal figure with revulsion.

'Wharf Cottages, wasn't it?' he said and, seeing Bravo-Alpha Two-Six, PC Baldev Singh, loading the black man brought down by Don Gearing's alsatian into the back of the Transit, he added: 'So that's two of our original trio back inside. It's just a pity Solomon wasn't at the party as well.'

'At least I reckon we've got the bitch who stabbed that lad at the festival,' Nash replied.

Calder raised his eyebrows and stared at the girl again. 'Well, she certainly fits the description on the box anyway,' he agreed. 'Good work, Nash. DI Torrington will be pleased. He's here at the moment too.'

Swinging round quickly, he glanced at the spot

where the plain car had been parked, but he was too late, for it was already pulling away. 'Typical CID,' he said with a grin, turning back to Nash. 'No nick, no interest. Still, he can see this "little treasure" later.'

Then his grin abruptly faded. Nash was wiping some of the blood off his hand with his handkerchief and swaying unsteadily as more dripped through his fingers. 'Here, let me have a look at that,' he snapped and, turning over the young officer's arm, he winced. The tear in the flesh was quite deep.

'The cow bit me,' Nash said, the disbelief still evident in his tone. 'Can you credit that? She actually bit me like some damned animal.'

'Yeah, pig,' the blonde snarled as she was dragged away by Jenny Major, 'and I'm HIV Positive too, so suck on that!'

Nash swallowed hard, his face white. 'Sarge, you don't think . . . ?'

'No, I don't!' Calder cut in, nevertheless conscious of the chill in his stomach at the thought. 'Let's just get you up to Casualty so they can do something about that wound, eh? You've done an excellent job, Nash, and I'll make sure it gets a mention. Now come on, I'll drop you at the hospital.'

'But what about the area car? That lot will come back and strip it if we leave it here.'

Calder grunted, remembering Daphne Young and thinking that he'd been faced with this problem only the night before. He depressed his radio's transmit button. 'Bravo-Alpha-Sierra One-Zero to Control.'

'Go ahead, skipper.'

'Two bodies coming in for Janice Lawson, Phil,' he said, 'but Two-Two has an arm injury from a bite and needs hospital treatment. I'll take him, but can you get Three-Two over to Fox Way to pick up the car?'

'Will do, skipper.'

Grandad (Three-Two) arrived within ten minutes, dropped off by the Transit, and he winked at Nash. 'She obviously liked you, Trev,' he chortled, after hearing the story, 'otherwise she wouldn't have tried eating you!'

Nash seemed a lot happier after his wound had been cleaned and bandaged, but the promise of a jab in his behind from the pretty Irish nurse brought more of a flush to his face than his other cheeks.

'You'll do,' Calder grinned, leaving him to the redhead's tender mercies. 'Just don't get a hard-on when she puts the needle in, eh?'

'Sarge?' Nash queried anxiously. 'Do you think that bitch was HIV?'

'Don't talk so wet,' Calder growled with a confidence he didn't feel. 'She was only trying to frighten you.'

Despite his reassurance, once he had pulled the curtain across the cubicle behind him, Calder went over to the young nurse as she was preparing her syringe from a cabinet and took her by the elbow a short distance to tell her his fears. 'So what happens now?' he said.

She nodded at the syringe in her hand. 'Well, in addition to the normal precautions we take following an injury of this sort, we'll put him on a Triple Therapy course, which includes AZT tablets,' she replied quietly. 'It's a recognised treatment.'

He looked perplexed. 'But I thought there was no cure for . . .'

She shook her head. 'I never said there was. We do

what we can, that's all, but he'll also be referred to the Sexual Health Clinic and will receive proper counselling.'

He snorted his contempt. 'Counselling? What a load of codswallop. And how long before he will know whether or not he's infected?'

She hesitated and looked away briefly before meeting his gaze again. 'Between forty and a hundred and forty days.'

He closed his eyes tightly for a second. 'Oh great! And in the meantime he will have this hanging over him like a death sentence?'

She made a face. 'I'm sorry, I really am, but there's nothing else that can be done except perhaps try to find out whether the risk actually exists in the first place by getting the girl who bit him to provide a blood test.'

He scowled. 'And for that we would need her consent which she would never give. What a wonderful world we live in, eh?'

The foyer of the casualty department was crammed with walking wounded already and Calder was almost bowled over by a trolley being propelled across the room by two ambulance personnel, with a nurse running along beside it, steadying a connected drip.

'It's certainly a madhouse here this evening,' a voice commented beside him and turning, he saw Chief Inspector Maxwell leaning against one of the ceiling support pillars. She was in full uniform, but carried her hat.

'Hello, ma'am,' he said with a tired smile. 'It's even worse outside.'

'How's Nash?'

He shrugged. 'He's got a nasty bite on his arm, but

that in itself isn't serious. Trouble is, the girl that did it says she's HIV and apparently he's going to have to wait for months before he knows whether or not he's been infected. Nurse suggested we got a sample of her blood, but that little bitch wouldn't even give you the time of day.'

'What about a court order?'

He brightened a little. 'I didn't realise we could get one for that.'

'I'm not sure we can, but it's worth trying. I'll speak to the Crown Prosecution Service tomorrow. Now let's drive, shall we? I want to talk to you.'

Another ambulance was turning into the hospital entrance, its siren wailing, as Calder pulled out of the car park for the second time in two nights and he turned automatically towards the town centre.

'So,' his passenger said sharply. 'How was it?'

'How was what?'

'The meaning of life. What do you think?'

He threw her a puzzled glance. 'I don't know what you're getting at.'

'The interview with the boss.'

'Oh, Mr. Rhymes, you mean.' He shrugged. 'Fine. Told me not to be a naughty boy in future and to be especially nice to Mr. Maybe.'

She chuckled. 'I did have a word with him, you know.'

'Did you, ma'am? Why was that?'

'Just cut out all this ma'am stuff, James. There's no one else here. And don't be such a prat. It doesn't wash with me.'

He grinned with something akin to genuine humour. Good old Rosy. She was so refreshingly normal and he always enjoyed her company. 'Where do you want to go then?' he said. 'Whole town's our oyster tonight.'

The radio cut in before she could answer. 'Any mobile vicinity George & Dragon. Fire in progress.'

'That will do nicely,' Maxwell said and he responded by putting his foot hard down.

The George & Dragon was an old coaching inn on the other side of town and by the time they got there the place was a smouldering ruin. The fire service had three appliances on site, but it was all a waste of time and the station officer in his white helmet simply shrugged as they pulled up.

'Arson?' Calder queried through the open window.

'Damned right it was,' Dennis Sale growled, stepping out from behind one of the fire-engines. 'A crowd of hop-heads from the festival were refused admittance, so they tossed a couple of Molotov cocktails through the toilet window. Paper towels and stacked boxes of toilet rolls seem to have done the rest.'

'They obviously came prepared then. Anyone hurt?'

Sale shook his head. 'Licensee got 'em out in time, but he's pig-sick over it and swearing vengeance. Trouble is, I think he means it.'

'Then I think I'd better have a word with him,' Maxwell said, getting out of the car. 'You might as well wait here, James.'

'Big guy with red hair over by the fish and chip shop,' Sale told her, pointing across the road. 'Name's Arthur Lacey. I'll introduce you to him, if you like.'

She nodded, then frowned. 'Your DI not here then?'

Sale glanced around him quickly. 'He was a moment ago, ma'am,' he replied, leading the way across the road. 'Probably scouting around for witnesses.'

In fact, Torrington appeared at the car window the moment Maxwell and Sale were out of earshot. 'Got your message about Solomon, Jim,' he said. 'Sorry I didn't contact you earlier, but I've had a lot on and I assumed you just wanted to confirm what I had already suspected.'

Remembering Baseheart's suggestion that Torrington should be encouraged to blunder off in the wrong direction Calder nodded. 'More or less, yes, but I also wanted to let you know that we evidently had Solomon in custody earlier, though we didn't realise it at the time.'

The detective stared at him. 'You had him in? When?'

Calder told him briefly what had happened and he whistled softly. 'What a bummer. Still, your shift certainly struck oil tonight by nicking one of the bastard's cohorts. Sorry I had to shoot off from the scene. Had another job on.'

'We got two of them actually,' Calder corrected, ignoring his apology. 'The black guy with the Afro cut? He was one as well. All we need to do now is lift the main man again.'

Torrington nodded. 'He'll come eventually. Still, I have to say that Nash did a bloody good job this time. I'll get him a mention in despatches.' There was the suggestion of a smile. 'How is our future commissioner?'

'A bit sore. The bitch sunk her teeth into his arm. Is she the one you're after for the stabbing?'

"No doubt about it, but she got rid of the knife

somewhere. Still, she had enough coke and amphets on her to keep her spaced out for a month. Admitted straight away what the stuff was, though we'll have to get Forensic to analyse it, of course. It's a nice little charge to hold her on until she coughs the stabbing.'

Calder raised his eyebrows. 'Why, are you going for supplying?'

Torrington nodded. 'Seems like a good idea and according to Drug Squad, as she's a coke addict she's likely to be selling the amphetamines to pay for her own habit.'

Calder looked thoughtful for a moment. 'The word is that someone is handing out hallucinogens free to the festival crowd, trying to get them stoned enough to cause some aggro.'

The other grunted. 'Yeah, so I believe.' He clapped Calder on the arm and laughed without humour. 'Tell Richard that and he's bound to think Solomon's behind it.'

'Solomon probably is,' Calder murmured as his colleague walked away. Then he turned as Maxwell reappeared from the other side of the road.

'Right, James,' she snapped. 'Might as well resume, eh? All in CID's capable hands. Was that DI Torrington who just walked away?'

Calder nodded and she snorted her displeasure. 'He didn't stay around long.'

'Got a lot on apparently.'

'Haven't we all? And it's going to get a lot worse before it gets any better.'

'Bravo-Alpha Three-One,' Control called, as if they had heard her. 'Attend fight at The Feathers. Two-Three and Two-Six back him up please.'

'I think we'll leave that,' Maxwell said firmly, sensing his interest. 'Let's just cruise, eh?'

They had only just pulled away again when the packet of Polos appeared under Calder's nose.

'Good for the digestion,' Maxwell said as he took one, 'and a crabby sod like you needs all the relief he can get.'

'Nothing wrong with me,' he replied. 'It's all the others.'

'So, what's this between you and Inspector Maybe then?'

He shrugged. 'We just don't like each other, that's all.'

'Pull over.'

'What?'

'I said pull over.'

He shook his head in resignation and turned into an alleyway at the rear of TW Bolton's Chemist's Shop.

'Turn the engine off.'

'Why, are you going to seduce me?'

'Don't be a prick all your life, James.'

She swivelled round in the seat to face him. 'This business with you and Douglas Maybe has got to stop or it will rip your shift apart. It's already the subject of locker-room gossip and your own officers don't know which way they're up because of it.'

'Don't you think I know that?'

'So what's the problem between the pair of you? Come on, James, I've read your file. I know you must have been transferred from the NCS for more than just old age. So has that got anything to do with it?'

His face was cold and hard as he stared through the windscreen at the little flashing red security light in the rear window of the chemist's shop. 'That's between Inspector Maybe and me,' he answered quietly.

She snorted. 'It may have been once, but not anymore, it isn't. Not when it's affecting the efficiency of this station. We've got enough problems with this damned strike looming without having to sort out internal feuds between supervisors as well!'

He threw her a swift sideways glance. He knew he would have to tell her sooner or later, for Rosy wasn't the sort to give up, and now was probably as good a time as any.

'Well?'

'Thank you Bravo-Alpha Three-One,' the radio acknowledged in the background. 'Mobiles attending The Feathers, please cancel. One in custody . . . Two-Six, please now attend Worsham Avenue. Report of intruders on premises. X-ray Delta One-Four (Dog Van) and Bravo-Alpha Five-Two (CID) attending also.'

He turned the radio down. 'I'll tell you on condition that this conversation goes no further, but remains strictly between ourselves. I don't want everything raked up again.'

She frowned, obviously not too happy with that arrangement. 'I shouldn't agree to pre-conditions, but seeing as it's you, okay, this one's off the record.'

He tapped the steering wheel with his fingers for a few moments as he turned things over in his mind. 'Remember a girl named Jenny Marchant?' he said finally.

She hesitated a second and then snapped her fingers. 'The young police constable who committed suicide at the Police Training Centre?'

'The very same. Well, Maybe was seeing to her.'

'I beg your pardon?'

'Okay, having an affair with her, if you prefer.'

'Douglas Maybe?' she breathed incredulously. 'I don't believe it.'

He emitted a cynical laugh. 'Oh you'd be surprised. Bit of a stag is our Torchy. Likes 'em young and nubile by all accounts.'

He paused for a moment to collect his thoughts, then continued in a more sober tone. 'I happened to be on a senior sergeants' course there myself at the time and Maybe was an instructor in Probationer Training. Jenny, then just nineteen, was one of his students on her initial course, and more importantly as far as I was concerned, she was also the daughter of an old army mucker of mine and had only joined the job as a result of speaking to me.

'It was common knowledge the pair of them were at it and they were often seen in the evenings huddled together in local pubs, trying to be discreet. What Jenny saw in someone like Maybe I'll never know, but I suspect she was flattered by his attentions and probably thought that being bonked by her course inspector would improve her final appraisal grade. Whatever the reason, the whole thing disgusted me and I had a word with her one evening in a quiet corner. But she was infatuated with the man and refused to listen. Then ironically, a week later, it seems he got tired of her and broke off the affair. The same night the silly little idiot took an overdose of Paracetamol. Whether she meant to top herself or was just trying to make a point with a bit of theatre, I don't know, but the fact is that she went into a coma from which she never recovered.'

He smoothed his face with the palm of one hand.

'The business shook me up a lot, I can tell you. I felt somehow I had let Jenny's parents down. Then, when I heard Maybe had put in a report suggesting she may have taken her own life because she couldn't cope with her course workload, I blew a fuse and spoke to the Commandant. But I put myself out on a limb, for I had no real proof anything had been going on and Jenny hadn't left a note of any sort. As for Maybe, he strenuously denied he'd had an affair with her and had the gall to claim he had only been out with her in the evenings to help her with her depression! As a result, his name could not be tied in with her death and, after the Coroner's Inquest had recorded the suicide verdict, a very shallow internal enquiry was conducted before the whole bloody thing was swept under the carpet.

'Mind you, the powers-that-be couldn't have thought too much of Maybe's story for after a decent interval he was posted from the Training Centre to shift duties at Hardingham, apparently on "career grounds". He never forgave me for reporting his misbehaviour to the boss or for the fact that his wife divorced him soon afterwards, demanding a larger than average financial settlement for her silence about his years of infidelity!'

'So how come you were moved off the NCS?'

'What does my personal file say?'

'You mean you've never seen it? Everyone has a right of access to their personal records now, you know that, don't you?'

He made a face. 'Not interested. The only things that are put on your P/F are what the powers-that-be want you to see anyway.' He tapped his forehead. 'They keep the real heavy stuff, all the non-provable anti-things, up here, so that they can put the knife in quietly without anyone knowing.'

'That's a load of rubbish.'

'Is it? Then what does my file say?'

'The official explanation is that you had been on specialist departments too long and, like Douglas Maybe, needed further career development.'

He chuckled softly. 'That really is rich. Adding my army service to time served in this outfit, I only had a few years to do when my transfer to Hardingham actually took place, so I can't see what sort of career development they thought I needed.'

'All right, then what was the real reason, do you think?'

He shrugged. 'It was down to me, I suppose. I continued to tick to everyone about the way the Marchant enquiry had been handled and in the end I was summoned to headquarters by the Director of Personnel and given a polite bollocking for making unfounded allegations against a fellow officer. Nothing was put on paper and I could see I was actually being given a gypsy's warning to forget about the case which had already caused the force a lot of embarrassment. I lost my rag a bit and said a few things I shouldn't have done.'

'You mean, as usual, you engaged mouth before operating brain?'

'Well, you know me. Bit of a prat at times. Anyway, the upshot of it all was that three months later I found myself posted to Hardingham and someone in HQ Personnel, either with not too much savvy or a warped sense of humour, stuck me on Inspector Maybe's shift.'

'And he's made life difficult for you ever since?'

'Tried to, yeah.' He shrugged. 'But I can handle that. What I can't handle is him fouling up a good collar just to get back at me.'

'Meaning?'

He sighed heavily. 'Look, I know I lost my temper with him in the office, but it wasn't about Nash getting preferential treatment or my disobeying some crazy local instruction. What really made me blow my top was the fact that Maybe had released three prisoners we had arrested on drugs charges before we'd had any chance of interviewing them. And the real bummer is that one of them, a villain who calls himself Solomon, is a bloody anarchist who's actually come to Hardingham to cause mayhem at the festival!'

She frowned. 'Did Mr. Rhymes know about this when he saw you? I certainly didn't.'

'I doubt it and he didn't say anything to me. It wouldn't be something anyone would pick up just by glancing through the custody records and I am pretty sure Maybe wouldn't have put it in his report.'

'He didn't. So what made you keep it back yourself?'

'It's not my place to go around bleating about my own governor.'

'Your old hang-up about loyalty.'

'It isn't a question of loyalty. I just don't do that sort of thing and you wouldn't like it if I did. Anyway, the damage is done now. I shall just have to find a way of nailing Solomon for something else. We've already pulled in the two who were with him on the original bust for other offences, one of them being the girl who stabbed that lad at the festival, so I'm quite sure Solomon will come eventually.'

'All this is pretty awful, James. By rights I should do something about it.'

He shook his head firmly. 'We agreed this conversation would be in confidence and I'm holding you to that. After all, I haven't done anything wrong so you're not being compromised in any way.'

'All right, you've made your point, but what about a change of shift? I can arrange it, you know?'

'No way. There are some good lads and lassies on this shift and I'm not going to desert them.'

'The eternal masochist?'

'Perhaps, but what you see is what you get.'

She nodded briskly. 'Okay, James. Well, as you say, I did promise that our conversation would be in confidence and therefore I have no option but to keep it that way. However, if things between you and Maybe don't improve soon, I'll have no choice but to take some sort of action to resolve the problem. Do you understand?'

'Thanks for that anyway.'

She smiled, studying him for a second or two. 'Now, what about you?'

It was his turn to look surprised. 'What about me?'

'You look bloody dreadful and you know it. When are you going to stop punishing yourself?'

'I don't know what you're on about.'

'Yes, you do. I don't need the letters MD after my name to know you're near the edge. You're working too hard, smoking too much, not eating properly and probably hitting the bottle when you're on your own.'

'So what? I'm over eighteen!'

She hesitated briefly, then plunged in again. 'Look, James, I know life's given you a pretty raw deal, but playing with the self-destruct button isn't the answer.'

He scowled. 'Going in for psychology now, are we, ma'am?'

She ignored the remark and resorted to an even blunter approach: 'Don't you think it's about time you let Maggie go and stopped feeling guilty because she's dead and you're still alive?'

He glared at her. 'Maggie's none of your damned business!' he snapped angrily.

'She is when I see a good man going down the tubes because he hasn't got the guts to face up to life anymore. Maggie wouldn't have wanted it that way.'

'And how the hell do you know what Maggie would have wanted?'

'Because I was the closest friend she ever had. That's why I was a bridesmaid at your wedding. Remember? But she's gone now, James, and you've got to start living again. Her death was not your fault, really it wasn't.'

He slammed the palms of his hands against the steering wheel, making her jump. 'Not my fault?' he said savagely. 'So where was I when she died, eh? At bloody work, as usual, on yet another crime operation. The same place I always was when she needed me. While she lay there dying, I was swanning around the countryside looking for a couple of escapees from stir. Couldn't face it in the end, you see, so I used the job as an excuse, somewhere to hide, just like I've always done.'

She snorted. 'What a load of bloody nonsense! The hospice themselves didn't know she was failing until an hour before she died. She was in a coma, for heaven's sake; had been for three months. You couldn't be expected to be there twenty- four hours a day. You tried to though, didn't you? The staff at the hospice told me how you used to come off duty every day and sit by her bed until you fell asleep.'

He started to say something, but she cut him off. 'No, just hear me out. Even your own boss knew you were driving yourself to the wall. He tried to tell you, but true to form, you wouldn't listen, would you? That's why you had to be signed off for three months after Maggie had gone, suffering from an internal haemorrhage and nervous exhaustion. I know exactly what happened, James. If you remember, I visited you at home several times when you were on the sick and if I needed any further reminding, it's all in your personal file.'

'Finished?' he finally managed to interject.

'No, I haven't. You've got nothing to be ashamed of, James. You just want there to be something, don't you? You need someone to blame so you can feed off your own bitterness and it's convenient to blame yourself because God is too far away.'

He swore and, starting the engine, engaged gear noisily. 'I don't have to listen to all this psychological crap,' he snarled, driving forward slightly before reversing back into a yard entrance to turn round.

'Then don't,' she retorted as he swung back to the junction with the main road and waited for a couple of cars to pass. 'Just go on wearing yourself down until they bury you too. Then see if anyone gives a damn. Now just drop me back at the nick. I'm through bothering with you!'

The radio barked out its messages incessantly throughout the short journey across town, but it was the only conversation that took place in the car, for both of them sat in morose silence, busy with their own thoughts and, as their anger cooled, each privately wishing they could take back some of the things they had said.

A powerful Traffic patrol car was parked in the lay-by at the front of the police station when they got back and the two crew members, a tall thin woman and a short over-weight male sergeant, were walking quickly down the steps to their vehicle as Calder pulled in behind it. The pair nodded in perfunctory fashion to Maxwell when they saw her get out of the supervision car (once it would have been a salute, Calder mused), then glanced at each other curiously as she slammed the door behind her with unnecessary force and mounted the steps two at a time.

Before Calder could drive off again the sergeant came over to his window and leaning on the sill, peered in with a big grin on his face. 'What's up with Rosy then, Jim?' he chortled. 'Try to touch her aspidistra, did you?'

'Go play on the motorway, Digby!' Calder snarled back. 'Preferably among the articulated lorries!' Then he pulled away so quickly that he almost took the other with him.

'What an arse-hole,' Digby muttered, rubbing his knee and staring after the fast disappearing police car.

His crew-mate, who had been within earshot during the short exchange, shook her head firmly. 'Wrong, Sarge,' she replied, opening the Traffic car door and climbing into the driving seat, 'you're the arse-hole . . . with respect, of course.'

It took Calder a long time to cool down completely and he drove around in aimless fashion for over half an hour, his mind in turmoil. Rosy had certainly managed to touch a nerve – probably because he liked her so much and she was closer to him through her friendship with Maggie than anyone – and whether this had been deliberate or accidental, it had nevertheless given him a severe jolt. He angrily resented her interference and yet part of that anger was directed against himself because he knew she was right but didn't want to hear the truth. He had let his health go to pot. He was eaten up with bitterness and unjustified self-recriminations. Not to put too fine a point on it, he had been wallowing in his own self-inflicted misery ever since Maggie's death and it was about time he stopped feeling sorry for himself and got on with his life. Yeah, that was all very well in theory, but after so long in the same dismal rut how did he climb out of it and where was the incentive to try?

'Bravo-Alpha Two-Five? Confirming you are now on meal break?'

Shaken out of his reverie by the metallic voice of the radio, which had maintained an uneasy silence for some while, Calder noted that dusk was closing in and switched on his lights. An area car, Two-Three, he thought, flashed him as it passed by on the other side of the road and he waved in acknowledgement before pulling into a bus stop lay-by and climbing out of the vehicle. He needed to clear his head, but the sultry night air provided little relief and after a few moments he got back into the car and lit a cigarette, watching groups of youngsters milling about on the wide pavement outside The Mason's Arms public house opposite. Most of them had pint pots in their hands and shouldn't have been out in the street with them, but the pub seemed to be heaving and as they were behaving themselves he let them get on with it. He needed to do something more profitable with his time anyway and he had been meaning to check on young Maurice Stone long before now.

Tossing the cigarette out of the window, he radioed Control. Jackie Holt acknowledged this time and he made the rendezvous arrangements with Stone on talk-through before easing out of the lay-by and allowing a bus to pull into the space he shouldn't have been occupying in the first place.

Maurice was waiting for him at the front of the Town Hall and the young bobby looked pretty embarrassed when he got out of the car.

'Evenin', Maurice,' he said. 'Over the sulks yet?'

Stone shuffled his feet uncomfortably. 'Sorry about that, Sarge,' he said. 'I was out of order.'

'You certainly were, especially with that nasty dig about racism. The old "you did it 'cos I'm black" routine has been a bit over-played during the last few years. People are getting bored with it.'

Stone nodded. 'Yeah, I know. It just come out, that's all. It won't happen again.'

Calder clapped him on the arm. 'I know it won't, Maurice, and I can understand your disappointment about the area car, but you will get an opportunity this set of nights, I promise you. Now, how's the wife?'

'Not too good. The baby won't come which means it's a caesarean tomorrow morning at nine o'clock.'

Calder frowned and glanced at the luminous dial of his watch. 'Right, then you finish at midnight tonight so you can be on hand at the hospital.'

'No, Sarge, I . . .'

'Listen, Maurice,' Calder snapped harshly, thinking of Maggie. 'You'll do as I say. Janet will need you there when she comes round afterwards.'

'But what about cover tonight? You're already stretched.'

'I think we've had this conversation before,' Calder replied. 'You finish at midnight. Understand? Manpower's my problem. Now, on your bike.'

Stone nodded. 'Thanks for this, Sarge.'

Calder's emitted a dry chuckle. 'Forget it,' he said. 'I'd do the same for a white man!'

Stone's face widened into a broad grin. '*Touché*, Sarge,' he responded with a short laugh of his own and climbing on to his bicycle, pedalled away slowly towards the top end of the street.

Calder was still smiling to himself when he returned to his car, but his expression soon changed. What made him suddenly remember Baseheart's sealed envelope and the fact that it still had to be dropped off at his home he had no idea, but when he reached in the back to pick it up his hands found only the stitched vinyl seat. Snapping on the interior light he searched frantically, even tilting both the front seats forward to check the floor. But it was a waste of time; the envelope had gone. His mind flashed back to the fracas at the council tip and he tasted the surge of acid in his throat. That had been the only time he had left the car unlocked and unattended, which meant that while he had been helping Nash with his prisoner someone else had been helping themselves to the envelope on the back seat!

7

Sleep did not come easily to Calder when he finished duty at six o'clock the next morning. The madness that had hit the town shortly after dark the previous night, with pub and street fights, shop break-ins and car thefts sending the exhausted shift racing from one location to another, may have prevented him from dwelling too much on the loss of the precious envelope, but he was given plenty of opportunity for reflection once he got home. Tossing and turning in bed as he tried to shut out the noises of the awakening street and ignore the rivulets of perspiration running down his body with the rising heat of the day, he eventually managed to drift off, but he awoke again at just after eleven-thirty, his eyelids stuck together and his head throbbing like someone suffering from a dose of the 'flu.

It was then that he made up his mind to re-visit the scene of Nash's arrest in the vain hope that whoever had stolen the envelope from his car may have discarded the thing on finding it contained nothing of value. But all he succeeded in doing was attracting curious glances from a couple of council workmen at the tip as he wandered aimlessly among the piles of rubbish and ruining one of his shoes when he stepped into a pool of oil leaking from an overturned drum.

He couldn't face lunch when he got back to his bungalow again, making do with strong coffee and a cigarette instead, but after sitting at the breakfast bar brooding over his major *faux pas* for nearly half an hour he was unable to stand the silence of the little kitchen anymore. In an effort to take his mind off things he went through to the lounge and turned on the television, but almost immediately he snapped it off again when the red face of the Home Secretary, Peter Walsh MP, filled the screen in the middle of a heated discussion with top interviewer, Anton Brace, about the impending police strike. Even the radio wasn't any better, for every channel appeared to be obsessed with the same subject and in desperation he turned to the whisky bottle, taking his second refill to his bedroom and leaving it on the dressing-table while he tried to wash away his sorrows in the shower. He was actually still in the shower when the doorbell rang at a little after one o'clock.

Cursing under his breath and suspecting that his neighbour's children were yet again calling on him to retrieve their ball after kicking it over his back garden fence, he draped a towel round his loins and dripped water and soap suds all the way to the front door.

The face of the attractive young woman standing on the doorstep reddened appreciably and she lowered her gaze to stare at her feet, one hand thrust out in front of her proffering a police warrant card. He noted a big racing-green Rover saloon car, presumably hers, parked outside.

'Sergeant Calder?' she queried sharply and when he nodded she added: 'DS Jane Sullivan, Special Branch. I need to talk to you.'

He gripped his towel more tightly and frowned, feeling a total fool. 'Well, I'm in the . . . er . . . shower,' he said, his own embarrassment evident in his hesitant tone. 'Bit difficult really.'

She raised her head and cool green eyes studied him frankly. 'I promise I won't rape you, Sergeant Calder,' she replied with a tight smile. 'But perhaps you might want to get some clothes on in case the neighbours start to talk.'

He shrugged and stepped to one side. 'Suit yourself. If you go through to the lounge on your right, I'll be with you in a moment.'

He was there ten minutes later, finding her studying a photograph on the mantelpiece showing him in army battledress.

'Armagh, Northern Ireland,' he said in answer to her unspoken question. 'I was there during the so-called Troubles before I joined this outfit.'

She smiled with a little more warmth this time, her green eyes sparkling and a dimple in her small rounded chin deepening as her lips parted.

'My, weren't you young then?'

'That's how we all start out,' he said grimly. 'But some of us age quicker than others.'

Her smile started to fade and he held up his hand apologetically. 'Sorry, I wasn't getting at you. I'm just tired, that's all. Please sit down.'

She propped herself on the edge of the two-seater settee and smoothed her brown shoulder-length hair back from her face, looking more like a bank clerk in her neat two-piece blue suit than a Special Branch detective.

'Richard said you might contact me if he couldn't do so himself,' he went on, opening up the conversation, 'though I must admit I didn't expect you as soon as this.'

She looked at him strangely. 'You've spoken to him recently?'

He nodded. 'Look, would you like some tea, coffee or something?'

She shook her head with slight impatience. 'No thank you. When did you speak to Mr. Baseheart?'

He sat down in the armchair opposite. 'Yesterday evening.'

'Yes, but what time?'

'Between seven and seven-thirty. So why the interrogation?'

Her face was now very serious. 'Richard . . . Chief Inspector Baseheart, seems to have disappeared!'

'What? You've got to be joking?'

'I wish I were. We have very strict reporting-in rules on the department, especially when we're on a job. He should have contacted me at nine o'clock this morning for our regular briefing, but he never turned up at the office and there's no reply at his home.'

He shrugged. 'Well, maybe he got delayed.'

'Sergeant Calder, I've . . .'

'Jim.'

'Jim then, I've heard nothing from him for almost twenty-four hours. He's left no messages at HQ or on my own personal answer-phone and he does not appear to be at home either. Something's wrong, I know it. Where did you last see him?'

Calder was beginning to feel anxious himself now and the more he thought about it the worse it became. 'He asked me to meet him at a derelict bakery near the local railway sidings, place called Peter's Pantry.

It used to be one of our tea-spots when we were beat bobbies together.'

'And obviously he turned up?'

'Of course he turned up. In fact, we had quite an interesting conversation. Then I drove off and that was it.'

'You left the premises before him?'

'Yes, he thought it best that we weren't seen departing at the same time.'

'Did he give you anything?'

Calder's stomach churned violently and he reached for his cigarettes, lighting one for himself when she refused the proffered packet.

'Well, Jim, did he?'

He stood up and stared out of the window, wishing he was anywhere but in his neat little bungalow at that precise moment in time. Finally he nodded. 'A large bulky envelope.'

'Thank goodness for that anyway. He said he was going to ask you to hold on to it for him, but he didn't tell me when he had arranged to meet you. Where is the envelope now?'

'I wish I knew.'

She started and he saw the alarm in her eyes. 'What do you mean? You're not saying you've lost it?'

'It was stolen from the supervision car when I was out on patrol last night.'

She jumped to her feet. 'Bloody hell, Jim! Do you know what was in that envelope?'

'I have some idea, yes.'

'Then how could you be so negligent with it?'

He turned on her angrily. 'Don't you come that high and mighty attitude with me, miss. I didn't want the friggin' thing in the first place. I only agreed

153

to look after it as a personal favour to Richard.'

She sat down heavily, her face white. 'You can have no conception just how serious this is,' she said in a low shocked voice. 'That envelope was Mr. Baseheart's insurance, his way of putting a stop to something. He didn't intend using it against anyone. It was his bargaining counter and if it falls into the wrong hands it could set the whole force alight!'

His eyes narrowed. 'Bargaining counter? I don't like the sound of that.'

She shook her head irritably. 'No, no, no. You've got it all wrong. It's nothing like you think. It's all to do with politics.'

'I'm listening.'

She hesitated, biting her lip. 'I just don't know what to do anymore. I have no idea how much Richard has told you or how much he intended you should be told.'

He grunted and bent over to crush his unfinished cigarette in an ashtray on the coffee table. 'Then I'll make it easy for you, even if it does mean I won't learn as much from you as a result. Richard told me precious little. He spoke mainly in riddles and I'm still not much wiser than I was before he gave me the envelope.'

She nodded slowly. 'Thanks for your honesty, but before I drop myself in it completely I think we should try and find Richard Baseheart.'

'And if we can't?'

'Can we cross that bridge when we come to it?'

He grunted and glanced at his watch. 'Okay, then we'd better get started. I've got to be back on duty for six o'clock tonight.'

She stood up again and smoothed the creases out

of her skirt. 'So, what do you suggest as our first move?'

He smiled wryly. 'You're the detective. I'm only a woodentop, but I would have thought we should initially pay a visit to his home and see if he's answering his door now.'

'Right, then I suggest we go in my car.'

Looking at his own battered heap through the window, which he could see she had blocked in the driveway with her gleaming new Rover, he considered it best not to argue.

Baseheart owned an old thatched cottage in the village of Great Mannington, four miles from Hardingham. He had moved there ten years before, a few months after his wife, Helen, had walked out on him, leaving him with the job of selling their home in the suburbs of Hardingham so she could start a new life with her new man in Canada.

The cottage stood at the very end of the straggling main street conveniently adjoining the only hostelry the village boasted. It had a small Victorian-style kitchen garden at the front which was now ablaze with a multitude of summer-flowering perennials and a paved yard at the back, enclosed by a high wall. There was no garage of any sort, only a hard-standing to one side of the garden which was empty, and there was no sign of Baseheart's silver-grey Mercedes in the roadway outside.

Things certainly did not look very promising. Nevertheless, Calder rapped on the front door repeatedly before giving up and wandering round the back. As he followed the wall along he tried to peer in through the windows but insufficient light penetrated the thick leaded panes and he was unable to see clearly into any of the rooms, while the solid rear door proved to be securely locked.

'Seems like we've got no choice but to force an entry,' he said when he finally returned to the front garden.

Sullivan raised her eyebrows. 'We can't do that.'

'Then what do you suggest? We can hardly report Richard missing without making sure he's not at home first. We'd look damned fools.'

'He can't be at home. His new Mercedes isn't here and I know he was supposed to be collecting it yesterday.'

Calder bent to examine a side window which seemed a little loose. 'That doesn't mean anything. He could easily have parked it in a lock-up round the corner and even now he might be lying on the floor inside after suffering a heart attack or something?'

'Well, he wasn't earlier . . .'

Calder straightened up and turned to face her as her voice trailed off. 'And how do you know that?'

She bit her lip, obviously regretting the indiscreet admission. 'Because . . . because I have this,' she muttered and held up a key.

He nodded slowly in understanding, treating her to a brief knowing smile. 'Why didn't you say before?' he said, taking it from her.

Her face flushed a bright crimson. 'It's nothing like that,' she blurted. 'Richard and I are simply good friends. I . . . I majored in modern history at University and he has a keen interest in the military campaigns of the early nineteenth century.'

He sighed as he turned the key in the front door. 'Listen, Jane, I don't care whether you majored in palmistry or whether Richard has been bonking you to death on the hearth rug,' he said. 'All I'm interested in doing is finding him. So shall we get on with it, eh?'

There were two pints of milk and a pile of neatly stacked unopened letters on the telephone table just inside the door and Calder waited while Sullivan punched the immobilisation code for the alarm system into the plastic box on the wall.

'Well, it doesn't look as though he's been home today,' he said. 'I assume you put the milk and letters there?'

She nodded. 'I meant to put the milk in the 'fridge', but . . .'

He cut her off. 'You have a look round down here and I'll take upstairs,' he said.

'I've already done all this, you know.'

'Then let's do it again, eh?' he said sharply and went for the narrow staircase without giving her a chance to reply.

Ten minutes later he joined her in the little sitting-room and cast his eye over the flowery chintzes and oak bookshelves sagging under the weight of innumerable volumes on European history and the Napoleonic wars.

'Bed's not been slept in anyway,' he said.

'I could have told you that,' she replied coldly.

'Yes, but did you look any further than the bed?'

'I don't follow you.'

For reply he strode out of the room to the kitchen. She went after him and found him checking inside the washing-machine. 'What the devil are you up to?'

He leaned back against the work surface and drummed his fingers against the casing of the washing-machine behind him. 'I've known Richard for a long time. We shared the same residential block at the police training centre and he is one of the most fastidious men I have ever met, especially about personal hygiene.'

'I would certainly agree with you there, but what about it?'

'The dirty-linen basket upstairs is empty, as is the washing-machine which is also bone-dry inside, and I noticed when I went round the back that there is no washing hanging up on the line.'

'So Richard has done it all. What's so significant about that?'

'It indicates that he didn't come home at all last night.'

'But we know that already from the milk I found standing on the doorstep and the pile of letters I cleared up off the door mat .'

He shook his head firmly. 'That only tells us he hasn't been back since the milk and post were delivered, say about 0430 hours if you use the milk as a guide. But what is there to say that he didn't return home and shoot out again before those deliveries, eh? Well, I'll tell you. Richard would never have come home and gone out again, no matter how urgent the job, without changing his shirt, socks and under-wear, but there's no trace of any soiled clothing at all. Furthermore, the flannel, soap and towels in the bathroom are not even damp and it is patently obvious that neither the shower or bath have been used recently. All this suggests that he hasn't re-turned here since leaving the house yesterday to go on duty.'

She raised her eyebrows again. 'Quite the little detective, aren't you?' she said acidly.

'Used to think so once, love,' he retorted, 'but that's another story.'

She glanced down quickly at her feet. 'Sorry, Jim, that remark was totally uncalled for and I take it back. I'm just so very worried, that's all.'

'You and me both,' he admitted, 'and by rights we should be reporting this business to headquarters straight away . . .'

'No!' she cut in sharply.

'Why not?'

She hesitated. 'Well, surely before doing anything we should first check out the derelict where you had your rendezvous with him yesterday evening. What if he injured himself as he was leaving. Struck his head on a projecting pipe or something. He might be lying there concussed?'

He gave her an old-fashioned look. 'It's hardly likely, is it?'

'Maybe not, but we should at least eliminate it as a possibility and I would have thought it was standard missing person procedure anyway.'

He pursed his lips thoughtfully. 'Why do I get the impression that you are just playing for time, eh?' he said. 'Trying to delay the inevitable for as long as possible?'

'That's not it at all. I would simply prefer to do a thorough job before we send the balloon up. After all, the derelict was the last place we can put Richard before he dropped out of sight.'

He grunted. 'Okay, but after that I want some answers from you and they'd better be good.'

There was no sign of Baseheart at Peter's Pantry, just a set of tyre marks left in the soft earth by his car as he had obviously reversed out of the yard from the rough ground where he had been parked. The building itself contained little of interest, apart from evidence in a corner of an upstairs office that the place had recently been used by junkies. The floor round several overturned boxes was littered with the cardboard tips of cannabis joints and there were a couple of broken hypodermic syringes lying in a dark corner.

Relieved that they had found no trace of the SB man, even though it put them back to square one, they returned to Calder's bungalow where he made some strong coffee and stared at Sullivan fixedly for a minute or two over the top of his steaming mug as they sat opposite each other in the lounge.

'Well?' he said at length. 'How about telling me what this is all about and where Richard was going after he left me yesterday evening?'

She took a sip from the coffee mug cupped between both hands and shook her head. 'I can't. Not until I've spoken to Richard anyway.'

'Then I will have no option but to ring the nick and report him missing.'

She stared at him and he noted the flicker of alarm back in her big green eyes. 'No, you mustn't do that. The job Richard and I are on is highly sensitive and it has reached a critical stage. There may be a perfectly reasonable explanation for his failure to make contact and if we take precipitate action now it could ruin everything. We must allow him a little more time to surface.'

Calder deposited his mug on the floor beside the chair and pulled out his cigarettes. 'This is getting worse. First I take possession of incriminating evidence that should have been lodged in a crime property store; then I lose the bloody envelope containing it; now you're asking me to suppress the fact that a senior policeman and a very close friend of mine has disappeared. For all we know he could be in real trouble right this minute.'

She shook her head and set her own mug on the chair arm as he lit up. 'If he is it won't be the sort of physical trouble you envisage. Please, give him a few more hours.'

He studied her askance. 'On one condition; you tell me what all this is about and who he was going to see last night.'

'That's just not possible. I . . .'

'Then that's it!' he snapped and without waiting for her to say anything else he was on his feet and striding across the room to the door.

'Jim!' she shouted after him. 'What the hell are you doing?'

He ignored her and when she reached the hall he was already standing by the telephone table with the telephone receiver in his hand. 'Either you talk to me now,' he threatened, 'or I talk to the station and report Richard missing. It's your choice.'

'But . . . but you can't.'

'Watch me!'

She clenched her fists, her face ashen. 'You bastard!' she said with feeling.

He shrugged. 'I've been called a lot worse. So, what's it to be?'

'All right, all right,' she snapped. 'I'll tell you what you want to know, but only if you give me your word you'll keep your mouth shut about Richard until I say.'

He replaced the receiver with a grim smile. 'Agreed, but what you have to tell me had better be good.'

'Oh, you'll love it,' she retorted with heavy sarcasm. 'Every little shitty detail.'

She immediately slumped on to the settee when they returned to the lounge, eyeing him warily as he dropped into the chair opposite.

'More coffee?' he queried.

'Let's just get on with it,' she snapped. 'But before I start I think you'd better tell me what you know already.'

He nodded thoughtfully. 'Well, from what Richard said I gather the pair of you are investigating some sort of conspiracy to do with the threatened police strike. He led me to believe certain powerful people wanted the strike to happen for political reasons and that they were manipulating Willy Justice to make sure a settlement was not achieved.'

'Go on.'

He half closed his eyes, trying to remember all that the SB man had told him in as near accurate detail as possible. 'He said there were conspirators inside as well as outside the service. They all had their own individual agendas and not everyone knew all of those involved. Some were working through intermediaries. I also gathered from him that he didn't trust his own colleagues, present company excepted, and because of this he feared the surveillance material in the envelope he gave me might go missing if it were put in a crime property store.'

'No fear of that now you've lost it for him, is there?' she cut in acidly.

His face reddened. 'I think you've already made your point on that,' he snapped back, 'and you couldn't make me feel any worse about it than I do at the moment.'

She looked down at her feet. 'I know and I apologise.' She stared at him again. 'Anything else Richard told you?'

He shook his head, still thinking. 'No, that's about it. Oh yes, except that he was going to see someone after he had seen me to try and stop things happening.'

She nodded. 'I know about that, but what I don't know, and have to have to find out, is whether he actually got there. That's my next move.'

'So who was this person?'

She got as far as opening her mouth before the doorbell rang. Calder swore and lurched to his feet. 'Hang on a minute,' he snapped. 'I'll just see who this is. Probably some kids about a football.'

But it wasn't and when he opened the door it was to find Chief Inspector Rosalind Maxwell standing on the doorstep, a civilian coat over her uniform.

'Hello, Jim,' she said with a brief smile. 'Glad you're at home. I've been trying to ring you all afternoon.'

He thought quickly. 'Yes, I've . . . er . . . been out.'

She made a face. 'I've got some bad news, I'm afraid. I thought you should be aware before you went on duty tonight. Can I come in?'

Inwardly he thought, 'Shit!' But he tried not to show his annoyance and stood to one side. 'Of course. The lounge is on your right. I . . . I have someone with me at the moment though.'

Maxwell stopped short when she saw Jane Sullivan and her eyes narrowed as he made the introductions.

'Jane, this is Ros . . . Chief Inspector Rosalind Maxwell,' he said quickly, then: 'Jane Sullivan, ma'am, a friend.'

The handshakes were only perfunctory. 'Can we talk . . . privately,' Maxwell said coldly.

He glanced quizzically at Sullivan and then back at his boss, puzzled by the sudden drop in temperature. 'Yes, yes, of course. Excuse me a moment, will you, Jane?'

Leaning against one of the cupboard units in the kitchen, Maxwell studied him critically for a moment. 'So who's she?' she queried sharply.

He looked bewildered. 'I've told you, a friend. Why?'

'Bit young for you, isn't she?'

'I beg your pardon?'

She shook her head quickly and bit her lip. 'Sorry, I shouldn't have said that. Forget it.'

He glared at her. 'No, I won't forget it. With respect, it's none of your damned business.'

She held up both hands in front of her in a defensive gesture. 'I've already said I'm sorry. Now let's just leave it there, shall we?'

He continued to glare at her for a second and then nodded reluctantly 'Okay. Consider it forgotten. So what's this bad news you have for me and why did you need to deliver it personally?'

'I didn't need to deliver it personally, but as I've already told you, I couldn't raise you on the telephone. Since I was out this way I thought I'd call instead. That is all right, isn't it? I mean, I do have your permission, don't I?'

Now it was his turn to feel uncomfortable. 'Don't talk wet. I'm a bit on edge at the moment, that's all.'

She pursed her lips for a second, then said abruptly: 'I came to tell you that Janet Stone lost her baby this morning!'

'Oh, bloody hell, no! How's Maurice taken it?'

'How do you expect? He's devastated. I'm afraid he

won't be in a fit state to come on tonight. I've given him some compassionate leave.'

Calder sighed heavily and ran a hand through his hair. 'How's Janet?'

'Not very good at the moment. She's under sedation.'

'Poor old Maurice. I shall have to go and see him. Does Inspector Maybe know?'

'Not yet. He rang in sick this morning.'

'Nothing trivial, I hope?'

She smiled faintly. 'Now you're being unkind.'

'Unkind? You know why he's chucked in the towel as well as I do. It's the strike Friday night and he is terrified of being seen as either a strike breaker or a strike supporter so he's taken the easy way out.'

'I'm sure you're quite wrong there. If that was the case why would he go sick tonight?'

He laughed. 'Well, it would be a bit flaming obvious if he did it on the night of the strike, wouldn't it?'

She shook her head gravely. 'You really are a dreadful cynic, James.'

'Perhaps I've got good reason to be.'

She eased herself away from the kitchen unit and glanced at her watch. 'Yes, well I think I should be going. I've got a pre-strike briefing with Mr. Rhymes in half an hour.' She smiled tightly. 'I'll see you tonight. If you're not too tired by then, that is.'

He scowled. 'As I've already told you, Jane is just a friend.'

'And as you've also so eloquently told me, it's none of my business anyway, eh?"

He winced and followed her to the door. 'Yeah, well I apologise again about that. I was a bit rude.'

She gave a tight smile. 'No more rude than usual,

James,' she retorted sweetly and marching off down the path to her car she half-turned and called back: 'Oh yes, and thanks for the . . . tea!'

But this time her sarcasm fell on deaf ears, for at the same moment he noticed Jane Sullivan's car was no longer parked outside. With an oath he rushed back to the lounge, to find she had left a note on the coffee table before making the most of her opportunity to slip away.

'Don't think badly of me, Jim, but there's something I must do before we talk. I'm holding you to your promise not to report Richard missing. I'll be in touch soon.
    Jane.'

He crushed the note in his hand savagely, recognising that he had been out-manoeuvred again. 'Bitch!' he said aloud. 'Conniving little bitch!'

8

There was thunder in the air when Calder locked the front door of his bungalow to go on duty, but apart from a distant angry rumble it didn't amount to anything and the weather remained uncomfortably hot and humid. Promising another pig of a night, he thought irritably.

He passed a few dozen half-naked youngsters on his way into town, several of the girls topless as well as the boys. All of them were obviously from the festival and stoned out of their minds. He swore as he swerved to avoid one teenage boy who ran directly out in front of his car, eyes wide and staring. But he didn't stop. On his own it would have been pointless and it would also have been pretty risky dressed as he was in part uniform.

He scowled and, glancing in his rear-view mirror, saw the lad he had just missed cavorting with a few of his cronies in the middle of the road. Then he saw movement out of the corner of his eye and braked hard as a whole crowd of fantasy figures in brightly patterned trousers and floppy hats strolled from one side of the road to the other just yards in front of him, most of them pulling infantile faces and making obscene gestures in his direction as they went.

He pulled out his handkerchief and wiped the perspiration from his forehead as he drove on, conscious of the accelerated thudding of his heart. Bloody Nora, things were starting to get out of hand. It was almost as if someone had opened the doors of every lunatic asylum in the country and let all the inmates loose. And to think that the police were actually poised to take strike action the following night. Maybe the members of the National Police Union needed locking up in an asylum themselves!

Calder didn't follow his usual route to the station, for he had left early to make a couple of welfare calls on the way and his first stop was Merridale Avenue on the south side of town where Maurice Stone had a small flat.

Stone was in the middle of a solitary drinking session and he only grudgingly opened the door to him. There were beer cans all over the living-room floor and Calder made a face when he followed him inside.

'This help, does it?' he queried, staring at the young officer fixedly.

Stone shrugged. 'Seemed like a good idea when I started,' he retorted in a slurred voice. 'Want one?'

'Don't be an arse-hole, Maurice,' Calder snapped deliberately.

Stone staggered to his feet slopping drink all over the carpet, his face set and belligerent. Calder didn't even flinch. 'Going to hit me, are you, Maurice?' he said quietly. 'Because if you are, you'd better make it a good one before I return the compliment!'

Stone stood there swaying for a moment, his free hand clenched into a great ball of a fist and his glass still dribbling beer on to the carpet.

'Well?' Calder persisted. 'What's it to be? Stupidity or some strong coffee?'

For a few seconds it was very definitely touch and go. Then the big man seemed to suddenly lose all his strength and slumping back into the chair promptly emptied the remaining contents of his glass into his lap.

Calder closed his eyes in resignation and took the glass from him. 'Coffee then,' he said firmly and headed for the kitchen.

It was a good hour before Stone could be sobered up enough to make him see some sense and then Calder listened with the patience that comes with age and experience to the outpouring of grief that was the inevitable consequence. Janet, it seemed, was still in hospital and would be for at least another couple of nights. Tough as he was physically, Maurice just couldn't handle the mental trauma of their loss. They had been trying for a baby for a lot longer than Calder had realised, but his macho pride had apparently kept Maurice from confiding in anyone about it before. Now, when it seemed their prayers were at last to be answered, their hopes had been cruelly dashed at the final hour.

Calder had no counselling skills, but in his gruff clumsy way he made more headway than he would have thought possible. It was heavy going though and he was more relieved than he cared to admit when a knock on the door heralded the arrival of Stone's sister, Maureen, enabling him to leave the problem with her. Nevertheless, he felt he had at least achieved something by calling on the young bobby and Stone's brief handshake and whispered, 'Thanks for the visit, Sarge,' was strangely moving as he made his way to his car.

His next port of call was a three-storey Victorian terrace directly opposite the municipal park, where Taffy Jones had been lodging for the past three months, and he was on the point of rapping on the door when the little Welshman actually came up behind him on the doorstep. He was in his running kit and the sweat was pouring down him as he forced a grin and reached past his sergeant to let himself in the front door with his key.

'You can do all this jogging when you're suspended, skipper,' Jones said. 'Plenty of time, see? Coming in then?'

The hallway was dark, smelling of damp and recently boiled cabbage, and Calder made a face as he followed him up the stairs to his bedsit on the first floor.

'So, how are you coping?' he growled, depositing himself on a two-seater settee while the young bobby bent down and plugged in the kettle by the fireplace.

'Coping? Oh, you know, bearing up under the strain and all that. Bit of a bastard though, isn't it? Can't even defend yourself nowadays, can you?' Jones half-turned. 'And you shouldn't be here at all, should you? If they find out, you'll be in the cart and no mistake.' He grinned, but there was no humour in it. '*Persona non grata* when you're suspended, see. Cut off from everyone. Not allowed to play with the other boys and girls anymore in case they get a dose of what you've caught. Only things they don't cut off at this stage are your balls. But someone probably does that later.'

Calder nodded slowly. Behind the bravado and the jokes he sensed the deep bitterness. 'Don't let it get to you, Taff . . .' he began, then broke off and picked up some coloured brochures from the arm of the settee. One carried the Royal Navy ensign and a photograph of an aircraft carrier on the high seas, and he frowned. 'What's all this then?'

Jones turned again, then shrugged when he saw what he was holding. 'Been making a few enquiries, that's all.'

'You're not thinking of resigning from the force?'

The Welshman stood up with two mugs of tea and set one on the floor beside Calder. 'Can't at the moment, can I?' he replied and sat down on the edge of the small bed opposite. 'Not allowed to when you're on suspension. Navy wouldn't even consider me at the moment, mind, not with this bloody thing hanging over me. I'm a criminal, see. I belt inoffensive members of the public who are going about their lawful business kicking women police officers to bits.'

'You haven't answered my question.'

Jones took a sip of his tea and sighed. 'That's my plan when this is all over, yes.'

'Then you're a bloody fool.'

The other leaned forward, his expression suddenly intense. 'Am I, Sergeant? Am I really? Just think about it for a moment. A violent toe-rag savagely beats up a young policewoman, then goes for me with a piece of lead pipe and I get suspended from duty for arresting him. Something wrong there, don't you think?'

Calder grunted. 'You know what they say : if you can't stand a joke, you shouldn't have joined.'

There was a grim nod of acknowledgement. 'Well, maybe I don't find it funny anymore. And I'm not the only one either. Talk to any copper nowadays and you'll get the same message. There's no point to the job nowadays. It's all gone to pot.'

'Now you're talking wet.'

Jones shook his head firmly. 'I don't think so and neither do you really. Morale is at the lowest I've ever seen it in five years. None of us knows what our role is anymore. The public complain about everything we do, the courts not only look for any excuse they can find to let villains off the hook, but dip into the poor box to pay them for the crimes they've committed as well. As for the bloody government, they seem hell bent on beating us over the head with every stick they can find. The wheel's about to come off this outfit and no one will give a shit until it's too late.'

Calder waited patiently for his outburst to come to an end and then made a wry face. 'Your suspension bring all this on, did it?'

'No, it's been coming on for some time. This was the final straw.' Jones raised one hand edge on to his throat. 'I've had it up to here, Sarge. Sorry, but that's the way it is.'

Calder nodded and stood up, looking at his watch and only finishing half his mug of tea. 'I understand how you feel, Taff, I really do, but be patient and don't do anything rash. You know I'll back you as much as I can in this investigation thing. Just tell the truth when they eventually interview you and don't lose your rag. Okay?'

The Welshman also stood up and thrust out a hand. 'Thanks for calling by, Sarge,' he said quietly. 'Appreciate the thought.' He grinned with something akin to genuine humour. 'You're not a bad bloke for an Englishman, you know.'

Calder had intended making Daphne Young his last

visit, but time had caught up with him and reluctantly he headed straight for the station, feeling more down than he had felt for a long time. With Richard Baseheart's disappearance, the loss of the all important envelope and the impending police strike, he had enough on his plate and he really hadn't needed to be reminded of the depressing plight of Maurice Stone and Taffy Jones. But duty was duty and as shift sergeant he took his welfare responsibilities very seriously. 'Too bloody seriously,' Maggie's soft Geordie voice seemed to say and he turned his head quickly, half expecting to see her sitting beside him in the front passenger seat.

Then suddenly the blast of a horn awakened him to reality and he swung hard left to miss the police Traffic car as it raced out of the rear entrance of the police station, its roof lights flashing furiously. Stopped at an angle in the yard he closed his eyes tightly for a second and took a deep breath. You're going to pieces, Jim, he mused. Get a hold of yourself. Re-engaging first gear, he drove straight across the yard and parked facing forward, contrary to regulations, in the first vacant bay he could see, now aware for the first time that Chief Inspector Maxwell was standing by her own BMW car parked two spaces along and staring at him fixedly.

'Shit!' he breathed as she sauntered over to him.

'That was rather close, James,' she said sharply. 'A bit more care please.'

He nodded and turned off the engine, surprised by her strangely hostile manner. 'Sorry ma'am. Mind was on something else, I'm afraid.'

She made a wry face. 'Yes, I can imagine. Well, you'd better get it back on track fast. You have someone in the nick waiting to see you after briefing.'

'To see me? Who on earth's that?'

'A Mr. Raymond Darling . . . and he isn't, by the way.'

'Isn't what?'

She smiled coldly. 'A darling. He's from the Regional Complaints Department. One of the new civilian investigators, I gather.' She turned back towards her car. 'So you'd better get your skates on, hadn't you?'

'Independent investigators!' Calder muttered to himself as he pushed his warrant card into the security lock by the back door. Yet another cross for the police to bear. Still, it had been on the cards for some time and was all part of the popular trend, started years before with the creation of an independent Crown Prosecution Service, to make the most accountable police service in the world even more accountable. Like other long-service bobbies he resented the changes, but he was shrewd enough to appreciate that the old system of police officers investigating other police officers had been pretty hard to defend, especially with the anti-lobby constantly making allegations of police corruption. At least no one could now accuse the police of fixing cases in their favour. No, he thought darkly as he headed for the sergeants' office, but the trouble was, from what he had heard over the bush telegraph things were actually starting to work the other way. Spurious complaints were being accepted on the flimsiest pieces of evidence and innocent bobbies sent up the steps just to prove a political point. Thank heavens he was nearing the end of his service!

Tom Lester had his coat on when he strode through the doorway and the day tour sergeant seemed even more anxious to be off than usual. Calder immediately saw why. A thin be-spectacled man with sparse ginger hair and a neat grey suit was sitting in the far corner of the room, his briefcase on his lap and a mug of tea in one hand.

'Mr. Darling,' Lester said quickly in warning. 'From the RCD. Wants to see you.'

Calder grunted and nodded in the other's direction. 'What's he doing in here? There's a perfectly good waiting-room along the corridor.'

Lester's eyes widened and he made a face at his colleague.

'I'll leave you with it,' he said with heavy emphasis, then on his way to the door, added: 'Nothing special to report. Same old problems as yesterday. It's all on the magic box anyway.' Then he was gone, for once not even whistling.

'Sergeant . . . er . . . Calder, isn't it?' Grey Suit had left his chair and mug of tea and was hovering almost at his elbow.

Calder looked up from the paperwork on his desk and studied him as he would have inspected an insect. 'Yes, Mr. Darling. What can I do for you?'

Pale blue eyes returned his gaze coldly and his visitor adjusted his glasses over his thin hawk-like nose. 'I need to interview you regarding an incident involving one of your officers.'

'PC Jones?'

'Exactly. Nothing for you to worry about. Just a witness statement actually.'

Calder's mouth tightened. 'That's assuming I wish to make one.'

The other smiled frostily and shook his head. 'You have no choice, Sergeant,' he said with surprising firmness. 'Under the new Police Act you can be required to make a statement, whether you wish to do so or not.'

'What about my civil rights as a citizen?'

Another frosty smile. 'Shall we stop playing games, Sergeant,' the investigator said quietly. 'I have a job to do and I intend doing it.'

'And so do I, Mr. Darling,' Calder growled. 'And right now I have a shift to brief. I'll see you in here when I've finished.'

Darling nodded. 'Of course, but as soon as you can please. I've had a long day.'

Calder actually completed the briefing in record time on this occasion, but not out of any sympathy for Mr. Darling's apparent fatigue, but because he was given no option by Chief Inspector Maxwell who put in a timely appearance and imposed her own guillotine at an appropriate moment.

'I understand from Mr. Darling that you are being awkward, James,' she said when the last of the shift had disappeared.

Calder scowled. 'I didn't like his approach.'

She closed the briefing room door. 'You don't have to like anything about him,' she snapped. 'All you have to do is give him a bloody statement. So do it!'

He nodded. 'Whatever you say, ma'am, but just one small point: I thought a complaint against a police officer by someone already arrested for a criminal offence couldn't be investigated until the complainant had been weighed off by the court?'

She hesitated as if he had caught her on the wrong foot. 'The man has already been dealt with.'

'But that's impossible. He was only arrested the night before last. There's no way all witnesses could have been seen and case papers prepared for court in that time.'

She nodded unhappily. 'He was dealt with on CPS advice when he appeared for remand.'

Calder's eyes narrowed.

'What first time in? That's unprecedented in a case like this.'

She nodded. 'I know it's unusual, but he was prepared to plead guilty there and then to a charge of Drunk and Disorderly and the CPS solicitor decided to accept it.'

'Drunk and . . . ?' he blasted incredulously, but she cut him off with an irritable wave of her hand.

'Apparently it was felt that going for an ABH or Assault on Police, which happened in the dark in the midst of a melee, would have been difficult to prove and in view of all the circumstances CPS decided it wasn't in the public interest to go for a protracted costly prosecution.'

Calder controlled himself with an effort. 'No, but it was in the public interest to suspend Taffy Jones even before he'd had a hearing, wasn't it?' he said harshly.

'That's automatic under the new Police Act, as well you know,' she retorted.

'Doesn't make it right,' he persisted stubbornly. 'And what about Daphne?'

She made a face. 'Her injuries were seen by the court as only minor and the sort of thing that goes with the territory.'

'Easy for someone to say that when their arse is stuck in a comfortable chair and they don't have to risk their own neck,' he grated. 'So what did the scumbag get?'

'As it was his first offence, a conditional discharge and two hundred and fifty pounds compensation, with three months to pay.'

'So that's the value of a policewoman today, is it? Two hundred and fifty quid! The whole thing bloody stinks!'

He made to push past her to the door, but she checked him sharply. 'Cool it, James, and that's an order! You won't help Taffy Jones if you go storming in to see Mr. Darling. For heaven's sake, use your head, man, or you'll play right into his hands.'

He nodded, an ironic gleam in his eyes as he remembered that he himself had handed out almost identical advice to the little Welshman just a short time before. 'Don't worry,' he retorted. 'I wouldn't give the cretin that satisfaction.'

Despite Calder's bold assurance, the gruelling two hour long interview that followed certainly tested his resolve. Perhaps because of the antagonism he had displayed previously, Darling adopted an aggressive provocative approach towards him that was clearly designed to get under his skin and he had to use every ounce of self-control he possessed to stop himself biting back.

In fact, as it turned out, the little man's wimpish bespectacled appearance belied a surprisingly forceful personality, coupled with the keen calculating mind of an accomplished interviewer and it quickly dawned on Calder that he had dangerously underestimated the other's professional competence. With this realisation came a change of tack on his part and as the verbal thrust and parry began to intensify he was forced to treat his antagonist with a new kind of grudging respect.

It was a peculiar feeling, however, sitting on the wrong side of the desk in his own office being quizzed by a civilian instead of the other way about. In twenty-two year's service he had carried out innumerable interviews in all sorts of situations and he thought he had mastered all the techniques. Now he was on the receiving end he felt strangely vulnerable and defensive, just as he had felt in the past when appearing before interview boards for promotion or vacant departmental posts. Apparently sensing his feeling of vulnerability, Darling did his best to press home his advantage, trying to put words into his mouth and suggesting that Taffy Jones had actually attacked the complainant with unreasonable force, bent on vengeance for the assault on Daphne Young rather than the need to defend himself. When Calder grimly stuck to his guns and denied this the little man began to show signs of impatience and then irritation, the pale blue eyes frosting behind the spectacles and a muscle in one cheek twitching spasmodically.

'You are just trying to protect one of your own, aren't you?' he accused. 'It's the usual thing of closing ranks, isn't it?'

Calder shook his head. 'That's not true,' he replied, gaining comfort and some strength from the other's evident frustration. 'Taffy was faced with a violent man and did exactly what I would have done under the circumstances.'

Darling raised his eyebrows. 'Indeed? So as a supervisor you think it's okay for police officers to run around like yobs in uniform, lashing out at anyone they take a dislike to?'

The remark was intended to rile and this time the tactic succeeded. After being lulled into a false sense of security Calder went for the jugular vein before he could check himself. 'You want to try doing this job, Mr. Darling,' he grated, 'deal with the scum we have to deal with. Taffy Jones is a bloody good officer, but because of this crappy complaint the force is likely to lose him for good.'

The pale blue eyes sharpened. 'And why should you think that, Sergeant?'

'Because he told me so.' The moment he blurted the reply Calder realised he had dropped himself in the mire and seeing Darling abruptly stiffen he inwardly cursed himself for a fool.

'And when did he tell you that?' the other said softly.

Calder knew he had been cornered and could do little but shrug his shoulders in resignation. 'When I visited him this evening.'

Darling nodded slowly, his eyes hard and judgmental. 'Let me get this straight, Sergeant. You not only visited an officer currently on suspension, but one who is subject of a criminal investigation in which you are involved as a key witness?'

Calder's mouth tightened. 'It was a welfare call, nothing more.'

'And you expect me to believe that?'

'I don't really care what you believe, Mr. Darling. That's what happened.'

'But it doesn't look good, does it?'

Calder shrugged again. 'I've never worried about what things look like. My conscience is clear and that's all that matters.'

'I shall have to report this breach, you know that, don't you?'

Calder grunted. 'Report what you like, Mr. Darling,' he said, 'but I have a shift to supervise, so can we now get on with my written statement? Unless,' he added dryly, 'you want to have me investigated for conspiracy to pervert the course of justice, in which case, I will say nothing without my solicitor being present.'

Darling gave a thin smile, the conspiracy idea obviously appealing to him, but instead of pursuing the issue further, he drew a blank statement form from his briefcase and began to head it up. 'I take it you don't object to me writing your statement for you . . . at your dictation, of course?' he queried.

Calder shook his head. 'As long as it's what I want to say and not what you want me to say,' he replied grimly. 'You can't be too careful nowadays!'

'James, you're a damned fool!' Chief Inspector Maxwell snapped when she ran into him as he was in the process of kitting up to go out after the interview. 'I've just been speaking to Mr. Darling. Fancy going to visit Taffy Jones. You know it was absolutely taboo under the new Police Act.'

Calder checked his torch and adjusted his personal radio in its harness. 'I'm sick of hearing about this new Police Act,' he retorted. 'A man doesn't suddenly become a leper just because he's on suspension and right now Taffy needs all the support he can get.'

She drew in her breath in an exasperated hiss. 'Support, yes, but not a visit from a main witness in the case. The RCD are going to think you went there so the pair of you could get your stories straight.'

'You know I didn't.'

'I'm not the RCD.'

'With respect, you're beginning to sound as if you are.'

She snorted. 'Grow up, man. I'm trying to help you. You've got to distance yourself from Taffy Jones until this business is all over. If you don't and he falls down you're likely to go down with him.'

He clipped on his side-baton and picked up his flat uniformed cap, his eyes glittering. 'You mean let him stew in his own juice, even though I know he's a bloody good officer who is likely to be crucified by the system just for doing his job?'

She shook her head irritably. 'You're missing the whole point of what I'm saying. The best thing you can do for Taffy at the moment is to keep away from him and remain an impartial witness. Let things take their natural course.'

'You know he's going to resign even if he's cleared, don't you?'

'No, I didn't, but that's his decision anyway. Nothing to do with anyone else.'

'So meanwhile, we just chuck him on the scrap heap and forget he ever existed?'

'It's not like that at all and you damned well know it. But it's essential that all complaints like this are seen to be investigated thoroughly and independently, otherwise the police will lose all credibility with the public.'

He emitted a hard cynical laugh. 'Thoroughly and independently, yes, but what about fairly? You haven't mentioned anything about that, have you? And the reason you haven't is because fairness doesn't enter into it anymore, does it? The system isn't interested in justice, only in satisfying the anti-police lobby. It just wants a sacrifice to prove a political point.'

'That's absolute rubbish.'

'Is it? Well, we'll see. But I'll tell you this for nothing: I'm not going to abandon one of my bobbies just to please the RCD. I'd be the last person to protect a bent copper, but I'm not about to stand by while an innocent one goes down the tubes either.'

Maxwell's face was set and angry. 'This discussion is at an end, Sergeant,' she snapped. 'If you won't listen to reason, I'll put it another way. You will not visit PC Jones again. You will stay away from his home completely and that is a direct order. Do you understand?'

Calder nodded. 'Oh I understand, ma'am,' he retorted. 'I understand only too well and I'm just glad I never aspired to become a governor.'

She bit her lip hard as he turned back towards his open locker, his barb going in deeply. 'James!' she said almost in desperation. 'For heaven's sake, man, I'm only trying to help you.'

He half-turned. 'Me or the system, ma'am?' he replied with a bitter smile.

'You bastard,' she breathed, her face colouring up. 'You thick stupid bastard. I just hope that cheap little trollop of yours is prepared to stay with you when they chuck you out on your ear without a pension!' Then before he could say anything further she spun on her heel and marched from the room.

Calder embraced the muggy evening air with the passion of a man just released from prison, anxious to put as much distance between himself and the station as possible. But when he climbed into the supervisory car and pulled out of the yard into the still busy street his mind was in a whirl; a hopeless confusion of anxiety, uncertainty and incomprehension that came and went like sparks of light whizzing round inside a cylinder, making no sense at all and settling so very briefly that he was denied the opportunity of focusing on any issue long enough to even begin to come to any real conclusion.

It was as though his whole world had begun to cave in and with it his ability to think rationally and logically. The Solomon thing; Richard Basehcart's disappearance; the conspiracy that Baseheart and Sullivan had been investigating; the loss of the vital envelope; Sullivan's rapid departure to heaven knew where; the impending strike; the complaint against Taffy Jones; Maurice Stone's tragic loss; and now to cap it all, the sudden hostility of Rosy Maxwell towards him. What a bloody week!

Turning down the radio after first booking himself on with Control, he pulled into the same alleyway where he had sat with Rosy Maxwell the previous night and lit a cigarette, listening with half an ear to the metallic buzz of traffic over the air.

'Received Two-One. Traffic mobile en route to you . . . Two-Three attend domestic Colonial Road. Believed two Asian families involved . . . Two-Six back her up please . . . Received Three-Two. Now go to Old Place Yard. Winos causing trouble . . . Two-Two ABA Salter's Shoes, Gorton Street . . . Thank you Bravo- Alpha Five-Two . . . PC Nash (Two-Two), CID now backing you up . . .'

So it went, on and on and on, a confused tangle of messages, call-signs and names that rattled around the inside of the car with the thoughts in his brain. For the first time in his service he neglected to reach for the radio transmit button to offer assistance, but just let the whole lot wash over him as if he were no longer part of it; anaesthetised by the constant hubbub and drifting in an unreal world of his own. For some reason Phil Davies in the control room didn't call him and it was only when the butt of his cigarette suddenly burned his fingers that he abruptly snapped out of his lethargy and, tossing the thing out of the window with a couple of choice swear-words, started the car's engine.

Porter-Nash seemed pleased to see him when he drew up outside Salter's Shop and he strode over to meet him as he got out of the car, shouting above the din of the audible alarm. 'Seems all secure, Sarge,' he said and jerked his head towards the premises. 'Five-Two, DC Jarvis, is round the back.'

Calder nodded and drew him to a quieter spot away from the shop. 'And how are you tonight?'

Nash shrugged and glanced at his bandaged wrist. 'What, the bite, you mean? Bit sore, but I'll live . . . unless I end up with Aids, that is.'

Calder stared at him keenly. 'Do you know if the bitch was HIV positive?'

Nash shook his head. 'Not yet. But apparently she provided a blood test in the end, so I'll probably know in a couple of days.'

Calder pressed his arm reassuringly. 'Keep your spirits up,' he said. 'We'll speak again later. I'm just going to pop and see Daphne Young.'

Nash nodded. 'How's Maurice Stone?'

'Pretty rough, but he should survive, given time.'

'I just hope *we* can. What with him, Taffy and

Daphne out of action and three others already borrowed for the festival, there isn't much of our shift left at the moment.'

Calder climbed into his car and laughed without humour. 'And Inspector Maybe on sick, don't forget him.'

Nash grinned. 'Sorry, Sarge,' he replied, 'but I already have, I'm afraid!'

It was gone nine-thirty when Calder finally pulled up outside Daphne Young's small semi in Tabitha Close, just behind the police station, but as he had expected she was still up, her boyfriend having only just left in his dilapidated sports car.

'Sorry to call so late, Daphne,' he apologised, conscious of the fact that she was clad in a blue towelling dressing-gown and appeared ready for bed, 'but we've got a lot on at the moment.'

She grinned and pulled the dressing-gown more closely about her. 'No problem, Sarge,' she replied. 'Actually, I'm rather glad you weren't any earlier. Could've been awkward and you know I keep late hours anyway.'

Thinking of the boyfriend who had just left, Calder scratched his nose, looking down at his feet with some embarrassment, and the chirpy ex-Wren chuckled. 'And just in case you're wondering, I do wear clothes from time to time when I'm not in uniform, even if you only seem to see me in dressing-gowns lately. Now, can I get you some tea or coffee?'

Calder hesitated, thinking of the amount he had already drunk on his previous two welfare visits, then shook his head. 'No thanks. I reckon I've had enough of that stuff tonight.'

'Well, how about a slice of home-made sponge?'

His face brightened, well aware of her reputation in that quarter. 'Now you're talking.'

Settling in the armchair by the television, he idly stared at the flickering screen as she busied herself in the kitchen. The regular weekly *News Chat* interview was well underway, with the tubby beetle-browed Leader of the Opposition, Kenneth Granger MP, sparring with TV's own gaunt raven-haired character-assassin, Anton Brace, and he wasn't surprised to learn what the subject was about when he turned up the sound.

'. . . and since this government has been in power,' Granger said forcefully, smoothing his mop of shiny blond hair back from one ear with a podgy hand, 'we have seen crime go through the roof and police morale hit rock-bottom. If the police are to be expected to deal with the problems society faces they must be given the proper resources.'

'So are you saying your party would provide increased police funding if it came to power?' Brace cut in, one finger carefully stroking his thin upper lip.

Granger smiled and his curious amber coloured eyes seemed to be mocking his interrogator. 'We would certainly set funding at a realistic level,' he replied smoothly, 'something this government has consistently failed to do throughout its whole disastrous term in office and despite all its election promises.'

'But would you increase funding?' Brace persisted, his smile just as insincere as he lazily scratched one eye-lid.

Granger's own smile was undiminished. 'I think you will find that our manifesto is very clear about the importance we place on a properly funded police force, Anton,' he patronised.

Brace was unimpressed. 'You still haven't answered my question. Does that mean an increase?'

But, true to form, Granger had no intention of committing himself or his party on such a sensitive issue, especially as their previous record on public service expenditure when in power had been just as dismal. 'It means that under our ministry the police would not be put in a position where they have to resort to strike action to get the support they need,' he said.

He raised a hand in an impatient gesture as Brace tried to cut in again. 'No, please, let me finish. You have to remember that for the first time in nearly a century this country finds itself on the brink of a potentially disastrous police strike in the Prime Minister's own constituency, simply because of government intransigence. Once again the government has refused to listen, refused to see sense and refused to acknowledge that they are leading us on the road to ruin.' Using a classic, if risky, interview technique he stared directly at the camera to emphasise his point. 'In short, we have a government that has demonstrated it is totally unfit for office, led by a Prime Minister who has lost all credibility even in his own constituency. It's time for a change.'

'Cake for the sergeant?' Daphne Young announced in a sombre voice.

Calder grinned and shut off the television as she set a plate, dwarfed by an enormous slice of jam sponge, on the little coffee table in front of him.

'I've given up listening to that,' she said after taking a sip from the cup of coffee she had made herself.

'None of them say what they really mean. Bit like senior officers in the services really.'

'I hope that doesn't include me,' he commented, starting on the sponge.

She chuckled mischievously. 'You're not a senior *hofficer*, Sarge. You're everyone's maiden aunt.'

'I'm not sure I like that description.'

She laughed outright, the bruises and cuts on her still slightly swollen face giving her an almost comic clown-like appearance. 'Oh, I don't know. I think it's rather nice. Beneath that gruff exterior and all that.'

He grunted, apparently still not convinced, then abruptly changed the subject. 'Anyway, what about you? How are you feeling now?'

She sat down on a pouffe on the other side of the table. 'A lot better, thanks, but I still look like a freshly mugged banana in the shower.'

He finished the last of his cake and grinned again. 'Well I'll have to take your word for that. I only popped round to see if you needed anything.'

She shook her head. 'No, nothing, thanks and it was very nice of you to call. Actually, apart from my boyfriend, Paul, of course, you're the second one today.'

'The second one?'

She sipped her coffee. 'Yes, Chief Inspector Maxwell was here this afternoon. We had quite a chat.'

'Oh?'

The mischief (never far from Daphne Young) was back in her eyes. 'Yes, women's talk, you know.'

He cleared his throat. 'Oh yeah, right.'

'Your name came up quite a lot too,' she went on innocently.

'My name?'

'Yes, she seems to be very interested in you.'

He frowned. 'Interested? What do you mean?'

'Oh come on, Sarge,' she exclaimed with another chuckle, 'surely you know?'

He set his empty sponge plate down on the coffee table. 'What the hell are you talking about, Daphne? Know what?'

'Well you must realise she's carrying a torch for you?'

He stared at her as if she had mouthed an obscenity. 'Carrying a torch for me?' He snorted. 'Don't be so bloody ridiculous.'

She shook her head mildly. 'All right, scoff if you must, but I happen to know it's true. Us women can tell these things.'

He could feel his face reddening as he hastily got to his feet and he was furious with himself. Anyone would think he was some spotty adolescent kid who blushed at the slightest provocation, instead of a fifty year old veteran who had seen so much in life that he should have lost the capacity to be embarrassed by anything.

'It's easy to see you're improving,' he growled, anxious to put an end to this particular conversation. 'Either that or the kick you got in the head has done something to your brain.'

She also stood up, her grin even wider than before. 'Jim and Rosy,' she murmured reflectively. 'Has a nice ring to it though, doesn't it?'

He scowled ferociously and turned towards the hall door. 'Don't be so damned cheeky, young lady. Give you youngsters an inch and you take a bloody mile.'

'Thanks for coming, Sarge,' she called after him as

he tripped over the doorstep on his way out. Then she added with a chuckle: 'Have a really nice night, won't you?'

Back in the security of his car, Calder took a deep breath and sat there for a moment, staring unseeing through the windscreen and trying to convince himself Daphne had been up to her usual leg-pulling nonsense, nothing more than that. Rosy carrying a torch for him? It was too daft for words.

He started the engine and pulled away quickly, scared his contemptuous dismissal of the possibility would not stand up to in-depth analysis and determined not to put it to the test. But the brain is its own master and as he drove his thoughts kept returning to the same subject.

Come to think of it, Rosy had been showing a lot of interest in him and his problems lately, even accompanying him out on patrol. He shook his head irritably. So what? She was a bloody chief inspector, for heaven's sake. He wouldn't have thought it untoward if she had been a man, would he? So why should it be any different because she was a woman?

Yes, but what about the personal visit she had made to his home regarding Maurice Stone's baby? That had been completely unwarranted, hadn't it? No senior officer he'd worked with before had ever done anything like that. They would have left it to the control room to telephone him. Then there were her bitchy remarks about Jane Sullivan and her coldness towards him after she had found her sitting in his bungalow. Jealousy maybe? It all added up.

'Balls!' he said aloud. 'What would she want with a dried-up old war-horse like me?'

Ah, but perhaps she liked older men and though

younger than him she was still no spring chicken herself. Furthermore, some women seemed to fancy a bit of rough on occasions and maybe he fitted the bill as far as she was concerned.

Yes, and what about his own feelings towards her? What did they amount to? He snorted. Nothing at all! Never had and never would. He'd always liked her, of course, but only as a friend. She was fun to be with, for goodness sake. Well, up until lately, that was. And she had been a very good friend to Maggie too. There was nothing more to it than that. Or was there?

Did he actually like her in another way, too. Worse still, had he always liked her that way, even when Maggie was alive? She was certainly a very attractive woman and he had to admit that since the first time they'd met there had been those little electrical discharges between them whenever they were close to each other, pleasurable tingling sensations that aroused him and made his heart thump uncomfortably. He shook his head fiercely. No! He refused to accept any of that nonsense. He'd always loved Maggie, had always been totally loyal to her. Rosy was just a friend, that was all, and if he had ever felt anything towards her it was nothing more than plain old sexual attraction, as with any other good- looking woman. Yet if that was the case, why was he so much on the defensive against the insidious voice in his brain which suggested otherwise?

Shit, he thought as he turned into the police station yard. This latest complication was the very last thing he needed on top of everything else and he was still thinking about it when he entered the office and heard his telephone ring.

'Yeah, Sergeant Calder?' he barked irritably.

'Been trying to get you, Jim,' a familiar voice said sharply. 'Meet me in half an hour at your place.'

The speaker was Jane Sullivan and even as it dawned on him the telephone went dead.

9

Jane Sullivan was sitting in her car outside Calder's bungalow when he arrived, this time she was dressed in a grey pinstripe trouser suit. 'Nice of you to put in an appearance again,' he said with heavy sarcasm and, showing her into the lighted hall, closed the front door behind her.

She smiled slightly, her face strangely pale. 'Sorry I ran out on you, Jim,' she replied, following him through to the lounge, 'but I had to check on something before we went any further. I hope my being here didn't give your lady-friend the wrong idea.'

His eyes narrowed and he stared at her suspiciously, but her face looked innocent enough. 'She's not my lady-friend,' he snapped. 'She's my boss. All right?'

She shrugged. 'Maybe, but she'd like to be a lot more than that, I could tell. It stuck out a mile.'

'And you women can read these things at a glance, right?'

She looked surprised that he needed confirmation of such an obvious fact. 'Of course. But I didn't have to be blessed with a woman's intuition to know what was on her mind. It was written all over her face. Anyway, you yourself must have thought it a bit odd for a chief inspector to call on you personally the way she did. She had to have an ulterior motive and she certainly took great exception to my presence.'

He grunted. 'Well, I could hardly tell her who you were, could I? That would have dropped us both in it. Now can we forget Rosy Maxwell and talk about why you suddenly took off the way you did?'

Before she could answer his radio rasped asthmatically and he held up his hand to silence her. 'Any mobile vicinity The Feathers Pub? Fight in progress . . . Received, Two-Three and Two-Six, thank you. Transit already en route.'

The radio went dead, then almost immediately rasped again. 'Three-One, attend St. Mary's Church, Cable Street. Kids from the Festival causing damage. Two-Zero, back him up please . . . Thank you X-ray-Delta One-Four. Obliged if you could start making your way.'

Calder made a face. 'I can't be long. The pot is beginning to bubble.'

She nodded and sat on the edge of the settee, her face deadly serious again. 'I took off, as you called it, because I wanted to check whether Richard turned up for the meeting he was due to attend last night. I thought if we could at least establish that, we would be a little further forward.'

'And?'

She shook her head. 'Apparently he never arrived.'

'So who was this meeting with?'

She bit her lip as if still reluctant to tell him.

'Well?' he snapped irritably.

She sighed. 'He'd arranged to see Deputy Commissioner Stephen Turner at regional headquarters.'

'Turner? Whatever for?'

She didn't answer at first, but carried on with what

she had been about to say before his interruption. 'When I checked with Mr. Turner's secretary, she confirmed that Richard's name was in the diary for an eight-thirty appointment, but for some reason he didn't show and her boss went home somewhat annoyed at being kept late for nothing. Apparently Turner has already drafted a snotty memo to Richard, demanding an explanation.'

Calder shook his head quickly, looking totally confused. 'I don't understand this. When Richard told me about his appointment he implied he was going to see one of the people involved in the conspiracy. "Make him see sense" was the way I think he put it.'

She said nothing, but regarded him with an unwavering stare, waiting patiently for the penny to drop, and when it did his eyes widened appreciably. 'Turner?' he breathed. 'You're not suggesting he's involved in this conspiracy?'

Her face was bleak. 'Not only him, but the Commissioner as well. It's very much a top level thing.'

Calder sat down heavily in the opposite armchair and pulled out his packet of cigarettes, his hand visibly trembling. 'I can't believe I'm hearing this.'

'But surely you suspected some of the conspirators were high up in the service?' she replied, watching him critically.

He lit a cigarette and drew down the smoke like a medical casualty taking his first gulp from the oxygen mask. 'Yeah, but not that bloody high up, I didn't.'

'No one is immune from temptation, Jim,' she reminded him.

He gave her an old-fashioned look and exhaled the ingested smoke in a long continuous plume. 'Maybe, but I can't see what Harding and Turner could possibly gain from a police strike in their own force area. It would be like committing *hara kiri*!'

She smoothed away non-existent creases from her trousers with both hands. 'Not necessarily. This whole thing's very complicated and there's still a lot I haven't told you.'

Before she could continue, the voice of the radio intruded yet again. 'Bravo-Alpha-Sierra One-Zero receiving?'

Calder simply sat there staring at her.

'Sierra One-Zero? Sergeant Calder?'

She nodded towards his radio. 'They're calling you.'

Like a man in a dream he pressed the transmit button of his remote microphone. 'Sierra One-Zero. Go ahead.'

'Yes, Sarge, please rendezvous Bravo-Sierra Two at Bravo-Alpha as soon as possible.'

'Blast!' he exclaimed after acknowledging the instruction to return to the station. 'What the hell does Rosy Maxwell want now?'

'You'll have to go.'

He stubbed out his unfinished cigarette in an ashtray on the arm of the chair and climbed quickly to his feet. 'Of course I'll have to go, but she certainly picks her moments.' He scowled. 'I suppose you'll disappear again now, leaving me right up a gum-tree after the bombshell you've just dropped?'

She shook her head. 'We need to sort out some sort of plan of action PDQ. But before we can do that you have to be given a much more thorough briefing and I certainly can't do that right this minute.' She hesitated. 'Unfortunately I live about twenty-five miles away which is no good at all, but if you like I could always stay here until you got back? I could easily doss down on the settee.'

'Sierra One-Zero. From Bravo-Sierra Two. ETA please?'

He swore again, reaching towards the remote microphone. 'Okay, we'll do that. But forget the settee. You can use the spare bedroom. It's the second door on the left.' Then he added: 'For Pete's sake don't show yourself though. I've got enough problems at the moment without people thinking I've got myself . . .'

'A bit of spare?'

'Something like that, yes.'

'Sierra One-Zero.'

'All right!' he snarled into the microphone. 'Sierra One-Zero. ETA five minutes!'

He took a deep breath and turned for the door. 'You will be here when I get back?'

She nodded with another faint smile. 'I might even cook you breakfast.'

Calder was on automatic pilot for the short journey back to the police station, his mind in the grip of a cold tight fist and his thoughts centred on the appalling revelations of Jane Sullivan rather than on his driving. It didn't occur to him that Jane could be wrong or might even have been making the whole thing up. Why should she? He knew with the instinctive feeling that comes with age and experience that it was all fact.

And as he thought about the situation and the implications it had for a police service he had held in such high regard for so long, another sizeable chunk of jigsaw fell into place with a sickening jolt.

His own boss, Superintendent George Rhymes, must have been dragged into the conspiracy too. That was what his meeting with Turner had obviously been about. Turner was using him as a link man between himself and Willy Justice so he didn't have to get his own hands dirty and Rhymes had agreed to sell him his soul in return for the renewal of his service contract. Now the conversation he had overheard between the two senior officers began to make sense and key phrases flashed through his mind in rapid succession: 'What about the press? The Commissioner sees it as a golden opportunity to redress the balance. Will you speak to our man and reassure him? We don't want any wavering, do we? Make sure Justice (obviously meaning Willy Justice) does prevail.' No wonder Turner had laughed. The pun had been intentional.

Calder felt physically sick. If the Commissioner, Turner, Rhymes and Willy Justice were all in this together who else might be involved, inside as well as outside the service? And who the hell could Jane and himself trust? But the biggest question of all had to be why? What on earth did high-ranking police officers expect to gain from the strike, especially as they themselves were likely to be criticised for lack of police cover if it went ahead? None of it made sense. He just hoped Jane Sullivan would be able to throw some light on things when he got home later. In the meantime, however, he had to put such questions to the back of his mind. He had more pressing problems to deal with and one of those problems, in the shape of a very sour-faced Chief Inspector Maxwell, was already waiting from him on the front steps of the police station when he finally drove up.

'You took your time, James,' she snapped. 'I've been standing here for at least ten minutes.'

'Made it as quickly as I could,' he growled morosely. 'So, where's the fire?'

'Fire?' she said, settling into the front passenger seat. 'What are you on about?'

He shrugged. 'The way Control were playing it I thought it had to be a fire at the very least.'

She grunted, unimpressed by his sarcasm. 'Well, for your information, there is no fire, just a potential riot, that's all.'

He raised his eyebrows. 'That's different anyway.'

'Just drive, James,' she instructed in a hard brittle voice. 'I'm in no mood for your witticisms tonight.'

'Fine, so where do you want me to drive to?'

'The tow-path at Hillier's Bridge. We've got a little problem with some of our locals.'

He nodded and eased out into the traffic after the Hardingham police GP (or general purpose) Transit, which had just that moment raced by the station, its blue light flashing. 'The Residents Action Group from the Warren Estate no doubt,' he commented. 'The day shift have already had some trouble with them, I gather.'

She grunted again. 'Well, we've certainly got trouble with them now. They're threatening to march on the Festival and close it down themselves. I've got some uniform down there from your shift and Superintendent MacIntyre, who's running the Festival operation itself, has deployed a few officers on his side of the bridge just in case. But I suspect that straight talking is the only way we'll win this one.'

He swung hard left into the labyrinth of streets that formed the town's Victorian heart, taking corners and plunging into dark alleyways at a speed that was exhilarating and yet made her wince.

'I hope you know where you're going,' she said tightly, gripping the edges of her seat.

'Trust me,' he replied, swinging out to avoid a projecting doorstep. 'Short-cut. We'll be there before the Transit.'

'Pity you didn't know of any short-cuts when Control told you to meet me.'

He nodded quickly. 'Sorry, but I was tied up.'

She threw him a swift penetrating glance.

'So where were you?'

'I had to attend to a personal matter,' he replied before he could stop himself.

'I might have known it,' she breathed. 'That girl again, wasn't it?'

He changed down and, eyes searching a minor cross-roads, accelerated over it into a street lined with factories. 'I think we've already agreed that that is my business, ma'am.'

'Not when it impinges on your duty time, it isn't.'

He gritted his teeth to hold back the remark that was on the tip of his tongue and turned right at the next 'T' junction to follow a narrow road through a run-down council estate choked with so many parked vehicles that it looked like a used-car lot.

For a few minutes neither of them spoke and the awkward silence which followed was relieved only by the sound of the car's engine and the sickening thud of large insects ploughing into the windscreen. Then, shortly after turning left on to the canal tow-path, Calder shifted uncomfortably in his seat and emitted a long drawn-out sigh of resignation.

'Look, I'm not sleeping with her, you know,' he blurted, surprised not only by his own candour, but by the fact that he had felt it necessary to make the point at all. He was seriously tempted to say a lot more as well. To tell her precisely who Jane Sullivan was and unload the whole damned conspiracy mess on her, but he knew he couldn't, not yet anyway.

She stiffened again. 'Why should it interest me if you are?' she retorted tartly.

'Well, you do keep on about her.'

'Only because, as an old friend, I don't like to see you making a fool of yourself.'

He gave a short cynical laugh. 'Is that why you've been such a bitch towards me lately?'

She glared at him. 'Don't be so damned impertinent.'

The car swerved slightly as his grip on the steering wheel tightened. 'Impertinent?' he blazed. 'What a bloody sauce. You're the one who became all pally and told me to drop the ma'am bit. Remember? It wasn't my idea. You want to play the big cheese? Fine with me. But you can't have it both ways.'

'I don't want it both ways,' she exclaimed, her exasperation showing. 'You just don't understand, do you? You're too thick to see anything unless it comes right out and hits you!'

'Oh, is that so?' he threw back at her. 'Well, maybe I understand a lot more than you think, a whole lot more. And I'll tell you this, it frightens the hell out of me!'

Abruptly her anger vanished and she stared at him with a renewed and almost hungry intensity. 'What do you mean by that?'

He shook his head irritably. 'Forget it. My mouth runs away with me sometimes.'

But she had no intention of forgetting it. 'What frightens the hell out of you?'

He glanced at her quickly, then back at the wind-screen. 'You do,' he snarled. 'Now let's drop the subject. I'm probably barking up the wrong tree anyway.'

She snorted. 'You're probably not.'

He swallowed hard, desperate to extricate himself from the situation, but acutely conscious of the fact that he was only plunging himself in deeper. What was it his old sergeant had once told him all those years ago? 'When you're in a hole, stop digging.' Well, he was certainly in one now and getting out was proving to be more difficult than he would ever have imagined.

'Whether I am or not,' he said finally, 'the whole thing's impossible anyway so, as I said, let's just forget it. Okay?'

'Why should it be impossible?' She seemed to lean closer to him in her seat and he was ashamed to feel his skin prickle in a way it had not done since Maggie's death. He pulled away from her slightly and tried to keep his mind on his driving. 'I said, why should it be impossible?'

Through the windscreen Wharf Cottages were coming up fast on their left. He reckoned it could only be about a quarter of a mile to Hillier's Bridge now and the throb of beat music from the festival site was getting louder all the time. He accelerated even more and the car began to bounce noticeably.

'Why are you always running from things, Jim?' she said quietly, apparently sensing what he was up to.

'Just leave it,' he said harshly.

'Not until you answer my question,' she continued doggedly, but she was already out of time and he breathed a sigh of relief as the lamplit buttresses of

Hillier's Bridge suddenly appeared directly ahead round a sharp bend. 'Damn you!' she finished and slammed back angrily into her seat, finally forced to admit defeat.

There was a police accident unit from the Traffic Department parked on the hump of the bridge itself, almost completely blocking the way. Its powerful roof spotlight was trained on a large crowd which had assembled on the tow-path and seemed to be expanding by the minute as more people joined it from the unmade road connecting with the brightly-lit houses of the Warren Estate. In front of the vehicle half a dozen uniformed bobbies were drawn up in a thin line across the bridge entrance, their side-handled batons in their hands as they faced the potential mob with obvious unease. On the other side of the canal, just a few hundred yards from the brilliantly-lit festival site, which still hammered out its discordant message, another larger police contingent sat in two parked Transit vans, waiting for something to happen. Press camera bulbs flashed when Calder pulled up and he saw at least one video camera trained on them from the edge of the crowd.

'Seems to be a bit of a stand-off at the moment,' he observed, relieved to be back with practical policing problems again.

Maxwell angrily tore open her seat-belt and threw the car door wide, glaring at a press photographer who suddenly rushed forward to snap her picture, as if trying to turn him to stone. 'We don't want a bloody stand-off. We want a dispersal,' she snapped and climbed out of the vehicle. 'So let's just make sure we get one, shall we?'

He emitted a soft whistle as she stalked away,

watching her brush aside a couple of eager reporters who had had the temerity to try and intercept her. 'Bit close, that one, Jim,' he murmured and reaching into the back seat to grab his flat cap and baton, made to follow her. As he did so, his gaze fastened on the blue flashing beacon and blazing headlights of a large white police van bearing down on them along the tow-path. So, he mused, the Hardingham GP Transit that had raced past them at the police station had finally made it and he put on his best scowl as he got out of the car. 'Turn that bloody beacon off,' he barked through the driver's window as the Transit slithered to a stop inches from his rear bumper. 'Do you want to start a war?'

The young flaxen-haired bobby behind the wheel grinned and promptly shut everything down. 'Sorry, Sarge,' he said and threw a quick glance over his shoulder at the three special constables in the back. 'Just trying to give our volunteers a bit of excitement.'

There was a chortle of laughter from them, but the burly bearded figure in the front passenger seat was anything but amused. 'Mad bastard!' PC Potter growled. 'Ought to be soddin' well certified.'

Calder repressed a grin. Dave Judd, normally the area beat man on Bravo-Alpha Three-Three but seconded to the Transit on night-turn, was well-known for his spirited driving and though he was very proficient at it, he took a great delight in frightening the daylights out of his passengers. Poor old Grandad was the last person he should have had with him on a shout and Calder guessed that the repartee between the two en route must have been pretty colourful, to say the least. 'Just stay in the wagon,' he instructed sharply as one of the specials got up to open the back doors. 'We'll call you if we need you.'

Chief Inspector Maxwell was already engaged in earnest conversation with a small fat man a short distance from the crowd when Calder turned round and he smiled grimly. George Appleyard, Chairman of the Warren Estate Residents' Association, was the archetypal pain in the backside. A printer by trade and a militant member of the local union, he was a man of limited intelligence, but had an ego the size of a bus, thriving on aggravation, especially if it brought him into conflict with the establishment. He had always hated authority and had never forgiven the police for interfering in his paedophile activities, which had resulted in a series of convictions and a two year prison sentence, courtesy of the NCS, when he was living in the Northern Region. Now he was in his element and it showed in the way he thrust out his belly aggressively towards Maxwell and glared at her with his little piggy eyes. Calder had a strong desire to grab him by the scruff of the neck and pitch him into the canal, but instead he smiled as he joined the heated discussion.

'. . . and the residents have no intention of letting this racket continue for another night,' Appleyard was saying loudly, playing to the restless crowd and the attendant press reporters, 'so either you shut the noise down or we'll do it for you!'

'Evening, George,' Calder said convivially before Maxwell could respond. 'Up to your usual tricks then?'

Appleyard turned his head sharply, a sneer on his fat face. 'Well, well, well, if it isn't Mister Jim Calder,' he said. 'The force is certainly scraping the bottom of the barrel tonight.'

'And no one knows more about the bottoms of barrels than you, do they, George?' Calder replied with a grim smile.

Maxwell looked nonplussed by the obvious innuendo and Appleyard's sneer was replaced by a scowl. 'And what do you mean by that?' he demanded.

Calder shrugged. 'Oh nothing really, George. Just an observation, that's all. How are the wife and kids?'

Now Appleyard looked nonplussed. 'I haven't got any kids,' he retorted.

Calder appeared genuinely taken aback. 'No kids, George? But I thought you'd always liked children? In fact, I was only saying to a colleague the other day that once you had settled in down here you were bound to try for some at the first opportunity.'

Appleyard caught on now all right and he licked his lips, glancing round quickly at the crowd a few yards away. 'You'd better watch your mouth, Calder,' he warned, lowering his voice and jabbing a forefinger in his direction. 'I could have you up for that.'

More flashes from the battery of cameras and some of the reporters moved closer, sensing the new antagonism that was developing and trying to hear what was being said.

'Have me, George?' Calder replied innocently. 'Have me for what exactly?'

Maxwell held up one hand, obviously unaware of Appleyard's previous history and concerned that things could get out of hand. 'Can we stop this?' she said tersely. 'I don't know what it's all about, but it's getting us nowhere.'

Appleyard ignored her. 'Think I don't know what you're implying, Calder?' he hissed between partially closed teeth. 'One word from you to anyone about me and I'll have you up for slander faster than you can blink.'

Calder emitted a short hard laugh. 'I won't have to say anything to anyone, George,' he responded. 'The court will do all that for me.'

'Sergeant! That's enough!' Maxwell snapped, watching out of the corner of her eye as a couple of reporters edged ever closer, one with a radio microphone in his hand.

'Court?' Appleyard went on. 'What has court got to do with anything? I've done nothing wrong.'

Calder shook his head. 'Maybe not . . . yet,' he agreed, then went on very deliberately: 'But I promise you this, if we end up with a problem down here tonight you'll be the first one who's arrested and you know as well as I do that if you're convicted your previous history will come out for all to hear.' He smiled again. 'I wonder what your nice neighbours would say if they were to find out they had a convicted paedophile in their midst, eh?'

A press camera flashed just feet away.

'Not so loud,' the little man choked, swallowing hard. 'Keep your bloody voice down.'

'I will if you will, George,' Calder replied.

'You bastard,' Appleyard grated, then turned on Maxwell who had become strangely silent after her sharp censure of Calder a few moments before. 'You heard him, Inspector. He threatened me. Aren't you going to do something?'

But Maxwell was no longer interested in what he had to say. Whether this was due to the revulsion she felt towards him after the shock disclosure about his unsavoury past, the fact that she had suddenly tumbled to Calder's strategy or because the little man had unwittingly demoted her in rank, was not apparent. The gaze that met his was bleak and uncompromising. 'I think we've made our position perfectly clear, Mister Appleyard,' she said coldly, 'and if you'll pardon the pun, the ball is now in your court.'

Appleyard smouldered with rage, but acutely conscious of the number of reporters in the immediate vicinity he tried hard to control the visible signs. 'You think you've won, don't you, Sergeant?' he said, glaring at Calder with undisguised hatred. 'Well there'll be other times, I promise you, so you'd better watch yourself from now on.'

'Look forward to it, George,' Calder replied and, turning his back on him in a dismissive gesture, he grinned broadly as he strolled over towards the line of bobbies by the bridge.

It was evident that Maxwell was far from pleased, however. 'Don't you ever put me in a position like that again, James,' she breathed. 'What you did was totally out of order.'

He glanced at her, unrepentant. 'What about the means justifying the end and all that?'

'Don't you dare patronise me,' she snapped, nodding curtly at a local reporter, but ignoring his request for an interview. 'You're fresh out of brownie points after tonight, just remember that.'

'If I ever had any in the first place,' Calder muttered to himself and stared after her as she strode through the police lines and past the Traffic Department's accident unit to the opposite side of the canal.

'Governor seems a bit uptight tonight, Sarge,' a voice said at his elbow. PC Baldev Singh, Bravo-Alpha Two-Six, was grinning at him like the proverbial Cheshire Cat.

'Probably a touch of PMT,' another voice from the police line chortled.

Calder scowled. 'Any more funny comments and I'll have you lot standing here all night,' he rapped. 'So shut it!'

'Any idea how long we'll be here, Sarge?' the bobby beside Singh queried. Gerry Stoddard, Bravo-Alpha Two-Zero, was the shift's most junior member. A freckle-faced twenty-year-old with curly ginger hair and a desperate attempt at a military moustache, he was their unofficial mascot and he hated it with as much of a passion as he hated standing still for more than two or three minutes at a time.

Calder stared at him. 'Well now, Gerry,' he replied slowly, 'that all depends on our Mr. Appleyard, but I have a feeling that things will wind down very shortly.'

'And what makes you think that?'

Calder smiled grimly, staring past him to the bank on the opposite side of the canal where Maxwell seemed to be locked in discussion with a number of other uniformed officers. 'Call it sixth-sense, lad,' he replied, tapping his nose significantly. 'Comes with service.'

In fact, Appleyard capitulated a lot sooner than even Calder had expected, perhaps fifteen minutes later, when one or two verbal exchanges between a few militant members of the crowd and the line of police officers blocking the bridge looked as if they might develop into something more serious. Desperately hauling himself up on to a pile of bricks and rubble on the estate side of the tow-path and banging a tin lid loudly to attract attention, he told his supporters their point had been made 'before the world's press' and there was, therefore, no need for any further action.

At first there was angry opposition to his words and Calder was delighted to hear the little fat man actually having to plead with those he had previously incited to take the law into their own hands not to resort to violence. For a while it was touch and go, with one or two hotheads in the crowd determined to whip things up even more, but in the end, as Calder and his thin blue line waited tensely in the wings, the drift back to the Warren Estate began. First it was in twos and threes and then in large sullen groups, one of which included Appleyard himself who continued to glare balefully in Calder's direction as he went. Within twenty minutes only a hard core of activists remained, shouting abuse and threats at the impassive bobbies, but lacking the physical courage to actually take them on. Then even they began to disperse and Calder was not surprised to see them head away from the Warren Estate back towards the centre of the town. He had already guessed that a substantial number of those in the crowd had not been local residents in the first place.

'Rent-A-Mob?' Maxwell spoke sharply behind him.

He turned to face her. 'Looks like it,' he replied, then followed her as she moved away from the police line.

'Which means we'll be hearing from them again later?'

'Or tomorrow when the strike is on and there's hardly anyone around to stop them.'

'A frightening thought,' she murmured over her shoulder, then stopped by his car and turned to face him. 'Still, at least your gamble with master Appleyard seems to have paid off,' and there was the suggestion of a sparkle in her eyes as she added, 'even though it was a reprehensible tactic, of course.'

He considered her remark for a moment, surprised at how quickly she had mellowed after their last acrimonious conversation. Talk about unpredictable. 'Is that supposed to be some sort of a compliment?' he ventured warily.

'Some sort, yes, but don't let it go to your head.' She hesitated, gnawing her lip for a second. 'Look, James, I want to . . . er . . . apologise about earlier. It was inexcusable and unprofessional, especially in my position. Unfortunately my emotions tend to get in the way sometimes, but I had no right to . . .'

'Forget it, Rosy,' he cut in hastily, staring down at his feet in embarrassment. 'My fault too.'

'I promise I won't come on to you again.'

He smiled wryly. 'Maybe an old dog like me enjoys being flattered sometimes.'

She gave a short laugh and opened the car door. 'Maybe you're right. But for the moment can I have your keys. I'll drive myself back. I'd like you to stay on here for a bit until you think it's okay to stand everyone down.'

He nodded and handed them over. Just for a second her hand brushed his and he felt that same tiny thrill of electrical current pass between them. He pulled away as if he had touched a hot stove, hoping she hadn't noticed anything, though aware of her gaze fastening on him briefly. But then the awkward moment was past and she had climbed into the driving seat.

'Oh, by the way, James,' she said quietly, staring up at him with a gleam of white teeth, 'it's a well known fact, you know, that old dogs are often the best.'

Then she had slammed the door and was speeding off along the tow-path towards the opposite exit, leaving him staring after the car's rapidly disappearing tail-lights as he tried to get his tangled emotions into some sort of order and failing dismally.

10

It was after one o'clock in the morning before Calder decided it was safe to stand down his small group at the bridge, an hour after the Traffic mobile and the other officers deployed from the festival ground had been withdrawn. Neither Appleyard and his supporters or the rent-a-mob crowd had reappeared and a quick reconnoitre of the Warren Estate had found only deserted streets, with most of the houses in darkness. Even the music from the festival seemed to have packed in for the night and where earlier there had been a confused mass of brilliant flashing lights there was now a black void, scattered with tiny glittering pin-points like earthbound stars. It was as if some massive Heavenly generator had been switched off, reducing the festival to an inert mass without the creative energy to continue, and although the new tranquillity was certainly welcome, it had an eerie feel to it, as if the night were holding its breath.

Joining the Transit for a couple of hour's patrol after warning Dave Judd to keep his speed down, Calder lapsed into a morose silence of his own, his mind returning to the subject of Rosy Maxwell as he tried to analyse his feelings towards her. He couldn't help wondering if she would end up as another of his missed opportunities or whether he was well out of the relationship in the first place. It didn't seem right to be thinking about another woman after Maggie; it was like, well, dumping her memory and it made him feel guilty and even a little ashamed. But he couldn't help it. Rosy had awakened something in him that he'd thought was dead. Hope for the future maybe? A new life? He desperately wanted it and yet he couldn't reconcile the idea with his thoughts of Maggie. He couldn't just bury her memory and carry on with his life as if nothing had happened, could he? But on the other hand he couldn't mourn for ever and surely she would understand? What was it Rosy had said? 'It's about time you let Maggie go . . . You've got to start living again.' Was it so terrible to do just that?

'Penny for your thoughts, Sarge?' Tom Merrick, one of the specials sitting beside him in the back of the Transit, jerked him out of his reverie.

He took the cigarette from the proffered packet and accepted the light, forcing a smile. 'Thanks, Tom, I was miles away.'

The thin grey-haired volunteer, or 'hobby-bobby' as some of the regular officers chose to call any member of what had now actually become a part-paid auxiliary force, lit his own cigarette and grinned. 'Sorry to bring you back from wherever you were, but you didn't seem to be enjoying it anyway.'

Calder grunted. 'That obvious, was it?'

His gaze travelled round the shadowy interior of the Transit, illuminated every now and then by street lights as they trundled by. Two other specials shared the discomfort of the hard bench seats with which the rear of the vehicle was equipped: Les Baker, a portly bank executive, who had a passion for boiled sweets and was busily engaged in searching his pockets for any of the striped humbugs he had missed, and Mary Anderson, a dour middle-aged teacher, who stared perpetually out of the back windows, lost in thought, just as Calder had been.

They were nice genuine people, but he couldn't understand why they did the job in the first place, especially on nights like this when they were required to ride around in a noisy smelly museum-piece, because the powers-that-be considered the station's general purpose run-about to be a less provocative patrol vehicle than the plusher protected Transits which had been designed for the task.

In the days when they had originally joined the Special Constabulary, there had been no pay attached to the job at all and even now the annual allowance was only a pittance. So what was the attraction? Why on earth would people do a full day's work and then come out in their uniforms to take on yobs, drunks and all the other rubbish that haunted the streets of every large town? Just for the fun of it? He shook his head slowly. He would never understand it in a million years. Like most of his colleagues he could not help feeling more than a little resentment towards them for doing the job as part-time volunteers, enabling the government to get policing on the cheap and keep down the pay of regular officers. He wondered what the specials would do if the police strike actually happened; incur the wrath of the regulars by taking their place or quietly keep out of the way? It was an interesting issue but one he had no intention of raising for debate.

He once more lapsed into thoughtful silence, this

time focusing directly on the strike and what Jane Sullivan had told him. To think that the Commissioner and the Deputy Commissioner were locked in some unholy conspiracy to make it happen and that his own governor, George Rhymes, whom he had always held in such high regard, had actually agreed to be the middle man for the sake of prolonging his own career. He could hardly believe it. And if they had gone so far down that road, how much further would they be prepared to go to keep the whole thing quiet? Perhaps they had already found out about Baseheart and had decided to silence him for good. It would certainly explain his disappearance, but if that was the case, they probably also knew about Jane Sullivan which meant she could be in real jeopardy now.

He was conscious of the fact that he was sweating more than was justified by the heat in the Transit, and the next second he jumped as the cigarette he was holding burned down to his fingers for the second time that night. 'Shit', he exclaimed, before adding quickly, 'Oh, sorry, Mary.'

There were chortles of laughter inside the Transit and Dave Judd threw a quick glance behind him. 'Soap and water, Sarge?' he said.

Calder scowled at the back of his head. 'You concentrate on your driving, me lad,' he retorted, trying to maintain his good humour, though his stomach was doing cartwheels. 'I know this isn't one of our newest Transits, but I don't want you reshaping it.'

'Exactly!' Grandad joined in. 'Not like you did the CID car you borrowed last week.'

'That wasn't me,' Judd protested.

'You mean you won't admit to it,' Grandad

continued good-naturedly, but Calder was no longer listening.

In fact, he was horrified at the direction in which his thoughts had taken him and the conclusions he had drawn. It was ridiculous to even think such things. Okay, so Harding and Turner might have stepped out of line, but as both Jane Sullivan and Richard Baseheart himself had intimated previously, it was all to do with politics and that was a long way from the poisoned umbrellas and exploding pens of the espionage and crime thrillers that crammed the bookshops. He had to get a grip on himself – he'd said that more than once in the last few days – or he could easily end up as a guest of the funny farm.

'Can't trust anyone these days, can you, Sarge?'

'Eh?' Calder jumped again, for a second thinking Grandad had been reading his mind or that he had inadvertently started talking aloud.

Then he relaxed as Potter continued. 'Take young Judd here, for instance. Just because he says he didn't crunch the CID car, doesn't mean he's innocent. Everyone knows what a bloody awful driver he is. Couldn't have been anyone else.' Clowning, he lightly cuffed Judd round the ear and there was more laughter in the back.

Calder permitted himself a smile that was more in relief than good humour, but almost at the same moment it froze and grabbing the wire mesh partition separating the driving area from the rest of the vehicle, he stared through the windscreen. 'After them!' he rapped as the group of youngsters standing half in the shadow of the bus shelter split and ran.

Judd didn't argue and the Transit roared as he

slammed into a lower gear and tried to achieve Concorde status.

'Oh my life, nought to sixty in three days!' Grandad exclaimed, then added: 'Which ones do you want, skipper?'

Calder grimly held on to the wire mesh, studying the road ahead. 'Forget the two running down Laycock Street,' he shouted. 'Go for the guy with the long blond hair and the two with him.'

'Frazer's Passage,' Judd said gleefully as the trio darted into a narrow slit between two shops. 'It's a dead end.'

He spun the wheel and, sending the Transit up on to the pavement, headed for the opening.

'Bloody hell!' Grandad yelled, holding his cap in front of his face. 'Is it wide enough?'

'Soon find out,' Judd responded and raced through, sending a pile of cardboard boxes stacked up for refuse collection spinning into the air.

Something sticky from the boxes hit the edge of the windscreen with an obscene 'smack,' but, pumping the windscreen-wash, Judd flicked on the wipers and kept going, though how he could possibly see anything through the glutinous substance spreading across his field of vision was a mystery.

The alleyway bored its way between overhanging buildings like a tunnel and through the smeared windscreen Calder glimpsed the two figures running hell for leather about twenty yards in front of them. 'Stop!' he yelled at Judd.

'What?' The young bobby darted a glance over his shoulder.

'I said stop!'

Which is exactly what Judd did, sending Grandad

slamming forward within the webbing of his seat-belt and the specials tumbling across the floor into the partition. Calder was down the vehicle and out the back doors even as the rest of the crew were picking themselves up.

Solomon emerged from the shallow doorway, smoothing his golden locks back from his face, and Calder nodded with grim satisfaction. 'Waiting for us to fly past so you could sneak away again?' he said. 'Well this time you've got nowhere to run.'

The big man towered over him, holding up one hand to shield his eyes as his glasses reflected the light of a torch directed on him by Mary Anderson. That same old uneasy feeling Calder had experienced before in his presence returned with a vengeance and he stepped back a couple of paces.

Solomon gave a faint knowing smile. 'Strive not with a man without cause, if he have done thee no harm,' he murmured piously.

'You can cut out the Biblical quotes,' Calder snapped. 'I can guess what you were up to just now and when I find what you were pushing, even personal friendship with the Pope won't help you.'

Solomon shook his head slowly. 'Save me from all them that persecute me,' he said solemnly and without being told he walked to the Transit and climbed in the back.

'Watch him,' Calder said to Grandad, then swung on his heel and went quickly round to the front of the Transit where the sound of shouting and swearing had suddenly erupted. In the still blazing headlights he saw Dave Judd and the other two specials struggling up against a wall with the two youths who had run off.

'Oi,' one yelled at him from behind Les Baker's confining bulk, 'we ain't done nothin'.'

'Shut it!' Calder rapped and peered at him closely before moving on to the second youth being restrained by Dave Judd and Tom Merrick a couple of yards away. 'Well, I certainly recognise these two,' he went on. 'Couple of the rent-a-mob crowd who were down at the tow-path if I'm not mistaken.'

There was the metallic snap of handcuffs being applied and, leaving the second youth securely anchored to Judd's wrist, Merrick delved in his pocket and opened the palm of his hand in the beam of one of the Transit's headlights. 'That's not all, Sarge,' he said excitedly. 'While we were chasing them they were chucking these out of their pockets like nobody's business.'

The slim silver-foil strips glittered in his hand and selecting one and peeling back the foil, Calder discovered the strip held a row of six small circular tablets that looked to be orange or red in colour when he studied them more closely with his flashlight. 'LSD, d'ye think?' Merrick exclaimed.

Calder frowned. 'There's no way of telling what they are just by looking at them, Tom,' he replied. 'They'll have to be submitted for forensic analysis first.' He stared at the prisoner held by Judd, a skinny lank-haired youth dressed in a sweatshirt and jeans. 'So what are these then?'

The youngster gave a derisory laugh. 'Smarties? What do you think they are?'

Calder nodded and stared along the alleyway. The headlights of the Transit picked out a litter of silver strips scattered all over the place. 'Good enough for a bust anyway, son,' he replied with grim satisfaction.

Then to Merrick: 'Better collect that lot up, Tom. But first help Les cuff the other one. I've got someone else to speak to.'

Solomon was sitting very erect in the back of the Transit close to the open doors, the hand that was nearest the end of the bench seat held behind him as if he had a lumber problem.

Calder reached forward without ceremony and yanked his arm into view, immediately grasping and turning the wrist so that the clenched palm was uppermost. Silver-foil glittered between the closed fingers. 'Give me!' he rapped.

The big man tensed and Calder felt the hidden strength in his wrist sinews start to work against him. The rimless glasses turned towards him and the thin lips parted in a chilling smile, but he met the intimidating stare with an expression of rigid determination. 'We can always do it the hard way,' he breathed, sensing Grandad's reassuring bulk move closer.

For a moment longer Solomon continued to resist him as if to make a point, but then quite suddenly he shrugged his shoulders and relaxing his taut muscles opened his fingers to reveal three silver-foil strips in his palm.

'Thank you,' Calder said curtly. 'Mary, have a look on the ground by the Transit's rear step, will you? I suspect you'll find a lot more of them down there.'

He watched out of the corner of his eye as she bent down, then heard her exclamation.

'You're right, Sarge. There's about a dozen here.'

Calder tutted loudly. 'Well, well, well. Trying to get rid of the evidence, were we, Solomon old son?'

The other's face remained impassive. 'Blessed is he whose transgression is forgiven,' he said softly.

'Well somehow I don't think yours will be,' Calder retorted and motioning him to hold out both wrists slapped handcuffs on him with business-like efficiency.

It was painfully evident when Steve Torrington was admitted to the custody suite that something was very amiss with him. Usually immaculate to the extreme, he now looked strangely dishevelled; his face was noticeably drawn, with more than a trace of five-o'clock shadow, and his eyes had the wild glint of someone with major worries on his mind.

He arrived just after Calder and Judd had finished searching their three prisoners and booking them in with the custody officer, Janice Lawson. His dark eyes narrowed appreciably when he saw Solomon standing there, briefly meeting the big man's contemptuous stare, then fastening on the haul of tablets contained in their sealed plastic property bags on the long custody office desk.

'Forgive them, for they know not what they do,' Solomon murmured blasphemously as he was led away through the opposite door to the cells.

'Well done, Jim,' Torrington said, following the blond giant with his eyes, 'You finally nailed him then?'

Despite the detective's praise his tone lacked sincerity, his sour expression reminiscent of someone who has just learned that a close friend has won the National Lottery. Calder smiled faintly, accepting as a veteran of the system the inevitability of CID resentment over a good arrest by any member of the uniform branch. 'Thank you, sir,' he replied. 'Us woodentops do have our moments, you know.'

Torrington nodded, but for a change the little dig met with no response, only a thoughtful, even distant frown, as if the little weasel-faced detective was preoccupied with something. 'Can I have a word, Jim?' he said, turning back to the door.

Surprised by the lack of reaction, Calder shrugged and followed him into the passageway beyond, pulling the door to behind him. 'Well?' he queried. 'What's the problem?'

Torrington leaned back against the electronically controlled security door which shut off the custody suite from the rest of the police station. 'No problem, Jim,' he replied. 'Just professional interest in what you've got, that's all.'

'Professional interest or professional envy?' Calder said pointedly.

Torrington forced a smile this time, but it was only a half-hearted effort and lacked the usual warmth. 'Maybe a bit of both,' he admitted. 'You've certainly done yourself proud with this one.'

Calder reached behind him to close the door completely. 'Yeah, I must admit, I am quite pleased with myself,' he replied. 'I reckon we've nabbed the source of the freebie hallucinogens that have been flooding the festival in the last few days.'

'Solomon?'

'Looks very much like it. He was one of a group huddled in a bus shelter in West Street. They all took off when they clocked us, but for once he chose the wrong escape route and we nailed him and two of the others in a blind alley.'

'Had the stuff on him, did he?'

Calder nodded. 'Caught him trying to dump some of it and when he was searched we found that in addition to his pockets being crammed with it, he had a body belt concealed inside the waistband of his jeans bulging with nice little silver-foil wrappers. Got him banged to rights this time without a doubt. He was obviously dishing the amphets out to his select little band of pushers when we saw him.'

'There's always a chance that your amphets might not turn out to be what you think they are, of course.'

Calder snorted. 'Yeah, maybe I've bagged up a couple of hundred vitamin tablets Solomon was dolling out as a good Samaritan to undernourished drug addicts. Or maybe they're even Smarties like one of the other little shits taunted. Get real, Steve. You know as well as I do what those things are likely to be. The forensic analysis is just going to be a formality.'

Torrington still did not seem to be convinced. 'Much cash on your three prisoners, was there?'

Calder frowned, sensing what the question was leading up to. 'No, very little actually, just a few notes each.'

'Might be difficult proving a charge of supplying then. No evidence of any gain involved. You could be left with just using an illegal substance.'

'With that sort of quantity? Oh, come on!'

Torrington shrugged. 'You know what the courts are like as well as I do. Don't forget, if all three of them were in possession you may have a job proving who was actually doing the supplying.'

'Thanks for your confidence. You're a real Job's Comforter, aren't you? Maybe you should even think of representing the three of them as their brief.'

Torrington smiled thinly. 'Maybe I should, but I'm a bit too busy for that at the moment,' he joked, though again with very little real humour.

Calder studied him keenly. 'What's eating you, Steve? Okay, so uniform have got themselves a better than average bust, but surely you're not that pissed off about it?'

Torrington ran a hand through his disordered hair which didn't look as though it had seen a comb for some time. 'I'm not pissed off about it at all, but I do think I should take the whole thing over. With all the implications involved it has to be a CID job now.'

'Like hell it does.' Calder thrust out his neck aggressively, suddenly tumbling to what the detective was up to. 'You're not pinching this one, Steve. This is a uniform case and that's the way it's going to stay.'

Torrington sighed and tried to smile again. 'Jim, Jim,' he said reassuringly, clapping him on one arm. 'This is me you're talking to. I wouldn't let you lose by it, you know that. No one can take the original collar away from you and your crew, but you can't afford to tie up half your section on what is likely to be a protracted enquiry, you must see my point?'

Calder shook his head firmly, his lips tightly compressed and a hostile gleam in his eyes. 'No way and that's final. I'm not losing yet another job to CID.'

'You forget, you owe me one.'

'What do you mean?'

Torrington looked uncomfortable, but he pressed on anyway. 'The collar I took off you as a favour a couple of nights ago. Remember? And the report I put into the boss to get you off the hook with Douglas Maybe?'

Calder seemed about ready to explode. 'You bastard.'

'Now, now, Jim. Don't push things too far. I'm still the DI.'

'And you're still a devious little shit too.'

Torrington hesitated, then went on again. 'I must confess there is another reason why I need to take over this case.'

'Ah, now we get down to it.'

'Yes, but it has nothing to do with nicking jobs off the uniform branch. The fact is that Solomon is now known to be a bosom associate of the girl, Caroline Dubois, who stabbed that lad at the festival ground.'

'Another uniform arrest.'

'No one is disputing that. I realise young Nash got himself bitten for his trouble, but it's CID who are lumbered with the investigation and we still haven't found the knife. Point is, Dubois has actually been dossing with Solomon at his rented tip of a house and we have reliable information he not only knows where the weapon is, but was also involved in the assault – sort of egged Dubois on – so he needs to be interviewed at length.'

'But what's to stop you chatting to Solomon about the stabbing as a separate issue?'

'Well, it would make things very complicated. Far better to have one team doing the whole business, especially as Dubois was almost certainly one of your man's drug-pushing team as well. Being an ex-CID man yourself you must see that.'

Calder's anger subsided in the face of the cold logic of his argument and he nodded. 'You're the DI,' he growled. 'You can do whatever you bloody well want anyway.'

Torrington smiled again, but apparently more with relief than anything else, as if a great weight had been lifted from his shoulders. 'Cheer up, Jim,' he said reassuringly. 'You won't lose by it, I promise. All I need from you and your crew are some statements of evidence and then we can get to it. In the meantime, I don't want Solomon interviewed by anyone until I've had a chance of chatting to him myself.'

'Then you'd better tell that to Drug Squad yourself, since I seem to be off the case now,' Calder retorted, his bitterness painfully evident. 'I asked Control to radio for their assistance and DS Fuller is already on his way up here from the festival ground. He's very interested in master Solomon, I can tell you.'

Torrington's eyes were suddenly hooded and thoughtful. 'He's not the only one, Jim,' he replied softly. 'Not by a long chalk.'

Calder's stomach felt as though his throat had been cut by the time he managed to finish documenting all three prisoners under Janice Lawson's watchful eye and was able to head back to his office for a break, but Fate permitted him just one gulp of coffee from his flask before the telephone rang. It was Bill Brookes, the civilian station duty officer, affectionately known to all as Gunner.

'Sorry to disturb you, Sergeant,' the gruff ex-Guards RSM barked in his ultra-correct manner. 'But there's a . . . a gentleman at the desk to see you.'

The deliberate hesitation over the word 'gentleman' was indication enough that in Gunner's eyes the visitor was anything but and Calder smiled to himself. 'Bit late, or early if you like, for a caller, isn't it?' he replied, glancing at the clock on the wall which, though ten minutes fast, still put the time at three o'clock in the morning. 'Who is he?'

Brookes cleared his throat. 'Gave his name as Sable, Sergeant,' he replied. 'Says he's an old friend.'

Calder paused in the act of taking a mammoth bite from his cheese sandwich. 'Sable?' he echoed. "Not Eddie Sable?'

'The same, Sergeant.'

'Well, I'm damned. That name's a blast from the past and no mistake.'

'Beg your pardon, Sergeant?'

Calder chewed slowly. 'Oh . . . er . . . forget it, Gunner. Tell him I'll be along right away.'

'Very good, Sergeant.'

Calder shook his head slowly several times as he replaced the receiver. Eddie Sable, he mused, his mind peeling back the years. The best nose in Fleet Street and one who had been a thorn in the side of the police at many a major investigation, mainly because of his uncanny knack of unearthing things and asking awkward questions almost before an enquiry was properly underway. He had crossed swords with the shrewd 'Queen of Hacks,' as Sable brazenly chose to call himself, on many occasions in the old days. Yet there had been a feeling of mutual respect and trust between the pair of them. This had often resulted in the confidential exchange of information at a time when any police officer below the rank of inspector would have had his testimonials removed by brute force for even talking to the press, let alone actually discussing the progress of a case with them.

He had last seen the old reprobate shortly after joining the National Crime Squad and that had to be at least five years ago. He frowned as he headed for the door, then snapped his fingers. Yes, the Buckner Case, that was it. Sable had been working for one of the big national papers, chief crime correspondent or something, and he had linked the London gangland boss, Larry Buckner, who was on trial for three contract killings, with Peter Dalston, the oil magnate and friend of the Chancellor of the Exchequer. He chuckled. The balloon had gone up on that occasion all right and it was one of the main reasons for the ultimate collapse of the government of the day.

He frowned again as he made his way along the corridor to the front of the station, hungrily finishing his cheese sandwich as he went. So what could have prompted someone like Eddie Sable to drop into Hardingham police station at three o'clock in the morning after the passage of so many years? It had to be something pretty big and smelly to bring him all the way down from the Smoke and the fact that he had asked for him personally suggested he was calling in a favour, which certainly bode ill for someone.

The rotund, balding little man in the crumpled white linen suit and green suede shoes was standing in the reception foyer reading the posters on the notice board when Calder opened the connecting door. He didn't even turn at the sound of the door, but nevertheless seemed to sense the other's presence. 'I can't believe the Ministry are still warning the public about Colorado Beetle,' he said. 'Time someone changed these notices, I think. They must have historical value by now.'

Calder grinned. 'I expect you can remember them when they first came out, Eddie,' he quipped.

The little man turned smartly to face him, exposing a mauve silk shirt front and a hideous yellow and red spotted bow-tie, with a matching handkerchief in his top pocket, proof enough that even time itself had failed to dampen his flamboyant spirit. 'Jimbo, dear boy,' he exclaimed, his chubby florid face split into a broad grin and both hands extended in a characteristically effeminate gesture. 'Let me look at you.'

Calder allowed himself to be gripped all the way up to his elbows, conscious of Gunner's disapproving stare through the counter hatch. Then, as he tried to disentangle himself, the hands slid down his arms to grip both wrists tightly. 'Why you've hardly changed at all. The old locks a bit depleted and a little more weight around the middle, but still frightfully macho.'

Calder winced and pulled himself free. 'Neither have you, Eddie,' he said with feeling. 'Still the same disgusting aftershave and appalling dress sense.'

The journalist chuckled. 'It's the extrovert in me, Jimbo,' he replied, then nodding with meaning towards the counter he whispered behind one hand. 'But I don't think Blue-chin over there approves.'

Calder opened the door wide. 'Then I think you'd better come through before you cause more of a stir than you have already,' he said dryly. 'And stop calling me bloody Jimbo.'

Sable grinned again and, briefly turning to pick up a leather briefcase from one of the chairs behind him, winked extravagantly in Gunner's direction before ducking under Calder's arm into the corridor beyond.

'Did you have to be quite so camp back there?' Calder protested as Sable drew up a chair to face him across his office desk. 'That was well over the top even for you.'

Sable chuckled again. 'Sorry, James, but these

right-wing Neanderthals get right up my nose. What was your man? Ex-army?'

Calder nodded. 'Guards regiment. Regimental sergeant major.'

'Might have known it. Must be something they're fed on. Had me for a poof as soon as I walked in the door, you know, and made no effort to conceal what he thought of me either. So I decided I would provide him with the exact stereotype he expected and really charm his taste-buds.'

Calder grunted. 'Well if it's of any interest to you my reputation on station is now shot to buggery.'

Sable made a face and raised his eyebrows. 'Shot to buggery?' he murmured. 'Now there's an intriguing thought.'

Calder gave up on him and rummaging in a drawer of his desk produced a mug which he set down beside his own. 'Coffee?' he queried, reaching for his flask.

The journalist nodded and pulled a small hip flask from his jacket pocket. 'Milk?' he replied with a grin and poured a generous measure of whisky into Calder's already half-full mug before helping himself to one of his cheese sandwiches.

'So?' Calder went on, sitting back in his chair. 'Why the courtesy visit after all these years?'

Abruptly Sable's face became very serious and, unzipping his briefcase, he withdrew a large bulky envelope which he tossed on to the desk in front of him. 'You should learn to lock your police car when you park up, James,' he admonished.

For several seconds Calder simply sat there gaping at the familiar envelope, which bore his name on the front in a heavy black hand and the words 'Named

Distribution Only Strictly Confidential' stamped in red in the top right-hand corner.

'Where the hell . . . ?' he blurted.

'Let's just say a public-spirited citizen,' Sable cut in.

Calder lurched forward in his chair, almost knocking over his coffee. 'Public-spirited, my arse,' he snarled, glaring at him. 'This is stolen property, so whoever handed it to you is a bloody criminal.'

Sable took a sip from his mug, keeping his eyes firmly fixed on Calder's face. 'World's full of them, dear boy,' he said, 'and in high places too judging by what's in the envelope.'

Calder turned it over and glanced at the flap. No surprise that it had been torn open and resealed. 'So you've been through the stuff then?' he commented.

Sable gave a short derisory laugh. 'Be your age, James,' he said. 'What do you think?'

'Even though you knew that it was police property and marked strictly confidential?'

The other shrugged. 'The envelope had already been opened, dear boy. I just had a rummage through.'

'So your greasy little sneak-thief has seen it all too?'

'One or two of the documents almost certainly which was undoubtedly the reason he thought it had a good resale value if offered to the right person. Not the tapes, though, as he is one of the jetsam and flotsam of our poor uncaring society without access to either audio or video equipment or even a roof over his head, for that matter.'

'A bloody left-wing drop-out, you mean.'

Sable sighed. 'Actually quite a nice boy really, if a little mixed up about life.'

'And how come he knew to approach you? Unless that's a silly question.'

Sable beamed. 'An old queen like me must take his pleasures where he can find them, James, and sometimes there's an unexpected bonus, as on this occasion, for example.'

Calder's expression adequately registered his feelings. 'You're disgusting, Eddie, you know that, don't you?'

Another sigh. 'Needs of the flesh, dear boy, needs of the flesh. Anyway, when I saw that the envelope was addressed to you I thought to myself, it's my old friend and confidant, James Calder Esquire. He'll be in trouble over losing this, so I must get it back to him as soon as possible.'

'Yeah, but not until you'd made copies, I bet.'

Sable chuckled again. 'You have a very cynical distrusting nature, James. It spoils your overall persona.'

Calder slipped the envelope into his top drawer out of sight and studied the journalist expectantly. 'So why make a personal visit? You could have mailed the thing to me.'

Sable flicked crumbs off his lapel and dabbed his mouth with the red and yellow spotted handkerchief he had delicately removed from his top pocket. 'I thought we could help each other, dear boy, just like old times.'

'You've got to be joking.'

'I never joke about money, James, and this story is the pot of gold that could secure my retirement.'

'You think your editor will give you that big a bonus?'

'I don't work for an editor anymore. I am an

independent now, with my own news agency.' He delved into an inside pocket and handed over a small business card. ' "Sable News". Has a nice ring to it, don't you think?'

'And I suppose you're going to market this story for all it's worth, eh? To hell with the consequences?'

Sable shook his head slowly and leaned forward across the desk. 'You still don't get it, do you, James? Have you any idea what kind of story this is? How much it is likely to be worth? This isn't just corruption, dear boy. It is mega, mega corruption, involving people in the highest positions.'

He broke off, reading the puzzlement in Calder's expression and suddenly tumbling to the truth. 'Good Lord, James, you haven't actually seen what's in the envelope, have you?' he exclaimed. 'You have absolutely no idea what I'm talking about?'

Calder cleared his throat and made a grimace. 'I know some of it, but not all, not yet.'

Sable whistled incredulously. 'But the envelope was addressed to you, presumably by the Special Branch man, Baseheart, whose name is all over this stuff as senior investigating officer. Do you mean to tell me he just sent it to you out of the blue?'

'I agreed to look after it for him,' Calder blurted before he could stop himself.

Sable wasn't just incredulous now; he was completely staggered. 'James,' he breathed, leaning forward again, 'are you telling me you agreed to look after a sealed envelope without knowing what was actually in it? I can't believe this of a shrewd battle-scarred veteran like you.'

'I'd trust Richard Baseheart with my life.'

Sable snorted. 'When this lot finally hits the tabloids, dear boy, you might have to, figuratively speaking, for heads won't just roll, they'll be blasted off shoulders!'

Calder felt sick. Everything seemed to be coming down on him. He almost wished the envelope had not been brought back at all. It was like holding on to a parcel bomb without knowing exactly when it was timed to go off. 'You still haven't told me why you're here,' he said quietly. 'You didn't return this thing to me out of brotherly love.'

'How very astute of you, James. Got to pay the rent and all that.'

'More likely the rent-boys. So what's the offer?'

'Precisely this. I leave you out of the affair completely; refuse to say how I managed to get hold of the envelope in the first place, giving you the opportunity of dumping it back on good old Richard Baseheart. In return, you get me an in with the man himself or his oppo' . . . er . . . Detective Sergeant Jane Sullivan, who also seems to feature highly in this case. All I want is a little off-the-record guidance. Clear up a few loose ends before I file copy. This way, your friend gets the chance to submit his investigation file to the appropriate authority before the balloon goes up.'

'You're asking him to stab the Commissioner in the back and sell his own force down the river?'

'Seems to me from what I've learned already that your commissioner is deserving of all he gets and not only him either. After all, justice has to be done and he's not exempt from the rule of law just because he's commissioner.'

'Don't give me the moral justice bit, Eddie. You're

not pushing this for the sake of justice. You're only interested in the pay-off.'

Sable's face darkened. 'I've never denied I'm in this business for money, James,' he said sharply. 'But strange as it may seem, I also believe in what I'm doing by exposing the bad guys and so do you. You've always been an honest copper, that's why I took to you in your Crime Squad days, and I know that, unpalatable though this whole thing may be to you, you couldn't allow it to be cuffed anyway.'

Calder didn't answer him, for he knew that the shrewd little journalist had summed him up to a tee. But his heart was racing now and his throat had begun to dry up. Trapped, he thought to himself, and no way out. Even if he had been the sort of ruthless self-centred bastard who was prepared to give Richard up to someone like Eddie Sable just to save his own skin, and he wasn't, he didn't know where the SB man could be found anyway and he could never drop Jane Sullivan in the cart, especially as she was in much the same invidious situation as himself. Yet if he did nothing and the story broke, he would be seen as having aided and abetted the conspiracy by not reporting what he had found out. More importantly, he would never be able to live with his own conscience for not doing something about it.

What he needed was time. Maybe Richard would turn up in the next few hours to take the responsibility back off him or alternatively he and Jane Sullivan might be able to work out something between them. In any event, as he didn't even know the full extent of the conspiracy there was no way he could make a decision about anything until he had had the opportunity of going through what was in the envelope.

'Cat got your tongue, dear boy?' Sable murmured, cutting in on his thoughts. 'What's it to be? The Sable way or do you want to go down with the ship?'

Calder stared at him. 'I'll need a few hours to get hold of Richard,' he lied. 'He's working on something at the moment.'

The other pursed his lips thoughtfully, then frowned. 'I can't hold off for long, James,' he warned. 'This is much too big. But I am prepared to be a little more patient if it means I can clear up one or to loose ends with Richard Baseheart before tackling the naughty boys involved. Muck me about though and I could get very bitchy.' He smiled. 'I'm staying at the Railway Hotel. I'll expect to hear from you by lunchtime.'

'That doesn't give me enough time.'

'Okay, three o'clock.'

'That's still not long enough.'

Sable sighed and stood up. 'I have every faith in you, dear boy,' he said, turning for the door. 'Oh, by the way, lovely cheese sandwich.'

11

For several minutes after Calder had shown Eddie
Sable out of the station under the still disapproving
stare of Bill Brookes he stood on the entrance steps,
staring down into the street and listening to the
murmur of traffic on the by-pass. A large moth
fluttered inside the blue 'police' lamp hanging above
the main doors of the building, distracting him for a
moment, and he reflected ironically on the fact that
even in the modern high-tech police service, with its
sophisticated communication systems, computerised
criminal records and DNA profiling, there was a
reluctance to abandon the old *Dixon of Dock Green*
image completely. Even after so many years, there
still seemed to be a secret hankering for a return to
the sort of solid, uncomplicated 'clip round the ear'
style of policing the traditional blue lamp continued
to represent. I *wish*, he mused, wondering whether the
top level whizz-kids in the service regarded heretics
as more of a threat to their reformist ideas than
dinosaurs.

Then abruptly the moth escaped, fluttering away
with his thoughts on the heavy humid air, and jolting
him back to reality. Dawn had already broken with
the usual eruption of bird song and the world was

starting to wake up after the lull in street activity that had followed the near riot at Hillier's Bridge and the arrest of Solomon and his cohorts. A milk float hummed past the station on the first deliveries of the morning, the bottles clinking merrily in their crates as it went, and a red post office van pulled out from a side street opposite and headed towards the centre of town, presumably en route to the main sorting office.

From where he stood, Calder could see the still lamplit gates of the municipal park and he remembered with a feeling of bitterness that it was there where it had all started. If only he had not agreed to take that fateful stroll with Richard Baseheart perhaps none of this business would ever have happened – well, it would still have happened, but at least he would not have been involved in it – or was he just being a total coward? 'Where the hell are you, Richard?' he said softly, turning back into the station. 'The shit's about to hit the fan!'

Bill Brookes was standing by the notice board as he passed through the foyer, apparently acting on Eddie Sable's dig about Colorado Beetle and taking down the faded Ministry of Agriculture notice. 'Not really a friend of yours, was he, Sergeant?' he queried, half turning, with an anxious judgmental look on his craggy face.

Calder paused in mid-stride and looked at him. 'Sorry, Gunner,' he said. 'What are you talking about?'

'The . . . er . . . gentleman who just left.'

Calder permitted himself a fleeting smile. 'Eddie Sable, you mean? Why, didn't you like him?'

Brookes stiffened, his face hardening. 'Ravin' poof,

Sergeant,' he replied, 'that's what he was, bloody arse-bandit.'

'That's a bit intolerant of you, isn't it, Gunner?'

The ex-Guardsman cleared his throat and squared his shoulders. 'Can't help it, Sergeant. Them queers is an affront to common decency. Should be locked up.'

Calder sighed wearily. He wasn't really in the mood for one of Brookes' well-known religious diatribes on moral values right at that moment, even though he knew the man was sincere in his beliefs and he didn't entirely disagree with him. 'Don't worry about it, Gunner,' he said dryly as he opened the connecting door with his security card. 'It will all come right at Armageddon.'

Thinking of things Biblical put him in mind of Solomon and instead of returning directly to his office he went the other way and called in to see Janice Lawson in the custody suite for an update on his three prisoners. The denim-clad hippy type, weighed down with beads and earrings, almost collided with him on the way out and initially held the security door open for him to pass through until he recognised him.

'Jim, my man,' Detective Sergeant Herbert Fuller exclaimed, now allowing the door to slam shut behind him. 'How's it all going for my favourite woodentop?'

Calder grinned and reaching forward, tugged on a lock of his frizzy, black shoulder-length hair which was held back from his face by a wide red and green patterned bandanna. 'Taken a liking to perms now, Herbie?' he queried.

The Drug Squad man leaned back against the door with the sole of one sandal-shod foot resting against the kick-plate and his arms folded across his chest. 'And where do you think you're off to?' he said airily.

'Out of the way, hop-head,' Calder ordered, still grinning. 'I've got to check on my prisoners.'

Fuller opened his eyes wide in mock surprise. 'Your prisoners?' he echoed. 'And all the time I thought they belonged to Steve Torrington.'

Calder frowned. 'Being difficult, is he?' he queried.

Fuller's good-humour vanished and he straightened up with a snort. 'Don't know what's got into the man. You called me in, right? As per normal procedure. And what do I find? The bastard has actually had a quick chat with my man, Solomon, then had him banged up for the night with instructions that he is not to be disturbed until after breakfast. Keeps talking about prisoners' rights under PACE to a proper rest and bloody Janice Lawson has actually sided with him.'

Calder sighed. 'Good old PACE, eh? Well, it doesn't really surprise me, but you can't blame Janice. As custody sergeant, she has to treat The Police And Criminal Evidence Act as her bible. More than her life's worth not to.'

'Maybe, but Steve Torrington? Shit, Jim, since when has he been interested in prisoner's rights?'

'It's got nothing to do with prisoner's rights. Steve's got a bee in his bonnet about the festival stabbing. Thinks Solomon is implicated in some way and is frightened to death someone else might get him to cough.'

'And meanwhile we have a major pusher in custody with what looks like a ton of LSD and I can't even have a few itsy-bitsy words in his shell-like?'

Calder leaned back against the opposite wall of the corridor. 'Sorry, Herbie, nothing to do with me. I don't know what's got into the man lately. Maybe it's the wrong time of the month, eh?'

They both laughed uproariously, then Calder's face became suddenly serious. 'This guy, Solomon, have you had a chance to see his d/f yet? It's a bit tasty.'

Fuller nodded. 'Very bad dude as Bob Grady would say. I gather SB were interested in him at one time. All I know is that he appears to be the source of the evil stuff that's doing the rounds at the festival. And it's mega bad, Jim. We've had scores of cases so far, and the kids taking it turn into regular Jekyll and Hyde's; violent psychos, who think they're invincible and are prepared to take on all-comers. The worrying thing is that it's being handed out on a free gratis basis, which means it's available to virtually anyone. So this can't be a buck-making enterprise, but is obviously being done for the sole purpose of creating maximum mayhem. Bloody frightening thought I can tell you.'

Calder studied him for a moment. 'So what are you going to do?'

'What can I do? No point in going to my boss, is there? He can't overrule PACE and anyway he's got too much on his plate at the festival at the moment. I shall just have to hope the Lab turns up a positive analysis at something more than the speed of a snail. Then I can push for my interview later today.'

'And meanwhile the stuff is still doing the rounds?'

Fuller moved away from the door and headed off along the corridor. 'Tell me about it, Jim,' he said, then called back over his shoulder. 'Oh, by the way, it was still a bloody good pull. Congratulations.'

A check with Janice Lawson confirmed Fuller's tale of woe. 'Nothing I can do, Jim,' she said. 'Okay, you could argue the point that the DI is over the top on his PACE interpretation, but once he starts insisting on a prisoner's right to a proper night's sleep before a full interview, I daren't go against that.'

'Has Solomon asked for a solicitor yet?' Calder queried.

She frowned. 'No, and that surprises me. Someone like him would normally demand representation straight-away. But he hasn't even asked for a 'phone call or anyone to be told he's here. All he keeps doing is quoting from the Bible. Drives you crackers.'

'Perhaps he is?'

'What, crackers? No, I don't think so. But I do think he's dangerous and he certainly gives me the creeps. I've told Pete Robinson, the gaoler, not to go in his cell for any reason on his own.'

'What about the other two characters?'

She laughed. 'Sleeping like babies. They came in shouting the odds, but when Solomon told them to shut it they did just that. Not a peep out of them since.'

Calder looked at his watch, turning back towards the door. 'Yeah,' he growled. 'Well, as it's already after five, I shan't be long following their example I can tell you.'

But he had reckoned without his persistent run of bad luck which seemed determined to make sure nothing went according to plan. When, at a little after six-twenty, he slipped behind the wheel of his car in the police station yard and turned the key in the ignition he was not really surprised that nothing happened, especially as he had left the interior light on all night and he already knew his battery was on its last legs anyway. Several more attempts produced the same result and, cursing volubly, he clambered from the vehicle and directed a vicious kick at the door.

'Having trouble, James?' a familiar voice drawled.

Scowling, he turned and stared at Rosy Maxwell who was standing by her BMW car with the door half open. 'Won't bloody start,' he snarled, stating the obvious.

'Kicking the door helps, does it?' she queried mildly.

Feeling more than a little silly, he gave her a sheepish grin. 'Let's it know how I feel,' he replied and, ducking into the car to retrieve his lunchbox and the now re-sealed Baseheart envelope from the front seat, he slammed the door and locked it.

'Do you want to try a jump-start with my car?' she said.

He shook his head. 'No point sodding about with it this time of the morning,' he replied. 'The battery's totally dead. Should have changed it twelve months ago. I'll buy a new one this afternoon and fit it when I come on tonight. Thanks anyway.'

'Give you a lift home then?'

'No, honestly. It would be well out of your way. I'll get one of the day-turn to do the honours.'

'Don't be so bloody daft. You might have to wait ages. Jump in.'

He hesitated, then nodded. The idea of hanging round the station waiting for someone to take him was not the most appealing thing in the world. 'Thanks a lot . . . if you don't mind.'

'What's in the envelope?' she queried as they pulled out of the yard on to the main road.

He started, realising that he had the thing clutched to his chest as if it were a cheque from the National Lottery. 'Oh . . . er . . . nothing really. One or two appraisals that are overdue. Thought I'd work on them this afternoon.'

She made a face. 'You shouldn't be taking work home, James. Not after the sort of shifts we're doing.'

'I don't mind, really.'

She shrugged. 'Well, if you want to be a hero . . . Oh, by the way, I forgot to tell you, Inspector Maybe will be back on duty tonight.'

He stared at her. 'Maybe? I thought he was sick?'

She gave a throaty chuckle. 'So did he, but I ran into him doing some late-night shopping when I was out and about last night, just before the Appleyard saga, in fact. He looked a bit miffed when I appeared, especially when I told him he obviously felt a lot better and would no doubt be keen to return to duty at six this evening.'

He was grinning from ear to ear now. 'And he agreed?'

'What alternative did he have? Hands laden with groceries and a four-pack?'

'Which means he'll now have to choose which side he's going to be on. Strikers or non-strikers. I bet his arse is going half a crown sixpence.'

'James, do you mind!'

He cleared his throat. 'Sorry, slip of the tongue.' Then he added: 'But at least this means you'll be able to get a night off.'

She snorted. 'Night off? What on the eve of a major police strike? You've got to be joking.'

'Do you think they will strike when it comes to it?'

'Certain they will. Mr. Rhymes has been locked in discussions with Willie Justice all day and apparently can't get anywhere with the man.'

I bet he can't, he thought grimly, remembering the

conversation he had heard between Rhymes and Deputy Commissioner Stephen Turner.

'And what will you be doing when they strike at ten o'clock tonight?' she went on.

He grunted. 'You've no need to ask me that and you know it.'

She swung the car across the road outside his bungalow and pulled up sharply, her eyes studying the street, almost certainly looking for Jane Sullivan's distinctive Rover car. Calder couldn't conceal a brief smirk as he opened the car door, pleased with his foresight in telling Jane to put the thing in his garage where it couldn't be seen.

'So, it's you and me versus the rest then, is it?' she said in a noticeably brighter tone.

'And Inspector Maybe,' he replied, climbing out of the car and slamming the door behind him.

She leaned across the seat and grinned through the open window. 'Of course, and Inspector Maybe. Incidentally, James, how will you get back to the station tonight? Would you like me to pick you up?'

He turned to stare at her. 'No, no, no,' he said hastily, 'that won't be necessary. I'll get one of my shift to do the honours on their way in, honestly.'

'Suit yourself, but don't be late.'

He watched her car pull away and regain its correct side of the road, heading for the circle at the end of the long cul-de-sac where she would have known from past experience that she could turn in one continuous manoeuvre. As she disappeared round the slight bend in the road he walked quickly up the garden path to the front door, keen to get to grips with the contents of Baseheart's envelope which he held securely under one arm and wondering if Jane Sullivan was up and about yet.

The feeling of panic hit him the moment he inserted his key in the lock. It wouldn't turn even a fraction. Jane must have put the catch down. Whether she had done it inadvertently or deliberately, it meant he was trapped on his own front doorstep with the prospect of Rosy Maxwell driving back down the road any second and querying why he couldn't get in.

Withdrawing the key, he hammered the knocker repeatedly, glancing along the road as he did so. To his relief there was an almost immediate response, but even as feet thumped along the hall inside he heard the sound of a car approaching from the far end of the cul-de-sac. Inwardly he groaned. 'Come on, Jane,' he breathed aloud as he heard her fumble with the lock, but it took her several seconds to shift the stubborn catch and Maxwell's car was already in sight, cruising towards him.

Then at last there was a sharp click and the door swung open, but already it was too late. Before he could dart through and slam it behind him Maxwell had drawn up outside the bungalow and stopped just as Jane Sullivan appeared boldly in the doorway. She was barefoot and clad in one of his old dressing-gowns, secured by a loosely tied belt, and even as he opened his mouth to warn her to get back inside Maxwell rapped his name.

Closing his eyes briefly in resignation, he tossed his envelope on to the adjacent hall table and turned back towards the road, feeling Maxwell's eyes boring into him all the way. She was leaning across the seat, her face hard and unsmiling and one arm extended with his lunchbox in her hand.

'You forgot this,' she said tightly. 'Obviously you were in too big a hurry to get indoors. And now I realise why. See you, James.'

He only just caught the lunchbox as it was flicked through the window, then stepped back quickly as she slammed the gearstick forward, revved the engine mercilessly and sent the car rocketing forward, leaving the strong smell of burning rubber in her wake as she headed back towards the main road.

'Sorry, Jim,' Sullivan said quietly when he returned to the bungalow and closed the door behind him. 'I must have put the snip down on the door by accident when I checked it before going to bed.'

He leaned back against the door and exhaled in one long continuous breath, studying her for a moment. She was clutching the dressing-gown very tightly about her slender body, but even so part of one shapely thigh protruded through a gap. 'Well, you certainly gave Rosy something to think about,' he commented, glancing down at her leg. 'And probably half the estate as well.'

Seeing the direction of his gaze, she quickly pulled the lower parts of the dressing-gown together. 'I said I was sorry,' she replied. 'But how was I to know she would be driving you home?'

He grinned suddenly. 'Don't worry about it, Jane,' he said. 'Besides, I haven't had as nice a home-coming as that for a long time.'

'You have a mucky mind,' she retorted, her face reddening, then quickly nodded towards the envelope on the hall table. 'What's all that about. Got yourself an early Christmas present?'

He picked it up and weighed it carefully in his hands. 'I think you'll agree that this is the Christmas present to beat all Christmas presents,' he said, 'but there's one hell of a catch to it.'

Her jaw dropped as the light of understanding dawned in her large green eyes. 'Richard's envelope,' she breathed. 'You've actually got it back, haven't you?'

He nodded grimly. 'In a manner of speaking, yes. I'll tell you all about it when we've had a bite to eat. Now didn't you say something last night about cooking breakfast?'

'So, let's take a look at Pandora's collection,' Sullivan said an hour and a half later and tearing open Richard Baseheart's envelope, which Calder had earlier resealed, she tipped the contents out on to the coffee-table.

Calder had felt very tired on arriving home, but after a shave, a shower and a superb breakfast prepared by Jane Sullivan with all the aplomb of an experienced transport cafe 'chef', the fatigue had quite literally fallen away from him and he had dismissed all thoughts of sleep from his mind. Now, seated on the edge of the settee in his lounge dressed in slacks and a casual shirt, he watched Sullivan, back inside her more respectable pinstripe trouser suit, carry out a quick inventory of the envelope's contents.

He waited patiently, surprised by the amount of material that was there: five audio cassettes, three reels of film, six 35mm film cartridges, all held in individual plastic bags, together with one loose VHS video cassette and a bundle of original notes, statement forms and collections of photographs clipped together in neat files. Significantly all the plastic bags, with the exception of those containing the 35mm film cartridges, appeared to have been torn open and then resealed with staples.

'Bloody Nora,' he breathed. 'Have we got to go right through this lot?'

She smiled thinly and returned all the items to the envelope, save the VHS video cassette. 'Only this,' she said, holding up the cassette. 'It is an edited copy of the original tapes and should explain most of what you need to know.' She sighed. 'It's damned unfortunate that most of the stuff seems to have been tampered with, for this will almost certainly affect its subsequent evidential value if we ever have to go to court. Any good brief could successfully argue that the integrity of the material had been compromised.'

'That's why Richard should have deposited it all in a proper police tape or crime property store at the very beginning,' he pointed out. 'At least then we could have proved handling continuity.'

She nodded. 'Well, for reasons you already know that was obviously out of the question, but at least it's all here which is a relief anyway.'

'That's supposed to reassure me?' he replied gloomily. 'Eddie Sable still has the story and we have only hours to find Richard or face the biggest scandal to hit Fleet Street for a long time.'

'Perhaps he's bluffing?'

He stared at her incredulously. 'Bluffing? Why should he do that, when he has all the information he needs?'

'Then why is he so desperate to see Richard?'

He shrugged. 'To put the meat on the bones, I suppose. Clear up any ambiguities and all that.'

She climbed to her feet and taking the video cassette across to his television, inserted it in the video recorder underneath. 'And if he can't get hold of Richard do you think he'll risk going to press with the disjointed material he's got?'

'Bloody sure he will. He's got more than enough for a major story.'

She switched on the television and pressed the mute button to lose the sound, then straightened up to face him. 'But he's only got copies of it all and that sort of material would certainly be challenged in any court of law on the grounds of admissibility. He could face a heavy libel action if he went ahead and published, not to mention theft and breach of copyright.'

His harsh disparaging laugh cut her off in the midst of her desperate straw-clutching. 'Get real, Jane. Eddie Sable won't worry about infinitesimal things like libel and breach of copyright. This story is far too big for that. As for theft, how can he be done for that when he took the trouble to return all the original stuff to us? Furthermore, if he were to be hauled up for anything, all he's got to do to prove his case is call us and demand production of the original material, whether it's been compromised or not. I don't know about you, but I've never committed perjury in my life and I'm not about to start now.'

She returned to the settee with the television's infra-red control unit in one hand and switched the set on to stand-by mode. 'Despite what you say, I still don't think we can talk to the press about this business. That has to be Richard's province.'

'I agree with you there, but what if Richard still fails to turn up before Sable's deadline? What then?'

She bit her lip, her face suddenly very pale again. It was apparent that she was under an even bigger strain than Calder himself, for there was the personal

dimension to the business as well, with Richard Baseheart's actual disappearance obviously still weighing
very heavily on her mind.

He took one of her hands in his. 'Sorry to be such
a pessimist,' he said gently, 'but we do need help. We
can't keep this thing quiet any longer, you must realise
that.'

'You think something's happened to Richard, don't
you?' she answered.

He released her hand and sighed. 'I don't know
what to think, Jane, I really don't. But we can't simply
stick our heads in the sand and hope this business will
go away. We must report it today.'

She emitted a deep trembling sigh and nodded
quickly. 'I realise that now, but let me run the tape
before we do anything else, so you can see just how
big a tiger we have by the tail.'

'That's why I didn't go to bed.'

Another quick nod, then she half-turned on the
settee to face him.

'First a bit of necessary background. You will know
already that Richard and I only unearthed the present
conspiracy by accident. What you won't know is how
that happened.'

'I'm listening.'

She stood up and began pacing the room, tapping
the infra-red control unit against her chin as she did
so.

'Several weeks ago,' she went on, 'Richard's boss,
Superintendent John Briggs, was approached by the
Home Office through Deputy Commissioner Turner
and asked to set up a very sensitive surveillance
operation on a well-known public figure. Full
authority was given for this, including any telephone

taps and vehicle buggings deemed necessary, and Briggs handed the job to Richard Baseheart with instructions to involve as few SB people as possible. Richard selected me, partially because of my expertise in electronic surveillance techniques and partially because of my experience on the department.'

'Go on.'

'The target on this occasion was a very keen golfer and it was during one of his visits to a particularly select west London golf club that I managed to video a revealing conversation between himself and his invited guest which really put the cat among the pigeons as far as our enquiry was concerned and persuaded Richard to extend his surveillance to other quarters.' She shrugged. 'Once we had embarked on this course it was a bit like tugging at a loose thread on a pullover; the more we pulled, the more it unravelled. Before long we were tangled up in something far more sinister and far-reaching than we had ever envisaged.'

'So, who was your target?'

She hesitated, then stared at him fixedly, anticipating his reaction. 'Kenneth Granger MP, leader of the main opposition party.'

Calder closed his eyes tightly for a second. 'Let me get this straight. You've been carrying out surveillance on one of the most powerful elected members of parliament? The man tipped for the post of Prime Minister if his party wins the next general election?'

She lowered her gaze. 'We had no choice. There was a suggestion that he was involved in activities and associations incompatible with his position as a member of parliament and the Home Office wanted clarification of the situation.'

'You mean they wanted enough dirt on him to use in their pre-election campaign.'

She flinched. 'Maybe you're right, but once an allegation is made that could affect national security we have no option but to investigate, whatever we might think privately.'

'Okay, I see your point, but what I don't see is how Granger fits into this conspiracy. Don't tell me our own Commissioner, John Harding, was his golfing partner?'

She laughed. 'Harding? No way. I doubt whether he knows one end of a golf club from the other. He's simply the pawn in this business. A high level one, but a pawn nevertheless.'

He shook his head. 'I'm even more bewildered than before.'

She directed the infra-red control unit at the television and pressed two buttons in succession. 'Watch the tape,' she said.

There must have been a fly on the lens when Jane Sullivan had first set up her camera, a tiny hyper-active speck that moved backwards and forwards over the faces of the two men, as they sat talking on a low rustic bench with a bottle of wine and two glasses on a small table between them. Behind them strong sunlight was reflected in the windows of what appeared to be a large conservatory and in their open-necked shirts and slacks, they could easily have been mistaken for a couple of old friends having an innocent drink together on a hot summer's day. Exactly what they were discussing was not evident, since Sullivan kept the video on mute.

'The terrace of the members' clubhouse,' she

explained abruptly, holding a close-up of both men on "pause." 'We managed to get an observation van, disguised as a caterer's wagon, parked just a few yards from where they were sitting and we were lucky to have some new state of the art surveillance kit that worked like a dream. Recognise anyone?'

Calder gave a low whistle. The chubby florid-faced man on the left was too often on television to be mistaken for anyone other than Kenneth Granger MP, and he had been expecting to see him anyway. What he hadn't been expecting was his white-haired companion, whose thin pinched face, deep-set eyes and hooked nose were unmistakable. 'Well, I'll be damned!' he breathed. 'Charles Simmonds, Chairman of the Police Authority. He only visited the nick last week.'

'The pair of them go back a long way apparently,' Sullivan explained. 'Friends since public school and then through university where they both studied politics.' She made a wry face. 'Now they keep in touch, very discreetly, of course, through functions at their respective Masonic lodges and the occasional round of golf.'

'Nothing criminal about that,' he commented. 'Lots of men belong to Masonic lodges and play golf.'

She nodded grimly. 'Yes, but lots of men don't have the sort of conversations that these two had.' She aimed the remote control at the video and pressed the fast-forward button. 'We'll skip all their preliminary chat and get right down to the nitty . . . ah, here we are. This is the important bit coming up now.' The film's rapid advance was suddenly halted as she pressed "play", the picture going into spasm for a few seconds before steadying and running at normal speed, accompanied by surprisingly clear sound.

'So,' Simmonds said, reaching for his glass, 'what's this proposition you have for me, Kenneth? I must admit I was rather intrigued by your 'phone call.'

Granger nodded, taking a few sips from the glass he already held in his hand before returning it to the table. 'How would you like to get rid of John Harding?' he said abruptly.

For a moment Simmonds looked shocked, jerking his head sideways to stare at him. 'The Commissioner?' he exclaimed, then glanced around him quickly and lowered his voice. 'What the devil are you up to?'

Granger gave a thin smile. 'You haven't answered my question, Charles.'

Simmonds set his glass on the arm of the bench beside him and frowned thoughtfully. 'Well, it's no secret that we share a mutual dislike of each other, always have. Man lives in the past, that's his trouble and he has about as much drive and imagination as a tortoise with Alzheimer's.'

'So if his departure could be . . . arranged you wouldn't be averse to the idea?'

Simmonds ran the palm of one hand down his long thin face, as if trying to come to terms with what Granger was saying. 'I'm not sure we should be having this conversation, Kenneth,' he replied.

'Then you're not interested?'

Simmonds threw him another sideways glance. 'I didn't say that,' he replied. 'But I'd be very surprised if it could be achieved. Harding may be an ornery, dyed-in-the-wool traditionalist, who obstructs the Police Authority at every turn, but he has an impeccable reputation and quite a few friends in high places, so he wouldn't be easy to dislodge. Believe me, if it were otherwise I would have done it long before now.'

Granger nodded. 'Funny thing about reputations though, Charles, is that they are made to be broken and as for friends, they will soon turn sour if they are let down. Were Harding to drop a major clanger that severely embarrassed the present government, for example, I suspect his demise as commissioner would be pretty rapid and that would leave the way open for you to appoint a successor of your own choosing, would it not?'

Simmonds shook his head. 'Nice idea, but you forget that the Home Secretary has to approve every chief officer appointment. The Authority, through its chairperson, only recommends. Even if Harding were to go we are bound to end up with a replacement favoured by this same bloody awful government.'

The MP's amber eyes gleamed. 'Not if Harding's *faux pas* were to precipitate the fall of the government and the election of an administration of an entirely different colour.'

There was a noticeable change in Simmond's demeanour. Now he was really listening. 'Go on.'

Granger pursed his lips reflectively before replying. 'How would you describe the state of morale in your police force at the moment?' he said.

'Morale?' Simmonds appeared momentarily thrown by the other's sudden change of tack, but then he recovered and shrugged. 'Pretty abysmal, like every other police force in the country just now. Police work is no longer the rewarding well-paid profession it once was. There's a lot of bitterness and resentment among the rank and file over the recent reductions in pay and loss of allowances, while the government's constant cost-cutting has thrown chief officers into a real spin.'

'In short, the boys and girls in blue are not happy?' Granger patronised.

Simmonds threw him a sharp suspicious glance. 'You seem almost pleased at the thought.'

The MP didn't confirm or deny the fact, but studied him intently. 'Just imagine what would happen if your Central Region finally decided it had had enough and opted to take industrial action.'

Simmonds made a grimace. 'A frightening prospect,' he replied. 'There would be absolute carnage.'

Granger smiled again. 'Exactly, but, apart from the immediate obvious breakdown in law and order, there would be another more important knock-on effect. Although the police would come in for considerable stick because of their strike action, it would be the government that would really get it in the neck, especially our unfortunate Prime Minister, the Rt Hon Duncan James MP, whose country retreat actually happens to be on the outskirts of Hardingham, in the eastern part of his large middle-class constituency.'

Simmonds shrugged. 'The government have weathered storms before.'

'Not one like this they haven't. Just think about it, Charles. Their misguided cost-cutting policies would be seen by the public as having directly precipitated the strike and their position would become completely untenable. Under severe pressure from the opposition parties, Duncan James would have no option but to call a general election or subject his cabinet to the inevitable no confidence vote in the House, either of which he would certainly lose.'

'Enabling your party to take over the reins of government with yourself as PM, I take it?'

'Precisely, but with an administration much more sympathetic to the needs of the public services and, more importantly, to Police Authority chairpersons like Charles Simmonds.'

The Chairman made a wry face. 'Interesting hypothesis, but it is only hypothesis,' he replied. 'Of all the public services, the police are the least likely to go on strike. It's against everything they stand for.'

'Stood for,' Granger corrected patiently. 'Things have changed, man, and with discontent in the force already at a record high I am quite sure the National Police Union could be encouraged to take such action. All that is needed, in fact, is for the screw to be turned just one little extra notch.'

'And how would you see that being done?'

Granger's smile was suddenly very smug. 'I rather thought a top-level announcement abolishing all paid overtime, coming as it would on top of recent pay reductions and loss of personal allowances, might have just the right effect.'

Simmonds raised an eyebrow, then emitted a short hard laugh. 'The right effect?' he echoed. 'More likely World War Three!' He shook his head. 'Well, you've certainly done your homework, Kenneth, I'll give you that, and for a while your little scheme did sound really promising, but there's no way things can be made to happen as you envisage. The Commissioner is the only one who can put a stop to paid overtime and he's hardly going to do that when he knows full well what the outcome is likely to be. He may be past his sell-by date, but he's not a complete fool.'

Granger's smug expression remained undiminished. 'Ah, but what if he could be persuaded by someone he trusts implicitly that there was not the remotest possibility of a strike? That it was all to be part of an elaborate ruse, fully supported by the National Police Union, to put pressure on the government to change its mind on its budgetary cut-backs? After all, it would be logical to assume that a police strike in the PM's own constituency is the very last thing the government would want and that they are bound to cave-in well before any walk-out is due to begin.'

Simmonds hesitated and screwing up his eyes ran the palm of one hand down his face again. Obviously Granger was getting through at last and the MP quickly pressed home his advantage.

'Don't forget, Charles,' he went on smoothly, 'Harding has been pushed into a corner by the government's latest decision to plunder existing budgets and he is desperate to find a way out. Cutting services is his only other option and that's the last thing any chief officer wants to do because it would result in a public outcry and lead to accusations of bad management.'

'And you really believe he can be persuaded to gamble his all on a brinkmanship strategy?'

'I'm positive he can. Harding may not be as politically devious as most of his colleagues, but he is a courageous man who can be relied upon to take a calculated risk.' A darker smile. 'Unfortunately, he will be dealing with a government equally as intransigent as himself, so in the final analysis he will be seen as having misjudged the situation and end up actually going over the brink to his ultimate destruction.'

Simmonds was silent for a moment, apparently still considering the plausible arguments Granger had put forward. 'It could work,' he said at length, then glanced at him quickly. 'But you have omitted one small detail.'

'Which is?'

'Who you have in mind to play the part of Brutus.'

'That's where you come in. I'm sure you can think of someone who has Harding's ear and could make the necessary moves on our behalf?'

Simmonds nodded. 'As a matter of fact, I think I know just the man.'

'Ah, but would he be prepared to do it?'

Simmonds snorted disparagingly. 'Deputy Commissioner Stephen Wilson Turner would be prepared to do anything that is of benefit to Stephen Wilson Turner,' he replied. 'He's the Commissioner's number two, with specific responsibility for the operational management of the force and very much his confidant.'

'Powerful position.'

'Oh, it's that all right and he's thirsting for more of the same.'

'Excellent material for our purposes then?'

'The very best. Sees himself as the next commissioner . . . somewhere.'

'Has he the ability?'

Simmonds shrugged. 'Perhaps. Very high IQ and excellent academic qualifications. Graduate entrant. Distinguished himself on the Special Course and rose rapidly under the accelerated promotion scheme. Totally ruthless and unlovable though and at present politically naive.'

'Not your choice for commissioner, then?'

'Not exactly. I've someone else in mind. But he needn't know that.'

Granger chuckled. 'And he can hardly complain after the event, can he?'

Simmonds also laughed. 'Be a damned fool if he did.'

Granger's face suddenly became very serious. 'Could prove complicated if he were aware that you and I had met though.'

Simmonds nodded. 'I understand perfectly. I will be making much the same point to Turner about myself and the Commissioner.'

'So our man will be on his own then?'

'Seems like it, but command always is a lonely position, is it not?'

Sullivan pressed a button on the infra-red control unit and the television screen went blank. 'Had enough?' she said grimly.

Calder lurched to his feet. 'I need a drink,' he replied. 'A large one.'

12

'Better?' Sullivan asked acidly as Calder finished the double whisky and sat back in his chair.

He made a rueful face, remembering Rosy Maxwell's dig about him hitting the bottle off duty. 'Not really, but I needed it all the same. You should have joined me.'

She shook her head. 'No thanks. I think one of us at least ought to stay sober, don't you?'

He scowled at the reproof and, pulling out his cigarettes, twirled a long filter-tip between his fingers for several seconds before lighting it. Somewhere outside children began squealing and he guessed the youngsters next door were at the hose again. After what he had just viewed on the video their mischievous laughter, joined shortly afterwards by the musical jingle of the ice-cream van, seemed part of a trivial alien world from which he had suddenly become disconnected, the umbilical cord linking him to normality having been severed at a stroke, leaving him trapped inside a nightmare from which he had no way of escaping.

'What else have you got on your damned tapes?' he said suddenly.

Sullivan shrugged. 'Nothing that you don't know

about already. We missed the first meeting between Simmonds and Turner. Couldn't get a bug in place quick enough. But we did pick up on their second rendezvous and got there before they did.'

She played with the infra-red control unit and the tape whirred for several seconds, then abruptly stopped. The television screen illuminated to reveal a large grassed area, bordered by lines of trees with a lake in the middle distance. Children played on the grass and a young couple sat on a seat entwined in a passionate embrace. There were ducks too, waddling along the edge of the lake, and a man in a short-sleeved blue shirt and grey flannels appeared to be feeding them from a paper bag.

The camera homed in on him and even though it was a back view Calder recognised Charles Simmonds immediately. 'Feeding ducks in a park?' he said incredulously. 'I don't believe it.'

Sullivan nodded with just the trace of an ironic smile. 'Collingborne, a couple of miles from police HQ,' she replied, then added: 'I think this conspiracy thing has gone to his head and he sees himself as one of the old Cold War spies like Philby.'

He snorted. 'I reckon you're all in the same mould as far as that's concerned, what with secret meetings, surveillance cameras, bugging devices and mystery parcels. It's about time everyone stopped playing silly games and got on with what they're paid to do.'

She coloured up. 'This is what SB are paid to do, James,' she retorted, 'and if we hadn't been doing it this business would never have come to light in the first place.'

'Maybe it would have been better if it hadn't,' he growled.

'Just watch the video,' she said tightly.

Even as she spoke another figure, dressed in a blue blazer, light coloured trousers and dark glasses, appeared centre stage, walking in short quick steps across the grass from left to right of the television screen. Deputy Commissioner Stephen Turner was plainly uneasy and he glanced about him repeatedly as he approached the Police Authority man.

'Ah, Stephen,' Simmonds barked suddenly, but without turning round. 'Good of you to come.'

'Chairman,' Turner acknowledged coldly, then added: 'But did we really have to meet like this? I feel like some damned criminal planning a robbery.'

Simmonds slipped his paper bag into his pocket and, brushing his hands free of crumbs, turned to face him. 'So would you rather we'd had our meeting in your office at police headquarters?' he said sharply.

'No, of course not.'

'Well there you are then and, as I've already told you, it's essential that we are discreet to ensure my involvement in this matter does not come to the attention of the Commissioner. If he were to find out that I am behind the current proposal he would reject it out of hand and you would lose all credibility in his eyes.'

'I understand that.'

'Good, so let's make this conversation as short as possible, shall we? What did Harding have to say?'

Turner threw a worried searching glance across the grass, staring directly at the concealed camera, but apparently seeing nothing. 'He took some persuading, but he's on board now.'

The video picture froze for a moment as Sullivan depressed the 'pause' button. 'And we've got it all on audio tape,' she said grimly. 'At least we got that job done in time.'

Calder stared at her. 'You bugged the Commissioner's office?' hc exclaimed.

'How else could we have secured the necessary evidence? We installed the device straight after Simmonds' meeting with Granger.'

'But . . . but the Commissioner's own office?'

She didn't answer him, depressing the video 'pause' button a second time so that he was forced to turn back to the screen without pursuing his point.

'Then he did agree to the proposal in the end?' Simmonds queried.

A curt nod from Turner. 'Naturally. He trusts me implicitly.'

Simmonds shook his head slowly. 'Put not your trust in princes,' he murmured, unwittingly obliging the camera by strolling towards it.

Turner scowled and quickly followed him. 'Let's just leave the Bible out of it, shall we?' he snapped. 'I don't exactly enjoy doing this, you know.'

'Nonsense,' Simmonds cut in and stopped abruptly. 'You don't give a damn about anything as long as you get what you want. We're two of a kind, you and I.'

Turner studied him narrowly. 'And will I get what I want?'

Simmonds gave a short laugh. 'I think you'll make an excellent commissioner, Stephen.'

The other grunted. 'As long as we understand each other, Chairman . . .'

'Charles, please.'

Turner's thin mouth twisted into a cynical smile. 'Charles then.'

Simmonds laughed again. 'I think we have always

understood each other Stephen,' he said, picking up on his previous comment. 'That's why we have exchanged confidences in the past. You don't rate John Harding anymore than I do. He's a battleship commander in a high-tech nuclear fleet; a Luddite, who has found it impossible to change with the times.'

'He's still a formidable adversary.'

'No reason for him to know you and he are adversaries, is there? Now tell me the programme you have in mind for our little project.'

More nervous glances from Turner around the immediate vicinity, then he went on in a rush as if anxious to get the discussion over and done with as quickly as possible. 'A memo will be issued by the Commissioner freezing all paid overtime at the end of this month,' he said, 'just as soon as the proposal has been floated before the members of the force policy committee at their meeting on Monday.'

'And you're sure the members will agree to it?'

'Positive. As you must already know, most chief officer positions nationally have now been civilianised and every force policy committee is therefore dominated by civilian principal officers who have little or no sympathy with the perspective of rank and file police officers. They'll be right behind the Commissioner on this one, you can count on it.'

'But if the policy committee meeting is on Monday, why wait until the end of this month to implement the proposal? Why not issue the memo straightaway?'

Turner faced the hidden camera again and his face wore a triumphant smile. 'To ensure maximum impact.'

'Go on.'

'As you reminded me when we last met,

Hardingham is in the PM's own constituency and any police strike there will not only embarrass the government, but cause considerable personal embarrassment to the man himself.'

'So?'

Turner's smile broadened. 'An annual rave festival is scheduled to take place as usual on the edge of the town next month. The withdrawal of police coverage during an event of this size would have particularly disastrous consequences and make the PM's embarrassment all the more acute. By delaying the memo, we reduce negotiation time and make a strike during the festival all the more likely.'

Simmonds raised his eyebrows, plainly very impressed. 'Capital!' he exclaimed. 'Brilliant idea! I can certainly see why you come across as commissioner material, Stephen. But I must admit, I am surprised that Harding has agreed to everything so readily.'

'He has swallowed the idea that the government will back down well before zero hour and he believes that my recommendation to hold back the memo until the end of the month is designed to put them under maximum pressure to agree a settlement before the festival actually takes place.'

'Silly man.'

'Very, because once he's started the process he will be locked into it and he's not the sort of person for U-turns.'

'No, I agree entirely. In fact, knowing him as I do, I wouldn't be surprised if he isn't actually a blood-line relative of the chap who led the fatal Charge of the Light Brigade.'

Both men laughed briefly, then Simmonds blew his nose on a large red handkerchief. 'But what about the

National Police Union?' he said, dabbing his nostrils tenderly. 'Have they actually got the balls to take this all the way?'

Turner nodded. 'The Central Region Branch Executive Committee is dominated by militants just looking for an opportunity to use their new industrial muscle and their chairman, Constable Willy Justice, is an egotistical windbag who sees himself as a future member of the National Executive and can therefore be played like a harp.'

'To our tune rather than John Harding's, I trust?'

'Most definitely, although on my assurance as his intermediary, the Commissioner is under the illusion that the NPU will be working with him on this one, for the good of the service and all that, and will be merely threatening to strike without any real intention of doing so.'

'And when he finally realises his mistake?'

'It will be too late and the region will be in chaos.'

Simmonds sighed contentedly. 'Exit Mr. John Harding to the obscurity of a retirement cottage. The prospect gives me a nice warm feeling.' Then his voice hardened. 'Just so long as nothing goes wrong.'

'What could possibly go wrong?' Turner retorted hastily, evidently sensing the sudden menace in his tone. 'I have the whole thing sewn up.'

'Like hell you have!' Sullivan breathed and switched off.

For a few moments Calder continued to stare at the blank television screen like someone at the cinema waiting for the second feature to start. Then he stubbed out his cigarette in an ashtray on the arm of his chair and poured himself another measure of whisky.

'You intend going on duty tonight after guzzling another one of those?' Sullivan snapped.

He looked at the glass halfway to his lips, then set it back down on the coffee table with an irritable bang. 'Okay, so you've made your point. I won't touch anymore. But now I'll make mine. We've got to report this shit without any further argument. Why the hell Richard left it so long before trying to see Turner when he must have had all the evidence he needed several weeks ago, I'll never understand.'

'He would have seen him if Turner hadn't gone on leave soon after the policy committee meeting. He had no choice but to keep everything on ice until the damned man came back.' She gave a short laugh. 'And as for you and I reporting it all now, that's fine, but who to? Stephen Turner himself perhaps? That was Richard's plan, don't forget. Tell the Deputy Commissioner what he had on him and persuade him to call a halt before it was too late. And what happened? Richard simply disappeared!'

Calder visibly started. 'What the hell are you implying?' he breathed. 'That Turner rubbed him out?' He laughed, but his attempt at derision had a shaky edge to it as he remembered his own thoughts in the police Transit the night before. 'Come on, woman, this is the police service, not some Mafia syndicate in New York.'

She leaned towards him, her face set and deadly earnest. 'Jim,' she said quietly, but with uncompromising firmness, 'we are dealing with powerful ruthless men here, men who have clawed and hacked their way through armies of colleagues to get to the very top of the tree and who cannot afford the slightest hint of scandal. Despite what we've been told, what if

Richard did actually manage to see Turner and tell him about the evidence in his possession? What would a man like Turner do? Say, "Okay, Chief Inspector, you've got me, so I'll stop being a naughty boy now and call everything off"'?'

Calder lurched to his feet and began pacing the room. 'So you're saying what? That Turner clubbed him over the head with his desk paperweight or stabbed him with his fountain pen before carting his body off to local woodland in the boot of his chauffeur-driven limo'? Get real, Jane. You've been reading too many thrillers lately.'

'All right, then. Where is Richard? Tell me that!' she blazed, tears in her eyes. 'For heaven's sake, Jim, he's been missing for about forty hours now.'

He wheeled to face her. 'Exactly! And whose idea was it to keep things quiet for a while, eh? Yours, miss, that's who. And now we can't wait any longer. We've got to report the whole sordid business before Eddie Sable goes public.'

She swallowed hard, then to his open-mouthed astonishment reached forward, picked up his whisky glass and drained it in almost a single gulp. 'Right,' she said in a voice partially strangled by the harshness of the spirit, 'so who do we know high enough up the ladder who has sufficient clout and can be trusted without question?'

'Rosy Maxwell,' he said quietly.

'What, your love-sick chief inspector?'

'The very same.' He glanced at his watch. 'And knowing her she'll be up and about well before lunchtime today which means we'll have to get weaving if we want to catch her before she goes out.'

'Why not ring her?'

'Because for a start, I don't happen to know her bloody number and secondly, if I were to contact the control room for it, that would set the tongues wagging from here to headquarters. No, we'll have to call round on spec. I know where she lives.'

'*We'll* have to call round?'

'Of course. I'll need you and your tapes to back up my story.'

She emitted a low whistle. 'After what she saw a few hours ago I bet she'll love me turning up on her doorstep.'

He made a feeble attempt at humour. 'Don't worry. You'll be okay if you avoid direct eye contact. Then she can't turn you to stone!'

They left in Sullivan's car ten minutes later and, en route to Rosy Maxwell's, paid a further visit to Baseheart's home. But it was a waste of time. The place was still empty and lifeless, more milk building up on the doorstep and post choking the letter-box. Inside, the house was oppressively warm and airless, the windows all tightly closed and no evidence of anyone having been there since their last visit.

It was a different story when they pulled up in front of Maxwell's thatched country cottage a few miles outside the town. She was very much in residence and, clad in shorts and a skimpy cotton top, busily engaged in cutting the dead heads off flowers in her front garden. Calder couldn't help but admire her long slender legs and trim bare waistline as he opened the wooden gate and went ahead of Sullivan up the gravel path. It was the first time for quite awhile (not since Maggie had died, in fact) that he had seen Rosy so casually dressed and she looked a real stunner. In spite of the serious nature of his errand, the sight of her made his heart begin to beat a lot faster, while his mouth became very dry and he felt a hardness in his loins that he was unable to control. Bloody Nora, Jim, he mused with a sense of shock, this one really is turning your clock back on, isn't she? And after all these years too. You had better keep a tight control of yourself, my lad, before you start behaving like some idiot teenager.

Maxwell had taken little notice of their car drawing up in the road outside, but she turned her head quickly when she heard the gate open and her face registered first astonishment and then angry indignation. 'You've got a nerve coming here . . . with her,' she grated, the secateurs in her hand pointing towards him as if she were contemplating stabbing him with them.

Calder held up both hands in a conciliatory gesture. 'You've got it all wrong, Rosy,' he said, 'and we've got to talk.'

She straightened up, her eyes flashing dangerously. 'We haven't got to do anything when it's on my turf, James,' she snapped, 'and I have nothing to talk to you about anyway, so kindly get off my property and take your trollop with you!'

He didn't answer, simply staring at her as if mesmerised. Her nipples were clearly visible, hard and sharp against the thin fabric of her top, and he couldn't help thinking that she had the most delectable navel he had ever seen.

She sensed his interest and glowered at him. 'When you've finished mentally undressing me like some grubby schoolboy,' she said, 'the gate is right behind you.'

He couldn't help grinning. 'Sorry, but I haven't seen you dressed like this for quite some time.'

She snorted her contempt. 'What do you think I wear off duty on a hot summer's day then? My bloody uniform?' She nodded towards Sullivan. 'At least it's a damned sight more than she was wearing earlier this morning.'

His grin vanished. 'I can explain that.'

She waved the secateurs angrily. 'I don't want to hear it. In the words of the prophet, just foxtrot-oscar, will you?'

Before Calder could say anything further Sullivan pushed past him and thrust her warrant card out in front of her. 'Detective Sergeant Jane Sullivan, Special Branch,' she snapped.

Maxwell raised her eyebrows. 'Is that supposed to impress me? Because if it is, it doesn't.'

Sullivan stood her ground. 'I'm here on official business.'

'Don't tell me,' Maxwell interjected. 'You and James have decided to get married and you want me to be matron of honour?'

Calder chuckled at the sarcasm and slowly shook his head. 'Dressed like that you couldn't be a matron of anything,' he commented.

'It's official-official,' Sullivan persisted, silencing him with an irritable glance. 'We have a serious problem and it needs to be reported.'

Maxwell's anger started to evaporate, her eyes narrowing. 'So why come to me? You have your own chain of command for that.' She stared at Calder. 'And what has it to do with one of my sergeants?'

'I got caught up in it by accident,' Calder replied quietly, 'and now it's way over both our heads.'

'That will teach you to indulge in pillow talk,'

Maxwell sniped, putting two and two together to make five. She turned on Sullivan. 'And you should know better as a member of that particular department than to gossip about things you're dealing with.'

Calder shook his head wearily. 'You're barking up totally the wrong tree, Rosy,' he said. 'We need an hour or so of your time to explain.'

She stared at both of them in turn, pursing her lips thoughtfully, then abruptly nodded. 'Then you'd better come in, hadn't you?' she said. 'But I'm warning you, this had better be good.'

Calder glanced round the small front garden at the little heaps of weeds and amputated flower heads, and nodded. 'That's not quite how I would describe it,' he replied dryly, 'but it's certainly a bit more important than dead-heading dwarf dahlias!'

Despite her initial hostility, Maxwell proved to be a very good listener. Apart from asking the occasional question in a low shocked voice, she sat in silence while Jane Sullivan first unloaded the facts of the case, (including Calder's own involvement), and then ran the video footage he had seen earlier, plus an additional extract from one of the audio tapes of Turner's revealing conversation with John Harding which he hadn't heard. In the little sitting-room with the heavy curtains closed against the sunlight there was absolute silence when the television screen finally went blank and both Calder and Sullivan waited impatiently for Maxwell's response which seemed to them to be a long time in coming. In fact, only when Calder got to his feet and pulled back the curtains did she finally stir, releasing her breath in a long drawn-out sigh, but saying nothing.

'So what do you think?' Sullivan said finally, unable to wait any longer.

Maxwell gave a harsh laugh. 'What do I think?' she echoed. 'Forgive me, but, after what I've just seen and heard, I'm finding that process a little difficult.'

'At least you have one consolation,' Calder pointed out with a half-hearted grin.

She raised her eyebrows. 'Do I, James? And what's that?'

'You now know Jane and I are not having an affair.'

She considered his answer for a moment and then nodded gravely. 'Thank you, James,' she said. 'Faced with the knowledge that the whole top echelon of this police force is currently engaged in a conspiracy to bring down the government, a senior police officer has gone missing and a notorious Fleet Street hack is about to go public on the whole thing in just a few hours, that really is a comfort!'

Sullivan glared at him, finding his feeble attempt at humour misplaced on this occasion. 'We had to report this to someone,' she said, staring at Maxwell expectantly. 'Jim said we could trust you and that you had the sort of pull that was necessary.'

Maxwell raised her eyebrows again and treated Calder to a cold smile. 'Well, thank you, James,' she said with emphasis. 'It's nice to know you think so highly of me.'

He stared down at the floor, the grin back on his face. 'Every confidence, Rosy, you know that.'

'Can we get on?' Sullivan grated. 'We haven't much time.'

'No, we certainly haven't,' Maxwell snapped, 'and you're a couple of bloody idiots for not reporting this earlier. Why the hell you dithered for so long is beyond me. Not only have you compromised your-selves by keeping quiet, but you've made it virtually impossible for anything to be done to stop the strike. And heaven knows what may have happened to Richard Baseheart in the two days he's been missing . . .'

She broke off, suddenly noticing the tears glistening in Sullivan's eyes.

Calder coughed loudly. 'She and Richard Baseheart were . . . er . . . going together,' he explained.

Maxwell winced. 'Oh!' she said in a low voice. 'Sorry, I didn't realise.' Then clearing her throat she quickly changed the subject. 'But really, I don't know what you think I can do about the situation. It seems to me that the most we can hope for is a salvage or damage limitation job, though with John Harding at the helm it's going to be very difficult. He's not the easiest man to deal with and he certainly won't bow to pressure, even if it means curtains for himself.'

Calder nodded grimly. 'We're well aware of that, but perhaps you could do something behind the scenes. I'm not into all this politics stuff, but I know you used to have some connections at the Home Office.'

'Ah, Juliet Grey, you mean? Yes, I still keep in touch with her.' A bitter smile. 'Used to bring her to police do's once. Then the usual stories started to circulate. You know, the score. Two unmarried women of our age going around together which automatically meant we had to be a couple of dykes, that sort of thing. So we stopped the socialising. Charming culture we have in the service when you think about it. As a matter of fact Juliet only lives a short drive from here.' She looked at her watch thoughtfully. 'I could be at her home in half an hour and I happen to know she's actually there on a week's leave at prescnt.' She warmed to the idea the more she thought about her friend's nice Georgian house, with its thick wall to wall carpets, beautiful antique furniture and pot-pourri perfumes of peach, lemon and apple blossom. 'I can certainly seek her advice, but I can't see her coming up with any instant solutions.'

'At least it's a step in the right direction anyway,' Sullivan ventured, drying her eyes. 'Perhaps she could bring some pressure to bear on the Commissioner through a minister before it's too late. After all, Harding has only to withdraw his damned memo and the crisis is over.'

Maxwell frowned. 'Maybe, but I have to say I don't like doing things this way. I've always held John Harding in the highest regard. Old school tie perhaps, but honest to a fault and above all a copper's copper who knows what it's like to stand in the rain.'

'He's all of those things,' Sullivan said, 'but with the government's latest cuts he's at the end of his tether. This is the last ditch stand of a tired desperate man who can no longer deliver the service required of him with the reduced budget he's been given. He sees the threat of a police strike as the only way to make the government see sense.'

Maxwell shook her head. 'But to take part in a . . . a conspiracy? It's unpardonable.'

Sullivan nodded. 'I'm not trying to defend him, but you have to look at it from his perspective. He still naively believes that the strike will never actually take place and he's not doing this for himself, but for the force and the public. The tragic thing is, he's been manipulated by his own number two right from the start and he just can't see it.'

Maxwell glanced at her watch again. 'That's as maybe, but the end result will still be the same, a total breakdown of law and order. And if that happens he will carry the can for it, you can be certain of that. Now, we really do need to get things moving and first off, Richard Baseheart's disappearance must be reported so that a proper full-blooded investigation can get underway.

'Jane, I suggest you get on with that through your own department at headquarters. No need to mention the precise nature of the operation at this stage. Let's get the missing person circulation done first and then the search procedures and enquiries can start. By the time all that's underway Juliet should have obtained some sort of directive from her lords and masters.'

'And Eddie Sable?' Calder queried. 'He won't simply go away, you know.'

'I realise that, James, but regardless of what either of you may think I don't believe Sable is ready to go for the jugular vein just yet. Okay, so he's obviously been through the tapes and got hold of a lot of information, but it's all a bit piecemeal and needs putting into some sort of logical sequence. Also he desperately needs an interview to go with his story and my guess is that, despite the threats he made, he will hang on a bit longer in the hope of button-holing Richard Baseheart.'

'And when news of Richard's disappearance hits the papers, as it surely must once the misper – the missing person – enquiry gets going?' Sullivan interjected. 'What then? He'll have to go for it.'

Maxwell shook her head. 'He knows he has an exclusive on this one and he's too long in the tooth to go jumping in before he has all the facts. The only danger is that in the absence of Richard he will go all out to get hold of you instead, so you must keep out of his way at all costs.'

'He could go direct to the Commissioner, perhaps even one of the other conspirators?' Calder pointed out.

'Not before he's exhausted every other avenue. He'll want to hit them right between the eyes with solid irrefutable facts and, as he admitted to you, there are some loose ends he has to tie up.'

'So we play delaying tactics?'

She stood up suddenly. 'Exactly, James. Put him off for as long as you can and I'll try and hurry things along through Juliet. Oh yes, and I'll need the file on all of this too.'

Sullivan looked startled. 'I'm not sure that would be a good idea, ma'am.'

Maxwell flushed and her eyes glittered. 'You have no choice, young lady It's not your personal property, but evidence of a police investigation. Anyway, if I am to secure Juliet's help I'm sure she will want a damned sight more than just my word on things.'

Sullivan bit her lip, looked at Calder, then nodded. 'Of course, I just don't want us to lose it again.'

Maxwell's smile was pure ice. 'I'm not in the habit of losing files, Sergeant,' she said tightly. 'Now I'd better get going.'

Calder stared at her long legs and grinned. 'Dressed like that you're likely to get everybody going,' he remarked.

'After I've changed, I mean!' she snapped coldly. 'Be good enough to see yourselves out.'

Neither Calder or Sullivan spoke during the short drive back to his bungalow, for both were totally wrapped up in their own thoughts. When the car finally came to a halt in front of his driveway, however, Sullivan voiced the fear that was as much in the forefront of Calder's mind as it was her own. 'Something terrible has happened to Richard, hasn't it?' she said.

Calder patted her knee like a Dutch uncle. 'Let's not anticipate the worst, eh?' he replied, forcing a smile. 'Knowing that wily old bugger, he's probably lying low for some very good reason known only to himself and laughing at our antics trying to find him.'

'That's balls and you know it. Richard would never have put me through all this. He would have left a note or contacted me on my answerphone at home. Something, anyway.'

'Okay, I'm worried about him as much as you are, but I still say we should not jump to conclusions and the best way you can help him is to go back to headquarters and let your DI know he's missing.'

'We haven't a DI at the moment,' she cut in. 'He's on secondment to Interpol in Paris. That's part of the problem in the department at present. There isn't anyone I can go to.'

He scowled. 'What a bloody force this is,' he breathed. 'Half the bosses on leave, secondment or bloody courses, and the other half up to their necks in a conspiracy!' He thought a second and then added: 'Okay, then as your own governor's away in Arnhem Land or whatever, you'll have to see someone else up the ladder.'

'Superintendent McDowell is the only one who springs to mind. He's Force Liaison Officer, Specialist Squads.'

'There you are then.'

'And he's also very great with Deputy Commissioner Stephen Turner.'

'So what? Turner will have to be informed about Richard's disappearance anyway, as will the Commissioner.'

'But they'll want to know what case he was working on.'

'All right, then tell them. Turner was the one who gave Richard the assignment in the first place, if I recall. You don't have to venture beyond the original brief Turner already knows about. Neither he or Harding will be aware of Granger's involvement in the conspiracy anyway, so the fact that you and Richard were carrying out a surveillance operation on the Leader of the Opposition won't set any alarm bells jangling in their minds.'

'And when they ask to see the surveillance material?'

'You say Richard took it with him, which is what did actually happen as far as you are concerned.'

'That really is sailing close to the wind.'

He climbed out of the car and turned to stare back at her. 'So what's changed? You've been doing that ever since you first learned about the conspiracy. Maybe Richard did what he did with the best of intentions, but this affair should still have been reported to someone right at the start.'

She nodded and started the engine again. 'Okay, I'll do my level best. Wish me luck.'

He watched her car swing round in a tight U-turn

to flash back down the road with a purr of the powerful engine. Then he turned towards his driveway, rummaging in his pocket for the front door key, and it was at that moment that he heard the faint ring of his telephone.

'Calder,' he answered, bursting into the hall and snatching up the receiver breathlessly as the front door slammed back against the wall.

'James?'

'Rosy?'

'I think you'd better come down to the nick right away.'

His stomach churned. 'Trouble?'

'I've just had a call from the control room. They couldn't raise George Rhymes. Apparently he's at some community meeting re the rave festival.'

'And?' came a trifle impatiently.

'Traffic have just pulled in two young joy-riders on the by-pass. They were in possession of Richard Baseheart's Mercedes.'

'Shit! And Richard?'

'Heaven knows!'

13

The silver-grey Mercedes was parked in the large garage of the police station yard and when Calder arrived twenty minutes later, somewhat ignominiously in a local taxi, he found a small group of police officers gathered curiously around the vehicle. The car appeared to have suffered substantial front end damage, plus a set of deep score marks down one side, and Dennis Sale was already engaged in a careful examination of the driver's seat while Maxwell, now dressed smartly in a business-like blue suit and high-heeled shoes, stood to one side, watching him.

'Had to run 'em off the road, ma'am,' Sergeant Digby said ponderously. 'Little shits led us a merry chase, I can tell you.'

Maxwell nodded, but Calder totally ignored the man. He had never liked the bumptious Traffic sergeant and saw no reason to change his opinion simply because the man had been a passenger in the powerful patrol car that had managed to overhaul the teenage joy-riders.

'Where are the prisoners now, Brenda?' Sale asked the young policewoman standing in the background.

'In the cells, Sarge,' she said. 'Bit bruised, that's all.'

'I'll be interviewing them shortly,' Digby said pompously.

Calder glanced sideways at Sale and their eyes met briefly. 'That should be an enlightening experience for them,' Calder muttered dryly.

Sale straightened up, trying hard to hide his smirk. 'I think it would be best if CID did the interviewing, Donald,' he said. 'There could be more to this than just the taking of a motor, especially since the registered owner is a police officer and he can't be located.'

'Hey, come on,' Digby protested, 'this is our collar. I'm not having CID pinch it.'

Calder smiled to himself, remembering that that had been his own reaction toward Steve Torrington after the arrest of Solomon earlier on and thinking how lame and childish that sort of protest actually sounded.

'DI Torrington and his team will be taking it over and that's final,' Maxwell interjected firmly. 'You've done your bit with the original arrest, Sergeant, and a very good piece of work it was too, but we can't have an expensive Traffic mobile off the road with the crew carrying out lengthy interviews when they should be on patrol.'

Digby started to say something in reply, but thought better of it.

'Have you checked the car thoroughly?' Sale went on, oblivious to his colleague's indignation.

Digby was in the sulks and didn't answer, but Brenda James nodded. 'As far as we can without spoiling things for the Scenes of Crime boys. Boot's empty and very clean, if that's what you're worried about. No sign of any violence.'

'Pair of 'em are banged to rights as far as I can see,'

Digby grumbled. 'Don't see why we need a Scenes of Crime examination. Don't normally do it on nicked cars anymore.'

Calder threw him an angry glance. 'Where did you pick them up?' he queried.

'Saw the car first on the by-pass,' James replied. 'It was heading south towards the motorway. We chased it for about three miles to the Talisman Lane turn-off. That's where we put it in the ditch.'

'What made you think it was nicked? I gather it hasn't been reported as such.'

She laughed. 'Two little greasers in a brand new Merc?' she echoed. 'That wasn't difficult to fathom and they confirmed our suspicions by taking off at speed the second they clocked us. A Moving RO check revealed the car was registered in the name of someone called Richard Baseheart. Found out later that he's actually a headquarters SB man.'

'They had a bloody nerve taking a nicked car for a spin along the by-pass in broad daylight.'

'Not in the state they were in. Both of them were pretty spaced out on something and one had a pocket-load of weed.'

Sale grunted and slipped a piece of chewing gum into his mouth. 'And we don't yet know where they nicked the car from?' he queried.

'One of them told us in the patrol car that some guy in a local pub had offered to sell it to them for a grand and they were just doing a test run to see if they liked it.'

'It must have really taxed their brains to come up with such an original and plausible explanation as that,' Maxwell commented sarcastically.

James laughed again. 'Couple of kids, that's all,

ma'am. Just half a brain between them. But the court will no doubt believe them, same as usual.' Then she frowned and pulled a set of ignition keys from her pocket. 'Interesting thing though is they didn't have to hot-wire the car. They actually had the keys.'

Calder tensed and exchanged glances with Maxwell, but said nothing.

'What's so special about that?' Digby butted in, obviously now over his chagrin and anxious to get back into the limelight. 'People are always leaving keys in the ignition.'

Calder threw him a look of disbelief. 'Donald,' he said patiently. 'The owner of the Mercedes is a senior officer on Special Branch, the car is brand new and I happen to know it's his pride and joy. Do you honestly think he would have left the keys in the ignition?'

'So how the hell did these two tearaways manage to get hold of them in the first place?' Digby snarled. 'Answer me that, Sherlock.'

'That is exactly what we have to find out, Sergeant,' Maxwell said sharply. 'And we can do without your juvenile behaviour in the meantime. Do I make myself clear?'

Digby swallowed hard. 'Yes, ma'am,' he said in a small voice.

'Good. Then we'll leave it with you, Dennis. My compliments to DI Torrington when he deigns to put in an appearance. Sergeant Calder, a word if you please.'

Calder felt the eyes of the others staring at him curiously as he followed Maxwell to the back entrance of the police station and he made a wry face when they finally reached her office on the first floor and he closed the door behind him. 'That wasn't very clever,' he said. 'They're bound to wonder what you wanted to see me about. Tongues will be on overdrive by tonight.'

She studied him coldly. 'Canteen gossip is the least of my worries, James,' she replied, facing him across her desk and dropping her own car ignition keys on to the polished teak top. 'I'm rather more concerned about how we handle this joy-riding episode, for it puts us in one hell of a position.'

'Things are certainly beginning to look pretty dodgy, I agree.'

'Pretty dodgy?' she snorted. 'That really has to be the understatement of the week. In fact, this latest development puts a different complexion on the whole damned business. Before, any enquiry team could have regarded Richard Baseheart more or less as AWOL; a missing officer we needed to trace. Okay, so in view of his job, his disappearance would have caused more than a ripple of concern anyway and all the stops would have been pulled out to try and find him, but the team could have adopted a fairly open-minded approach. After all, people drop out of sight every day for a variety of reasons; women (or men) troubles, money matters, work pressures, even mental breakdowns. But now, with his car turning up the way it has, there is every reason to fear he has come to serious harm, maybe even become a victim of violent crime.'

'Don't you think I realise this?'

'I'm sure you do, but I hope you also realise that by keeping what we know to ourselves we are with-holding evidence and that could be seen as a criminal offence later.' She leaned back against the wall, hands resting on the radiator behind her. 'Look, we're getting deeper and deeper into this thing. By rights I should have unloaded the lot on George Rhymes, let him take responsibility for it.'

He snorted. 'Rhymes? Oh, that would be really wonderful! Why don't you just put a memo into the Commissioner and have done with it? Shit, Rosy, didn't you listen at all to what Jane Sullivan was telling you? Good old George is a key member of the bloody conspiracy. If you so much as hint at what we've found out he'll be on the blower to Turner faster than you can pull up your tights.'

'So what? From what I've heard, Richard Baseheart had already intended going straight to Turner himself.'

He shook his head impatiently. 'Yes, but that was right at the start of the business when Richard thought he might be able to put a stop to things before they really got going. I think we all agree that his original plan of action was seriously flawed and, as you yourself pointed out earlier, it's far too late to call a halt to the strike now anyway. What we can and must do though is to make sure this whole rotten affair is properly investigated, especially now Richard has so very mysteriously disappeared.'

She stared at him with narrowed eyes. 'You're not seriously suggesting his disappearance could be down to one of our conspirators?'

He shrugged. 'I don't know what to think anymore. When Jane Sullivan suggested the possibility I laughed at her. I said she'd been reading too many thriller novels, but now . . . I just don't know.'

Her face noticeably paled. 'That's the most ridiculous thing I've ever heard,' she snapped, but he could see from her expression that she didn't think anything of the sort.

'Is it?'

'Of course it is. Richard's disappearance may or may not be connected with the investigation, but certainly not in the way you're insinuating. That's totally ludicrous. It's more likely that he's lying low for some reason or that he's had an unfortunate accident in the course of his enquiries.'

'So how did those two little toe-rags get hold of his car *and* the keys?'

She frowned heavily. 'How the hell should I know? You were the last person to speak to him, it seems. Maybe something happened at that derelict building.'

'Peter's Pantry?'

She nodded and he shook his head. 'If it did, there was no sign of anything untoward when I re-visited the place with Jane Sullivan afterwards. Certainly the car was not there, so Richard must have got away all right, but as to what may have happened afterwards, that is anybody's guess.'

'But according to Sullivan he never kept his appointment with Stephen Turner at headquarters.'

'So Turner's secretary told her.'

'Which means Turner and the rest of the conspirators would have known nothing about the surveillance material he had in his possession and therefore would have had no reason to see him as any sort of threat to them.'

He raised his hands, palms upwards in a deprecating gesture. 'Okay, okay, whatever you like, but spilling the beans to George Rhymes would still be a pointless exercise. It won't help us to actually find Richard and it could be downright harmful to the major enquiry that will eventually have to be undertaken.'

'I wish you'd never told me about this damned

affair, James,' she said heavily. 'It puts me right on the spot and no mistake.'

He grunted. 'Well, if you haven't got the balls to stay with it, Jane and I will just have to do the necessary on our own then.'

'Women don't have balls, James,' she pointed out tartly. 'Those particular encumbrances are reserved for the male gender. And don't talk like a fool. I have no intention of walking away from my responsibilities. But nothing says I have to like them.'

She smoothed her skirt and picked up a leather handbag from the desk, glancing quickly at her watch. 'Look, it's time I was calling on Juliet. This car business has already delayed me for far too long. I'll see you later tonight when you're back on duty.' She studied him for a moment, concern evident on her face. 'In the meantime, don't you think you should get some sleep? You look a bit grey around the gills and I'm assuming you haven't been to bed since yesterday morning.'

He provided the ghost of a smile. 'I'll manage. Probably get a couple of hours on the sofa this afternoon.'

She glanced at her watch again, apparently unconvinced.

'Well, you haven't got much time left. I'll drop you off at home on my way to Juliet's if you like.'

He shook his head firmly. 'Thanks anyway. Got to try and get my motor going first.'

She frowned. 'You'll never do it and get some sleep in as well. Don't forget, the strike is supposed to take place tonight. You'll need all your wits about you for that.'

'I said I'll manage,' he retorted irritably. 'Now just leave it, will you?'

She pushed past him into the corridor. 'Suit yourself,' she snapped tight-lipped. 'Just don't fall asleep on the job, that's all.'

'Don't worry,' he called after her as she clattered down the stairs. 'I'll have Inspector Maybe to hold my hand and that's enough to keep anyone awake!'

Calder found that the task of fixing his car was a lot more onerous and time-consuming than he had anticipated. The ancient battery was actually cracked and encrusted with a combination of gunk and congealed acid which had formed a virtual lava flow down one side and collected on the metal plate underneath in a hard sediment, while the terminal screws were so heavily rusted that he thought at first they were immovable. It was a wonder the thing had even carried on working for so long and he vowed that in future he would take a little more interest in car maintenance than he had up until now.

Twice losing flesh from his hands when his screwdriver slipped, he struggled for almost half an hour before he managed to unscrew the terminal connections and wrench the battery from the plate to which it had become almost fused. Borrowing the spare CID car he then had to drive halfway across the town to the tyre, battery and exhaust centre to pick up a replacement, only to find himself on the end of a roasting from the shift inspector, Janet Moore, when he got back because uniform had needed the car for a local pre-arranged surveillance job.

By the time he had cleaned the battery plate and fitted the new battery he had dirt and grease up to his elbows, battery acid in the cuts to his hands and a far from charitable outlook on life in general. In fact, he was in no mood for conversation with anyone and just wanted to get home, take a shower and grab some sleep before the long night shift began. But Fate had other ideas and he had only just closed the bonnet lid with much greater force than was needed when the powerful brand new Volvo estate pulled up alongside and a voice hailed him through the open window.

'Giving it the kiss of life then, Jim?'

Jerking round belligerently Calder saw Steve Torrington staring at him from behind the wheel. 'Get stuffed, sir,' he responded, eyeing the flashy metallic blue car with undisguised envy.

Torrington switched off and climbed out. 'No need to be rude, Jim,' he replied. 'Only being conversational.'

'Well, I'm not in the mood for conversation, if you don't mind,' Calder retorted and ducking into his own car tried the engine, some of his bad temper evaporating when it started first time.

'Perhaps you should buy yourself a new one,' Torrington went on. 'Nice little BM sports or something.'

'Maybe I would if I was a rich DI,' Calder said dryly, 'but seeing as I'm a skint woodentop, I think I'll stick to this one.'

Leaving his engine running he leaned back against the driver's door, wiping his hands on an already oily rag and eyeing the detective critically.

Torrington looked even more ill than when they had last crossed swords in the custody office. His normally dark complexion was now almost grey, his eyes exhibiting a weary haunted expression and seeming to have sunk deeper into his thin face so that the cheekbones had gained an unhealthy prominence.

'You look awful,' Calder observed.

The other sighed. 'Thanks. A bit of friendly re-assurance always goes a long way. You don't exactly look the picture of health yourself. We're both obviously working too hard.'

Calder nodded towards the back of the police station. 'So, how are you doing with Solomon and his cohorts? Any coughs yet?'

Torrington shook his head. 'He's a hard nut to crack and we found absolutely zilch when we searched the place he's supposed to be renting in Riverside. As for the other two, they're just small-fry pushers who don't seem to know anything about anything.'

'And the stuff we found on them?'

He shrugged 'Still waiting for the Lab.'

'Bugger it! I thought we had made special arrange-ments for the festival so that analysis jobs could be speeded up?'

'We did, but the Lab's inundated with work at present and they've only got so many staff to do the business. We'll just have to be patient, that's all.'

'Until we run out of time and Solomon simply walks.'.

'Oh, I don't think there's any fear of that. We've got enough to hold him on for a while.'

'So what about Drug Squad? Have you let them in yet? Herbie Fuller is pretty desperate and by rights they should have been involved at the start.'

Torrington scowled. 'Sod Drug Squad. I'm more interested in Solomon's involvement in the festival stabbing than in some bloody dope-dealing job.'

Calder also scowled, his own personal resentment over the way Torrington had taken the arrest off him once more surfacing with a vengeance. 'You're doing this all wrong, Steve . . .' he began, but the detective cut him short.

'Don't push it, Jim,' he rapped. 'I'm in no mood for bloody debates.'

'You won't have any choice if this thing goes pear-shaped. I'm surprised Custody aren't squealing their heads off by now, especially if no solicitor's been allowed in yet.'

'Don't worry, they've been burning my ears already, but the boss has given authority for Solomon to be kept incommunicado for the present and we still have a bit of time before we need to ask for extended detention.'

Calder started. 'George Rhymes has actually consented to denying him access to a solicitor? That must be a first. On what grounds?'

Torrington smiled thinly. 'Serious arrestable offence, Jim, and I'm surprised you are worried about such things. Thinking of taking up the bar when you retire, eh?'

'I'm just curious as to how you managed it.'

Another shrug. 'Nothing startling about that. As I explained when you first brought your three bodies in, Solomon is believed to have been Dubois' accomplice when she did the stabbing and he was almost certainly responsible for the subsequent disposal of the knife. The boss quite rightly accepted my argument that we needed to search the scum-bag's house for the weapon as well as to interview three other toe-rags who had been staying there at the time. Obviously, as a practical copper himself, he appreciated that to do this properly we needed to be sure word wouldn't get out in advance – like through a bent brief, for example. Perfectly reasonable request and quite legal in fact.'

Calder slowly shook his head. 'You really are a jammy bugger, aren't you?' he breathed. 'I reckon if you fell into a cess-pit you'd still come up smelling of roses. But even you can't keep a solicitor away indefinitely.'

Torrington looked at his watch. 'True, but we still have a couple more enquiries to make and George Rhymes has too much on his plate already re the impending strike to be worrying too much about the so-called rights of someone like Solomon who hasn't even asked for a brief in the first place. I'm pretty sure we'll be able to stretch things out a bit longer anyway'

'And the other two irks?'

'Oh they're long gone.'

'Long gone? Long gone where?'

'Chucked 'em out on police bail, pending the results of the Lab analysis.'

Calder swore. 'Oh that's just great! I hope you're not expecting to see them again, because there's no way they'll turn up on the bail date.'

Torrington's eyes roved absently round the yard as if he were suddenly bored with the conversation. 'I'm really not interested one way or the other, Jim, and we had no power to keep them in any longer anyway.' His voice trailed off as his gaze fastened on the Scenes of Crime officer examining the boot lid of the Mercedes parked in the open garage, and he visibly started. 'Hey, what the hell's Richard Baseheart's car doing in here?'

Calder straightened up and stared in the same

direction, raising his eyebrows in surprise. 'You mean you don't know?'

'How could I? I've only just come in.'

'Well, it seems that a couple of joy-riders were nicked by Traffic driving the thing down the by-pass this afternoon. They hadn't even bothered to change the plates.'

'The bastards. Where did they nick it from?'

'We don't know yet. Dennis Sale is dealing with the job so you'd better speak to him.'

'But where's Richard?'

Calder shrugged. 'That's the problem. We don't know. He seems to have completely vanished.'

Torrington's jaw dropped. 'Vanished? What the hell do you mean vanished?'

'Simply that. He can't be located either at headquarters or at home.'

The detective gave a low whistle. 'I don't like the sound of that.'

'Nor does anyone else. And Rosy Maxwell has instructed Traffic that you will be dealing with the case.'

'Quite right, too.' He turned on his heel. 'Then I'd better get on with it, hadn't I?'

'Yeah, you do that,' Calder murmured, staring after the CID man as he strode purposefully towards the back door of the police station. 'I hope you get further than we have!'

Something was bugging Calder as he drove slowly home, something his mental antenna had picked up along the way which he couldn't quite put his finger on. He was pretty sure it was connected with Base-heart's car – the circumstances of its recovery perhaps or a comment someone had made about it – but his mind refused to give up the information and the more he tried to focus on the issue the deeper it sank into the black pool of his subconscious.

In the end he had no choice but to admit defeat and by then he was actually turning into his own road and had more important things to think about anyway.

A white Peugeot estate was parked directly outside his bungalow and his heart sank when he got closer and saw the portly man in the lime-green suit and white casual shoes sitting on the low boundary wall like some flamboyant garden gnome.

'Jimbo, dear boy,' Eddie Sable hailed him, quickly wriggling off his perch and crossing the brown lawn to the car as Calder swung into the driveway. 'Thought you'd be home soon to don the old kit for the night's fun and games.'

Calder yanked savagely on the handbrake, as if seeking to wrench it from its mountings, and stared at the tubby journalist through his open window with undisguised hostility. 'I've told you before to stop calling me Jimbo,' he grated, switching off the engine 'And how the hell did you get hold of my home address?'

Sable stepped nimbly to one side to avoid being hit by the door as it was flung wide open with exactly that intention. 'All things are known to the press, dear boy,' he replied smugly without answering the question.

'In that case, you've no need to hound me,' Calder retorted, pushing past him and striding towards the front door. 'You can find out all the information you want on your own.'

Sable hurried after him. 'You said you would contact me by three o'clock, James,' he said reprovingly, 'so what about it? We had a deal, remember?'

Calder slipped his key in the door. 'No, you had the deal, not me,' he corrected over his shoulder. 'I've got nothing to say to you. Okay? So why don't you just creep back under your bloody stone?'

Sable made an irritable clucking noise with his tongue. 'Now that sort of abusive attitude won't help you or your force out of this mess, you know.'

Halfway through the door, Calder turned on him angrily. 'Sod the force and sod you too!' he snarled. 'Now piss off before I lose my rag completely!'

Sable was unmoved by the outburst and stood on the doorstep with one foot pressed cheekily against the door. 'I gather Richard Baseheart's still missing then?' he said innocently.

Calder's narrowed eyes jerked from the offending foot, which he had been about to stamp on heavily, to Sable's watchful face. 'What do you know about that?' he breathed, his anger beginning to subside as intense curiosity took over.

The journalist shrugged. 'Word gets round, dear boy, and not everyone is as reticent as yourself, particularly if the . . . er . . . return is worthwhile.'

Calder noticed that the elderly woman spraying her roses in the garden next door was staring over the fence, obviously intrigued by the colourful appearance and effeminate mannerisms of his visitor. Sable was certainly doing wonders for his reputation with the neighbours. He quickly opened the door wide. 'You'd better come in,' he snapped, 'but only for a minute. I'm about done in and I must get my head down.'

The moment he had shown Sable into the lounge

he turned on him. 'So you've been told all about the misper enquiry, have you?'

The journalist beamed and, inserting his hand in his pocket, produced a crumpled sheet of paper which he held up in front of him. 'Got a copy of the actual message, dear boy.'

Even from where he stood Calder recognised the printed format of a missing person circulation. Jane Sullivan must have moved really fast to get that pushed out so soon and the fact that it bore the easily recognisable endorsement in bold block capitals, indicating that it was for police eyes only, hadn't stopped someone breaching confidentiality and making use of a photo-copier to earn a quick buck.

'All looks pretty sinister to me,' Sable went on, 'especially as I hear that you have now also recovered the man's Mercedes car in possession of two young tearaways. This affair is getting more interesting by the hour.'

His disclosure that he knew about the car as well came as only a slight surprise to Calder, for he was fast losing the capacity to be surprised by anything the wily little journalist managed to discover, but he was unable to mask the resentment he felt over the man's undoubted investigative skills. 'If you know so much about everything,' he said sarcastically, 'including the fact that I couldn't arrange a meet between you and Richard Baseheart even if I wanted to, why have you bothered to come here moaning about broken appointments?'

Sable smoothed each eyebrow in turn with one podgy finger. 'Well, it seems to me that if Richard can't be traced, his oppo', Jane Sullivan, might be amenable to a little chat instead. I thought perhaps you could set something up. For old-time's sake and all that. I assume you know her quite well?'

'Not a chance.'

A deep sigh. 'I could, of course, ring the Special Branch office at your headquarters and speak to her myself.'

Calder shook his head. 'The switchboard wouldn't put you through to SB and if it was that easy you'd have done it by now anyway.'

Sable frowned. 'How very astute of you, James. So you won't even speak to the lady for me?'

'Absolutely not and if that's why you've been camping outside my bungalow half the afternoon you've wasted your time.'

'Well it was worth a try,' the little man replied, 'and who knows, I might bump into her myself sooner or later anyway.'

'I wouldn't advise it.'

'Why? Spirited lady, is she?'

Calder waved a hand towards the door. 'Time you were leaving, Eddie,' he said grimly.

Sable didn't move. 'What if I were to tell you that I'd acquired some important new information which I am willing to trade in return for a meet with Jane Sullivan? Would that persuade you to reconsider your decision?'

'What sort of information?'

The other hesitated, tugging at one ear lobe and apparently choosing his words very carefully when he finally replied. 'My sources tell me you have a particularly rotten apple in your basket, a fifth-columnist I believe they're called in polite circles, who needs to be rooted out before irreparable damage is caused.'

Calder gave a short cynical laugh. 'Well that

certainly comes as no surprise. Judging by what's on Baseheart's tapes we have several of those.'

Sable waggled a finger demonstratively. 'Ah, but I'm not referring to the top level conspiracy, James,' he replied. 'This is something completely different which coincidentally complements what your top brass are trying to initiate with the strike, but is likely to precipitate a much more dangerous situation than they had envisaged.'

'You're talking in bloody riddles, just like someone else I know.'

'Okay, putting it quite simply, you have a close colleague who is actually working with the opposition and from what my sources tell me this may have a lot more to do with Richard Baseheart's disappearance than the political game being played out in the corridors of power.'

Calder grabbed him by the shoulder. 'What the hell do you mean by that?' he snapped.

Sable made a grimace and gently extricated himself from the other's grip, smoothing the sleeve of his jacket as he did so. 'I don't have all the details yet,' he replied. 'But I expect to get them very soon.'

'And this rotten apple you talk about, do you have a name?'

'That would be part of the trade I suggested.'

Calder shook his head firmly. 'I've told you, there will be no trade so you can forget it.'

Sable's face darkened appreciably. 'Well if that's your attitude, James, we've nothing further to discuss,' he snapped and abruptly turning on his heel he stalked from the room.

Calder went after him and caught up with him by the front door. 'You have a public duty to tell me anything you know,' he said furiously and once more grabbed him by the shoulder.

Sable shook himself free a second time and turned to face him. 'Public duty?' he retorted, with a short derisory laugh. 'Don't give me that, James, not after what your own top brass have been up to. My only duty, dear boy, is to the truth, nothing more. I don't believe in God, I don't support the system and the only Queen I have any faith in is myself. Got it?'

He produced a business card from his jacket pocket and dropped it on to the adjacent telephone table as he opened the front door and stepped out into the sunshine. 'If you change your mind, dear boy,' he said, half turning again, 'you can reach me on my mobile number.'

'I won't,' Calder snapped back, 'so don't hold your breath.'

Sable wiggled his fingers at the nosy neighbour in a calculated alternative-style wave and beamed with satisfaction when she ducked out of sight behind her roses. 'Then you'll be very sorry, James,' he warned. 'Very sorry indeed.'

'Sorry?' Calder muttered bitterly, watching the pressman as he deliberately minced his way down the path to his car. 'What's new? I've been sorry half my bloody life!'

It was well after four o'clock before Calder's head finally touched a pillow as he tried to satisfy his body's desperate need for rest, but sleep completely eluded him. With the windows of his bedroom tightly closed to exclude as much of the normal street noise as possible, the temperature soon reached a level comparable with that of one of the hot houses at Kew

Gardens, and, as he tossed and turned on a mattress sodden with his own perspiration, his over-active mind constantly tortured him with Eddie Sable's ominous revelations: 'particularly rotten apple in your basket . . . fifth-columnist . . . working with the opposition . . . to do with Richard Baseheart's dis-appearance . . .'

At one stage he did manage to doze fractionally, but then the whispered questions started inside his head: 'Who is it? Male or female? Give me a name.' Face after face floated before his mind's eye: George Rhymes, Douglas Maybe, Rosy Maxwell, even Jane Sullivan. And all of them were laughing at him because he didn't know the answer. In the end he hauled himself up into a sitting position on the edge of the bed and sat there for a moment with his head in his hands, shivering, nauseated and dripping with perspiration, before he forced himself across the room and into the shower.

Even there the voices in his head didn't let up, however, and standing under the cold invigorating jets he tried to satisfy their craving for answers by logical analysis. So who was the most likely culprit? George Rhymes was already mixed up in the top-level con-spiracy and was therefore a distinct possibility. But George on the take? No, that was out of the question. Okay, the man had thrown in his lot with the con-spirators for his own ends, but that was a different sort of thing altogether. He would never sell the service or his colleagues for monetary gain. He thought too much of his job to do that.

What about Rosy Maxwell? She was ambitious, a touch ruthless and certainly a pretty shrewd cookie. But bent? No way. He had known her too long and anyway he liked her too much to even really consider the possibility. As he thought about her he remembered how she had looked in the garden, with her long slender legs and bare midriff and despite the cold water streaming down his body he began once again to feel disquieting stirrings in his loins. With a slightly embarrassed grin he shook his head quickly to banish the provocative image.

His thoughts then turned to Douglas Maybe and his expression hardened. Now there was a candidate suitable for consideration. Maybe had always been an untrustworthy self-seeking bastard, as his own past encounters with him had shown. Torchy would be capable of anything if it feathered his own nest or protected his own interests, wouldn't he? Yeah, but there again, Calder had to admit that he didn't like the man, so he was more prepared to think ill of him than anyone else. His so-called analysis was therefore flawed by inherent prejudice.

Jane Sullivan? He frowned. Again, that didn't add up. She obviously doted on Richard, so she wouldn't do anything to hurt him and if she was on the take she would hardly have made a point of enlisting Calder's help in relation to the top-level conspiracy. Unless, of course, she had done that specifically to draw attention away from something else she was doing? Yeah, and what about the car she was driving? A brand new top of the range Rover. That must have cost her a pretty penny, so how had she managed it on an SB sergeant's pay? Easy. She paid on the never-never like everyone else and after all, she was still single and with her detective allowance and regular overtime she had to be worth a few bob.

He turned off the shower with a scowl and stepped

on to the bath towel he had laid out neatly on the tiled floor. So much for his attempt at logical analysis. It wasn't anything of the sort. He was just clutching at straws with absolutely nothing to go on at all. For all he knew, Eddie Sable could have made the whole bloody thing up to try and get an 'in' with Jane Sullivan. To hell with it.

Drying himself off more vigorously than was really necessary, he slipped on his dressing-gown and stomped to the lounge. Attracted by the sunlight glittering on the bottles in his glass-fronted cocktail cabinet, he was on the point of succumbing to weakness and pouring himself a stiff whisky when he was saved by the bell. The hall telephone rang.

'Yeah?' he snapped into the receiver.

'Jim? It's me, Jane Sullivan. I'm still at headquarters. Are you in a position to talk?'

He grunted. 'More to the point, are you?'

'Yes, I'm on one of our secure SB 'phones, but I can't be long. Turner wants to see me in a few minutes and there's a bloody war going on up here. The place is on its head.'

'Was that before or after you got your misper circulation out? I've just seen it.' He smiled wryly. 'Bit surprised you included Eddie Sable in the distribution though.'

'Included who? Oh bloody hell, no. He hasn't seen it, has he?'

''Fraid so. We've got a leak down here somewhere . . . and worse.'

'Worse? What do you mean worse?'

He cleared his throat. 'Something Eddie Sable said. Tell you when I see you. Watch yourself though; he's got you targeted for interview.'

There was a strained silence for a moment and then she blurted. 'Is it true they've found Richard's car?'

He sighed, guessing that that was her real reason for ringing. 'Yeah. In possession of a couple of joy-riders. But no sign of Richard. Steve Torrington and his team are working on them at the moment.'

'It looks pretty bad, doesn't it?'

He didn't answer her. It didn't just look bad, it had to be bad now but, knowing how close she was to the SB man, he didn't want to upset her any more than she obviously was already.

'What are these two like?' she went on, apparently oblivious to the fact that he hadn't answered her previous question.

'The joy-riders, you mean? Haven't seen 'em myself, but from all accounts just a couple of kids. Hardly trained killers anyway.'

Silence and he broke it. 'You okay?'

A faint sob and then a snuffle, and he heard her clear her throat. 'I'll . . . I'll be fine.'

'What's going on up there?'

A long trembling sigh. 'Oh, Harding and Turner have been closeted now for over two hours with Willy Justice and the NPU reps.'

He pricked up his ears. 'Breakthrough likely then?'

There was a grim laugh. 'Hardly. When I said there was a war on up here, I meant it. Keeping my head down.'

'So why does Turner want to see you? Any chance he suspects we know?'

'Difficult to say. He's a strange character, creepy actually. But I don't think so. He's probably just going through the motions because one of his senior staff is missing.'

'Be careful.'

'Oh, I'm being that all right. Any news from your girlfriend?'

He grinned. The mischievous dig was a good sign. It showed she hadn't lost her sense of humour in spite of everything that had happened. 'Nothing as yet. Actually she thinks you are my girlfriend.'

'More like your daughter,' she retorted, then broke off suddenly. 'Got to go, Jim,' she said softly but urgently. 'Being paged. Catch you at the nick sometime tonight.' Then the line went dead.

Calder returned the receiver to its cradle and stared out through the hall window for a few moments. He felt a great almost overwhelming sense of frustration. No, not just frustration, inadequacy. He seemed to be nothing more than a passenger or observer in this bloody awful business. Seeing things happen, but being powerless to do anything about them. Yet at the end of the day he knew only too well that he was likely to be called to account for everything in just the same way as the conspirators themselves. He had been sucked in, tainted, and now all he could do was wait for the axe to fall. It was so unfair, but that was what life was like and he couldn't help ruefully calling to mind the well-worn job phrase he had used on Taffy Jones : 'If you can't stand a joke, you shouldn't have joined!'

14

The boards were going up on the shop windows everywhere and people seemed to be heading homeward at a much faster pace than usual. There was tension in the still sultry air, a sense of barely repressed panic that was spreading like an invisible cloud through the town, heavy and infectious.

Calder's face was grim as he drove to work along the emptying streets listening to the radio bleating out its doom-laden news bulletin. Commissioner John Harding had refused to meet the demands of the National Police Union, it said, and the Prime Minister had ruled out any kind of government intervention, curtly dismissing the suggestion from one backbencher in the House that troops should be used to break the deadlock.

The feared police walk-out was therefore expected to take place from ten o'clock that night unless a last minute agreement could be reached and NPU headquarters had warned that any attempt to supply mutual aid from other forces would result in an all-out national police strike. Intransigence was the popular word being used by all parties as each spokesman laid the blame for any resultant catastrophe on the other, but, while the verbal battles raged and the public bolted for home, the clocks ticked inexorably towards zero hour and the battening-down city had no choice but to hold its breath.

The little tobacconists on the corner of Commercial Street and Imperial Road was one of the few shops that still appeared to be open and, conscious of the fact that he was almost out of cigarettes, Calder finally turned off the radio and pulled up on a set of double yellow lines outside. The people streaming past paid hardly any attention to him and as he approached the shop a couple of skinheads – a tall thin boy with a purple Mohican hair-style and a girl with brilliant green hair and a silver spike through her nostrils – held the door open for him as they left. Calder smiled to himself, heartened by their unexpected courtesy and the fact that you could never judge by appearances.

'Ah, Sergeant Calder,' the bearded Sikh behind the counter greeted him, his face unusually grave.

'You'd better give us three packets of twenty, Singh,' Calder replied with grim humour. 'Going by the rest of the traders, it looks as though we're in for a siege.'

Singh Baines nodded and placed the packets in front of him, his expression cold and unfriendly. Calder raised his eyebrows. He had known the man for years, right back to when he was on the Crime Squad, and this sort of reception was unprecedented. 'You're very serious tonight,' he encouraged, digging out his wallet and handing over a couple of notes.

Singh operated the till and gave him his change without saying a word. Calder frowned. 'Something up, Singh?' he queried. 'Have I developed BO or what?'

'It's not you, Sergeant,' another voice joined in. 'It's what is happening in the town.'

Calder turned his head and nodded towards the plump sari-clad woman who had entered the shop through a curtain. 'Evening, Mrs. Baines.' he said. 'You mean the strike, don't you?'

She nodded. 'How can the police desert us like this?' she said, her anger surfacing. 'Who will we call when the young thugs break into our shop and attack us?'

Calder's face hardened. He felt embarrassed and ashamed. 'I . . . I'm sorry, Mrs. Baines,' he replied hesitantly. 'I don't agree with it either, but a lot of my colleagues feel very angry and let down.'

She shook her head firmly. 'They have no right to do this,' she exclaimed. 'We have always respected the police, but how can we trust them after they do this thing?'

Calder nodded. 'Rest assured, we won't all be striking, Mrs. Baines,' he said quietly, 'and I for one expect to be working as usual tonight.'

Her husband snorted, his eyes glittering behind his silver-framed spectacles. 'And you will be able to protect the whole town on your own, will you, Sergeant?' he said. 'Listen to them already.'

But Calder could already hear the shouts outside and, turning to stare through the glass front door, he saw a group of youths walking slowly past. They were only in their early teens, but they looked quite formidable in their tight jeans and heavy army-style boots.

'Kill the wogs, kill the wogs,' they chanted over and over again, stabbing their fingers at the shop front and then laughing uproariously.

'It's only empty air, Singh,' Calder said reassuringly. 'They're only kids.'

'Kids?' his irate wife exclaimed. 'Those kids can still loot and burn, Sergeant, and those kids and others like them will have the town to themselves once your brave colleagues turn their backs on us.'

Calder knew she was right and that it was an argument he couldn't win. He felt helpless and disgusted and, grabbing his cigarettes, he nodded to both of them as he turned towards the door. 'I . . . I'll call by myself during the night just to make sure you're okay,' he said. 'That's a promise.'

The woman's anger subsided and she sighed. 'I know you will, Sergeant Calder,' she said quietly, 'but in the meantime, we have to defend ourselves, yes?'

Calder wasn't surprised to see the heavy machete her husband raised from behind the counter and he refrained from coming out with the usual empty platitudes about not taking the law into your own hands, simply because he knew that after ten o'clock that night they would have no other option. But that didn't stop him feeling sick to the stomach when he left the shop and drove away, for he knew that the reaction of the frightened couple he had just left almost certainly mirrored that of the rest of the normally law-abiding population. Anarchy was just around the corner unless someone in a position of influence or authority decided to come to their senses. But if he needed anything to dash his hopes of a possible move in that direction, he got it when he turned into the service road at the back of the police station and found Willy Justice and a couple of his cronies from the NPU Regional Executive Committee, dressed in their police uniforms, already in place by the entrance to the yard.

To be fair, the trio were not yet trying to turn anyone away, but they had placed 'A' boards on the pavement on either side of the ramp announcing the imminent strike and were handing out leaflets to everyone going through. A two to three car queue had built up in front of Calder and he sounded his horn impatiently as he drew up.

'You seem keen to get to work, Jim,' Willy Justice boomed in through his open window when it was his turn to get the hard sell.

'It's sergeant to you,' Calder snapped. 'Now get out of my way before I run over your foot.'

Justice stepped back slightly and scowled. 'This is an official picket, *Sergeant*,' he retorted. 'We have a perfect right to be here.'

'Not until ten o'clock, you haven't.'

The big man smirked. 'We are merely putting our case to the comrades,' he replied.

Calder snorted. 'Comrades?' he echoed. 'Where do you think you are? Moscow's Red Square?'

The scowl returned to the other's bearded face. 'You won't think it's so funny later tonight when you haven't got any shift to supervise,' he sneered.

'No,' Calder said savagely. 'Neither will the people of Hardingham whom we've all sworn to protect and your rabble of a union want to use as cannon fodder. Now shift your fat arse before I get really angry.'

The union chairman moved aside only just in time, for the next second the car leaped forward with a screech of tyres, one of the wing mirrors catching his sleeve in the process and drawing a succession of curses from him as he bent down to retrieve the pile of leaflets he had dropped. Calder smiled with grim satisfaction as he swung into a vacant parking space and switched off, but his smile soon faded when he saw that he had parked next to an unpleasantly familiar blue Renault car. So, contrary to the consensus of opinion among his colleagues, Inspector Maybe had actually turned in on the night of the strike after all. Obviously Rosy's powers of persuasion had been too damned good by far which meant that the next twelve hours were likely to be even more of a penance than he had feared.

Already stressed up to the eye-balls and irritable through lack of sleep, the thought of Maybe breathing down his neck during what promised to be one of the most gruelling shifts of his service soured his mood even more and he completely ignored the polite greetings of the officers he passed en route to the sergeants' office. He could think only of getting the parade briefing over and done with as quickly as possible so that he could be out on the street before his inspector had a chance of rubbing him up the wrong way.

In fact, he was so fixed on his purpose that he even passed the Superintendent in the corridor without speaking and only pulled up when Rhymes barked at him. 'Sergeant, I'm talking to you!'

He stopped short and turned, his face reddening. Out of the corner of his eye he saw Inspector Maybe standing in the doorway of his office which Rhymes had apparently just left, a smirk on his face. 'Sorry, sir,' he muttered. 'I was miles away.'

Rhymes looked him up and down. 'I believe we discussed this apparent deafness of yours when you last visited my office, Sergeant,' he said sarcastically, 'and you made a similar excuse on that occasion. I wasn't aware that your sight was failing as well though.'

'I can only repeat my apology, sir,' Calder replied tightly. 'It won't happen again.'

Rhymes grunted and studied him with a perplexed frown. 'Are you okay, man?' he said in a quieter tone. 'You look ghastly.'

Calder forced a smile. So do you, George, he thought. You look as though you've aged ten years. Your conscience must be giving you hell at the moment, you poor stupid bastard. 'I'm fine, sir,' he replied. 'Not much sleep, that's all.'

The other nodded. 'Well, the way things are going you will only be doing four hours tonight anyway so you'll be able to catch up, won't you?'

Calder met his gaze steadily. 'I won't be joining the strike, sir,' he said. 'I shall be working on as normal.'

Rhymes nodded again. 'I would have expected nothing less from you,' he replied, a strange gleam in his eyes.

Surprisingly, he looked and sounded almost pleased with the answer and Calder couldn't help feeling a measure of sympathy for him. The damned fool didn't agree with the strike any more than he did. Even though Rhymes had allowed himself to be pressured by Turner into doing all he could to make it happen, in a perverse sort of way his better self secretly hoped the union's call would be ignored, despite the fact that it would probably mean he'd lose his one chance of an extension of service as a result.

'I'll be at home if you need me, Douglas,' Rhymes continued, staring over Calder's shoulder, 'but Chief

Inspector Maxwell will be on duty later and will keep me informed of developments.' He glanced at Calder again. 'Have a good night, James.'

'Oh, I'm sure I'll have that,' Calder murmured as the other strode off down the corridor. 'It's guaranteed.'

Then he turned sharply as Inspector Maybe made an impatient noise at his elbow. 'Mr. Rhymes feels we should keep any officers who decide to remain on duty after ten o'clock inside the station,' he said. 'Answer emergency calls only, that sort of strategy. It's for their own safety and we won't have the capacity to patrol the streets in the normal fashion anyway.'

Calder's mouth closed tightly and he threw him a contemptuous glance, knowing full well that for once it wasn't simply their safety that concerned old George. It was the need to demonstrate to his mentors that he was doing his bit to prevent the impact of the strike being damaged by a few stubborn well-meaning officers who were determined to carry on working anyway. 'Is that right, sir?' he said aloud. 'And no doubt you'll be setting your usual fine example for us all to follow?'

Maybe's face darkened appreciably. 'Just do it, Sergeant. Never mind the wisecracks,' he snapped, turning back to his office. 'And be here at ten. Understand?' Then the door slammed with a force that echoed for several seconds down the corridor.

Tom Lester met him in the doorway of the sergeants' office. 'What the hell was all that about?' he exclaimed.

Calder shrugged. 'Just Torchy throwing his toys out of the pram,' he said with a crooked grin. 'He'll probably sulk all night now.'

Lester shook his head and turned back into the office.

'You really do like chancing your arm, don't you, Jim?' he said. 'One of these days you'll go too far and really be in the shit.'

Calder's burst of cynical laughter made him jump and he stared at him in consternation. 'Have you been drinking?' he queried sharply.

Calder, still chuckling, clapped him on the arm. 'Tom, I think you're priceless,' he said.

The other grabbed his anorak from the back of his chair with a grunt, but made no immediate move for the door. 'Well, I'm glad you're in such fine humour,' he said grimly, 'because you'll need all of it in the next few hours.' He tapped a sheet of paper on his desk. 'Area beat intelligence, via the LIO, suggests major public disorder tonight. Rumour control has already been working overtime in the town and all sorts of stories are circulating.'

'Yeah,' Calder cut in, his face now very serious. 'I saw the shop windows being boarded up on the way in.'

Lester nodded and continued. 'Well, there's quite a bit of evidence to back up what's being said. A member of the public reported seeing gangs of yobs in a couple of vans carting away bricks and rubble from a building site in Ganges Road. There's also been a daylight raid on Moore's Outdoor Shop. You know, the place that sells the ex-Army kit and survival stuff? Apparently three or four masked thugs cleared the shop of knives, crowbars and pickaxe handles and gave Terry Moore, who's in his sixties, a thorough beating for trying to stop them. Then we've had a raid on the local dairy.'

'The dairy?'

'Yep. Sounds like the same two vans seen on the building site. They got away with quite a few crates of empty milk bottles.'

Calder fell in. 'Petrol bombs!'

'Exactly. Looks bad, I can tell you. These are not just isolated incidents either. They're part of an overall plan; the whole thing is being organised, Jim. The LIO has already been on to Criminal Intelligence and they believe an anarchist group is behind it all which spells real trouble.'

'Yeah, well at least with my bust of that nutter, Solomon, last night one of the main trouble-makers is under lock and key which should spoil some of their fun.'

'Not anymore he isn't.'

Calder started and his eyes narrowed. 'What do you mean?' he grated.

Lester made a grimace and sighed. 'He's off on his toes.'

'What? How the hell did that happen?'

Lester sighed. 'Steve Torrington went to re-interview him about two and a half hours ago and found him crouched on the floor of the toilet, apparently vomiting blood.' He shrugged. 'Les Moon in Custody called an ambulance and we packed him off to Hardingham General Hospital.'

'And then he just walked, I suppose?'

'Not exactly. We sent an escort with him, one of my best lads, Jamie Scott, but a few of Solomon's friends called by and were all over the youngster before he knew what was happening. Jamie looks as though he's been hit by the Eurostar Express and he's now on the sick.'

'And Solomon obviously made a miraculous recovery?'

'According to the Casualty doctor, who also got a good-hiding when he tried to intervene, your man demonstrated the agility of an antelope.'

Calder shook his head in despair. 'I just can't believe all this. Twice we've had that bastard in and twice he's got out. He seems to have the luck of the Devil.'

Lester nodded awkwardly. 'We've combed the town from end to end, of course. I've had everyone on it and we've sent out the usual alerts and circulations, but he seems to have vanished off the face of the earth.'

'I bet he'll reappear tonight,' Calder replied grimly.

Lester sighed. 'Sorry about this, Jim. No one is more upset about it than me, I can tell you. My governor's already torn my head off and I expect Douglas Maybe is loving every minute of our bad luck. But to be fair, no one could have foreseen this kind of thing happening in a month of Sundays.'

Calder ignored his apology and cruelly refrained from making any reply that would have eased his misery. 'What I can't understand is how Solomon's friends knew he was at the hospital,' he said, 'especially so soon after he'd been taken there. He's had no contact with the outside world since I nicked him, so how the hell could anyone have found out about it?'

'Dennis Sale reckons he must have someone on the inside.'

Calder made a grimace, but remembering Eddie Sable's earlier 'rotten apple' warning he didn't waste his breath making phoney indignation noises and simply let Lester carry on.

'Seems incredible, I know, but there you are. Anyway, Steve Torrington's been jumping up and down like a kid who's lost a new toy, so he's obviously the best man to look into the whys and wherefores of the thing.'

Calder's anger over the escape was abruptly tempered by a sense of vindictive pleasure at the thought of Torrington's chagrin, but it didn't lessen his hostility towards Lester. 'Yeah, well I've still got the problem of finding Solomon again,' he snapped, then glanced at his watch. 'So why don't you foxtrot-oscar and let me get on with it, eh?'

Unusually, his colleague still seemed in no hurry to disappear, but propping himself on the corner of the desk with his anorak crushed into a ball in his lap he stared at him as if anxious to say something, but feeling unsure of how it would be received. 'Jim, this strike . . .' he began.

Calder held up one hand to cut him off, making a noise like a leaking steam valve. 'Forget it, Tom,' he warned. 'I'm not striking and that's that. I don't want to discuss it anymore.'

The other gave a short exasperated sigh. 'Look, I've already told you what's in the wind. The whole town is set to explode tonight and even if some of your shift do decide to stay on you'll never have enough bobbies to deal with the sort of disorder you can expect. Furthermore, how are you going to operate when the control room closes down as well? Ted Appleby, the control room inspector, has already reported in sick, Sergeant Wilf Grey, his number two, is a hundred percent behind the strike and from what I hear, none of the civvies manning the radios are prepared to stab their police colleagues in the back by working on either.'

'So what am I supposed to do, eh? Just walk away from everything? Leave the town to burn?' Lester started to interject, but Calder went on before he could say anything. 'I called in at a tobacconists en route to work tonight and you know what? I felt bloody well ashamed to be wearing this uniform. After all the years I've served with this outfit I was actually ashamed to be a copper! Those people were frightened to death, Tom; terrified about what is likely to happen to them tonight.'

Lester's mouth tightened. 'That's not your problem, Jim. This strike is down to the government and the Commissioner. They're responsible for everything that happens, not us. We're only fighting for our rights.'

Calder erupted. 'Bollocks, Tom. That's just a cop-out and deep down you know it. It's the sort of humbug the IRA come out with when they blow up a shop and kill a dozen innocent civilians. Not their fault, oh no, it's down to the government for not giving in to them.'

Lester swore angrily. 'You can't compare us with a bunch of bloody terrorists, Jim. We're not going round killing people.'

'Maybe not directly, but it could amount to the same thing if we walk out on them tonight.'

Another exasperated sigh and Lester straightened up and headed for the door. 'Suit yourself then,' he muttered. 'As I've said before, it's your bloody funeral.'

Calder stared after him grimly. 'If things go pear-shaped tonight, it could be everyone's!' he retorted.

Briefing was a tense sombre affair, lacking any sort of vitality or humour, everyone busy with their own individual anxieties and unwilling to share them with anyone else. Several familiar faces were missing too. Apart from Taffy Jones, Daphne Young and Maurice Stone, who Calder already knew about, two others were now absent as well: Baldev Singh (Two-Six) and Eddie Talbot (Three-Four). 'Reported in sick,' Grandad announced with a cynical grin. 'More likely taken the easy way out,' Calder growled, disappointed with the pair of them.

It was not all bad news, however. On the plus side a number of specials, the three involved in the arrest of Solomon, together with their Section Officer, George Darby, and Special Constable Dick Weaver, had turned out to make up the numbers and for that he was grateful, but he wondered how long they would last when Willy Justice and his rabble really started to pile on the aggravation. Dealing with street violence was one thing, an accepted part of the job, but defying an official picket line was quite another, especially as many of the specials were themselves members of professional trade unions in their own full-time jobs and scabs were a particularly despised species. As for the regulars, there was no telling how many of them would remain on duty after ten o'clock, possibly none, which meant that he and Inspector Maybe could well end up having the station to themselves. A far from pleasing prospect.

As if to emphasise the point, there was another memo from Maybe lying on his desk when he returned to his office, once again tersely reminding him about his mountain of virtually untouched paperwork. Poor old Torchy, he mused. The man seemed to be living in a world of his own, untouched and uninfluenced by events around him. He was the type who would still be issuing memos about paperwork from the safety of his office when the town was a looted burning shell and the police station was under siege from mobs of rioters.

Screwing up the small note and tossing it into the wastepaper bin in disgust, Calder quickly kitted up and marched off down the corridor, the keys of the supervision car swinging in one hand. Whether Maybe liked it or not he had far more important priorities to attend to than clearing up an over-full in-tray and foremost of these had to be tracking down Solomon.

Even as he drove out of the police station yard, however, he knew he had set himself a near impossible task. Hardingham was not a small place and his quarry was hardly likely to risk walking boldly down the street, but would have gone to ground somewhere, to remain hidden until well after dark. Nevertheless, he had to make the effort, if only for his own peace of mind, and with his face set in a tired but determined mask and his sore gritty eyes probing every alleyway and doorway, he began a slow tour of the town, mentally willing Solomon to show himself.

As he drove he became even more conscious than on his way into work of the tension that hung like a miasma in the still air and the tangible signs of public unease were in far greater evidence too. Though only just after half-past six the pavements were almost clear of pedestrians and traffic was down to a mere trickle. True, a few people stood at bus stops and the taxi rank by the railway station still looked to be doing a brisk trade, but overall, with its emptying streets, closed boarded-up shops and deserted car parks,

Hardingam had the air of abandonment usually associated with some strife-torn Third World city waiting for the revolutionary army to march in.

Even the police radio system seemed traumatised and twice Calder called up Control, ostensibly for a situation update, but in reality to reassure himself that they were still there. It was far too quiet. At this time on a Friday night the town should have been humming, things should have been happening, especially as the rave festival was still in full swing. But, apart from a couple of minor traffic accidents and one or two shop alarms being triggered off by careless staff closing up, there was nothing, just a continuing exodus of people from the town and that unmistakable sense of apprehension in the heavy humid air that told him big trouble was brewing.

In desperation, after half-an-hour's fruitless cruising, he arranged a rendezvous with Porter-Nash and Jenny Major and had them join him for a thorough search of both Wharf Cottages and Solomon's rented flat in Riverside. But there was no trace of the anarchist. The row of derelicts was deserted, even the winos weren't at home, and after a brief argument over right of entry without a warrant, Riverside was found to contain just three shivering, bedraggled junkies suffering withdrawal symptoms and anxious to administer their next fix.

Parting company with his two colleagues, Calder finally paid a visit to the police post adjacent to the rave festival site. He was relieved to find that their Control had already received the circulation about Solomon and had passed out the details to all the officers on the ground, including Drug Squad.

'Mind you,' commented the thin bearded sergeant

manning the custom-built portakabin, ' I don't know what use that information will be after ten o'clock tonight, for there's likely to be no one here to do anything about it anyway.'

Calder lit himself a cigarette and leaned against the small radio console which connected the police post to festival control. 'So you're all going to walk out at the stroke of ten as well then?' he said. 'Doesn't that worry you?'

The other shrugged. 'Commissioner's brought it on himself,' he replied, popping a piece of chewing gum into his mouth. 'Not our fault.'

Calder nodded slowly. 'Yeah, they said much the same thing at Nuremberg,' he retorted, then broke off with a curse as a sudden blast of sound shook the portakabin from end to end and sent him straight to the window.

The festival site was only about three hundred yards away and the powerful amplifiers, which had just that second erupted in a screeching thudding cacophony to signify the resumption of the day's festivities after an apparent lull, not only impacted painfully on the eardrums, but made themselves felt as a persistent throbbing vibration through the ground itself. Crowds of weirdly dressed youngsters moved constantly in and out of the wide gateway which gave access to the vast fenced enclosure, their progress monitored by groups of uniformed private security guards who in reality could do little but watch, while the field outside was a jumbled mass of vehicles, tents, caravans and sleeping bags through which hundreds of other festival-goers moved like a constantly ebbing and flowing tide.

'How the hell do you put up with that row?' Calder

326

shouted, grimacing horribly as he made for the door.

The other sergeant grinned. 'Pardon?' he shouted back. 'I can't hear you above that row!'

Calder noticed that the sun was much lower on the horizon and the shadows were already beginning to lengthen as he climbed into the supervision car and headed back along the rutted track leading to the main road. Glancing quickly at his watch, he saw with a start that it was already almost nine o'clock. Soon it would be dark and then all hell would break loose, he was sure of it.

His stomach churned. He had to admit it, he was frightened to death at the thought of what might happen. He knew only too well what a rampaging mob could do, he'd seen enough of them in his service, but this was going to be different; a lot worse. At least on those other occasions it had been possible to call on all the physical and technical support the force had at its disposal, whilst he had been a mere minion, obeying orders and following the decisions someone else had made on a much higher rung of the ladder. Tonight there would be no back-up and it would all be down to him and a handful of officers at most. From past experience he knew he couldn't rely on Inspector Maybe while George Rhymes was already compromised. Though that still left Rosy Maxwell, it was likely she wouldn't even get back from her errand to her friend Juliet's in time. What a bloody situation.

The now shadowy streets were completely empty as he drove through the town centre and the only vehicles he met seemed to be police cars carrying out a last tour of inspection before heading back to the nick to comply with Maybe's instructions. Hardingham had become a ghost town.

Solomon was pushed to the back of his mind as he pulled up outside the tobacconists owned by Singh Baines. The shop, like its neighbours, was heavily boarded up, but there was a glimmer of light in the window of the flat above. He knocked several times before he saw a face appear at the window and a couple of minutes later the front door opened.

'Hello, Singh. Just checking on you as I promised,' Calder said, eyeing the machete in his hand.

The other nodded. 'Thank you, Sergeant,' he replied. 'But it is too quiet I think.'

Calder turned to stare up and down the empty street. 'Just keep your door locked and if there is any trouble I'll try and get someone to you as soon as I can,' he said.

Singh glanced briefly behind him at the sound of sobbing in the darkness of the shop. 'My wife,' he explained, slowly closing the door on him. 'She is very frightened.'

'Aren't we all?' Calder muttered as he turned back to his car.

The union pickets were out in force when Calder drove into the police station yard behind another area car and a loud cheer went up to acknowledge their return. It will be a different story when we have to drive out again, he mused, nodding to Porter-Nash and Grandad as he headed for the back door.

It was only a quarter to ten, but already everyone else was back in the briefing room, mugs of tea in their hands as they sat at the long table or drifted aimlessly round the large room, tense and silent. Calder nodded to them curtly, but only stayed long enough to make sure he had a full complement. There were a couple of other things he had to do first.

His first port of call was Rosy Maxwell's office on the next floor. He desperately needed to find out about the result of her meeting with her Home Office friend, Juliet, but he was disappointed. The office was in darkness and it was apparent from the tidy state of the desk and the empty out-tray that she hadn't been back since they had last spoken.

Mouthing a silent curse he left the office and carefully closed the door behind him. But instead of returning to the stairs he went in the opposite direction, heading towards the CID office and the distinctive smell of fried food which wafted tantalisingly along the corridor and set his taste-buds going.

He found Dennis Sale sitting at his desk finishing off a greasy looking bag of fish and chips. Propping himself on one corner Calder helped himself to a chip and made a face as he swallowed it. 'Ugh, bloody thing's cold,' he complained.

Dennis grinned. 'Must be the one I tried and spat out,' he replied with his mouth full.

Calder tore open a new packet of cigarettes and flicked one on to the table in front of the CID man. Sale scowled, then picking it up, dropped it into the congealed mass of left-overs and tossed the lot into the adjacent wastepaper bin.

'You know I've given that up, you bastard,' he said, gulping down the remains of his coffee and scowling even more as Calder lit up and gently released a puff of smoke in his direction.

'Sorry, Dennis, I forgot,' he replied. 'So how're we getting on with our two joy-riders?'

Sale sat back in his chair, his powerful stubby fingers clasped over his large stomach and his eyes studying Calder suspiciously. 'And why should you want to know that?'

Calder shrugged. 'Curious, that's all. ' He hesitated. 'And I'm also worried about Richard.'

Sale nodded. 'We all are. Apparently, the Deputy Commissioner has appointed a detective super', chap named Morris from the NCS, to oversee the enquiry. He should be joining us tomorrow morning. Know him, do you? Steve Torrington says he thinks he's new.'

Calder frowned, then shook his head slowly. 'Must be. Never heard of him. So there'll be an incident room on this one then?'

'Got to be really. Vanishing SB chief inspectors aren't that common.'

'And what are our little toe-rags saying?'

'Well, they've ditched their original story anyway. They claim they were given the keys to the car by a tall blond guy with glasses and told to get rid of it in the reservoir. Got fifty quid for their trouble. Then when they collected it they got to thinking that it was too good to dump, so they hid it in some woods at Bickstone. They intended taking it to a ringer they knew up north as soon as the police strike started and there was less chance of being stopped.'

'So how come they were actually caught driving the car south on the by-pass in broad daylight?'

'Usual thing. They bought some pot with their fifty quid, got high and decided to go for a spin. End of story.'

'And you believe them?'

Sale thought a moment, then nodded definitely. 'I reckon so. After all, why should they lie? They're banged to rights for nicking the car anyway.'

'Yeah, but not for murder.'

Sale stared at him, taken aback by his directness in naming what was on both their minds. He shook his head again. 'No, not these two. Not the type. They're scared shitless and now that the weed has worn off they're feeling too bloody rotten to make up stories anyway.' He grinned again. 'Shouldn't really have been interviewing them in the first place, but at least we got that out of them before the DI put the mockers on the thing.'

Calder raised his eyebrows. 'Steve stopped it?'

'No choice really, what with this detective super' en route and Janice Lawson jumping up and down about us interviewing unfit prisoners. You know PACE as well as I do.'

'And where did they pick the car up from? Do we know yet?'

Sale grunted. 'Wondered when you'd ask that. A derelict factory somewhere local apparently. We think it's over near the council tip, but neither of the kids were able to be more specific. They hail from Manchester apparently and were only down here for the festival.'

Calder's mouth suddenly felt very dry. Peter's Pantry was close to the council tip. Okay, so there were a number of other derelict properties down there too, but it seemed too much of a coincidence. The place had to be the old bakery, but if that were the case it suggested Richard had never left there at all. This opened up a whole new can of worms, especially as the building itself had already been thoroughly searched without any trace being found of him.

He felt Sale's eyes studying him intently and took

a grip on himself. 'And you haven't run them out there to try and pinpoint the premises?'

'We did think about that, but it's too late now. Even without PACE we'd have a problem with the police surgeon. He's examined the little shits and instructed that they must be allowed a proper period of rest. Apparently they're in poor physical shape after their ordeal and need time to recover!'

Calder grimaced. 'And Steve Torrington is actually happy with all of this?'

Sale snorted disparagingly. 'Steve Torrington doesn't seem happy with anything lately. He's been in a sour mood most of the week and uniform's loss of this character, Solomon, hasn't improved him, I can tell you. I don't know what's got into him. Maybe he's working too many hours, I dunno.'

Calder had more important things on his mind than the behavioural problems of a detective inspector, but he nodded anyway. 'Yeah,' he agreed absently. 'I thought he'd been a bit stressed out the last couple of days. Look, Dennis, I'd better get on. See you later, eh?'

Sale belched and rubbed his stomach as Calder stood up. 'Bloody fries,' he growled. 'I never seem to learn. Oh by the way, Jim.'

Calder made an irritable grimace and half-turned in the doorway.

'Yes, Dennis.'

'There's one other piece of information you may be interested in. I was waiting for Steve Torrington to come back, so we could decide what to do about it.'

'So, what is it?'

'I don't know whether I should tell you before I speak to Steve.'

Calder grasped the door frame loosely with both hands as he leaned his forehead against it, his eyes half closed in a gesture of frustration. He was well used to Sale's love of the dramatic which invariably involved saving the best morsels until last, but the detective also liked to stretch things out a bit and he had neither the time nor the inclination to play games. 'Why don't you just tell me, Dennis?' he said like someone humouring a small boy. 'Before dawn would be nice.'

The other belched again, then winced. 'Yeah, well when your mate, Solomon, did his amateur dramatic bit in the nick one of our little joy-riders was being escorted back to his cell after a spell in the exercise yard.'

'So?'

'He apparently clocked Solomon as he was being carted away on a stretcher by the ambulance crew.'

'And?'

The big man looked troubled. 'He's since fingered him as the blond guy who paid for Richard Baseheart's car to be dumped in the reservoir!'

Calder slowly straightened up and turned right round to face him. 'Say that again,' he breathed.

Sale's eyes met his and locked on. 'Looks like we find Solomon and we find where he dumped Richard . . . and why,' he said grimly.

Calder was in a partial daze as he made his way back down the corridor, deeply shaken by what Dennis Sale had told him. It was all too clear now what was most likely to have happened. Richard had been feuding with Solomon for so long that the two had obviously become bitter enemies. What better opportunity would the anarchist have had to settle old scores and to finish his enemy off for good than when Calder had left the SB man alone at Peter's Pantry after their rendezvous? It was very likely that Solomon frequented the area. Riverside, where he had his flat, was just a stone's throw away and during his earlier search of Peter's Pantry Calder had found enough evidence in one of the upstairs rooms to indicate that junkies used the place on a regular basis. What if the blond giant had been skulking around with his addict friends in the shadows of the building at the time of the rendezvous and had caught Richard off guard when he was on his own? It would have been easy for someone of Solomon's powerful build and violent nature to have overpowered a person like Richard and, after disposing of his body, the anarchist would certainly have wanted to get rid of the last bit of incriminating evidence, the SB man's Mercedes car. What better way of doing that than using two hop-heads for the job, knowing they needed money to buy their bloody fixes and wouldn't ask any questions?

Then abruptly Calder stopped dead, his mind teased and stimulated by his initial hypothesising now fully activated and propelling him off on another even more horrifying tack. What if Solomon's presence in Peter's Pantry at the critical time hadn't been co-incidental? What if someone in the know had told him Richard would be there? Someone who actually worked in the nick and who had perhaps seen the note Baseheart had left Calder and which he himself had not only carelessly forgotten to destroy, but had actually left in his drawer for anyone to read? His expression hardened. Yeah, and who was most likely to have raided his drawer? The same person who regularly went through his tray and left stupid notes. The same person who had had Solomon released the first time he was arrested. Inspector Douglas Maybe! 'You have a particularly rotten apple in your basket.' Eddie Sable's warning flashed through his brain like the flame of an acetylene torch. Douglas Maybe. It had to be him.

Without at first realising it Calder found himself on the ground floor again and, taking a deep breath, he made his way to the briefing room. He couldn't afford to let his suspicions show. He had to give Maybe more rope and that meant trying to carry on as normal. One other thing he had to do, however, and pretty soon, was to return to Peter's Pantry to carry out an even more thorough search. That wouldn't be easy on this night of all nights, especially with Maybe himself breathing down his neck the whole time.

Where the hell was Rosy, he asked himself? Guzzling bloody cocktails with her Home Office buddy while the nick fell apart? Come on, girl, he mused, get your arse back here before it's too late. Yeah, and what about Jane Sullivan? She'd said she would be over, but she still had not put in an appearance. Suddenly he felt very much alone.

His spirits got an unexpected lift when he stepped through the briefing room door, however, for, as his eyes roved slowly round the room, he noted that all the officers he had started with at six o'clock had stayed on duty. Not one of them had joined the strike. Even the specials were still there, white-faced, uneasy, but still there. Furthermore, two additional uniformed figures were sitting together at the end of the long table, two he had certainly not expected to see for a few more days at least.

'Evening, Sarge,' Daphne Young said with a grin, the heavy bruising on her face showing as pigment-like patches under the heavy make-up she had applied to disguise her injuries. Maurice Stone merely gave him a brief smile, then looked down at the table top.

Calder forced a scowl. 'What the hell are you two doing here?' he growled.

'Thought we'd join the fun and games tonight,' Young replied, meeting his stare with characteristic defiance.

'Well you can't,' he snapped, though he was unable to conceal the gleam of pride in his eyes. 'You're supposed to be sick and Maurice is on compassionate leave.'

Young tossed her head and glanced sideways at Stone. 'Is there anything wrong with you, Mauri?' she said. 'I can't see it.'

Stone now grinned broadly. 'Nothing wrong with me, Daphne,' he replied.

Young shrugged. 'Me neither,' she said. 'So there you are, Sarge. Both fit as fiddles.'

Calder nodded. 'What about your wife, Maurice?' he said, studying the big man carefully. 'She needs you at the moment.'

The other shook his head stubbornly. 'She's okay now, Sarge. Honest. Come to terms with it and all that. Anyway, my sister, Maureen, is with her.'

Calder stared at each of them in turn, then sighed heavily. 'Okay, okay,' he said. 'I'm too tired to argue, but,' and he waggled a finger in Young's direction, 'you are not going out on the street, Daphne, and that's final. Not in your physical condition. We can make good use of you in the control room.'

She pouted, started to say something, then changed her mind and grinned. 'Deal, Sarge,' she agreed.

Calder nodded again. 'But I do appreciate the pair of you turning out,' he said gruffly, strangely embarrassed by the unexpected show of loyalty. Then, staring round the room, he went on: 'And thanks to the rest of you for staying with it. I just hope you've picked the right side to be on.'

'It's the only side to be on, Sarge,' Jenny Major replied quietly and there was a murmur of agreement from the rest. 'But I must admit, I think we're on a hiding to nothing.'

As she spoke what sounded like a small stone clattered against one of the briefing room windows and the chant of 'Scab, scab, scab' filled the air from outside. It was ten-thirty.

15

Jenny Major's 'hiding to nothing' began at precisely ten-forty and Calder received the first call personally when he paid a visit to the control room with Daphne Young to check the staff situation.

Phil Davies was alone in the large air-conditioned, sound-proofed communication suite on the top floor. A lonely figure crouched over the only console that was manned in the midst of a clinical grey vastness of computer work-stations, radio and telephone equipment and television monitors; a grey vastness that emitted a continuous low hum and smelled of nothing but new carpets and warm plastic.

'Bravo-Alpha-Sierra One-Zero?' Davies was speaking quietly into the sensitive headset microphone that gave him access to both the radio and telephone communication systems, unaware of the faint clunk of the main door opening behind him as Calder let himself in with his security card. 'Sergeant Calder, are you receiving?'

'Yeah, I'm receiving,' Calder snapped at his elbow. 'Nice to see you still in the chair, Phil.'

Davies half-turned, not surprised and unimpressed by the other's sudden appearance. 'That was festival control,' he said grimly, tapping the relevant box on the computerised touch-screen to end the call. 'Two thirds of the personnel down there have walked off the job. The rest have had to lock themselves inside the control room building for their own safety and most of the site's own private security staff have joined them there. All hell's broken loose at the ground apparently: fights, fires and wholesale looting.'

'So it's started,' Calder said quietly.

'Oh, it's started all right,' Davies agreed, reaching towards the touch-screen to answer another incoming call, 'and festival control say it won't be long before the mobs hit the town centre. Some trouble-makers are apparently already heading our way.'

'What's the state of play elsewhere in the region? Have you heard?'

Davies shrugged, his hand poised over the screen. 'Same as here. Some on, some off. On the other half of the area Gratling nick only has seven working. Inspector's covering one of the area cars there, I'm told.'

Calder grunted, thinking of Inspector Maybe. Some hope of that here, he mused! Then aloud, he said: 'Yeah, but no one else has got a bloody rave festival, have they?'

Davies grinned and touched the screen. 'All part of life's rich tapestry, Sarge,' he replied, then to the caller: 'Hardingham Police. Can I help you?'

Calder watched him intently as he spoke to the person at the other end of the line, conscious of the fact that the whole screen was alight with flashing boxes indicating waiting calls. Without being told, Young made her way to the adjacent console and settled herself into the chair, donning the headset lying on the table top and plugging herself into the system.

'Yes, ma'am, we'll get someone over there as soon as we can . . . Yes, the force is officially on strike, but we are still maintaining emergency cover.'

Calder nodded approvingly. Good old Phil. No senseless point-scoring against the strikers. Instead, making the best of an appalling public relations *faux pas* and loyally trying to project the sort of caring professional image that the community had a right to expect of its police service.

'Yobs breaking into cars, East Street Multi-Storey, Sarge,' Davies explained over his shoulder. 'Who have you got downstairs to send?'

'Use Two-Eight,' Calder replied promptly and waited as he passed out the message on the radio.

Then as Davies reached forward to answer another incoming call he thrust a piece of paper under his nose. 'For your information, I've double-crewed three area cars, as per this new postings sheet,' he said quickly, 'and they will operate as Two-Zero, Two-Two and Two-Four. In view of the deteriorating situation out there I've taken the old GP Transit off the road completely and you'll now have two of our three protected PSU Transits, Two-Seven and Two-Eight. You'd have had Two-Nine as well if it hadn't been borrowed for the festival.'

'No foot patrols then?' Davies interjected.

Calder shook his head firmly. 'Too risky,' he replied. 'I don't even like using the area cars on the streets tonight because they're so vulnerable, but we need to show the flag as much as possible.' He nodded towards the console now occupied by Daphne Young. 'I'm leaving Daphne in here to give you a hand. She is control room trained and can at least take the incoming 'phone calls off you.'

Davies glanced at the young policewoman and nodded his thanks.

'That's a big help anyway,' he commented. 'So what's the strategy?'

'How about bluff?' Calder retorted with a grimace. 'It's all we've bloody-well got left.'

The control room man grinned and raising a hand in acknowledgement was almost immediately back in his own world. 'Police emergency. Can I help you? Yes, sir, we are on strike, but . . .'

Calder missed the rest of the conversation, for he had already turned and left the control room, but he only just reached the top of the stairs before his radio pack-set blasted. 'All available units, with the exception of Two-Eight, start making town centre. ABAs activating at several premises, Lower High Street. Details to follow. Keyholders being informed.'

As Davies acknowledged the responses Calder ran down the corridor to his office, stopping briefly in the doorway when he saw Jane Sullivan sitting at his desk, dressed in a skimpy black T-shirt and blue jeans.

'Jim,' she exclaimed. 'We've got to talk.'

'Then it will have to be in the car,' he said breathlessly, listening to the radio now pumping out information on the location of the alarm activations as he kitted up. 'World War III is just about starting out there.'

She nodded and jumping to her feet followed him back out of the door. 'We have to make another search of Peter's Pantry,' she continued, almost running to keep up with him as he strode quickly along the corridor.

'I know,' he threw over his shoulder. 'But not right at this moment, that's for sure.'

He glimpsed a figure descending the stairs to his

right and broke off, grabbing her arm and virtually propelling her through the doorway on the left as Inspector Maybe's voice called out sharply. 'Sergeant, where is everyone going? I thought I instructed . . .' But Calder had already disappeared in Sullivan's wake and they were through the door into the yard before Maybe had a chance to finish his sentence.

The scene outside was one of absolute pandemonium. Uniformed figures shouted to each other above a cacophony of blaring radios, revving engines and screeching tyres as they dodged among manoeuvring vehicles, pulling doors open and scrambling aboard even when the wheels had actually begun to roll. At the same time other vehicles raced across the yard towards the exit, slowing only briefly to edge their way through the shouting placard-waving crowd of pickets, who tried desperately to turn them back, then streaking off into the street with blue lights flashing and sirens screaming their defiance.

Calder and Sullivan were the last to leave some way behind the rest of the convoy and when they reached the exit, the pickets, growing bolder when faced with just one vehicle, crowded the arched tunnel-like opening, pushing against the car bonnet as Calder tried to move forward. Willy Justice's bearded face appeared at the driver's door, his big hands holding on to the wing mirror as he shouted something at Calder through the open window and the chant of 'Scab, scab, scab' was deafening and strangely unnerving in the confined space. Finally, the sheer weight of numbers and the risk of actually running over someone forced Calder to stop, but as a cheer went up from the crowd he forced his door open, trapping Justice against the wall, and grabbing the union chairman by the front of his shirt, held him up against the brickwork. At once the crowd fell silent, while invisible press cameras flashed repeatedly.

'If you ever get in my way again,' Calder snarled, 'I'll drive right over you, you great fat blather of lard!' Then, releasing him and running his gaze over the crowd gathered round his vehicle, most of whom were actually dressed in police uniform, he shook his head in disgust. 'You're a disgrace to the service,' he shouted. 'No better than the yobs out there who are trying to tear the town apart. I hope you can live with your consciences afterwards, that's all!'

'Bravo, James,' a familiar voice called and he glimpsed Eddie Sable, with a microphone held high in one hand, pushing his way to the front of the crowd accompanied by a man with a video camera on his shoulder.

Muttering an oath, he jumped back into his seat and slammed the car door. Then, quickly engaging first gear, he edged forward again. This time the crowd, with a general embarrassed shuffling of feet and a lowering of gazes, parted to let him drive on, but Sable managed to get to the front passenger door and grabbing the handle half opened it, stumbling along beside the slow-moving vehicle while Sullivan held on to the door arm-rest for all she was worth.

'Jane Sullivan?' the tenacious little man shouted through the open window and tried to push his microphone through while his colleague hobbled backwards just in front of the car, filming the struggle with evident glee. 'Is it true you are investigating . . .'

Sullivan managed to wind the window up with her other hand, almost trapping his microphone in the process, and as Sable jumped back, releasing the door, she slammed it shut properly, snapping down the lock. The next moment, narrowly missing the video man and half-blinded by a battery of flashing camera bulbs, they were clear of the crowd and had turned right in the narrow street outside the entrance, then right again on to the main road.

'That was damned close,' Sullivan gasped, falling back into the seat and fastening her seat-belt as Calder accelerated hard down the long drag towards the distant but clearly audible clangour of alarm bells in the town centre. 'We'll probably be on the tele' tonight or in tomorrow's papers.'

'Yeah,' he growled, 'Celebrities of the week.' He gave her a brief sideways glance. 'How'd you get on with Turner?'

She took a deep breath. 'As I expected, he wanted to know what Richard was dealing with when he went missing, so I just told him about the surveillance on Granger, nothing more. He wasn't very pleased when I said Richard still had the case file though, or that I had no information on the actual progress of the investigation.'

'D'ye think he suspected anything else?' he queried, swinging out to overtake a small black van and scanning the occupants briefly as he raced past.

'From the way he spoke I don't think he had an inkling of Granger's involvement in the conspiracy which means Richard couldn't have got to him at all.'

'He didn't,' he snapped back, speaking much quicker now as they drew closer to the town centre and the sound of the activated burglar alarms became more strident. 'Spoke to Dennis Sale tonight. Seems our two joy-riders picked up Richard's car from

Peter's Pantry and were paid to dispose of it by some character called Solomon.'

'Solomon?' she gasped, stiffening in her seat. 'Did you say Solomon? Surely not after all this time?'

'You know him then?'

'Know him?' she breathed. 'For a time he was almost part of my life. Richard was always trying to nail him, operation after operation, but he never got lucky.' Her voice trailed off and he could actually hear the anxiety in her voice when she continued. 'Jim, if that evil bastard has had anything to do with his disappearance . . .'

'Now don't go jumping to conclusions,' he cut in, making a clumsy attempt at reassurance. 'Wait until we've had another chance of searching that derelict and pulling Solomon in again.'

'Again? What do you mean by again?'

He made an irritable hissing noise. 'Had him in on drugs charges last night. Then bloody day-turn let him escape.'

'Escape? What, Solomon? You're joking! But . . . but how the hell did that happen?'

'Long story,' he replied grimly. 'But rest assured I'm working on it.'

She frowned, surprised and irritated by his peremptory dismissal of the issue and determined to get some answers to the questions that were piling up on the end of her tongue. Before she could pursue things any further, however, all conversation was halted by a large stone which suddenly crashed into the windscreen and bounced off into the night.

With an oath Calder swerved instinctively towards the pavement, mounted the kerb edge and crashed back on to the road, narrowly missing a lamp standard.

Another stone followed, this time smashing into the rear wing, and as he came to a halt he glimpsed a small group of youths running off down a side-street opposite.

'You okay?' he queried, once more throwing Sullivan a swift glance.

She laughed shakily, for the moment all thought of what they had been discussing pushed to the back of her mind. 'Just about, but I'm glad the windscreen held. Aren't we going after them?'

He shook his head and, pulling away from the kerb, listened with half an ear to the radio as Control acknowledged that Two-Eight had now resumed patrol from the East Street Multi-storey car park commitment which had apparently been a malicious call. 'No chance. That was too obvious a come-on. Chase after them and we'd find a whole army waiting for us down there.'

He drove round a cast-iron council wastebin which had apparently been torn from its concrete base and thrown into the middle of the road, then, on the approach to the High Street roundabout, swung hard left to miss the traffic bollards which had also been ripped from the ground and were now spread halfway across the junction in a still flickering tangle of electric wiring and dismembered plastic.

Beyond the hump of the roundabout Lower High Street was illuminated by pulsing blue light and as they negotiated a lethal obstacle-course of broken glass and other debris strewn over the road encircling the big green island, they saw one of the police Transits (Bravo-Alpha Two-Seven), parked at an angle in the middle of Hardingham's main shopping thoroughfare. Just a few yards further up the road two stationary area cars were clearly visible, each slued round at a crazy angle to the pavement with both front doors wide open. The headlights and roof beacons of all three vehicles had been left on and uniformed figures ran in and out of the shop doorways, torch beams probing the shadows.

The street itself was littered with pieces of broken wooden panelling, obviously torn from the shop windows, and the pavements were covered in broken glass which glittered coldly in the headlights of the vehicles. This, coupled with the deafening blast of multiple burglar alarms, provided an immediate testimony to the looting that had been interrupted only seconds before.

As they pulled up a third area car drove slowly towards them from the opposite end of the High Street, a flashlight scanning the shop fronts and alleyways from the front passenger window. Threading its way carefully between the other parked police vehicles it stopped alongside them.

'Bastards made off as we arrived,' Terry Watson shouted above the din created by the alarm bells. 'Obviously didn't expect any of us to turn up tonight in view of the strike.'

'And we certainly saw 'em off,' Gerry Stoddard joined in, leaning across from the front passenger seat. 'You ought to have seen 'em run, Sarge.'

'They'll be back.' Calder retorted, then broke off and turned up the volume of his pack-set as Control began calling again.

'Any mobile available to attend Chandler's Off-Licence, East Parade? Reported ram-raid in progress . . . Thank you Two-Eight . . . Five-One, CID also attending.'

There was the crash of gears and, even as Gerry

Stoddard reached for the remote microphone of his radio, Terry Watson was already sending his car screeching back the way they had come, mounting the pavement in reverse, pausing fractionally, then streaking off down the High Street like a rocket.

'Bloody mad-brain,' Calder exclaimed and, seeing the uniformed figures now also piling aboard the Transit, he jumped out into the roadway and grabbed the door of the big wagon before it could drive away. 'Just hold it right there,' he yelled at Dave Judd and raced round to the other side of the vehicle, waving his arms at one of the area cars in the act of trying to execute a U-turn over the pavement. He had already lost the second area car which had careered off down the High Street in the wake of Terry Watson's car as if trying to break through the sound barrier.

'What's up, Sarge?' Porter-Nash shouted through the front passenger window.

Calder scowled and glanced briefly at Dave Judd, who had left his vehicle and was now standing behind him, impatiently fidgeting from one foot to the other. 'You and the Transit will stay here until the key-holders have secured these premises and re-set their alarms,' he snapped. 'Then you're to remain in the High Street area unless specifically directed elsewhere by Control. Understand?'

'But, Sarge . . .' Judd protested.

'Sarge, nothing!' Calder rapped, turning on him angrily. 'I won't have this shift tearing all over the town like some ill-disciplined rabble, chasing shadows. That's exactly what the yobs want us to do and we're not falling for it.'

As if to back him up the radio barked again. 'Thank you, X-ray One-Four. All units attending

Chandlers, cancel. Premises in order. Malicious call.'

Judd noticeably relaxed. 'Sorry, Sarge,' he said with a sheepish grin and waved a hand at the still open back doors of the Transit. 'Come on you lot. We've been had.'

As the specials manning the vehicle clambered out Calder pressed the transmit button of his radio microphone. 'Bravo-Alpha-Sierra One-Zero to Control. Advise all units to resume patrol of areas designated at briefing. I have instructed Two-Seven and Two-Four to remain in Lower High Street until premises have been secured. I suspect our capability is being tested by the opposition so we must provide maximum visibility.'

Phil Davies acknowledged and passed out the instruction immediately, but that wasn't the end of the issue by any means, for within minutes, before Calder managed to return to his car, the radio was off again. 'Bravo-Alpha-Sierra One-Zero?'

'Go ahead, Phil.'

'This isn't Phil, Sergeant,' the voice blasted back. 'This is Inspector Maybe. 'All officers, except the two units in Lower High Street, will return to this station to await my instructions. There will be none of these provocative patrols. We will adhere to a response-only strategy. Is that clear?'

Reaching his car, Calder slumped back into the, driving seat and closed his eyes tightly for a second, mentally counting to ten while Sullivan shook her head in disbelief. 'Provocative patrols? What the hell's he talking about?' she exclaimed. 'The man's a complete idiot!'

'Tell me about it,' Calder replied grimly, 'and he's

now told every yobo within a few yards of a police radio that we're all going home.'

For a moment he massaged the small plastic remote microphone clipped to his shirt with one hand, considering his reply. Then abruptly he pressed the transmit button. 'One-Zero to Control,' he said in a carefully controlled voice. 'It is absolutely vital that we maintain a visible uniformed presence in the town to deter attacks on shop premises.'

The response was like a whiplash. 'Sergeant Calder, you will comply with my instructions to the letter. I will decide what is or is not vital. Return to the station immediately. That is an order!'

A couple of cars edged past them along the High Street, stopping close to the opposite kerb just beyond the Transit and several figures with cameras soon appeared in front of the smashed shop windows, flashes going in quick succession.

'Bloody press are everywhere,' Calder growled. 'They're going to have a field day over all this.'

'Bravo-Alpha-Sierra One-Zero,' the radio barked again. 'Acknowledge last instruction.'

Wearily he reached for the transmit button.

'What are you going to do?' Sullivan exclaimed. 'We have to check out that derelict.'

'What the hell can I do?' he retorted. 'He's the boss tonight.'

But Calder turned out to be wrong about that and before he could respond the radio was acknowledging another call. 'Received Bravo-Sierra Two. Will comply. Confirm your ETA two-zero minutes.'

A brief pause before Phil Davies was broadcasting another message and even the normally unemotional Welshman could not conceal the glee in his voice. 'All units disregard last instruction. Repeat, disregard. High visibility patrols to be maintained until further notice. Did you receive, Sierra One-Zero?'

Calder's face split into a broad grin of delight, his weariness falling away from him like an old skin as he quickly acknowledged the message then turned towards Sullivan. 'Rosy's on her way back,' he practically chortled, hammering the steering wheel with both hands. 'And she's stuffed poor old Torchy even before she arrives!'

'Thank heavens for that,' Sullivan replied. 'But before you gloat too much, I suggest you get moving. We've got unwelcome company.'

Calder had hardly noticed the white Peugeot estate drawing up alongside the Transit, blocking the road ahead completely, but the sight of Eddie Sable and his side-kick with the video camera now hurrying towards them galvanised him into immediate action.

Doing a Terry Watson-style departure, he reversed the car back to the roundabout, heedless of the broken glass from the shop windows crunching under the tyres or the tell-tale smell of burning oil coming from the engine. Then, skidding to a halt with the offside wheels close to the green island, he slammed the gearstick forward and powered off down Eastern Avenue towards the outskirts of the town and the by-pass.

'What was it you called that area car driver a moment ago?' Sullivan exclaimed, gripping the edges of her seat with both hands. 'Mad-brain, wasn't it? Talk about the pot calling the kettle black!'

Calder scowled at the reprimand, but didn't slacken his speed, his gaze repeatedly studying the rear-view mirror. 'Sometimes it pays to be a little mad,' he retorted, stiffening as he saw the headlights swing out on to Eastern Avenue about a quarter of a mile behind him. 'And seeing as Eddie Sable is now on our tail, this is one of them. Hold on to your bra-straps!'

Sullivan only noticed the side-street as he spoke and she was certain in her own mind that he would never be able to turn into it at the speed they were going. The fact that he accomplished the manoeuvre (with the sort of heavy braking that should by rights have stood the car on its nose and a voyage of discovery through the gears that produced some very interesting sounds from an incredulous box) was due more to luck than judgment. As the tyres squealed and slid on the dusty tarmac she stared in wide-eyed horror at the furniture store which seemed to be coming right at them. Then at the very last moment, with something akin to the start of a victory roll, the car managed to straighten up and she saw the large plate-glass window bristling with settees and armchairs leap away into the darkness behind them as they hurtled down a straight tree-lined avenue with their lights out.

'Lost 'em!' Calder snapped, studying the rear-view mirror again and switching his lights back on. 'Now let's get this building search over and done with before something else happens.'

Sullivan wriggled her behind more securely against the back of the seat, convinced that had she not been wearing a seat-belt, she would probably have ended up in the engine compartment. 'Do the press usually have that effect on you?' she queried tartly.

He slowed down in a more conventional fashion to turn into another side-street. 'Only when they hound me at the wrong time,' he replied. 'The last thing we want is for Eddie Sable to follow us to where we're going.'

She nodded. 'I just hope you can think up a good enough excuse when your speeding ticket arrives,' she said dryly.

He threw her a quick glance, then swore.

'Oh shit! That bloody speed camera in Eastern Avenue. I forgot all about it.'

She smiled slightly. 'I shouldn't worry. Maybe they've run out of film.'

'Knowing my luck, they've just put a fresh roll in.'

She shrugged. 'That's the price of being a celebrity, Jim. Everyone wants your picture.'

Peter's Pantry looked a lot more formidable now that night had fallen and Calder was reminded of Alfred Hitchcock's original version of the horror film, *Psycho*, when the ramshackle collection of buildings first appeared in his headlights. To make matters worse, as the car bumped its way along the track from the main road, the horizon beyond the railway sidings suddenly registered flickering illumination like the flashes of distant gunfire and this was immediately followed by a low grumbling sound.

'That's all we need tonight, a damned thunderstorm,' Sullivan commented anxiously. 'This place is spooky enough as it is.'

Conscious of the incessant chatter from his radio pack-set despite the reduced volume as Control despatched mobiles to one location after another, Calder shook his head and leaned forward slightly to peer up at the sky. 'It's exactly what we need,' he replied. 'Rain's always been the bobby's best friend and a good night's downpour will send the yobos packing quicker than anything. But we had some thunder earlier in the week and it came to nothing, so I expect the same thing will happen this time.'

Swinging to the right just inside the gateway of the old bakery he parked in the spot Richard Baseheart had previously chosen for his Mercedes and switched off. Then, turning the volume of his radio right down and plugging in the hated earpiece to mute its voice to external ears, he sat for a moment staring at the dark rectangle that was the side door to the bakery itself.

The night was very still. Even the music from the rave festival, which at one time would have been audible here as much as anywhere else despite the fact that the site was on the other side of town, had ceased. After living with so much noise for so many days Calder found the silence strangely unnerving. In fact, he felt a bit like one of the early nineteenth century explorers in Africa who, on hearing the native war drums suddenly stop beating, waited for the inevitable tribal attack.

'Well, are we going in or not?' Sullivan snapped suddenly, shaking him out of his reverie.

He grunted and reached for his torch on the back seat. 'Yeah, let's get it over with,' he replied, opening his door. 'You'll find a spare torch in the glove compartment, but since you don't have a radio, make sure you stay close to me. I don't want you going missing as well.'

He could have bitten his tongue for making such an insensitive remark, but she appeared not to have noticed and a second roll of thunder, closer this time, came at just the right moment to distract her attention as they made their way across the yard.

Some sort of rodent, possibly a rat, made off in a panic when they stepped through the doorway and shone their torches round the room in which Calder had had his fateful meeting with Baseheart a seeming eternity ago. Their feet crunched on the broken glass from the smashed windows as they made their way past the storerooms and the big walk-in refrigerator to the opposite door.

Beyond, a corridor flung its arms out on either side and other doorways could be seen opening off at regular intervals. The smell of dankness and decay was very strong and from somewhere to the right the same loud plopping of water that Calder had noticed before was clearly audible in the sepulchral stillness.

'We'll check the place room by room,' he said, the hostile atmosphere of the building burrowing into his senses and prompting him to speak in little more than a whisper. 'But watch your step. It's falling apart.'

'Received, Bravo-Alpha Two-Zero,' the radio murmured through the plastic earpiece, tickling his ear mischievously, 'Confirming, malicious call? Yes, understood. Standing by.'

In the world outside the aggravation continued. How much time had they got, he wondered, before the whole thing actually blew? Not long, he was pretty sure of that and he felt more than a little guilty prowling around this empty derelict while his shift played a non-stop game of cat-and-mouse with the scum now loose on the streets. Yet he knew he had no alternative; he had to satisfy himself that the building was the empty derelict it seemed to be.

Empty? He froze and gripped Sullivan's arm tightly, motioning her to do the same, but she had already stopped and, like him, extinguished her torch. The sound had been quite distinctive, the stealthy scraping of soft-soled shoes on a gritty wooden surface. Some-one was in the building with them, someone who knew

355

they were there and was trying very hard not to give his or her presence away.

Calder's heart was pounding madly and a nerve in his left knee had gone into spasm, making his leg tremble uncontrollably. Trying to ignore the discomfort he bent close to Sullivan's ear. 'Someone's here,' he breathed. 'Could be a wino, but we can't take any chances. Stay close. Keep your torch off.'

They moved on together, the beam of Calder's torch now just a trickle of light through his closed fingers, but providing sufficient illumination for them to see their way. They came to a staircase and paused to listen once more. Train noises from the railway sidings, clanks and rumbles, but nothing else. Calder once more switched off his torch completely and whispered in Sullivan's ear. 'I think our intruder is on this floor, hiding in one of the offices. Do you fancy going up top on your own? Make a bit of noise and so forth while I wait down here?'

There was no hesitation. 'No problem,' she whispered back.

'Sing out if you need me.'

But she had already brushed past him, her feet clomping on the bare wooden stairs and her torch back on and probing the blackness of the landing above her.

She reached the upper floor and he saw the light of her torch fade. Then her footsteps could be heard on the floorboards above his head, moving from room to room. He waited, his back against one banister, his eyes probing the blackness of the corridor.

'Bravo-Alpha Two-Two?' Control called.

Wincing at the sudden noise, which though inaudible externally made him jump and served as an unwelcome distraction, he switched the pack-set off. Still no movement in the gloom around him. Patience, Jim, he mused. Just remain motionless and wait.

Sullivan's footsteps once more moved across the floor above his head, then passed to the opposite end of the building. Otherwise the silence remained unbroken. He frowned. Perhaps he had imagined the noises earlier? Maybe his nerves? But no, there it was again, soft footsteps in the gloom immediately to his left. Very slowly he turned his head to study the slightly blacker rectangle of the office doorway, his other hand reaching towards his belt to unclip his baton as he inwardly cursed the government for deciding to outlaw the small CS gas-sprays the police had once been issued with.

Silence again, then Sullivan's footsteps growing louder above his head as she returned to the head of the stairs and the very next moment sudden movement as someone emerged quickly from the doorway, a vague shape in the gloom just feet away from him, moving fast. He started forward, switching on his torch as he did so, his baton ready in his other hand.

'Hold it right there!' he yelled, but the intruder must have already been aware of his presence, for something lunged out of the mix of shadows and torchlight, slamming against his head and sending him reeling back into the banister rail in an explosion of pain. His heel caught under the lip of the bottom stair and he almost tripped over, but then regaining his balance with an effort, he stumbled forward again, trying to clear the red mist from his eyes and conscious of a sticky wetness spreading down his face into his shirt collar. He had dropped his torch and one of his eyes was now clogged with what had to be blood from the wound to his head, but he was madder than he had ever been and determined to get to grips with his mystery assailant before he managed to get away.

The next blow missed his head, but caught him on the shoulder, sending a river of fire through every muscle and sinew, and making him drop his baton and pitch sideways into the wall. Before he knew it he was down on one knee, trying to pull himself up the wall with one arm, while he peered with his one good eye at the vague outline of his assailant standing over him in the blackness, motionless and waiting.

There would have been another final blow, he was quite certain of that, one that would very likely have cracked open his skull, but at that moment footsteps hammered on the stairs behind him and the powerful beam of a torch cut through the darkness, illuminating the whole length of the corridor and transfixing his assailant with the intensity of a laser.

Calder caught the glint of rimless spectacles in a heavily bearded face and then the giant standing over him dropped the broken chair leg he was holding and, raising one hand as if to hold back the light, turned on his heels and ran, his shoulder-length blond hair swinging from side to side as his long legs pounded down the corridor.

'You okay?' Sullivan exclaimed breathlessly, helping Calder to his feet a second later.

'Did you see him?' he snarled back through clenched teeth. 'The bastard, Solomon, did you see him?'

'Yes, I saw him,' she replied, examining his head wound with the torch. 'Have you got a clean handkerchief? You've got a nasty split there.'

Calder shook her off irritably. 'Never mind that. He's getting away.'

Gently but firmly she pressed him back against the wall and reaching in her pocket produced a handkerchief of her own. 'He's long gone, James. We'd never catch him now. Let me wipe some of that blood away.'

The throaty sound of a car engine made them both start and holding her handkerchief to his head Calder stumbled back along the corridor as she ran ahead of him towards the exit.

The police car was still parked where they had left it which was a relief at any rate, but they could see a pair of very bright rear lights in the process of disappearing at speed along the track leading to the main road.

'Swine had a motor parked somewhere close by,' Calder muttered and gingerly reached for the remote microphone of his radio with his other hand, gritting his teeth against the pain in his shoulder.

Sullivan checked him. 'Waste of time,' she pointed out. 'What are you going to tell Control? We don't have a registration number and we don't even know what he's driving, apart from the fact that it looked like some sort of large van.'

He hesitated, then, nodding in resignation, turned back into the room. 'Got to get my baton and torch,' he said, slumping back against the wall, but didn't argue when she offered to do it for him.

On returning a few moments later she found him still leaning against the wall, the handkerchief pressed to his head with one hand and his other arm clasped awkwardly across his chest.

'We'd better get you to the hospital,' she said firmly. 'You'll need a jab, maybe even stitches in that wound.'

'Balls,' he retorted ungraciously. 'It looks worse than it is, just a cut, that's all.'

'How can you tell that in here? And what about your arm? I can see from the way you're holding it that you've injured that as well.'

He flexed it experimentally. "It'll be okay. Just a bit sore. I can still use it.'

'I still think you need to go to hospital.'

He ignored her, levering himself away from the wall and rubbing his injured shoulder with his other hand. 'Just what was that bastard doing in this place?' he said sharply. 'I mean, the action will be in the town centre tonight, not out here.'

She shrugged and began wandering around the room, the beam of her torch tracing an erratic course over the cracked walls and rubbish-strewn floor. 'Maybe he was holed-up here. Though when I collected your things just now I did look in the room in which he'd been hiding and there's none of the usual signs of occupation, like bedding material or anything.'

He shook his head, then winced at the pain that immediately lanced through it. 'No, I can't see that arse-hole dossing in a place like this. He was here for something else, I'm certain of it.'

She swallowed hard. 'Richard?'

He turned his head towards her in the gloom. 'Maybe, I just don't know. But whatever it was we obviously interrupted him, otherwise he would have been away before we arrived.'

'But . . . but there's absolutely nothing here. I've checked every single room upstairs and, apart from a few joints and syringes, the place is completely empty. Oh, shit!'

Her sharp exclamation gave him a sudden start.

She had stopped short in front of the big built-in refrigerator, her torch directed at her feet.

'What is it?'

For reply she bent down very slowly and picked up something from the floor. He went on to one knee beside her and ignoring both his leaking wound and the pain in his shoulder took the object from her hand like a bomb-disposal man receiving an extracted charge from an explosive device. Conscious of a sick feeling in the pit of his stomach that had nothing to do with his recent injuries, he ran his fingers over the distinctive Meerschaum pipe with its Arab's head bowl.

'It's Richard's,' she whispered. 'I'd know it anywhere.'

He straightened up, his skin crawling and the muscular tremble back in his left leg. 'Where did you find it?'

She remained in her crouched position and directed her torch at a small mound of ceiling rubble in front of the refrigerator door. 'There. It must have been sticking out from amongst that lot. I . . . I caught it with my foot.'

He slipped the pipe into his trouser pocket. 'No wonder we didn't see it before.'

He pushed past her and shone his torch on the refrigerator door behind the rubble. It was still tightly closed and padlocked, but closer inspection revealed that the padlock was not actually engaged and appeared to be broken.

'I'm sure this was intact when I came here for my rendezvous with Richard,' he said, 'and it was certainly still in place when you and I did our search later, 'though I must admit I didn't check to see if it had been tampered with.'

'Neither did I. I just assumed the 'fridge was secure.'

He grunted. 'You wouldn't have known without physically examining it anyway. The whole thing was pushed together to give the impression that it was locked. We should have checked before though and I could kick myself for not doing it.'

She shivered, then stared at him fixedly. 'So let's do it now,' she said quietly, a noticeable tremor in her voice.

He nodded, knowing that she was thinking exactly what he was thinking and that his fears as to what might lay behind the door were as nothing compared to her own. Reaching forward, he slipped the hook of the padlock free and pulled the hasp back, holding the rusted lock tightly in one hand as he gripped the big steel handle. For a moment he hesitated, glancing over his shoulder at her motionless figure.

'Do it!' she snapped and he gritted his teeth and tugged on the handle.

The refrigerator door, though heavy and badly rusted at the edges, opened easily enough, but when it did they were both forced to step back hurriedly, for the smell that rushed out at them was not just indicative of stale air, but of something far worse. The source was not difficult to spot either, for the man in the beige, linen jacket was lying just inside the door, facing towards them. In the torchlight the wide open eyes stared back at them accusingly and the fingers of both hands were crooked against the unyielding floor as if he were actually trying to crawl towards them even though one side of his head had been completely smashed in. Detective Chief Inspector Richard Baseheart was no longer a missing person, but a very dead one!

16

The ambulance drove very slowly through the gateway of Peter's Pantry, then accelerated away down the track to the main road, its blue flashing beacon coming on at the end as it turned left towards the town and the local hospital.

Calder watched it go with a feeling of emptiness. At least Jane Sullivan was well and truly out of it all for now anyway, he mused, but where did that leave him? The cruel irony of the situation was certainly not lost on him. All he had agreed to do at the start of this damned business was to look after an envelope for an old friend and colleague. Now, with both the key players out of what had become a deadly game, he had actually been left holding on to the board, counters, dice and everything else.

Despite his bitterness, however, he didn't envy Jane her means of escape. Shock was a funny thing and although her collapse within seconds of their discovery of Richard Baseheart's body had not really surprised him, the fact that he had been unable to bring her round afterwards had given him a real fright on top of everything else that had happened. The police surgeon attending with the cavalry shortly afterwards to officially certify the SB man's death had seemed even more concerned about her. The low pulse, clammy skin and wide open eyes apparently suggested some sort of catatonic seizure and there was no telling if and when she would come out of it again, though quite what the accident unit of the local hospital would be able to do to speed her recovery was questionable.

'You should have gone as well,' Rosy Maxwell said quietly at his elbow, following the direction of his gaze. 'Even in the dark you look a total mess.'

He carefully felt the plaster the police surgeon had put in place over the deep cut on his head after cleaning him up in his car and winced, thinking that the doctor had said much the same thing. The tablets he had been given were now beginning to work, but they only served to dull the constant throbbing pain in his head and shoulder and he knew it would be a lot worse before the night was out. 'Just a knock, that's all,' he replied. 'I'll live.'

'But aside from your so-called knock you must be near to dropping anyway,' she persisted and there was real concern in her voice now. 'James, you obviously haven't had any proper sleep for over twenty-four hours. You can't go on like this, man. You'll kill yourself.'

'I said I'm okay,' he grated. 'Now get off my case, will you?' He nodded towards the floodlit doorway of the old bakery, abruptly changing the subject. 'How are they getting on in there?'

Maxwell sighed, realising she was wasting her time with him. 'Dennis Sale and one of his men, Robin Skinner, are still examining the scene. The Home Office Pathologist is apparently on his way and we're trying to get hold of one of the Scenes of Crime teams that isn't actually on strike.' She frowned. 'I can't think where Steve Torrington's got to. Control are still trying to raise him. But the DCI should be here shortly anyway and Detective Superintendent Graham Morris from the NCS is coming down now instead of in the morning.'

'That's nice of him,' Calder observed with heavy sarcasm. 'Has George Rhymes been told about this?'

'He's also on his way,' she replied, then added: 'Everyone seems to be on their way, in fact, and I think you should be too if you're so determined to be a hero. There's nothing more you can do here and the disorder in the town is getting serious.'

He stared past her at the police surgeon who was now climbing back into his car to head for home and acknowledged her comment with a grunt. He could hear his muted radio chattering away incessantly in the background. It hadn't stopped since he had turned the pack-set back on half an hour ago to report finding Richard Baseheart's body and he was only too well aware of the fact that things were getting out of hand. Rampaging mobs were now out in force, smashing up property and looting town centre shops. Several mobiles had already come under missile attack and it wouldn't be long before the mobs realised just how thin police resources on the ground actually were. Then heaven help the town.

'Yeah, I know. I'd better get out there,' he said, pulling himself together and feeling in his pocket for the keys to the supervision car.

She waved a hand towards an area car parked on the other side of the yard. 'I'm afraid you'll have to manage without Two-Zero. I've had to detail Stoddard and Watson to stay on here for the time being to secure the scene, so you're down by two more officers now.'

'Can't be helped,' he replied, then threw her a keen sideways glance. 'How did you get on with your friend, Juliet?'

She looked around her quickly, then lowered her voice. 'She has the file in her possession and should actually have spoken to the Home Secretary on the telephone by now.'

'You left it with her? What are we playing? Pass the parcel?'

'I had no choice, but she's hardly likely to lose the thing.'

'Not like me, you mean?' he cut in ruefully, but she didn't rise to the bait and simply carried on speaking.

'The fact is, Juliet will need to show it to him personally and as I gather he's presently staying with the PM at Duncan James' country retreat not a million miles away from here, it shouldn't present too much of a problem.'

'Then something should be happening soon?'

She emitted a short grim laugh. 'If I know Juliet, things will already be underway. She's a very re-sourceful lady with more pull than you can imagine.'

The next moment she nudged his arm in warning as footsteps approached across the gravel yard. 'Talk to you later,' she breathed, strolling off towards the side door of the derelict. 'Someone wants a word, I think. But remember what I've told you about keeping your cool.'

Douglas Maybe looked very different in his flat cap and Calder realised that it was only the second time he had seen him wearing it, mainly because their illustrious shift inspector never went out if he could avoid it. His mood was as sour as always, however, and Calder suspected that his stomach had turned a double somersault when Rosy Maxwell had visited him in his office to insist that he accompanied her to the murder scene.

'Well, Sergeant,' he sneered, 'feeling better now, are we?'

'A lot better, thank you, sir,' he said, trying to step round him to go to his car.

'Oh, good,' Maybe went on, blocking the manoeuvre. 'Then perhaps you wouldn't mind telling me what the hell you were doing here to stumble on the body of Richard Baseheart?' He emitted a short derogatory laugh. 'I mean, the town's in total uproar, mobiles are rushing from one commitment to another and where is the shift sergeant? Holed up in a derelict property with his radio switched off, playing doctors and nurses with some young tart!'

Calder studied his senior officer fixedly, only the gloom masking his undisguised contempt. 'You're incredible, you know that, don't you?' he said quietly. 'If you had taken the trouble to enquire you would have learned that Jane Sullivan is a detective sergeant on headquarters Special Branch. She and Richard Baseheart were going together.'

Initially, Maybe seemed taken aback, but it only lasted a moment. 'That still doesn't explain why you came here in the first place, Sergeant,' he snapped, 'and I demand an explanation now!'

'We were looking for an escaped villain if you must know,' Calder answered, his tone very brittle and his jaw thrust out belligerently as he faced him. 'The same villain who we now believe actually murdered Richard Baseheart. Surely you remember Solomon, the prisoner who escaped from custody earlier today? There's no way you can have forgotten him. After all, you were the one who chucked him out when Porter-Nash and I first arrested him for drug offences.' He poked his finger none too gently in Maybe's chest, advancing on him as the other nervously backed away. 'And if you hadn't chucked him out just to spite me, Richard Baseheart would be alive and well today, so you're in no position to demand explanations from anyone, *sir*, got it?'

'That's enough!' Rosy Maxwell had evidently not gone too far away and she now stepped smartly in between them, her tone hard and uncompromising. 'There's a man lying dead in there, the town is virtually under siege and the pair of you are still waging your own private war. I just can't believe it.'

Maybe was swallowing repeatedly as he tried to get his words out and when he finally managed it they were still directed at Calder, almost as if Maxwell were not there at all. 'That's a damned lie. I didn't release him to spite you. I did it because Steve Torrington asked me to. The man was one of his snouts. He . . . he needed him on the outside, not answering some piddling little charge of possessing cannabis.'

'Steve Torrington?' Calder gasped, pushing past Maxwell. 'That doesn't make any sense. Steve knew what Solomon was like. Bloody hell, he was part of the team that actually tried to nail him when he was on SB'

But his voice was faltering even before he'd finished the sentence, for suddenly the comment made by the LIO, Bob Grady, about the SB raid on Solomon's house two years before came unbidden into his mind: 'Richard Baseheart reckoned Solomon was tipped off from the inside.' At almost the same moment Eddie Sable's warning erupted from his sub-conscious like a mental hydrogen bomb: 'You have a particularly rotten apple in your basket, working with the opposition.'

He stared at Maxwell, unseeing. Steve Torrington? Surely not? The man was a fanatical thief-taker, a committed right-winger who despised villains and left-wing activists more than anything else in the world, a man who would nick his own grandmother to notch up another detection. There were few people less likely to be involved in corruption than Steve Torrington . . . and yet.

'What's the matter, Sergeant?' Maybe gloated, sensing that his words had somehow touched a nerve. 'Apology sticking in your throat, is it?'

Calder didn't seem to hear him. There was a coldness inside his head and his mind had now torn itself free of the fetters which had previously bound it, tossing other pointers up into the air like leaves in the vortex of a whirlwind.

What about Torrington's three hundred pound suits, his succession of expensive female companions and flashy cars, not to mention his big four-bed detached in the sticks? How had he managed to pay for all that on a DI's salary? Then there was the obsessive interest he had shown in Richard Baseheart's presence in Hardingham, his insistence on taking over the second drugs bust of Solomon and his sudden out-of-character concern about prisoner's rights, refusing to let anyone near the anarchist while he was in the cells. It all fitted so neatly into place. But there was worse and it was then that Calder suddenly remembered the thing that had been bothering him after his last conversation with Torrington in the police station yard. The CID man had immediately recognised the Mercedes car in the garage as belonging to Richard Baseheart, yet Richard had only taken delivery of the vehicle on the afternoon before he disappeared. Torrington could only have known it was Richard's car if he had actually seen it parked in Peter's Pantry and that raised other questions he just didn't want to think about. 'This may have a lot more to do with Richard Baseheart's disappearance than the political game.' Eddie Sable's voice mocked him from deep inside his head and he visibly shuddered.

'You okay, James?' Maxwell queried, peering at him anxiously.

He stared at her blankly for a moment, conscious of the fact that he must have been standing there with his mouth open for quite a few seconds.

'Yes, James,' Maybe mimicked, forgetting himself for a moment. 'Lost our tongue, have we?'

'Shut up, Douglas,' Maxwell said with feeling. 'James, I said are you all right?'

But Calder was already pushing past both of them, almost running to his car.

'James?' Maxwell exclaimed, starting after him. 'Where the hell are you going?'

'Something I've got to do,' he shouted over his shoulder and, flinging the car door open, clambered inside and started the engine. Then he was swinging away from them through the yard entrance, headlights blazing and wheels spitting gravel as he disappeared at speed down the track towards the main road.

'The man's crazy,' Maybe exclaimed. 'Stark raving mad!'

'I have a horrible feeling he has good reason to be,' Maxwell said grimly, 'and while you're trying to ponder that one out you can demonstrate how good a field manager you are.'

Maybe stared at her. 'Field manager? I don't understand.'

She treated him to a thin smile that went unnoticed in the gloom. 'Don't be so coy, Douglas,' she replied. 'I know how anxious you are to take command of the action in the town centre, so I've decided to release PC Watson from his duty here to be your driver for the night. It will put another car back on the road and provide the shift with an experienced senior officer on the ground.'

Maybe swallowed hard and there was a slight waver in his voice when he replied. 'But . . . but the crime scene will need to be protected.'

'Then we'll just have to make do with one officer instead of two. I have to wait for Superintendent Rhymes and the Home Office pathologist to arrive anyway and I suspect CID will be about for some time yet, at least until Detective Superintendent Morris and his team turn up. There'll be plenty of us on site to prevent unauthorised access.' She emitted a short hard laugh, sensing his growing panic 'Oh, don't worry if you forgot to bring a torch with you, Douglas. I'm sure PC Watson has a spare one in his car.'

Two fire-engines streaked over the cross-roads in front of Calder as he drove at speed through the outskirts of the town, their blue beacons flashing frantically and sirens wailing in familiar anguish. Then they were gone, leaving just a flickering bluc after-glow in the plate-glass windows of a row of unboarded shop fronts and a mournful echo chasing along the dark street, like the doom-laden cry of a banshee.

Simultaneously Phil Davies in the police control room announced a suspicious fire in progress at De Marne's Warehouse in Canal Street and, after despatching Two-Two to the scene, went on without drawing breath to send Two-Eight to a reported stone-throwing attack on the White Peacock chinese restaurant in the town centre and then Two-Four to another fire, suspected petrol bombs, at the Central Library just a street away. Two-Seven was apparently already dealing with a series of smash and grabs in the Queen's shopping mall and one of the few Traffic mobiles not supporting the strike, Tango Four-Six, had volunteered to attend a report of cars being set on fire on the Warren Housing Estate.

The town was about to erupt into the full-scale public disorder everyone had feared and, knowing that the thin blue line was now stretched to the limit, Calder hesitated at the cross-roads, almost changing direction at the last minute to go after the fast-fading sirens, but then with ruthless determination forcing himself to stick to his original objective.

Turning his back on the town and his small loyal team as they tried so desperately to hold things together hurt like hell and, as he sped away in the opposite direction, he couldn't shake off the feeling that he was running out on them. But though he may have felt like a deserter, deep down he knew that was not the case. The onerous task he had taken on board could not be left until later and he had an obligation, not only to Richard Baseheart and Jane Sullivan, but to the service as a whole to follow things through to the bitter end.

He swerved hard right to avoid a large gang of youths apparently playing basketball with the globe of a belisha beacon in the middle of the road and smiled to himself without humour. Anyway, as he had heard on the radio soon after leaving Peter's Pantry, Inspector Maybe was now mobile with Two-Zero. Obviously Rosy Maxwell's work. The shift, therefore, already had a supervisor on the ground to take charge of the police operation in the town and he couldn't think of a better man for the job.

There were fewer pickets on his arrival at the rear of the police station than there had been before and when he swung through the archway into the yard the shouts of 'scab' that went up, almost as an automatic response to the sight of the police vehicle, had no real force or conviction in them. Even Willy Justice appeared more subdued than usual and he put the strikers' lack of enthusiasm down to the noticeable absence of any press cameras to capture their performance.

Steve Torrington's Volvo was in its usual parking space, but there was no sign of the man himself and, having checked the driver's door and found it to be securely locked, he didn't waste any more time on the vehicle, but headed straight for the back door of the police station, turning his radio off as he did so.

The building itself was deathly still and most of the downstairs lights had been switched off. He found the atmosphere of the place strangely hostile, almost threatening, and his footsteps produced an unnatural hollow sound as he made his way along the patched linoleum floor to the small square hallway where the main corridors met at the foot of the stairs. Even at night the building was usually full of noises: the raucous laughter of bobbies on meal-break, the metallic chatter of a personal radio or the slam of a cabinet drawer or uniform-locker door. Tonight, however, there was nothing, just his footsteps, the muted sound of his own radio and the buzzing of flies inside the plastic covers of the strip lights. It was weird and somehow unnerving.

The stairs looked even less inviting than the hallway, but he didn't hesitate. Somewhere in Steve Torrington's office could be the damning evidence that would take the case rapidly building against the detective beyond mere suspicion: a diary or notebook entry, the copy of a telephone message, maybe even the trace of a call on his answerphone, anything to connect him with Solomon or, heaven forbid, implicate him in the murder of Richard Baseheart!

But Calder knew he hadn't much time, was probably already too late. Steve Torrington was a very shrewd calculating individual and meticulous in his attention to detail. It was most unlikely that he would have left any incriminating evidence lying around and, if he had, it was virtually certain that he would have got rid of it the moment he realised things were closing in around him. Nevertheless, Calder knew he had to try and if that meant risking his own career by tearing the DI's office apart, then so be it.

The odour of Dennis Sale's fish-and-chip supper still lingered in the air as he made his way quickly along the heavily carpeted first floor corridor towards the unlit CID general office, but when he got to the open doorway he detected another much stronger smell which he immediately recognised and his mouth tightened.

The arc-lamp on Steve Torrington's desk glowed

dimly through the blinds which had been pulled down over the windows of the partition separating his office from that of his team of detectives and Calder heard the clink of a glass.

He didn't knock, but threw the door wide and strode in. Steve Torrington was slouched behind his desk, a bottle of whisky in front of him and a nearly empty glass in one hand. He showed no surprise at Calder's dramatic entrance, but met his hostile stare levelly, the thin lips registering a bitter smile, the glass poised halfway to his lips.

For a few moments Calder was taken aback by the detective's physical appearance which, in the few short hours since they had last spoken, had deteriorated to such an extent that he no longer looked the same person. The weasel-like face now had the pallid shrunken appearance of a corpse and the dark eyes, once so sharp and watchful, had become dull and lifeless. His was the face of a man who had given up on life, who no longer cared about anything and this was reflected in the state of his clothes. The jacket of the expensive linen suit was so badly creased that it looked as though he had actually been sleeping in it, there were obvious stains down the front of his rumpled shirt and his silk tie hung in an untidy knot from his open collar.

'Hello, Jim,' he said in a slightly thickened voice. 'I wondered when you'd decide to show.' He tried to chuckle, but it only came out as an empty rattle. 'You've certainly been in the wars by the look of it. Who had the temerity to belt you then?'

'Let's cut out the crap, Steve,' Calder grated, 'You know why I'm here and a skinful won't help you on this one.'

Torrington shrugged and, pulling the whisky bottle towards him, tilted it towards his glass to pour himself another, slopping some of the amber coloured liquid on to the desk in the process. 'That wasn't my intention, Jim,' he replied. 'Bar was closed upstairs, so I thought I'd open up one of my own down here, that's all.' He fumbled around in one of his desk drawers and produced another glass. 'Want to join me?'

Calder's expression was one of absolute contempt. 'I wouldn't drink with you if you were the last person on earth,' he snapped. 'Not after what you've done.'

Torrington nodded and sitting back in his swivel chair he studied his colleague over the top of his glass as he cupped it between both hands and sipped the spirit slowly. 'Can't say as I blame you for that, Jim,' he said, making no attempt to defend himself against the unspecified accusation. 'I'd say the same if I were in your shoes. I just want you to try and understand.'

'Understand?' Calder cut in with a snarl, leaning on the desk with clenched fists, his head thrust towards him and his eyes narrowed dangerously. 'Understand what, Steve? Understand why you've been on the take all these years? Why you've been supplying a scumbag like Solomon with confidential information to help his bloody revolution? Why you've sold your own colleagues down the river? Why . . . ?' He choked on his words and straightened up, staring at the ceiling for a second, his teeth clenched tightly with emotion.

'I didn't murder Richard Baseheart, you know,' Torrington said quietly.

Calder stared at him with an expression in which loathing and incredulity were clearly mixed. 'No?' he rasped. 'But you still made it happen, didn't you? You panicked when you thought he was about to point the finger and got Solomon to shut him up for you.'

Torrington flared suddenly, slamming his glass down on the table and spilling more whisky over one hand. 'It wasn't like that, damn you!'

Calder's lips curled into a sneer. 'So what was it like, Steve?' he said. 'Why don't you tell me, eh? Think of it as a sort of rehearsal before you make your debut in the dock at Crown Court.'

Torrington sighed heavily, his anger abruptly subsiding, as if he hadn't the will to sustain it. 'I'm quite ready to face the music, Jim,' he replied in a more even tone. 'If I hadn't been, I would have bolted long before now.'

'So what do you want? A bloody commendation?' Calder said bitterly, then swaying suddenly, he clutched at the edge of the desk for support and carefully sat down on a small tubular chair behind him, leaning his head back against the wall with his eyes tightly closed for a second.

The strain of the past few days, coupled with lack of sleep and the injuries he had suffered as a result of Solomon's violent assault, were at last beginning to tell and the throbbing pains in his head and shoulder, which the police surgeon's earlier medication had only temporarily reduced, were now back with a vengeance accompanied by waves of nausea and a feeling of total exhaustion that left him almost too weak to stand up.

'You okay?' Torrington queried and he seemed genuinely anxious.

Calder opened his eyes and focused on him with difficulty. 'I'll survive,' he said, 'which is more than I can say for you when this lot gets out.'

The detective shrugged again. 'I'll just have to take

what's coming to me, Jim,' he replied. 'I simply can't live with my conscience any more.'

Calder smoothed his face with both hands. 'How the hell did you get into this mess, Steve?' he said wearily. 'You had it made and yet you threw it all away.'

Torrington stared into his whisky glass, swirling the liquid round and round. 'Money, Jim, plain and simple,' he replied. 'I suppose I've always lived above my means, spent more than I could afford so I could stay in the fast lane, but I always managed to keep my head above water. You know, bit of overtime here, some imaginative expense claims there. Then about seven years ago, when I was a DS on the Drug Squad, I met this bird at a party. She was a nurse at the local hospital and a real stunner. We got involved and started living together, but I couldn't keep up with her spending excesses and in the end I became a walking IOU, heading for a nervous breakdown.'

He took another sip of whisky. 'Then she introduced me to this guy, her brother she said, who was something big in the music industry. He offered to bail me out as a favour to his little sister and like a bloody fool I agreed. Trouble was, the only thing he turned out to be big in was cocaine.'

'Solomon.'

'Exactly, though he didn't call himself that then, and he soon started calling in the favour. Evidently he and my live-in lover had been planning this damned thing for months as a means of infiltrating the squad.'

'So why didn't you come clean with your boss before things got out of hand?'

'Not as easy as it sounds. I was a lot younger then and anxious for promotion. The thought of spilling the beans at that stage in my career scared me shit-less.'

'So you just went along with their demand for inside information. Thirty pieces of silver and all that?'

Torrington nodded bleakly. 'And I got in deeper and deeper until there was no way out. Nursy took off afterwards, of course. She'd done her bit and, surprise, surprise, she wasn't anyone's bloody sister. Solomon stuck to me like glue though and, when I got a transfer to SB, he started touching me for information about my new department's activities. By this time he had graduated from a pusher to a full-blown nutter in the anarchist movement with pretensions of spiritual greatness.'

'And had also come to the notice of Richard Baseheart?'

'Yeah. Richard saw him as a primary target and threw all the resources of the department into nailing him.'

'But you made sure he never did?'

'I had to. If Solomon had been nicked he would have taken me with him, so I did all I could to keep him out of Richard's clutches.'

'Including blowing the last SB operation that had been set up in Birmingham?'

Torrington grimaced. 'Yeah, but I thought I'd dropped myself in it there. Richard already suspected that Solomon had been tipped off about previous jobs from inside the department and he had narrowed the leak down to three of us who had been involved on each one: the DI, John Kidd, DS Jane Sullivan and me. Fortunately, I got promoted to DI here within a couple of weeks of the operation and managed to shake Solomon off my back. Then shortly afterwards

Richard was told by his boss to chill it with Solomon. As a result, he never really got the chance to pursue things, but I reckoned at the time that I had always been his chief suspect.'

A flash of blue light illuminated the office and was immediately followed by a distant roll of thunder. Both men glanced quickly at the window, then back at each other.

'So when Richard turned up in the canteen at the beginning of this week you thought he was doing his own rubber-heel on you?' Calder said.

'Investigating me?' Torrington shook his head. 'Not at that stage, no. I simply assumed he was managing the usual sort of SB surveillance operation at the festival and was just curious. But when I did my usual tour of the cells and took a look at the prisoners you said you and Nash had nicked, I nearly shit myself to find that one of them was Solomon, especially when he told me he would finger me for past indiscretions if I didn't get him out.'

'So you persuaded Maybe to do the honours, telling him in confidence that Solomon was one of your snouts?'

'It was the only way, because as DI I hadn't got the necessary station authority to do the job myself. Anyway, I thought I'd resolved the problem then, but as I was returning to my office I heard Maybe asking one of the shift where you were and the lad said in all innocence that he'd seen you going for a stroll in the park with Richard Baseheart. It was at that moment that I really began to suspect Richard's presence in Hardingham had something to do with Solomon, bearing in mind his previous paranoia about the man.'

'Which is why you bent my ear at the Cooper's Store break-in?'

'Yes, but only after I had found the note Richard had left you about the rendezvous at Peter's Pantry.'

'But that means you must have read the bloody thing before me?'

Another brief nod. 'I was on my way to your office when I clocked Richard leaving, though he didn't see me. When I spotted the envelope in the middle of your desk, I opened it, quickly read his message, then simply resealed it in another envelope.'

Calder closed his eyes again for a moment, but this time not through pain or fatigue, but because he was now way ahead of Torrington. 'And then you promptly went and passed this information on to Solomon?'

Torrington compressed his lips tightly and shuddered. 'How was I to know the mad bastard would kill him?' he said hopelessly. 'I only told him about the rendezvous to warn him something was going down. He knew I was going to tail you there, so there was no need for him to have gone anywhere near the place.'

Calder held up his hand to stop him. 'You followed me to Peter's Pantry?' he said, leaning forward in his chair. 'But if that's the case you must have still been there after I left, which means you must have been with Solomon when he murdered Richard?' He rose from the chair and leaned across the desk again. 'You bastard. You stood and watched, didn't you?'

Torrington swallowed hard, shaking his head furiously. 'No, no, it wasn't like that at all, you must believe me. Yes, I did follow you to the place and I also saw Richard hand you that large envelope before he took you inside the building, but I couldn't get any closer without giving myself away, so I never tried. The moment you left, I took off as well.'

'Why should I believe you?'

The detective took a deep breath. 'Because you yourself saw me at the scene of that punch-up involving Porter-Nash only minutes after you had left Peter's Pantry. There was no way I could have got there so quickly if I had been with Solomon at the time of the murder. In fact, I only found out about it when the swine met me the following day to tell me what had happened.'

Calder sat down again. 'And exactly what did he tell you?'

'He claimed Richard's death had been an accident; that there had been an argument between the two of them and Richard had fallen over and hit his head on the fridge door.'

'And you believed him?'

'I didn't know what to believe then. I was mixed up, horrified by what had happened and looking for a way out. When he said he would sort everything I . . . I just agreed and left him to it.'

Calder tugged his packet of cigarettes from his pocket and tapped the end of a long filter-tip several times on the packet without lighting up.

'Which is obviously what he was trying to do when Jane and I ran into him,' he reflected grimly. 'And he'd have got away with it too if we had arrived just a few minutes later, because the only other person who knew about the crime had washed his hands of the whole thing, that's right, isn't it, Steve?'

Torrington grimaced. 'I didn't kill Richard, Jim,' he repeated defensively.

Calder dropped his cigarettes as he lurched forward in his seat. 'You were a bloody policeman, Steve, a DI, and one of your own colleagues had been murdered; someone you knew, someone you had worked with. How could you simply walk away from that?'

He broke off, one hand clutching at his head as the pain lancing through the wound seemed about ready to remove the top of his skull. Torrington reached in his drawer and produced a small bottle which he tossed across to him.

'Do you think I wanted to?' he replied bitterly, and watched Calder swallow two Paracetamol with difficulty, then wince as the tablets went down. 'Do you think I found it easy? But shopping Solomon would have meant shopping myself and I was terrified of the consequences.'

Calder bent to pick up his cigarettes, then gingerly straightened, closing his eyes tightly again as he waited for the waves of nausea to subside.

'So you carried on protecting the murdering bastard,' he said, finally pocketing the cigarettes without lighting up. 'Even to the extent of devising a cunning little plan to actually spring him from custody when he was nicked the second time, never mind who got hurt in the process.'

'I had no choice. There was no way I could repeat my earlier trick because of the seriousness of the charges, but I had to make sure no one else got to speaking to him. Then the two joy-riders were arrested and I knew I couldn't risk them seeing and identifying Solomon who was in the same cell block.'

'So you slipped something to Solomon in his cell to

enable him to convince Janice Lawson he was having a haemorrhage and should be rushed to hospital?'

'Yeah, some raw liver dregs from the canteen. Crude but effective.'

Calder made a face. 'And warned his cronies where he would be?'

Torrington didn't confirm or deny the fact. 'As bad luck would have it, one of the joy-riders evidently clocked Solomon as he was being wheeled away and did just what I'd feared. By the time they'd managed to speak to anyone I'd got him out. I knew that so long as he managed to evade arrest and I could fix it so that the two tearaways were prevented from pin-pointing where they'd picked up the car, I was fairly safe.'

'But you didn't reckon on Jane Sullivan and myself doing the job for them?'

The detective gave a short harsh laugh. 'It was the last thing I expected, and when I heard on the air what had happened I knew·it was only a question of time before Solomon was brought in and the whole business came down on me like an avalanche of shit.'

Calder stared at the floor for a few moments his eyes distant and unseeing. 'The tragic irony of it all is that Richard wasn't after Solomon at all,' he said. 'In fact, he didn't even know that animal was here until I told him.'

'I know.'

Calder's head jerked up and his eyes focused on Torrington's face. 'What do you mean, you know?'

'Who do you think nicked the envelope off the back seat of your car at the council tip?'

Calder clenched his fists. 'You bastard!' he said. 'Do you realise what you put me through?'

'I can imagine and I'm sorry, but I was left with no choice. I had to find out what was in the thing.'

'Yeah, and having found out and realised you were off the hook, what did you do then, eh? Even though you knew about Richard Baseheart you still tried to make some easy money out of the envelope by offering it to Eddie Sable.'

Torrington shook his head vehemently again. 'You've got it all wrong,' he retorted. 'Yes, I'll admit to trying to make money out of the thing and, yes, I did go to Sable with it. I had been supplying him with information for years and knew he was a good payer who could be trusted to protect his source. But, as I told you just now, I didn't know Richard was dead until the following day, by which time I had already seen Eddie and handed over your damned envelope.'

'So you simply shed a few tears for Richard and banked the money Eddie had paid you, eh?'

Torrington visibly flinched. 'I did nothing of the sort. In fact, I tried to return the advance he had given me,' he replied. 'I told him I'd changed my mind and wanted nothing more to do with the business.'

'I bet he loved you for that?'

'He wouldn't agree to it, seemed to smell that there was an even bigger story to be had. When I wouldn't enlighten him and threw his money back at him he got pretty nasty, threatening to expose me at the first opportunity.'

Calder nodded. 'He tried to as well. Told me that there was a rotten apple in the nick and offered to give me a name in return for my co-operation in arranging an interview with DS Sullivan.'

'The treacherous little swine.'

Calder laughed derisively. 'Talk about the pot

calling the kettle black. You've turned treachery into an alternative art form.'

Torrington glared at him, his anger re-surfacing in spite of the guilt that weighed heavily on him. 'Look, I'm not proud of what I've done, Jim,' he snapped, 'but at least I'm trying to set the record straight.'

Calder's eyes blazed. 'Is that right?' he snarled. 'Well, let me tell you something. This is no confessional box and I'm no friggin' priest, so don't think you can wipe the slate clean simply by telling me what an arse-hole you are. I know that already.'

Torrington studied him warily. From the street outside sirens wailed and there was another loud clap of thunder. 'Okay, so what happens now?'

'What the hell do you think? You're an accessory to murder. Why should you be treated any different to anyone else?'

'I'm not asking to be treated any different, but I won't have the murder bit. I had nothing to do with that.'

'Maybe, but you aided and abetted Solomon afterwards, didn't you? And that's how the court will see it. Either way, you're going down, Steve, and that won't be any picnic when the other inmates find out you are ex-bill.'

Torrington nodded, then stared at him levelly. 'I know what's ahead of me, Jim,' he said grimly, 'and, as I've already told you, I'm ready to take my punishment. But there's something I have to do first.'

Calder snorted. 'Like what, for instance? Get a toothbrush and some clean underwear together?'

'I'll make a deal with you.'

'No deals. You're not in a bargaining position.'

'Oh I think I am. You know as well as I do that

386

nothing I've said to you in here is any good to you. It wasn't under caution and you've got absolutely no corroboration.'

Calder was on his feet again, fists clenched and face contorted into an expression of anger and pain. 'You little snide!'

Torrington held up one hand. 'No, hear me out. I'm not trying to slide out of it. I'll give the firm the confession it needs, under caution and on tape, but only after I've done what I have to do.'

Calder slumped back into his chair, fingers pressed against the side of his head. 'What guarantee do I have of that?'

'You don't, but if I give you Solomon you'll have his testimony anyway.'

Calder raised his head to stare at him. 'Solomon?' he breathed. 'You know where he is?'

Torrington looked at his watch. 'I know where he will be now he's created the mayhem he came for.'

'How do you know he's got what he wants?'

Torrington's face looked even more ghastly than before. 'I think you'd better look out of the window, Jim?' he breathed, staring sideways across the desk as more sirens wailed from the direction of the street.

Even before he got there Calder could see the glow. It lit up the night sky like a false sunset, devouring any stars that lay in its path and burning a long ragged hole in the deep black canopy. Armageddon had finally arrived and the whole town centre was ablaze!

17

Several long seconds elapsed before Calder reacted to the nightmare drama being played out before his horrified gaze just a mile from where he was standing. The shock of this new calamity, coming on top of the discovery of Baseheart's corpse and the realisation of Torrington's treachery, had a strange numbing effect on him, bringing with it a sense of unreality. In fact, he felt almost as though he were watching the finale of some epic disaster movie on a giant cinema screen and half-expected to see the camera zoom in for a mind-blowing close-up at any moment.

Then the boom of the tannoy abruptly destroyed the illusion and blew the cobwebs from his mind. 'Attention all personnel. This is an emergency,' Phil Davies announced coolly as if it were anything but. 'All available units to attend town centre immediately. Rendezvous with Bravo-Sierra Two junction of Eastern Avenue and Lower High Street. Major rioting in progress. Repetition to follow.'

But Calder needed no further incentive and he was stumbling through the general CID office even before the message could be repeated, one hand clutching his head while the other switched on his pack-set and roughly disconnected the hated earpiece.

'Wait,' Torrington yelled after him, snatching his own pack-set from a drawer, 'I'm coming with you.'

But the detective's words were virtually drowned by the blast of his own radio which was alive with activity as Phil Davies, having obviously already passed the same message out over the air, handled the multitude of incoming calls with the cool dexterity of a Wimbledon tennis player returning serves from a top seed on the Centre Court.

A brilliant flash of lightning illuminated the police station yard as the two men charged towards Calder's supervision car and the clap of thunder that followed seemed to be a lot closer than before. There was a dank smell in the air too and Calder thought he felt a few heavy drops of rain before he jerked the door open and threw himself inside. Torrington was hammering on the passenger door as he started to reverse and he jerked to a halt briefly to pull up the catch, hardly giving the CID man time to jump inside before he was screeching backwards, then swinging round towards the exit.

The pickets were still there, but away from the archway, gathered at the junction of the service road and the main drag staring towards the town and pointing excitedly. Calder slammed to a halt a few feet short of the junction and, throwing the door wide, scrambled out into the service road while Torrington exited more uncertainly from the other side.

'Are you lot just going to stand here while the whole town is gutted?' Calder yelled, striding towards the small crowd and roughly pushing two of the pickets aside who didn't move out of his way fast enough. 'What sort of cowardly shits are you?'

As he spoke Phil Davies was off again, but now for

the first time the tension was evident in his tone. 'Urgent assistance required, town centre. Police and fire service units now under heavy mob attack.'

'Hear that?' Calder yelled again, studying the faces around him. 'Your own colleagues are getting hammered out there. Don't you care what happens to them?'

But apart from some embarrassed shuffling of feet, his audience seemed incapable of saying or doing anything and in sudden fury at the lack of reaction from them and, heedless of the pain trying to rip his head apart, he grabbed a uniformed officer by the collar and shook him. 'We've already lost one copper, don't you realise that? He was murdered by the scum who are torching the town. Are you going to stand by while the same thing happens to the rest?'

Now at last the pickets began to mutter amongst themselves, their unease about the situation finally beginning to surface, and at the same moment Willy Justice's bulk pushed through the small crowd. 'Don't listen to him, comrades,' he shouted, obviously sensing that some of them were starting to waver. 'Scabs mean nothing to us. They deserve all they get.'

That was possibly the worst thing he could have said and the next flash of lightning neatly captured Calder's response as he turned on the union Chairman with an angry snarl that made Justice stumble backwards in alarm. But the big man was just not quick enough and Calder's closed fist struck him heavily on the jaw before he could get out of the way, sending him crashing into the perimeter wall of the police station where his legs buckled and he slumped to the ground in an undignified insensible heap.

'Bloody hell, Jim!' Torrington exclaimed

390

delightedly from his elbow as an involuntary gasp went up from the pickets. 'You've really gone and done it now!'

Calder was unrepentant and, turning on his heel, he strode away from him back to the car. 'Something I should have done a long time ago,' he growled and, rubbing his knuckles with his other hand, jumped back into the vehicle and rammed it into gear while Torrington was still climbing into the front passenger seat. Then, revving the engine brutally, he powered the car away like a dragster, callously leaving the CID man clinging to the inside of the front passenger door for a few seconds before he managed to wrestle it shut.

The moment they turned right on to the main drag the magnitude of the problem they faced immediately became apparent. Ahead of them in the darkness a fierce orange glare seemed to fill the space between the rows of tall buildings on each side of the wide black tongue of tarmacadam and even from so far away the clangour of alarm bells and a continuous tell-tale roaring sound, like the noise made by an excited crowd at a football match, could be heard all too clearly.

Then just half a mile down the road the seriousness of the situation was really rammed home to them when a crash-helmeted figure lunged from a doorway and hurled a flaming missile at their car, forcing Calder to take immediate evasive action. The petrol bomb hit the bonnet and exploded, showering glass and burning fragments over the windscreen. But no real damage appeared to have been caused and Calder made no attempt to stop and check, instead pressing the accelerator pedal even harder to the floor as a second petrol bomb appeared from the same spot, arced over the roof and exploded harmlessly several feet away.

This attack was immediately followed by a fusillade of stones which hammered into the bodywork from all sides like the discharge from an automatic firearm and what sounded very much like a large brick landed on the roof with a deafening crash before bouncing off again into the darkness.

Then they were at the roundabout and the glare from a barricade of blazing cars blocking the entrance to Lower High Street seared their eyes as Calder drove round the smashed traffic bollards on the wrong side of the road and mounted the corner of the opposite pavement to avoid the still smoking skeleton of a single-decker bus which straddled part of the road encircling the island.

Two fire-engines were stationed at the junction of Lower High Street and Eastern Avenue, hoses jetting torrents of water on to the burning cars from a safe distance. At the same time their crews desperately tried to shelter behind their own vehicles and the three police area cars, which had been hastily drawn up in a protective line, as a hail of bricks and petrol bombs rained down on them continuously from the middle of the roundabout where a large mob had collected.

Beyond the barricade the flames of burning buildings in Lower High Street leaped skywards unchecked and the scream of burglar alarms and the roar of the mob, combined with the thud of erupting petrol tanks and the crash of exploding shop windows, created a din that was as terrifying as the spectacle itself.

Edging round a cast-iron postbox and thumping down the kerb into Eastern Avenue, Calder's mind flashed back almost two-and-a-half decades to another town in another place across the Irish Sea and the young soldier who had faced a similar missile-throwing mob as he crouched behind his shield in the glare of a blazing barricade of stolen vehicles. Nothing ever changes, he thought grimly, only the excuse is different.

Drawing up behind the barrier of parked police vehicles, he scrambled from his seat without waiting for Torrington and keeping his head low picked his way amongst the litter of bricks and broken glass towards the bobbies crouched behind their area cars. He saw at once that they had all had the good sense to kit themselves out in the flame-proof overalls and protective helmets that all mobiles now carried in their vehicles as personal issue, and realised with a rueful smile that the shift sergeant was the only one who had neglected to take this most elementary of precautions.

'Hi there, Sarge,' Maurice Stone shouted at him cheerfully above the din, but ducked as several stones hammered the bonnet of the vehicle. 'Bit warm here at the moment.'

Calder gave him a quick smile, pleased to see the big man in a happier frame of mind, then glanced around at the other faces. 'Any injuries?'

'Only cuts and bruises,' Jenny Major replied from his right, raising her helmet visor, 'though we stink a bit from that inferno in Imperial Road.'

Calder visibly started. 'Imperial Road?' he queried a little too sharply, a cold watery feeling in the pit of his stomach despite the heat generated by the burning cars only yards away.

'Yes, that was some blaze I can tell you,' she went on. 'Around nine shops petrol bombed. Two-Seven and Two-Eight must still be escorting the fleet of ambulances being used to ferry the poor devils from the upstairs flats to the hospital.'

Calder thought of Singh's Tobacconists on the corner of Imperial Road and Commercial Street and inwardly cursed himself for leaving his radio off for so long in his eagerness to nail Torrington.

'Whole terrace was gutted,' John Powell joined in from his left, then swore as a stone bounced off his helmet. 'When Trevor and I broke off from there to head for this job hardly anything was left except brick walls.'

'But why target Imperial Road?' Calder queried. 'It's hardly the centre of town.'

Powell shook his head. 'Dunno. Maybe a diversion so they could hit the High Street. Apparently it all started at that Asian tobacconists shop. Mob torched the place and the fire spread to the Handy Stores next door. Lot of paraffin in there. Fire service had two appliances on the scene within five minutes apparently, but . . .' and he shrugged without finishing the sentence.

Calder closed his eyes tightly for a second. 'Anyone hurt?'

'Not as far as we know. We got the Asian family to the hospital by ambulance anyway, smoke inhalation or something, but they were pretty upset about it all.'

'I'll bet,' Calder replied. He couldn't help thinking of Mrs. Baines' bitterness towards the police and he blamed himself for letting the couple down so badly after all his promises, even though he knew he couldn't have done anything anyway. Then suddenly he snatched at the wing of the car for support, waves of nausea sweeping over him as the pain in his head hammered through his skull like a road-drill.

Jenny Major grabbed his arm to steady him and peered into his face anxiously. 'You've certainly had a nasty bang there, Sarge,' she said close to his ear. 'You okay?'

Calder pushed her away roughly, ignoring her concern and, gritting his teeth, half straightened. 'Just keep your heads down,' he snapped. 'I'd better find the governor.'

A group of senior fire-fighters had gathered under a shaded spotlight at the rear of one of the fire-engines and Rosy Maxwell, now clad like the other police officers in her protective kit, was standing to one side of them talking to the Station Officer in his distinctive white helmet. Calder wasn't surprised to find Inspector Maybe hovering nervously in the shadows behind them all, looking more than a little incongruous in his own flame-proofs and over-large helmet, but he soon came to life when he clapped eyes on Calder.

'Where the hell have you been, Sergeant?' he shouted, for a moment forgetting himself and pushing through the group of fire-fighters to venture out from behind the reassuring bulk of the fire-engine. 'We've been calling you half the night.'

'Leave it, Douglas,' Maxwell rapped, turning away from the fire officer. 'I'll deal with this.' Then to Calder: 'A word in private, if you please, James.'

There was a familiar satisfied smirk on Maybe's face as his sergeant was led away by the elbow and it was obvious that he was revelling in the roasting he felt sure the other was about to receive. But he was prevented from witnessing the expected dressing-down when Maxwell took Calder into the recessed doorway of a small shop.

'Right, James, it's quieter here and we can talk,' she said, showing no signs of relaxing her prickly demeanour. 'So, picking up on Inspector Maybe's point, exactly where have you been?'

Calder's face was a cold hard mask in the light trickling through the venetian blind on the shop door. 'Smelling out a rat,' he grated.

'Something to do with DI Torrington?'

He grunted, and she pursed her lips and nodded slowly. 'I wondered why you took off like a madman after that heated exchange with Inspector Maybe earlier. Going to tell me about it?'

Another missile of some sort smashed into the roof above their heads and they withdrew further into the recess. 'Torrington's bent,' Calder said tersely with one eye still on the street. 'He was the one responsible for stealing Richard's file from my car and sending it to Eddie Sable and he's also been in Solomon's pocket for years. That's why he had to get the bastard out of custody before we interviewed him.'

'Steve Torrington?' she echoed. 'I can hardly believe it. Hell's bells, James, you've certainly turned over some stones this time.'

'And that's not all either,' he snapped and quickly gave her the rest of it.

For a few moments after he had finished speaking she said nothing, apparently stunned by what he had told her and obviously thinking carefully about the implications. Calder waited patiently, listening to the noise around them and wishing, not for the first time, that he was a million miles away from it all.

Staring diagonally across the street towards the roundabout, he saw several youths break away from the mob to run straight at the line of police area cars and a petrol bomb flew through the air, exploding on the ground just a few feet away. It was immediately followed by another before three of the police officers crouching behind the cars left their positions to chase the youths off with batons swinging. From the opposite side of the road an army of press cameras flashed and one braver and more enterprising pressman almost collided with the retreating youths as he rushed out into the middle of the road with his video camera on his shoulder. Calder craned his neck to study the shadowy group of newshounds, but couldn't see Eddie Sable's distinctive figure among them.

'And where is Steve Torrington now?' Maxwell asked suddenly.

'He came here with me,' Calder replied, realising at once how negligent that sounded.

'Here?' she exclaimed. 'Are you mad? He should have been locked up. He could be an accessory to Richard Baseheart's murder!'

'Don't you think I realise that? But he offered to give me Solomon. He knows where the bastard is. Anyway, in the middle of his bloody confession all this blew up and I thought it was more important to answer the assistance call than ponce about with him at the nick.'

'Then I'd better talk to him. Whereabouts is he?'

Calder could see her peering round the edge of the window and his stomach churned as he moved up beside her. The distance between them and the line of emergency vehicles was only a matter of yards and he could see everyone clearly enough in the glare of the burning cars to know that Torrington was no longer there. 'The friggin' little toad!' he rasped.

Maxwell turned back into the recess with a sharp

grunt. 'Well, you didn't seriously expect him to wait around for you, did you?'

Calder shook his head several times. 'You don't understand. He had no need to come with me in the first place. He could just as easily have slipped away from the nick after I had left. So why do a runner now, especially on foot?'

She shrugged impatiently. 'We can worry about that later. Right now we've got more important things to think about. Like how to stop the whole town being burned to the ground.'

'We can't, not with the number of personnel we've got. All we're doing by standing around here is giving that scum a bloody target to throw things at while we do our best to protect our own arses. Sooner or later they're going to get braver and when that happens, they'll be all over us. Shit, Rosy, we're not even as well off as the British Army were when they faced the bloody Zulus at Rorke's Drift.'

'If I remember my history and a certain Nineteen-Sixties film epic accurately,' she retorted tightly, 'the British Army won that engagement.'

'Yeah,' he replied, nodding towards the police vehicles strung out in front of them. 'But they had more biscuit tins to use for cover than we have.'

Another bright flash of lightning lit up the doorway in which they were sheltering and she visibly jumped at the sudden loud clap of thunder. 'So what the hell do you suggest?' she shouted, clearly rattled and out of patience with their small talk.

'I suggest,' he snapped back, 'that what we need is a fully equipped, fully trained complement of police support units armed with riot shields and CS Gas, preferably from the Regional Public

Order Group, but we're not likely to get them, are we?'

'We might, I don't know,' she replied almost reluctantly. 'It depends on how things pan out. George Rhymes should be on to the Commissioner now.'

'But Harding daren't bring in PSU's from outside while there's a strike on. The only way he could do that would be to cave in to the NPU's demands first.'

'I realise that and so does George Rhymes.'

Calder gave her a critical sideways glance. 'You've spilled the beans to Rhymes, haven't you?' he accused.

She hesitated, biting her lip, then nodded quickly. 'I had no choice. Richard Baseheart's death has broken him, James. He blames himself for it. When he turned up at the scene of the murder he looked like an old man and he took me to one side and started to unload everything on me. I was left with no alternative but to admit we already knew about the conspiracy.'

'Which means that now Harding and Turner will know that we know. Bloody Nora, Rosy, they'll be covering their tracks faster than a dog burying its . . .'

'It doesn't matter,' she cut in hastily. 'The die's already cast. Juliet will have done her bit by now and if I know the Home Office, they'll move very fast on this one. They can't afford not to.'

Calder stared gloomily up and down the road. The crowd on the roundabout had grown appreciably and Eastern Avenue was now also filling up behind them. Even when the burning barricade across Lower High Street had been extinguished neither they or the fire service had anywhere to go, since they were trapped between two mobs of rioters.

'Then the Home Office or the Commissioner had better do something pretty fast,' he said, watching more petrol bombs arcing towards them. 'Or this won't end like the victory over the Zulus at Rorke's Drift, but the bloody massacre by them at Isandlwana!'

Reinforcements actually arrived ten minutes later, moments after Calder had pulled on the flame-proof overalls and protective helmet he had managed to retrieve from the boot of the supervision car under a hail of bricks and bottles. But the two pairs of powerful headlights that suddenly cut a wide swathe through the crowd gathered at the opposite end of Eastern Avenue and the flashing roof beacons that sent out brilliant wedges of phantasmic blue light into the darkness, like the rotor-blades of spectral helicopters, did not belong to the vanguard of a police support unit convoy, but to the two Hardingham Area Transits, Bravo-Alpha Two-Seven and Two-Eight, obviously just returning from the Imperial Road commitment.

Nevertheless, the formidable-looking, long-wheel-base Transits with their massive front-end grills, reinforced wheel-arches and steel-mesh windscreen protectors looked very impressive and when they swung in one behind the other, ten to fifteen yards back from the line of police area cars, to provide a defensive wall against the missiles now being hurled by the crowd massing in Eastern Avenue, one of the senior fire officers quickly stepped forward to speak to Maxwell. 'Don't those vehicles carry riot control equipment, Chief Inspector?' he queried keenly.

Maxwell nodded. 'They carry defensive shields anyway, Mr Metcalf,' she replied, breaking off as the side doors of both vehicles suddenly swung open from inside to allow a large number of what looked like rigid oblong sheets of transparent plastic to be dumped unceremoniously on the ground one after the other, in an untidy heap. ' As you can now see.'

The fire officer seemed heartened by the sight. 'So now that you have them,' he said, 'what are your chances of clearing the street sufficiently for my units to get through to Lower High Street? The barricade fire has almost been extinguished and I understand from Fire Control that two more appliances are already on their way here from another commitment. But we shall have to move immediately if we are to get to those burning shops in time.'

Maxwell turned to Calder. 'What do you think, James?' she rapped as individual officers ran forward to grab a shield each from the pile.

'Including those in the Trannies, we have a total of eight fully trained regulars and five specials here,' he replied.

She grimaced. 'Not even enough to make up one full police support unit then?'

'I think that's about to be rectified, ma'am,' he said, nudging her arm and pointing. The headlights of a third police Transit were approaching, this time from the direction of the roundabout on a similar route to that taken by Calder earlier, its single blue roof beacon flashing and siren wailing as it forced its way through the army of rioters trying to bring it to a halt by sheer weight of numbers.

'What the devil's that?' Maxwell exclaimed.

'Looks like the GP Tranny we were using on patrol the other night,' Calder replied, remembering, with a bitter taste in his mouth the arrest of Solomon and the two drug-pushers.

'What, the thing we use for post-runs and taking stray dogs to the kennels?'

'The very same, ma'am. It's usually taken out in preference to Two-Seven and Two-Eight because it's seen as less provocative than the protected Transits.'

'But who on earth . . . ?'

'My guess is that our strikers have had a change of heart. It seems as though there is some *esprit de corps* left in the job after all.'

Inspector Maybe snorted from his protected position at the rear of the fire-engine. '*Esprit de corps?*' he said. 'There must be a thousand rioters out there. We'll need a damned-sight more than *esprit de* bloody *corps* to send them packing.'

Calder ignored him and adjusting the straps of his helmet he carried out a quick head count as over a dozen police officers, dressed in the same flame-proof overalls and helmets, scrambled from the Transit and, ducking under a renewed barrage of bricks and bottles, snatched more of the shields from the pile before joining their colleagues crouching behind the other parked police vehicles.

The last of the new arrivals to leave the carrier, this time from the front passenger door, was Sergeant Lester off the day shift and he made a beeline for Calder, a broad grin on his face. 'How're the knuckles, Jim?' he exclaimed. 'Still sore?' Then, noting Maxwell's presence for the first time, he coughed loudly and nodded a brief, 'Evenin', ma'am,' before bending close to Calder's ear, and adding: 'Willy Justice is vowing to have your arse for what you did, *if* he can find anyone who'll admit to seeing anything, that is.'

Calder's eyes gleamed in the pool of light cast by the spotlamp. 'I'll worry about Willy Justice when this is all over,' he retorted ungraciously, though his rugged face wore the suggestion of a smile. 'Now how many converts did you bring with you? I made it thirteen. Must be an over-crowding offence there somewhere with that vehicle. Good job Traffic only has one mobile on.'

Lester chuckled at the dig. 'You never could flippin' well count, Jim,' he retorted, ducking quickly as what looked like a length of lead-piping hurtled over the area cars and smashed into the side of one of the Transits, missing his head by about a foot. 'There are actually fourteen, plus me.'

Calder half-turned towards Maxwell with a sense of satisfaction. 'There you are, ma'am,' he said. 'With our own troops that makes a total of twenty-seven, excluding the four of us here, so now we not only have the shields, but the bobbies to go with them as well. Looks like we're in business at last.'

'In business?' Maybe shouted before she could answer with more than a trace of panic in his voice. 'Are you mad? We can't possibly take on a thousand rioters with what amounts to just over one PSU.'

Calder stared at him fixedly, the contempt in which he held his inspector not for the first time nakedly exposed. 'I don't see why not,' he replied. 'Unlike the bad old days, everyone in the force is trained in public order tactics now, even the specials, so we've got the edge on that rabble to start with. A small disciplined team like ours, equipped with batons and shields, should be able to disperse them long enough for the fire service to get their units into Lower High Street. Then we can all fall back and protect their arses while they do the business.'

'Sounds good to me,' the fire chief commented. 'We're ready when you are.'

'And the barricades?' Maxwell queried, turning briefly to stare at him. 'You realise you'd have to ram straight through them with one of your tenders? I thought that was against fire service policy?'

Metcalf shrugged. 'Desperate situations call for desperate action, Chief Inspector,' he responded, then added: 'Though I must admit I would be happier to see an ambulance or two in the wings just in case.'

Maxwell nodded. 'I advised Ambulance Control to keep their units away from the scene until they were needed,' she replied. 'No point in risking their crews unnecessarily. They are kitted up and waiting on station. Three minute response time they say.'

The fire chief took a deep breath. 'Then I suggest we get on with it,' he said heavily. 'No sense putting it off any longer, is there?'

Like a condemned man seeking a reprieve from the final arbitrator, Maybe turned desperately to Maxwell. 'This is sheer lunacy, ma'am,' he exclaimed. 'You must see that? We should either wait here for proper reinforcements to arrive or . . . or withdraw completely.'

'And meanwhile the town burns to the ground?' she snapped. 'That's okay, is it?'

'But surely it's preferable to risking the lives of police and fire service personnel on some harebrained venture that has absolutely no chance of success?'

'What about the lives of people who might be trapped in flats above those burning buildings, Inspector?' Metcalf angrily interjected. 'We're paid to take risks; they're not!'

Maybe was shaking his head furiously now, forced to accept that his sentence was not going to be commuted, but determined to make a last-ditch stand anyway. 'I wish to place on record my total opposition to this madcap scheme,' he choked.

Maxwell nodded coldly. 'Consider it as recorded, Douglas,' she replied. 'But for the present, get yourself a shield with the rest of us. We move in five minutes!'

Calder was once again back in Northern Ireland, the scenario just the same as it had been during all those nights of rioting on Belfast's Falls Road so many years before. The never-ending barrage of bricks and lumps of stone hurtling out of an orange-lit blackness to smash into the polycarbonate shields of the advancing police serials with terrifying force; the burning paraffin-like smell of petrol bombs exploding around them in never ending succession, occasionally clawing at their shields with dripping molten fingers before dropping back into the river of fire that already lapped the sticky, melting road surface; the sweat pouring down the grim set faces that peered through misted visors as weary arms constantly struggled to keep the weighty shields upright; the deafening roar of the crowd as it hurled itself against them in tide-like surges; and the hoarse, strangely remote sound of his own voice, joined by that of Tom Lester, urging them forward against the enormous tightly-packed mass of bobbing heads and flailing arms that tried to wrench the shields from their grasp and force a way through.

Close behind him, Maxwell shouted instructions and words of encouragement through a megaphone as she used her own shield to try and bat off the missiles that flew over the heads of the shield teams before hitting the road in a deadly bouncing avalanche, while behind her the two PSU Transits, driven by Judd and Grandad, did their best to provide a measure of rearguard protection against any attack that might come from the smaller crowd in Eastern Avenue. Of Inspector Maybe, there was no sign and it later transpired that a glancing blow on the leg from a brick had quickly sent him limping to Grandad's Transit as a self-declared casualty only seconds after they had begun their offensive.

Calder wasn't particularly surprised by his inspector's disappearance and he didn't much care where he had disappeared to either. Not only was Rosy Maxwell doing a far better job anyway, but there were more serious things to worry about than an inveterate coward like Douglas Maybe! As he had foreseen, the initial police action had caught the rioters completely by surprise and they had fallen back in panic and confusion before the groups of advancing shields and the menacing quasi-military figures crouching behind them with batons at the ready. But it hadn't taken them long to recover and, urged on by agitators using megaphones equally as powerful as the one carried by Maxwell, they now hurled themselves against the police serials with renewed ferocity.

Already three bobbies had gone down under the force of the attacks, only to be rescued in the nick of time by the members of other serials, who closed ranks in front of them to enable them to regain their feet. Two more had ended up wreathed in flames after a couple of petrol bombs had exploded directly beneath their shields. Only their flame-proof overalls and the speed and efficiency of colleagues using the small fire-extinguishers with which all PSUs were equipped had prevented them from suffering serious burns, but the sight of the uniformed figures momentarily blazing like human torches was a horrific one, serving to unnerve the other members of the serials as much as it filled the rioters with vociferous delight.

As for Calder himself, only will-power had kept him going thus far and the new reserves of strength he had somehow managed to scrape together to get the police offensive underway were almost used up. The agonising pain in his head had been quietened, no doubt by Torrington's Paracetamol on top of the tablets given him by the police surgeon, but his brain now seemed to be enmeshed in icy cobwebs, giving rise to severe nausea and a familiar dreadful wooziness which hit him in waves like the effects of a skinful of malt whisky. He felt strangely disorientated, continually losing concentration and allowing his mind to take him off on weird backward trips into the past, raking up memories of school concerts and holidays in Cornwall with his parents as a boy and only returning to reality with the crash of a brick against his shield or the flare of a petrol bomb. He knew he couldn't last much longer, but it wasn't in his nature to quit like Douglas Maybe. Although, as officer in command it was Rosy Maxwell herself who had made the decision to take the offensive, she had only done so on his advice and he wasn't about to let her down and walk away from it all just because things had started to get tough.

But he had no illusions as to the growing seriousness of their predicament. The offensive had always been a calculated gamble, relying for its success not so much on the usual practised police tactics, but on speed and the element of surprise. That surprise had now been lost, with the rioters recovering a lot quicker than expected before the police had had time to withdraw. Such a small complement of officers, with no proper defensive equipment, like CS gas or baton rounds, to give them the edge and absolutely no prospect of any back-up, had as much chance of containing a mob of this size as King Canute trying to hold back the ocean. They were already starting to lose ground under the pressure of the crowd, with two of the serials well out of line with the others. It was only a matter of seconds before they lost the initiative altogether and the moment that happened the game would be over for every one of them; the gamble lost and the sacrifice they had made all for nothing.

With his mind locked into such a fatalistic negative mode it was small wonder that the sudden wail of sirens took a few seconds to register, but when it did, Calder felt the depleted adrenaline surging back into his veins with almost painful force. Flicking up the misted visor of his helmet to clear his vision, he risked a glance over his right shoulder and was just in time to see a fire-engine smash through the still smoking remains of the barricade that blocked the entrance to Lower High Street and disappear into the fiery gullet beyond, closely followed by three more in an impressive convoy of flashing blue lights.

'We've done it!' Maxwell shouted close to his ear. 'They're through!'

'Took 'em long enough,' Calder shouted back. 'Now let's get the hell out of here!'

Getting out, however, proved to be a lot more difficult than they had anticipated and the withdrawal itself was nothing like the orderly disciplined operation they had practised so many times in regular police support unit training. Even as Maxwell raised her megaphone to give the order to fall back the mob finally broke through *en masse*, sending police and rioters crashing to the ground in a tangle of bodies and shields.

From that point on it was little more than a battle for survival, with the police serials struggling desperately to fall back to the relative security of the Lower High Street barricade and the mob closing in around them determined at all costs to cut off their means of escape. Already the police vehicles they had been forced to leave behind in Eastern Avenue had been torched and the protected Transits at the scene were hemmed in so tightly that they were unable to move without physically running over the rioters jammed in their path. In the back of one of the big wagons Douglas Maybe's white face was clearly visible pressed up against the reinforced glass, his eyes wide and staring as he watched the carnage taking place outside, but Calder had no time to dwell on his cowardly behaviour, for the next instant he saw Maxwell go down just feet from the barricade with several figures on top of her.

Abandoning his cumbersome shield he stumbled to her aid, reaching her side at the same moment as Stone and Porter-Nash, and grabbing one of her female attackers by her long hair he pitched her into the road a few feet away. But the violent exertion was too much for him and the next second a wave of dizziness swept over him, making him lose his balance and fall on to one knee, lights flashing in front of his eyes. For a few moments the icy cobwebs were back, cloaking his brain, and he couldn't think where he was or what he should be doing. He was only dimly aware of the arm which suddenly clamped itself round his neck when another of the rioters sprang on to his back. But Maurice Stone was already there with his baton and a moment afterwards the arm went limp and the youth slid off him, to fold up into a heap over his legs.

'Come on, Sarge,' Stone yelled, hauling the apparently insensible assailant off him and yanking him to his feet with a broad grin. 'This is no place to tie your shoe-laces.'

The big man was supporting him with his shield arm as easily as someone might have supported a frail old man, his baton in his other hand swinging viciously at a group of rioters who now encircled them like jackals waiting to move in for the kill. A few feet away Nash was bending over Maxwell, supporting her as she tried unsuccessfully to struggle to her feet and immediately Calder tore himself free of Stone's grip and stumbled towards her, his mouth dry with anxiety. Suddenly he realised just how much he cared for her and he promised himself that, if they ever managed to get out of this mess, he would damned well tell her so. But even as he made the promise to himself his mind was off again, playing tricks on him. How could he care for another woman when he was married to Maggie? He screwed up his face tightly. But wasn't Maggie dead? He seemed to remember . . .

'Done her ankle in, that's all, Sarge,' Nash exclaimed, staring at him strangely. 'You okay?' Then in a more urgent tone: 'Hey, watch your back!'

But Stone was there yet again and his baton caught the youth, coming at him with the long-bladed knife, full in the face, almost definitely removing some of his teeth and making him drop the weapon and fall to his knees, blood pouring from his nose.

The other rioters took up a familiar chant, 'Kill the bill, kill the bill, kill the bill,' and edged closer. With a great effort Calder hauled his mind back to the present and, keeping his eyes firmly on one section of the group surrounding them, he somehow managed to retrieve his own baton from the ground and straighten up again, standing back to back with Stone and Nash to form a protective circle round Maxwell who was still unable to stand unaided. They were completely at the mercy of the crowd. The barricade, though only yards away, might as well have been three to four miles and the chance of any other member of the team coming to their assistance was not even a remote possibility, since everyone else plainly had problems of their own. In the words of the 'prophet', he thought, everything had gone to rat's shit and his marvellous plan was about to end up in the annals of history as only marginally less of a cock-up than the Second World War evacuation of British troops from Dunkirk!

For once, however, his natural pessimism turned out to be unjustified. Help was actually right on hand and it came from an entirely unexpected quarter. The sudden double-flash of sheet-lightning heralded the daddy of all thunderclaps directly overhead and as the gazes of police and rioters alike swept skywards it seemed as though some mighty celestial cistern had been flushed, releasing a deluge that would even have impressed Noah. In seconds the roundabout had become a shallow lake, with rain falling in visible lines as thick as bamboo canes that beat up off the glistening road surface in thousands of miniature waterspouts. More lightning and thunder followed in quick succession and, as the rain actually (and incredibly) increased in volume, the vast crowd choking the roundabout began to thin out, with the bulk of the rioters abruptly losing interest in the proceedings and running for cover.

'The best policeman in the world,' Calder shouted hoarsely and, heedless of the fact that he was already soaked through to his underclothes, he raised his baton to salute the angry flashes that turned the night on and off like some giant defective strip light.

Just seconds later the wail of sirens and the rapid pulsing of blue emergency beacons announced the approach of a whole convoy of armoured Transits which swept down Eastern Avenue and out on to the roundabout in a continuous stream. As the vehicles slammed to a stop, teams of helmeted riot police from the force's Regional Public Order Group, armed with shields and long batons, were disgorged through the side doors, forming up with practised ease into several dozen serials and moving in on the remnants of the crowd with determined business-like efficiency. The appearance of such formidable police reinforcements was too much even for the mob's hard-liners and in the intermittent flashes of sheet-lightning they could be seen making off in all directions, leaving behind what resembled a vacated battlefield, with the dozen or so weary battered bobbies who had not been able to reach the barricade standing or crouching in the pouring rain in shocked bewildered groups amidst a litter of bricks, broken glass, discarded weapons and abandoned PSU shields.

One particularly prolonged lightning flash revealed something else too. A tall thin figure, dressed in denims, fleeing into Western Avenue with long loping strides, his shoulder-length blond hair streaming out behind him as he ran. A figure that Calder recognised instantly as Solomon!

18

The sight of that fleeing figure was the very incentive that Calder needed and, like a terrier that has started a rat from cover, he went after him without a moment's hesitation, his mind crowded with images of Richard Baseheart, Jane Sullivan and people like the Singhs, whose lives had been totally destroyed along with their gutted homes and businesses because of this one twisted creature. But for once grim determination was not enough on its own, for his physical condition was not up to the task. He had only managed to stumble a few yards before his legs turned to rubber again and he was back on one knee, his senses swimming and vomit welling in his throat as he blinked repeatedly to clear his blurred vision and fought to keep his wandering thoughts on track.

'Don't be a bloody fool, James,' Maxwell shouted anxiously as she limped towards him on Nash's supporting arm. 'It's not worth it.'

Stone bent over him, one meathook resting on his shoulder. 'The governor's right, Sarge,' he advised firmly. 'You're in no fit state for the one minute mile . . . whoever you're chasing'

Calder shrugged himself free with surprising strength and struggled to his feet. 'Get out of my way,

Maurice,' he snarled and stumbling towards the two Hardingham Transits, still parked against the island in the centre of the roundabout with their engines ticking over, he hammered repeatedly on the front passenger door of Two-Seven until Dave Judd leaned across from the driving seat and unlocked it. Climbing up into the vehicle he unfastened his helmet straps and wrenched the thing off with a gasp of relief.

'I have need of your driving skills, David,' he gasped, dropping the helmet on the floor between his feet and pointing across the roundabout. 'Western Avenue . . . and quickly.'

One thing about Dave Judd was that he never argued when instructed to put his foot down. Now was no exception and they were in gear and pulling away even before Calder had managed to haul his seat-belt across his chest. The Transit accomplished an impossible U-turn, mounted the corner of the opposite pavement, scattering a small group of stragglers from the crowd as it did so, then roared off down Western Avenue with its powerful headlights blazing through the still thickening curtain of rain and its wipers going at full tilt.

'What are we looking for, Sarge?' Judd shouted above another loud clap of thunder.

'The arse-hole who engineered this mayhem,' Calder jerked through gritted teeth and leaning forward to grip the dashboard tightly with both hands, he peered closely through the windscreen, his still slightly blurred vision also hampered by the protective mesh screen and the rippling effect of the wipers trailing the continuous flood of water across the glass.

Lightning flashes revealed scores of phantom-like shapes flitting along both pavements or cutting across the road in front of them, but there was no sign of Solomon's distinctive figure and about a quarter of a mile down the road Calder slammed the dashboard with one closed fist. 'Lost the bastard,' he snarled. 'He can't have got this far on foot. Turn around and head back . . . slowly.'

Judd reduced speed, studying his mirrors, then swung the heavy vehicle in another tighter than comfort U-turn. 'Perhaps he saw us coming and dived in somewhere,' he said. 'What does he look like?'

'Well over six foot. Big guy with shoulder-length blond hair, dressed in denims. The one we busted for dope the other night.'

'What him, you mean?'

Calder shook off the icy cobwebs that were once more trying to wind themselves round his brain and jerked forward in his seat-belt as Judd pointed to the other side of the road. The pavement was now deserted except for a single figure that had suddenly darted out of a shop doorway and raced off in the opposite direction, feet kicking up water as they pounded the flooded street.

'After him, David!' Calder shouted hoarsely.

The instruction was unnecessary, for Judd was already going for another of his U-turns, but by the time he had straightened up the figure had vanished again. Calder swore and they came to an abrupt halt, the rain now lashing the roof of the Transit with the force of millions of tiny pebbles and the wipers thudding in a wild rhythm as they flew backwards and forwards across the streaming windscreen.

'Control to Bravo-Alpha-Sierra One-Zero,' the radio barked. 'From Bravo-Sierra Two, you are to return to the scene immediately.' Calder ignored the transmission.

'There!' Judd shouted again, slamming the Transit in gear and slithering away.

'Good man,' Calder breathed, for he had also seen what amounted to little more than a shadow caught fractionally by a shorter than usual flash of lightning, leaving another doorway a few yards in front of them before abruptly disappearing again.

'Bravo-Alpha Two-Seven,' the radio blasted again, 'Re last transmission, you and Sergeant Calder are to . . .' Calder turned his pack-set off and had the satisfaction of seeing Judd do the same.

'I bet I know where he's gone,' Judd said grimly, braking almost immediately to turn into an arched opening between a betting shop and a large derelict boarded-up building that looked as though it had once been a theatre or cinema. 'The side entrance to the old Regent,' he said. 'He's made the same mistake as he did with us before. It's a dead-end.'

The Transit's headlights revealed a bare stone-flagged passageway, some thirty feet long, totally enclosed by brick walls. It was plainly deserted. 'You sure he came in here?' Calder queried doubtfully.

Judd eased the Transit forward a few feet and stopped, completely blocking the entrance. 'Positive, Sarge.' He grinned. 'Perhaps he has a ticket for the next performance.'

Calder's door was too close to the wall for him to get out, so he hauled himself across the seat to follow Judd out of the driver's side instead. The young constable handed him a rubber-cased torch and, reaching back inside the vehicle, grabbed a heavy flashlamp for himself from behind his seat.

There were four small doors in the wall to their left, each about four feet apart, the first two signed 'Stalls' the third 'Circle,' and the fourth 'Balcony.' A quick examination revealed that all were secure, save the second door leading to the Stalls which had apparently been forced, then simply closed over. It opened after a determined tug with a scraping shuddering groan.

'Is there anybody there?' Judd intoned in a low ghostly voice, but his chuckle abruptly died when Calder turned on him.

'We're not playing games, David,' he grated. 'This bastard has already murdered one copper and he'd make it two if he got half the chance, so watch yourself.'

Beyond lay a large oblong room which extended lengthways on either side of them. To their left, some twenty feet away, a sea of paper, apparently made up of letters and newspapers that some wag or wags had still thought fit to deliver despite the obvious dereliction of the place, lay in front of the barred and bolted main entrance doors, glittering with shards of glass from the shattered ticket kiosk which occupied the adjacent corner. To their right, about the same distance away, a boxed sign, labelled 'Toilets,' leaned away from the wall at a crazy angle above a single door which had been jammed half open with a tubular chair, and between it and the external wall a wide flight of stairs, with the sign 'Circle & Bar' above, ascended into even heavier blackness.

The wall in front of them boasted three ornate gothic-style archways, separated from each other by smaller open kiosks. The middle archway, also signed 'Circle & Bar,' framed a further much wider ascending staircase, separated in the middle by a guard rail. The other two, each signed 'Stalls,' had just half a dozen steps leading down to padded double doors. Strangely enough, the foyer and stairs were all still fully carpeted, although if the torn stained condition of the foyer carpet was anything to go by, it was small wonder that no one had bothered to take any of them up. The whole place had the familiar derelict-smell of damp and decay.

'So, where did he go?' Calder growled softly. 'He certainly had plenty of choice.' He motioned Judd to stand still for a moment to listen, but apart from the rain lashing against the boarded-up windows the building gave no hint of life.

He frowned. This place would be like a rabbit-warren. For just the two of them to try and search it properly would be an impossible task. They needed help and quickly. He tapped Judd on the shoulder and bent closer to him. 'Nip outside and call for some back-up,' he said in the same low voice. 'Our friend may not know we're in here yet or how many of us there are and I don't want to give the game away before we're able to cover all possible exits.'

Judd nodded. 'And what are you going to do meanwhile?' he whispered.

Calder grunted. 'Have a quiet nose round,' he replied.

'Is that wise on your own, skipper?'

Calder gave a short humourless laugh. 'Wisdom was never my forte, David,' he replied.

Judd still seemed unhappy about the idea. 'Skipper,' he blurted. 'I really don't think you're in any state to . . .'

'Do it!' Calder snapped back and before Judd could

protest any further he moved away from him towards the stairs leading to the Stalls, the beam of his torch masked by his hand.

Standing at the back of the auditorium a few moments later he waited for his eyes to adjust to the darkness. He was surprised to find that it wasn't that difficult to see a little of his surroundings despite the absence of any external light. Almost immediately he was able to make out the rows of seats sloping away from him on either side of the aisle in which he was standing and before long he could even determine the outline of the open stage and a few blacker slashes that were obviously emergency exits. He advanced carefully down the aisle, his torch still masked and directed at his feet.

There was a loud bang somewhere above his head like the sound made by a heavy fire door closing and he froze, futilely studying the darkness pressing down on him from the great vaulted roof. He saw the faint outline of the Circle, raised on its big square columns above the Stalls, and a couple of boxes projecting from the right hand wall, but nothing more. There was another bang, then silence.

He swung back through the double doors into the foyer, stumbling into the door frame as he did so, then headed for the stairs leading to the Circle. Common sense dictated that he should wait for Judd to come back in, but he hadn't time. Even now Solomon could be disappearing through a fire-exit at the rear of the building, making good his escape while they pontificated at the front.

Gripping his torch more tightly in one hand and his baton in the other, he followed the curve of the stairs as quickly as his weary trembling legs and thumping head would allow, grateful for the carpet deadening his footsteps, but remembering the last time he had made a search of a derelict building and the way it had ended.

He reached the next floor and leaning against the wall for a moment, feeling sick and breathless, he risked using the naked beam of his torch to get some idea of his surroundings. He was in a second carpeted foyer, containing two more open kiosks, one of which had the word 'Bar' above it in brass. The shelves at the back of the bar were now empty, of course, but display cards continued to advertise a variety of drinks and he moistened dry lips, thinking of his bottle of whisky sitting at home.

To his right a staircase, signed 'Balcony,' rose into the darkness and moving out into the middle of the floor to face the stairs he had just climbed, he found yet another gothic archway in front of him, giving access to the Circle. Beyond it a second staircase, signed 'Upper Circle,' continued to climb ever upwards. At each end of the foyer single doors, one inscribed 'Gentlemen' in brass and the other presumably giving access to the 'Ladies,' were clearly visible and with his nerves the way they were now, he was almost tempted to use the facilities provided.

For a moment he stood there, listening to the muted rolls of thunder and watching the ghostly flashes of lightning illuminating the open doorway of the ladies toilet, which appeared to be one of the few areas of this dark creepy building which had not suffered the ignominy of boarded-up windows. Then as the thunder subsided again other noises became audible, this time from below, and he made a grimace. Dave Judd had obviously returned to the main foyer after making his radio call and was looking for him, and none to quietly by the sound of it. He didn't wait for the young constable to find him either, but went through the archway and up a short flight of stairs to the Circle.

The muffled shouting began just as he pushed through the double doors, apparently coming from immediately to his right. Extinguishing his torch, he stopped dead in the gangway, which extended out on either side of him between the upper and lower tiers of seats, and peered into the blackness, gripping the back of one seat to help him with his balance. He couldn't hear exactly what was being said, but the voice was that of a man and the anger in the tone was unmistakable. Then there was a crash and the shouting ended abruptly in a sharp agonised cry which was abruptly cut off.

'Sarge?' Judd's anxious voice called up from the Stalls. 'You okay?' Calder inwardly swore, his right hand tightening on the baton. 'Shut it, David, for Pete's sake,' he breathed to himself, but didn't raise his voice to answer him for fear of giving his own position away to anyone else.

'Sarge?' came again, then a door banged below. Judd was obviously making for the stairs. Talk about a bull in a china shop! Calder switched on his torch again and, masking the beam, edged his way along the gangway to the right until he met the outer aisle running along the wall from the top of the Circle to the front row. Turning left in the direction from which he fancied the shouting had originated, he tripped and almost fell on a short flight of loosely carpeted stairs, but managed to keep his feet by grabbing the back of a seat again. He reached an exit, found the door propped open by an abandoned fire-extinguisher and went through into a passageway.

There was a door on his immediate left and risking a little more light from the torch, he saw the word 'Private' at the top. The door frame was badly splintered near the handle and the lock mechanism appeared to have been completely smashed. To re-secure the door a padlock hasp and staple had been fitted, very recently from its pristine appearance, and the padlock now hung open on the staple, minus the key, suggesting that someone had just unlocked it and was still inside.

Remembering Peter's Pantry and the broken pad-lock on the refrigerator Calder hesitated. Perhaps he was being stupid doing this thing on his own? Maybe he should have waited for the cavalry to arrive? He scowled fiercely in the darkness. Yeah, and maybe he should have become a girl guide instead of a bloody copper! Pushing the door back very slowly until it tapped against the inside wall, he slipped through, switching his torch off as he did so.

'Sarge? Where the hell are you?' He winced at Dave Judd's voice. It sounded as if the young constable had actually reached the Circle foyer and he seemed determined to let the whole of Hardingham know about it. Still, it made no odds now anyway. If Solomon wasn't aware of their presence by this time he was either deaf or had already made good his escape.

Ignoring more calls from his well-meaning but uninitiated colleague, Calder eased the door shut behind him and listened for any other noises in the darkness around him. There was nothing and risking his torch again he saw that he was standing in a narrow uncarpeted corridor. An excuse for a staircase dropped away into the darkness immediately to his left, no doubt intended for staff use only, and just beyond it several closed doors attracted his attention. One of these particularly interested him, for it was labelled 'Manager' and there was a thin bar of light at the bottom. Altering his grip on the baton slightly so that it could be used for much closer body protection should he need it, he pushed the door open and stepped inside. For a moment he stood there, squinting in a bright flickering light as he leaned back against the door frame, his heart pounding with an unnatural force.

The room was about ten feet square and contained just a wooden desk and a rough-looking, metal document cabinet. The cabinet appeared to have been knocked over, possibly in a violent struggle, and the floor was scattered with familiar silver foil strips and small cellophane packets of what looked like white powder. A butane lamp stood in the middle of the desk and in its light the bloodied hand of the man who was slumped in the corner shook as he gripped the desk's rope-edge, apparently trying to pull himself upright, while his other hand clutched at the gory stab wound in his abdomen.

Steve Torrington was on the way out, that much was obvious. His eyes were wide and staring and his face twitched spasmodically as perspiration ran down his forehead and cheeks in continuous rivulets. Calder bent down beside him, using his own handkerchief to wipe some of the sweat away, but keeping hold of the same rope-edge to prevent himself losing his balance and pitching over. 'Did Solomon do this, Steve?' he said gently.

The detective nodded, his mouth working silently for a moment. 'Knew he'd come back for his dope,' he whispered. 'Riverside address just a blind . . . dossing here . . . thought I'd nail him and make amends for everything.'

'And how the hell did you ever think you could take him on your own, man?' Calder exclaimed, glancing cautiously behind him at the still open door.

Torrington nodded again and releasing the edge of the desk rummaged around clumsily under the drawer pedestal until his hand hit something, then swept it out across the floor. It was one of the CS gas-sprays that had once been issued to the police, then withdrawn when the government had got cold feet after a couple of civil actions for alleged injury.

'Keepsake from the good old days,' he said with a brief twisted grin. Calder took the small canister from him, studied it for a second then slipped it into his pocket. 'Never got chance to use it . . . bastard was ready for me . . . had a bloody great knife . . .'

His face contorted in agony and he coughed up a large quantity of blood. Calder started to wipe it away, but he shook his head several times and grabbed the front of his overalls with surprising strength, all but pulling him over on top of him. 'Nail him, Jim,' he said fiercely through clenched teeth. 'Check fire-escape . . . has a van out back, but won't get far . . . fixed sodding thing.' He sank back against the wall again, his eyes glazing over, but the twisted grin back on his thin lips as he tugged weakly at the blood-soaked lapel of his jacket. 'Pity about the suit.' Then the light left his eyes, his body convulsed once and he was gone.

For several seconds Calder stayed where he was,

staring at the dead man's face and torn by a confusion of feelings in which shock, regret and cold vengeful anger were all equally represented. Torrington may have been a bent copper, a traitor to the service and his own colleagues, but he had been a friend once, a good friend, and at the end he had genuinely tried to make amends for what he'd done. He hadn't deserved to die in a nondescript derelict with a knife in his belly, especially not at the hands of some arrogant psycho like Solomon, who seemed to think he had the God-given right to take life just whenever he felt like it, secure in the knowledge that under the present legal system he would never have to forfeit his own! It was time for a reckoning.

Calder heard the starter-motor turning over continuously as he gently closed Torrington's sightless eyes and he straightened up quicker than he should have done, gripping the edge of the desk for a few moments with both hands when the pain in his head returned in quivering spasms, accompanied by a familiar giddiness and nausea that made him want to vomit.

The sound was surprisingly loud and he saw why when he recovered sufficiently to stumble from the office along the corridor. There was a wide-open door at the end and the rain-washed fire-escape outside glistened in the beam of his torch. Directly below a large black van, almost certainly the same one that had raced away from Peter's Pantry before, was parked sideways on to partially broken down wrought-iron railings which separated the theatre building from a large public car park, the driver's door hanging open and the bonnet up.

There was no sign of Solomon with the vehicle,

which was hardly surprising under the circumstances, for the headlights and blue flashing beacons of a PSU Transit were clearly visible as the big wagon lumbered across the car park from the back-street entrance. But the problem was, if he had now abandoned his van and fled, where could he possibly have gone? The car park itself, which was otherwise empty of vehicles, was enclosed by high brick walls and another flash of lightning confirmed that the shining expanse of tarmac offered no place of concealment whatsoever.

Stepping out on to the fire-escape, Calder snapped his pack-set on again, intending to warn all units to keep a look out for the blond giant, and immediately intercepted a transmission from Control. 'Sierra One-Zero, Sergeant Calder, please come in!'

The exasperation in Phil Davies' normally monotone voice suggested that he had been calling for some time, but Calder wasn't given the chance to respond. He caught the glint of rimless spectacles out of the corner of his eye a fraction of a second before the tall figure lunged at him from his right. Solomon must have fled back up the fire-escape the moment he had spotted the police vehicle arriving, quickly concealing himself behind the outflung door when he heard Calder stumbling towards him, and it was evident that he had no intention of turning himself in.

The heavy haversack slammed into Calder's injured shoulder with all the force of a massive sandbag, knocking him off balance as he jerked round clumsily to defend himself and sending him pitching back into space. Moments later he found himself lying at the bottom of the fire-escape on a sodden spongy strip of grass which bordered the wall of the building inside the wrought-iron railings, the wind completely knocked out of him by the fall and the rain hammering on to his face with cruel stinging force.

Staring back up the fire-escape as if through a wet smeared windscreen, he saw a uniformed figure appear in the doorway, briefly pinpointed by flashlight beams from the car park before thundering down the irons steps towards him. It turned out to be Dave Judd and he reached his side a fraction of a second before Porter-Nash and Maurice Stone. 'Don't move, skipper,' Nash said quickly, as the three of them bent over him. 'We'll get an ambulance.'

The word 'ambulance' seemed to act as an immediate trigger and, surfacing through his woolly world, Calder met the spasms of pain and nausea with gritted teeth as he forced himself to his feet, using a pair of convenient shoulders for support. 'Never mind the bloody ambulance,' he snarled, staring belligerently at Judd. 'Where'd the bastard go?'

'I don't know, Sarge,' Judd replied. 'I saw no one in the corridor. But he can't get out of the place now anyway; it's covered front and back.'

Calder released Stone's supporting arm and scanned the length of the building where the torches of other officers flashed in the murk as they raced along the grass verge, presumably to secure the emergency exits at the far end. 'Check the offices inside,' he rapped at Judd. 'He could be hiding in one of them or he may have taken that narrow staircase to the lower floor.' He turned towards Stone and Nash. 'Any shields in the Transit?'

Stone shook his head. 'All at the riot scene, Sarge.'

Calder grimaced. 'Shit, just when they're bloody needed. Still, can't be helped, but the three of you had better watch yourselves. This one's armed with a knife and he's already opened up Steve Torrington like a kipper.'

'DI Torrington?' another familiar voice gasped. 'Good God, no!'

He turned quickly. Rosy Maxwell stood feet away, leaning awkwardly on a length of wood she had picked up from somewhere. 'Afraid so,' he retorted harshly. 'His body is in one of the offices, but we'll have to attend to him later.' Then to the three constables, 'Now move!'

Only when the trio were thumping back up the fire-escape did Calder allow his ferocious mask to slip, snatching at the adjacent handrail as he felt the bile rise in his throat, then vomiting on the grass in long agonising shudders. The rain felt warm and oily as it mixed with the sweat pouring down his face and he had to take several deep breaths to prevent himself from actually passing out. He'd certainly caused himself some damage in the last few hours, he reflected grimly, and his backward flip down the fire-escape had not exactly helped matters. He was sure he had done something to the muscles of one of his legs and his back felt as though it were on fire. Still, he had one consolation. At least his new injuries were painful enough in themselves to take his mind off his persistent splitting headache.

'You should have gone to hospital in the first place, man,' Maxwell snapped, tugging at his arm. 'Come back to the Transit with me.'

Calder shook himself free and glared at her. 'Like hell, I will,' he snarled and, grabbing the handrail of the fire-escape again, hauled himself up the steps after Judd and the others.

He reached the top as the next flash of lightning

came and the shout from the car park was almost drowned by the roll of thunder. 'There he is!'

The beam of a flashlight leaped out of the darkness to fasten on something above his head and, quickly staring up through the curtain of rain, he caught a glimpse of an indistinct shape moving along the edge of the roof. At the same moment he saw an iron ladder bolted to the wall just three feet away from him. So that was where the swine had gone.

'James, for God's sake, give it up!' Maxwell's voice was almost a shriek, but he ignored her and, stumbling across the landing, grabbed hold of the rung immediately above his head. The iron was cold, wet and slippery and not intended for heavy leather-soled boots. Solomon was probably wearing trainers. One foot slipped off the bottom rung as he hoisted himself up. But he regained his foothold and went for the next one, climbing slowly and painfully, like a mountaineer scaling a treacherous rock-face. He got halfway up before he slipped off his perch again, this time both feet skidding away from him leaving him hanging by his hands, while his senses spun and his stomach propelled searing acid up into his throat and mouth with the force of a fuel injector. Then as the toes of his boots scrabbled frantically for a grip he felt the ladder start to quiver uneasily, indicating that someone was climbing up after him.

He had only just managed to gain a secure foothold when there was a loud crack and he felt the right-hand side of the ladder pull away from the wall under him. He froze and, blinking hard to clear the rain from his vision, glanced down at the uniformed figure several rungs below as a lightning flash illuminated the side of the building. For some reason he couldn't seem to focus properly again and the lightning physically hurt his eyes. 'Go back down,' he shouted at the upturned blob of a face. 'It won't support both of us.'

The figure, hesitated and another section of the ladder came away by his right foot. 'Do it!' he yelled. 'Do it now!'

The figure retreated quickly and, taking a deep breath, Calder went for the next rung and then the next, bringing his feet up after him a lot more gingerly than before and expecting the whole thing to come apart in his hands at any second.

Miraculously, he reached the top without mishap, but he was caution itself as he raised his head above the balustrade that seemed to enclose the roof all the way round, very conscious of his vulnerability should Solomon be waiting to administer a *coup de grace* with a well-placed boot. There was no sign of the long-haired giant, however, and more lightning revealed just a bare rain-swept roof, rising in the centre to form a broad hipped cap with a flat top, like an Aztec temple, which had obviously been designed to accommodate the vaulted auditorium. There seemed to be nowhere to hide and for the first time Calder began to wonder whether the figure he thought he had spotted on the roof had just been a trick of the rain. Still, there was only one way to find out.

Feeling for the final rung of the ladder with the toe of his left boot, he gripped the top of the balustrade with both hands to hoist himself up, then swung his other leg over, straddling the coping for a moment before pivoting round completely to drop down the other side. The balustrade was only about three feet high, but the climb had almost destroyed him and his legs gave way the moment he tried to straighten up, bringing him to his knees in a pool of icy water where he crouched for several seconds, trying to marshall enough strength to get back on his feet.

Only by gripping the edge of the wall with both hands and hoisting himself up did he finally manage it, but even then it was touch and go as to whether he was actually going to stay on his feet or pitch back off the top of the building and he stood there swaying unsteadily for several seconds, staring across the roof to the fuzzy glare of the burning town as he tried to regain a proper sense of balance and clear his blurred vision. At the same time his hand automatically went to the deep pocket of his overalls for his torch and it was then that realisation dawned. In his haste to get after Solomon he had forgotten to retrieve not only his torch, but his baton as well which he had dropped in his tumble down the fire-escape. Great. Now he had no light and no means of defending himself even if he did corner Solomon.

Turning back to the balustrade as his eyes gradually returned to something like normal focus, he peered over, hoping to see the uniformed bobby he had ordered down climbing back up. He wasn't disappointed. The lad was just getting started. He could see his figure clinging to the ladder in the beams of several torches trained on the building from the car park, but it looked as though the climber was making very slow progress, no doubt due to the precarious hold the ladder had on the wall, and instinctively he knew he had no time to wait for him.

It was only sixth-sense that made him swing round, for Solomon had appeared from the darkness behind him with the stealth of a cat and though he managed to throw himself to one side, the long-bladed knife ripped through the sleeve of his tough police overalls, slicing his arm. The anarchist stumbled into the balustrade, temporarily thrown off balance, but he recovered almost immediately and Calder's clumsy side-step was not quick enough to prevent the blade cutting his arm again. 'I will repay, Sergeant Calder,' he hissed. 'I will repay.'

Calder backed away from him towards the far end of the roof, conscious of the blood trickling down his arm inside his torn sleeve as his hand trailed along the balustrade. 'You crazy murdering bastard,' he said hoarsely, trying to play for time. 'They'll love you at the funny farm. You'll get your own padded cell.'

A lightning flash illuminated the pale bearded face and the rimless glasses seemed to glitter with the cold diamond-like specks of an acetylene torch, but there was no sign of anger and no attempt to justify anything, simply the continuation of that relentless advance, as if this were not a human being at all, but an unfeeling android that had been programmed solely to destroy. Calder thought of Richard Baseheart and Steve Torrington and knew that he had no more chance of overpowering this maniac than they'd had, but he was sure as hell going to try and now was as good a time as any.

'Sarge, where are you?' Maurice Stone's distracting yell could not have been better timed, for it came at the precise moment that Calder chose to launch himself at the anarchist and Solomon's head was still half-turned towards the new threat when he slammed into him. The force of the impact sent the big man staggering backwards into the stone plinth supporting the roof of the auditorium, the knife flying from his hand and clattering away in the darkness as he fell heavily on to the steeply sloping tiled surface with the policeman on top of him.

In his weakened condition, however, Calder was no match for his powerful adversary, whose homicidal mania seemed to have given him superhuman strength, and their positions were quickly reversed, with the other now on top of him, one knee pressed against his chest pinning him down and both hands clamped tightly round his throat. Calder struggled with every ounce of strength he had left, wrenching at the steely wrists and twisting his hips violently backwards and forwards in an effort to dislodge the giant, but it was useless. In response, Solomon simply increased the pressure on his throat, steadily, and with cool deliberation, crushing the life out of him.

Starved of oxygen, with the blood pounding louder and louder inside his head and a gagging rattle forcing its way out of his constricted windpipe, Calder began to lose the will to fight anymore and to accept the inevitability of oblivion. But then, just as his senses began to spin away from him in a kaleidoscope of exploding colours, he glimpsed the torch flashing wildly way over to the right and somehow realised, even in his semi-conscious state, that Maurice Stone was stumbling around in the rain-lashed darkness, searching for him at the wrong end of the roof. That tiny bobbing light was like a spark of hope, restoring his dogged determination to cling to life for as long as possible and from somewhere deep inside him he managed to find the strength to make that one last effort to survive.

The relaxation of his victim's grasp on his own taut wrists when both arms dropped limply away lulled Solomon into a false sense of security and the last thing he expected was for one of those hands then to come up between his legs to grab his testicles through the crutch of his trousers in a savage twisting grip.

Mad, Solomon may have been, but immune to pain he wasn't. With a sharp, bubbling exclamation he immediately abandoned his vicious stranglehold to attend to his own nether regions, falling on to his knees doubled up in agony and leaving Calder clutching at the fire raging in his windpipe as he took down great lungfuls of air with loud whooping gasps, powerless to do or think of anything except satisfy his desperate need for oxygen.

On the far side of the roof the beam of Stone's torch lanced towards them, but passed overhead, failing to pick them out and, while Calder still struggled with his breathing, Solomon managed to stumble upright, snatching something from the floor at the same moment. Even in the darkness Calder knew the anarchist was once more holding the knife he had dropped. A flash of lightning produced a distant yell from Stone, indicating he had spotted them at last, but he looked like being too late, for as his feet pounded recklessly across the slippery roof, Solomon closed in for the kill.

It was the pain caused by something burrowing into his thigh that made Calder suddenly remember Torrington's CS gas-spray and his hand dived into his pocket as he threw himself to one side. The knife missed him by a hair's-breadth, but, true to form, Solomon recovered in an instant and turned on him before he could get back on his feet. Calder had no idea whether he was holding the CS gas-spray properly or even whether it would work after such a

435

long time; he just jabbed it out in front of him and pressed. This time Fate was with him.

The irritant cloud must have hit Solomon directly in the face from a distance of less than two feet and the effect was instantaneous, despite the protection afforded by his glasses. Even as Stone got to them, the beam of his torch warily trained on the anarchist, it was all over. With a desperate cry the blond giant once more allowed his knife to clatter harmlessly to his feet, his hands going straight for his eyes. Then, bent almost double, he staggered drunkenly around the roof, retching and gasping for breath and obviously temporarily blinded. In his panic he failed to appreciate just how close he was to the balustrade and blundered straight into it. Before either Calder or Stone could do anything he had lost his balance completely and with arms futilely flailing the air had pitched headlong over the top, his long scream of terror quickly fading into the rain.

Dragging himself to the balustrade a moment later, Calder saw the police torches rapidly converging on the scene from a dozen different directions at once and, as more lightning provided its own form of brilliant illumination, he glimpsed the anarchist draped, like a grotesque broken doll, over one of the upright sections of the iron railings, his body neatly skewered by the spikes and still jerking fitfully in the final stages of extremis.

Then the lightning was gone and the gruesome vision buried in the rain-leaden folds of the night. At last it was all over, the final act and the final scene played, the murders of Baseheart and Torrington avenged and judgment imposed by the highest court of all. 'For it is written, vengeance is mine,' Stone murmured solemnly in the gloom. 'I will repay, saith the Lord.'

'That's what our late friend, the prophet, said,' Calder's tortured voice rasped in reply as he continued to stare down into the torch-lit blackness while he swayed unsteadily on the roof's edge. 'Only he thought it was down to him to do the repaying.'

Stone emitted a hard grim laugh and moved closer to him. 'Well now, he was one dumb prophet who didn't know his Bible then, weren't he, Sarge?' he replied, and quickly made a grab for him as he passed out.

'Come on, Jim, you can make it. Keep trying. Don't give up.'

For so long there had been an eternity of nothing: immeasurable and incalculable . . . disembodied, unintelligible voices talking to each other in the midst of impenetrable blackness . . . noises all around him that he couldn't identify . . . strange sensations in his hands and feet . . . unfamiliar smells that caught the back of his throat and made him feel nauseous . . . conscious, yet unconscious and, through it all, unable to move, to speak or to see . . . a living nightmare from which there was no awakening, only an awareness of another plane without verbal contact or visual confirmation.

But now a voice that he could understand, speaking to him directly, breaking through the nothingness, and it was accompanied by a weird spinning feeling in his head, going faster . . . faster. A greyness was developing where the blackness had been; smoky, patchy, swirling around him like fog. Whitish blobs appeared and receded. He felt clammy and sick, his head throbbing with a familiar neuralgic type pain. Ironically he just wanted to drift back into the very same all-embracing darkness from which he had been trying to escape for so long, but he couldn't find it anymore.

Then the fog was almost gone and he was aware of a warm glow building in its place. The white blobs became blurred faces that suddenly snapped into focus, but the brightness of his surroundings hurt his eyes and he closed them with a low groan. He heard a swishing clinking sound, like a curtain being pulled, and when he opened his eyes again the light had been reduced to a more comfortable level. 'Welcome back, Sergeant Calder,' someone said. 'For awhile we didn't think you wanted to join us again.'

He blinked several times, focusing with difficulty. He appeared to be lying in a hospital bed, wired to more drips, bottles and electronic monitors than the hapless monster of Frankenstein. A uniformed nurse and a man in a long white coat, whom he assumed to be a doctor, stood beside the bed staring down at him and their faces wore the sort of self-indulgent smiles usually reserved for mothers after a successful birth.

Calder wanted to say something, but his throat seemed to be blocked by some sort of tube and he could only manage a strange rasping sound. 'You've been through a lot,' the doctor went on, studying him more closely. 'You need to rest now. I'll be back to see you later.'

Calder nodded, feeling strangely exhausted despite the fact that he had only just woken up, and, closing his eyes, he was almost immediately gone again.

Over the next few days he found himself drifting in a strange twilight world of half sleep and half wakefulness. His mind was heavy and confused, desperately trying to remember what had happened to him and to make sense of the disjointed flashbacks that repeatedly surfaced from his subconscious, then slipped away again like will-o-the-wisps before he could properly focus on them. And all the while white-coated doctors and smiling nurses floated in and out, doing their rounds. Visitors came and went too, nodding smiling, patting his hand and trying to make cheerful conversation. They were people he vaguely recognised, but was unable to respond to.

Bit by bit, however, he began to grow stronger and as he became more aware of himself and his surroundings, the flashbacks steadied into clearer mental pictures and his memory began to return to normal. For the first time he was able to recall everything that had happened to him, including his last violent struggle with Solomon on the roof of the Regent Theatre where he had passed out. Finally, de-wired and de-tubed from the apparatus beside his bed, he began to feel less like a Dalek and, shortly after an X-ray of his heavily bandaged head, he received an unexpected bonus. A hefty male nurse arrived to wheel him out of what was plainly the intensive care unit to a small, bright private room, where cool air played on his face from a partially open window and the smell of antiseptic was replaced by that of newly mown grass.

With his ears tuned to the sound of birdsong, he drifted off into a deep dreamless sleep and, when he awoke several hours later, it was to find a very welcome visitor sitting in a shaft of fragile evening sunlight beside his bed.

'Hello, James,' Rosy Maxwell said and her hand

reached out briefly to touch his own. She had a light anorak over her uniform which suggested she had come straight from work and although she looked very tired and there were tears in her eyes her face wore a delighted smile.

He smiled weakly in return. 'How's the ankle?' he said, conscious of a soreness in his throat.

She dried her eyes with a handkerchief and laughed. 'Oh, that's long been better, thanks,' she replied. 'Only a severe sprain, nothing more.'

'And what about Jane Sullivan?'

She made a face. 'Improving, but it will be a long hard haul. She's suffering from some kind of catatonic condition as a result of the dreadful shock she received and has been undergoing therapy for the past three weeks.'

He visibly started. 'Three weeks? But . . . but that's impossible.'

'Is it?' Maxwell leaned forward and laid a hand on his own again. 'James, don't you know? Haven't they told you yet?'

He made a wry face. 'Well, I haven't exactly been receptive to detailed explanations, have I?'

She bit her lip and stared down at the bedclothes for a moment before studying him intensely. 'James, you did yourself some real damage out there. The doctor thinks it must have happened when Solomon attacked you with the chair leg at Peter's Pantry. Incredible as it may seem, you were running around all those hours with a serious head injury. That's why you were behaving so strangely. I don't know the technical details, but apparently the hospital found some bleeding inside your skull and had to operate to drain it off. Fortunately, a scan showed no sign of a fracture, just a burst blood vessel or something, but the injury was bad enough to put you in a coma.'

'But for three weeks? I can hardly believe it.'

She snorted with sudden anger. 'Oh you can believe it all right. I've been visiting you almost every day since Maurice Stone brought you down off the roof of that damned theatre on his back with the ladder breaking under him the whole way. It was only when one of the nurses saw your toes twitching that Dr. Lawrence realised you were actually coming out of the coma.' Her eyes were filled with tears again and her mouth quivered uncontrollably as the weeks of strain broke through. 'I thought you were going to die, you bloody stupid idiot!'

Calder gripped her hand tightly while she dried her eyes and blew her nose, strangely touched, but not embarrassed by her emotional outburst. 'So I've missed all the fireworks then?' he said quietly.

She sighed heavily and put her handkerchief away. 'It's been quite a difficult time, I must admit,' she replied. 'The town centre was virtually gutted. It's going to cost millions to restore apparently and there are already heavy civil claims in the pipeline against both the NPU and the Police Authority, who are at loggerheads with each other over who should be held responsible for meeting them.'

'Any of the lads and lassies badly hurt?'

She shook her head with a wry smile. 'Only Douglas Maybe apparently.'

He glared at her, some of his old pugnacious spirit returning.

'Douglas Maybe? How could he get injured? He spent most of the night hiding in Grandad's bloody PSU van.'

441

'I know he did and so do a lot of others. There have been a number of complaints from the officers on your shift about the way he behaved and a discipline investigation is already underway. He's been on the sick ever since, allegedly suffering from depression, but he'll have to face the music eventually and I think he'll be for the high jump on this one.'

Calder's familiar scowl was back. 'Couldn't happen to a better man,' he growled. 'And the rest of the shift are definitely all okay?'

'Well, there were a lot of cuts, bruises and minor burns, quite a bit of post-traumatic stress too, but nothing major. There were no serious injuries to the public either, apart from smoke-inhalation. So we were all pretty lucky considering the circumstances.'

'All of us except Richard Baseheart and Steve Torrington, you mean,' he said, his tone very bitter.

She made a grimace, then eyed him carefully. 'What about Steve Torrington, Jim? They've got him down as a hero, but you and I know differently, don't we?'

He met her gaze and held it. 'At the end he was a hero and, unless you've any objections, I think it's best left that way. There must be enough shit flying around from this business already without that as well.'

She hesitated, then nodded. 'I'm inclined to agree with you there and, as I'm in the hot seat now anyway, I could do without more aggro.'

'Hot seat? What do you mean?'

With a slightly embarrassed smile she pulled back the collar of her anorak a little way to reveal one epaulette. In place of the three tin bath stars of chief inspector rank was a single imposing crown set on a red background. 'It's been all change in the force lately,' she explained. 'As you'd expect after all that's happened.'

He gave a low whistle. 'Superintendent?' he chuckled. 'Well, I'm damned.' He squeezed her hand even more tightly. 'Congratulations anyway. No one deserves it more than you.' Then he frowned again. 'But where's George Rhymes?'

Her smile faded and there was pain in her eyes. 'Dead,' she said bleakly. 'Poor damned fool topped himself after the riots. Car hosepipe job in his garage. Couldn't live with himself, it seems. I . . . I was already through the board and in the promotion pool, so it was a logical progression to his position.'

Calder was silent for a moment, thinking of a man he had once liked and admired, who had paid the ultimate price for someone else's misdeeds. 'Go on,' he said at length, leaning back against the pillows. 'You'd better fill me in on the rest.'

She stood up and walked slowly to the window, staring out into the sunlight. 'John Harding has gone, of course.'

'What already? That's a bit unprecedented, isn't it?'

She shrugged. 'The government needed a quick fix job, someone to blame. He was the ideal candidate. The official line is that he took early retirement on health grounds, but in reality he was left with no option but to go. He was badly mauled by the press for alleged mismanagement and in the end had to carry the can for everything. I hear down the grapevine that his capitulation to the NPU's demands over paid overtime hit him particularly hard, but without it we'd never have got the RPOG units deployed on the night of the riots, so in a way he made a brave decision.'

'He never knew he'd been set up then?'

She turned to face him again. 'Oh I think he suspected something of the sort at the end, but obviously realised the issue wasn't worth pursuing. The only comfort he can draw from the whole disastrous business is that the NPU came in for just as much stick as he did and, under pressure from the union's National Executive at the "Kremlin", Willy Justice had to resign his position as Chairman on the Regional Executive.' She turned back to him, managing another brief smile. 'Poor old Willy is now walking the beat in the remains of Hardingham town centre, so that should focus his mind a bit.'

Calder studied her keenly. 'And who's the new commissioner?'

She hesitated, and he tensed. 'Not Turner?'

She returned to her chair, crossing her legs and eyeing him cautiously. 'Well, he's acting-commissioner anyway until proper interviews have been set up.'

'You don't think he'll get the job?'

'Pre-ordained, I should imagine. The only good thing about it is that our dear Police Authority Chairman has exchanged one problem for another. John Harding may have gone, but Simmonds is not only saddled with the replacement he didn't want, but he's actually going to be forced into bed with him on the basis of "I won't tell if you don't".'

Calder stared at her aghast. 'You're saying Simmonds is actually still in post after all that's happened?'

She laughed dryly. 'Clever man, our Charles, and a born survivor too. He knows the government want to avoid a public scandal at all costs. They already have their sacrificial lamb for the Hardingham riots in John Harding. Any more sacrifices would be overkill and raise doubts about the competence of the Home Office to manage the police service effectively.'

Calder was now tuned into her wavelength and his face was grim. 'Then I take it Granger's mob didn't spring their vote of no confidence on the government after all?'

'How could they? Not with Richard Baseheart's envelope, crammed full of evidence fingering their esteemed leader, locked securely in the Home Secretary's safe.'

'Blackmail, eh?'

She laughed again without humour. 'Juliet put it another way. She said that Granger had come to an accommodation with the Prime Minister over the matter. As a result, though a few cosmetic criticisms of the government were made in Parliament by the opposition, most of the condemnation on both sides of the House was reserved for the rioters and tough new public order laws are on the way, together with a new bill to turn the clock back by outlawing future police strikes.'

'Which will be pushed through unopposed by the opposition, of course?'

'Largely, yes. In any event, the present administration are likely to have a very healthy majority and can look forward to a less sticky time with the opposition in the future for as long as Granger is in the chair.'

'So the government are as bent as the opposition?'

'Does that really surprise you after all you've been through? And anyway I suspect that from their perspective it's seen as all perfectly legitimate political manoeuvring.'

His face contorted into an even heavier frown than usual. 'But what about Eddie Sable? His exposé should have hit the tabloids like a neutron bomb. Obviously it didn't, otherwise everyone wouldn't be so happy.'

'Copy was never filed.'

'Never filed? You mean he actually agreed to bury it? That doesn't sound like Eddie.'

She shook her head. 'No, Jim, he ended up being buried himself. He was killed in the fire when the Railway Hotel was torched by some of the rioters.'

Calder winced. 'Good grief. Poor bastard.'

'He'd obviously left the stuff he'd copied from Richard Baseheart's envelope in his room. He rushed back there when he heard the hotel had gone up and like a damned fool tried to get back in to retrieve it.' She shrugged. 'Not much left of him apparently. All they found were a few bits of twisted plastic, evidently the remains of some video cassettes.'

His eyes narrowed to reflective slits. 'Mighty convenient for all the parties involved though, wasn't it?'

She frowned. 'What are you getting at?'

'Just that it seems a bit too neat. I don't suppose your friend, Juliet, accidentally dropped some lighter fuel in his bedroom?'

'Now you're being ridiculous.'

'Am I? I thought Jane Sullivan was being ridiculous when she first suggested that the top brass were involved in a conspiracy. Look how that turned out.'

She cupped one hand over his wrist. 'James,' she said patiently. 'Eddie Sable was the unfortunate victim of an arson which the NCS are still investigating along with all the others in the town. That's all there is to it. As for Juliet Grey, she is a short, thin bespectacled spinster of this parish who would run from her own shadow if she saw it on the landing. She is not a hit woman for MI6. Okay?'

He managed a wry smile. 'Maybe not, but we've already seen the lengths to which some politicians will go to get what they want.'

Maxwell stood up again and treated him to a severe glance. 'James, I'm getting seriously worried about you. Members of Her Majesty's Government and other ministers of the Crown may be prone to political chicanery of the most disreputable kind, but I hardly think they are likely to go around setting fire to hotels and burning pressmen to death in their rooms. So can we leave it there before you are packed off to the funny farm diagnosed as suffering from schizophrenic paranoià?'

He sighed and settled back against the pillows again, feeling very tired after all the talking. 'I'll reserve my own judgment,' he said a little distantly. 'But you're the boss and I really can't be bothered to argue anymore.'

She raised her eyebrows and nodded. 'Now that is a change for the better,' she replied.

Her perfume seemed to envelope him as her lips brushed his in a tender caress and suddenly he was no longer sleepy. 'Hey, what the hell are you doing?' he exclaimed, his heart pounding fit to burst. 'I'm a sick man.'

Her fingers stroked his face and her eyes stared intently into his from just inches away. 'Dr. Lawrence told me that he should be able to release you soon, provided you can be given constant care,' she said softly. 'So you're going to come and stay with me for a while until you're completely recovered.'

He swallowed hard. 'No, no, that's not a good idea,' he protested, the panic rising in his tone. 'I . . . I don't sleep very well in a strange bed . . .'

She bent closer and kissed him on the mouth again, her lips lingering provocatively. 'Who said anything about sleeping, James?' she whispered in his ear. 'I'm sure we can think of some much more imaginative therapy than that, don't you?'